THE ABBESS OF WHITBY

"Jill Dalladay immerses the reader in the turbulent world of seventh-century Britain, where everything is changing, and vividly tells the life story of the woman who played a key role in the creation of England: Hild of Whitby."

Edoardo Albert, author of *Edwin: High King of Britain*

* * *

"Jill Dalladay has presented us with a well crafted novel about one of the most enigmatic women in early Christian times in England. Hild was abbess and teacher at Whitby and is today venerated as a saint. From her pagan upbringing to her conversion to Christianity, her story is presented with a sharp eye for historic detail together with finely drawn characters. This is skilful and accomplished writing."

Peter Tremayne, author of The Sister Fidelma Mysteries

JILL DALLADAY is a classicist, historian, and former head teacher who pioneered the Cambridge Latin course. She lives in Whitby.

The ABBESS of Whitby

A NOVEL OF HILD OF NORTHUMBRIA

JILL DALLADAY

LION FICTION

Published by Lion Fiction
an imprint of
Lion Hudson plc
Wilkinson House, Jordan Hill Road
Oxford OX2 8DR, England
www.lionhudson.com/fiction

ISBN 978 1 78264 154 4
e-ISBN 978 1 78264 155 1

First edition 2015

Acknowledgments
Cover image: Doorway © duncan1890/
iStockphoto.com; Nun © Nilfur Barin/
Trevillion Images
A catalogue record for this book is available
from the British Library

Printed and bound in the UK, July 2015, LH26

For Roger

CONTENTS

FAMILY TREE

ROYAL FAMILIES OF NORTHUMBRIA

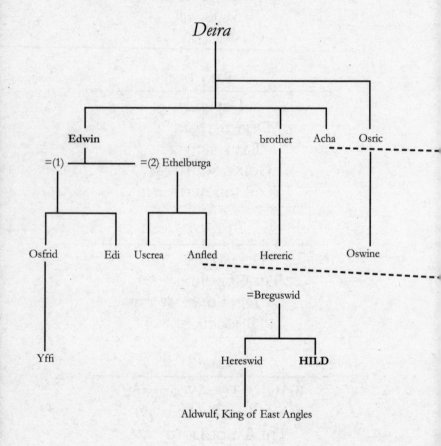

Deira

Edwin — =(1) ... =(2) Ethelburga — brother — Acha — Osric

Osfrid — Edi — Uscrea — Anfled — Hereric — Oswine

Yffi

=Breguswid

Hereswid — **HILD**

Aldwulf, King of East Angles

Bold indicates kings

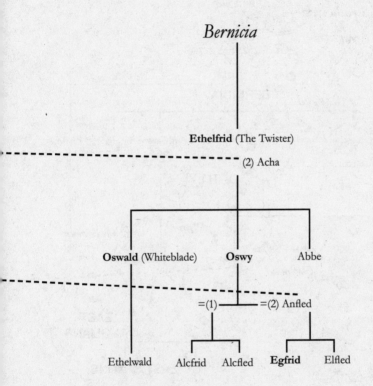

Bernicia

Ethelfrid (The Twister)

(2) Acha

Oswald (Whiteblade)   **Oswy**   Abbe

=(1) — =(2) Anfled

Ethelwald   Alcfrid   Alcfled   **Egfrid**   Elfled

THE PEOPLES OF 7TH CENTURY BRITAIN

Strathclyde Picts

Gododdin R. Tweed

Rheged BERNICIA

NORTHUMBRIA

R. Tees

DEIRA

Elmet

The Humber

Lindsey

Gwynedd

MERCIA

EAST ANGLIANS

EAST SAXONS

WEST SAXONS KENT

SOUTH SAXONS

------- Old Roman road

Britons in italics

Hild's Northumbria

Iona

BERNICIA

The Firth
Din Edin
Doon Hill
Abbe's Headland
R. Tweed
Lindisfarne
Melrose
Bamburgh
R. Tyne
South Shields
Jarrow
Hexham
Wearmouth
R. Wear
Isle of Hart
R. Tees
Whitby
R. Esk
Lastingham
R. Swale
Catterick
Hackness
DEIRA
R. Ure
Ripon
York
R. Derwent
Oldest Royal Hall
Woden's Shrine
Elmet
The Humber
Lindsey
Isle of Anglesey
Gwynedd
Chester
R. Trent
OLD ROMAN ROAD
Stamford
London
Canterbury

CHARACTERS

Characters in italics are invented

Deirans

Edwin, king of Northumbria

Ethelburga, his queen from Kent

Uscrea, their son

Anfled [Ani], their daughter

Osfrid and Edi, Edwin's sons by a former wife

Yffi, Osfrid's son

Breguswid, widow of Edwin's nephew, Hereric

Hereswid and Hild, her daughters

Coifi, Edwin's High Priest

Bass, Forthere, Lilla, and *Cutha*, Edwin's Companions, high-ranking thegns

"The Twister", Ethelfrid of Bernicia, Edwin's mortal enemy

Paulinus, the queen's chaplain from Canterbury

James, one of Paulinus's monks

Erpwald, son of King Redwald of East Anglia

Eomer, envoy from Cwichelm, king of the West Saxons

Begu, a slave girl

Cerdic, a Gododdin hostage

Caedmon, a British peasant

The Gododdin

Gwylget, the chief

Gerda, his wife

Rohan, Cerdic's steward

Brigit, his wife

Young Rohan, their son

Caitlin, their daughter

Wulfstan [Wulfi], Hild's son

Eata, Cerdic's spear bearer

Cuthbert, Cutha's son

Bernicians

Oswald, king of Bernicia

Oswy, his brother

Abbe, their sister

Alcfrid, Oswy's son by a former wife

Alcfled, Oswy's daughter by a former wife

Anfled of Deira, Oswy's queen

Egfrid, son of Oswy and Anfled

Elfled [Elfi], daughter of Oswy and Anfled

13

Romanus, the queen's chaplain from Canterbury

Aidan, summoned by Oswald from Iona to be bishop

In Hild's communities

Frigyd, a high-ranking widow
Oftfor, her son
Brother John, a blind scholar
Aetla, priest in training
Wilfrid, aspiring priest
Heiu, nun who founded Hartlepool
Ulf, steward of the royal estate at Hart
Sigebert, king of the East Saxons
Bosa, priest in training
Tatfrid, priest
Udric, steward at Whitby
Aldwulf, king of East Anglia, Hild's nephew

Monks, priests, etc.

Monks lived in communities but, in the Iona tradition, made pilgrimage in wild places to be close to God and serve the people. Priests started as monks but were ordained, first as deacons, then as priests, to administer the sacraments. Bishops lived in communities, under the rule of an abbot, but travelled widely with the king they served.

Utta, Adda, and Betti, three brothers trained by Aidan to be priests

Cedd, Chad, and Coelin, also brothers trained by Aidan to be priests

Finan, bishop after Aidan

Colman, bishop after Finan

Augustine of Canterbury, sent by Pope Gregory to convert Britain

Theodore, a later Bishop of Canterbury

Agilbert, a French bishop invited to the West Saxons

Wine, an Englishman consecrated bishop in his place

Pagan gods

Woden, supreme god, wielded the spear, attended by ravens
Thor, thunder and lightning, wielded the hammer
Freyr, goddess of childbirth
Eostre, goddess of spring
Hreth, goddess of vengeance

si quid in his cartis te dignum reddere grates
invenias domino maxime nunc moneo;
sin alias, vati veniam dignare canenti
iam tribuere pius: quod potuit cecinit.

If you find anything in these pages worthy of you,
I urge you to give heartfelt praise to God;
If not, graciously pardon the poet for his work;
he did his best.

* * *

From *On Abbots*, a poem by Aethelwulf,
ninth-century monk of Lindisfarne

It *couldn't be him. She trusted him. A man of years, family head, the people's lord, he communed with the gods, bringing peace, security, prosperity.*

It had to be him; the strength and cunning. Who else would defy Woden's taboos? Who else would murder a kinsman?

She'd known him kill without compunction, lash men, hang them, and never shed a tear.

"Men don't weep," her mother said, and believed it.

But they did. She'd seen their eyes spring in the mead hall when the scop's singing stirred their hearts. Or when a favourite horse crumpled. Or when they were banished from the king's hearth.

Never when they killed. Then, men would roar in triumph, gloat over booty, fawn on the warleader, clamour for more battle, more spoils. They wreaked havoc in the name of the gods: hammer-wielding Thor, or vengeful Hreth. Killing was their trade. Women wove the threads together and restored the fabric of peace.

It had to be him. His deeds ran through her memory, she saw his secret ways. But the risk, if she challenged him! To lose home, friends, livelihood, maybe life itself. Had she the daring?

It was for her father. No one else was left to act.

She stood up, squared her shoulders, and strode to confront the man she believed to be his murderer.

PART 1

1

DEIRA

Shivering, Hild burrowed into her cloak. The hilltop was an awesome place, shunned by all but the priest, closer to the gods than she had ever been. Clutching her sprig of rowan, she pressed it to her heart. It kept her safe, the Runetree. Safe against elves and ghosts, wolf's cry and owl's wings, and beasts of the undergrowth. Safe against the monstrous creature standing over her head, black against the fitful moon, moving almost, its leafy skirts crackling in the breeze. Was it alive? Was that what the old priest meant?

"To the place of gods." He'd pointed them up the hill. "You will find all you need. Build a great Moormaid for the fire. A Moormaid to die and bring life to the land. Guard her through the dark and bring her safe down."

She remembered the High Priest's finger beckoning her into the group of girls, but it was Eostre herself, goddess of fertility and birth, who chose her as leader. In the low rays of the setting sun, she'd drawn the long straw. She was the chosen one, goddess Eostre's maid, called to lead at the spring festival and serve the year through.

Old Coifi was right. They'd found everything to hand: a gleaming ball of mistletoe for the head; an ash branch forked by Woden's thunderbolt as the body; blackthorn and ivy to weave into the stiff skirt which glimmered with dew; the arms, hacked from alders with their eating knives.

She scanned their handiwork in the creeping light. The Moormaid stood skeletal and translucent, a fitting sacrifice. Their scratched and bleeding arms would be a badge of pride, proclaiming them the Spring Dancers, six girls on the cusp of womanhood. Today, through their offering, the Spring Goddess would unfurl the leaves, grow the crops, ripen the harvest and make the cattle bear…

If nothing marred the day…

If she played her part well.

A cockerel crowed. Hugging her knees, Hild looked below. The mist was unfurling in the sun's warmth. Dayglow touched the tips of the trees and the antlers adorning the king's rooftree. From thatched homesteads rose the din of morning: goats bleating, children splashing buckets, men hollering for hounds. She saw the king's door open. His herald emerged. Purification Night was over. Eostre's Day had come.

Hild set her team in place and they raised the ungainly figure onto their shoulders. As she led them down the hill, they sang the age-old song learned from their mothers at cookpot and washing stones:

At a springhead under a thorn
Was in the past a saving charm.
A maid stood there enthralled by love,
With love she will save all from harm…

"*Seven nights the maid lay on the moor,*" sang Hild, taking the solo part, beating out the rhythm, leading where the ground was smoothest. "*Fair was her food, what was her food?*"

"*The violet and the primrose good.*" The girls spluttered with effort.

Like a sprinter, the Moormaid leaned forward, driving them on. The girl at the back screamed and lost hold. The creature swayed wildly. Hild gasped. She would capsize… blight the crops… anger the goddess…

"*What was her drink?*" she sang, darting alongside to grip the prickly skirt.

"*Her drink was cool spring water…*" shrilled the girls. An echo rolled round the valley; women full of memories joined in as they converged on the place of sacrifice.

Down to the level, over the stream, past the swineherd's hut and the steward's lodging, beyond the slaughter pen and the king's hall, the Moormaid wafted on a wash of excitement to the place where three valleys met. The slopes were black with people.

Setting her down, the girls danced round her with abandon. On and on the chorus drove them, in and out they wove, back and forth, arms flung wide, hair streaming, bending backwards, twirling round and round. Elated, relieved, Hild felt passion spill from her like wine from a spinning cup, rising, whirling, flying. She could not see, she could not hear, she was all motion, all spirit…

Of every tree, of every tree,
The hawthorn bloweth fairest…

Erect at the front, King Edwin watched, chin jutting proudly, silver hair lifting in the breeze. His sword belt sparked with jewels, his gold armlets gleamed, and the chains round his neck dazzled like the sun's rays. Ranged up the slope behind him were brawny fighting men, thegns of the royal service, each hedged by leathercaps from his own warband. Beside the king were his Companions, senior thegns who were his intimates, sporting richly coloured cloaks and pommels bright with gems. Closest was white-haired Lilla, the king's childhood friend, lord of the lands around, whom Edwin was honouring with his presence for the spring festival. Hild saw the royal party as a blur of brightness each time she whirled past.

My love she'll be, my love she'll be…

Still as a rock inside the dancing girls, a white-robed priest stood by the Moormaid, knife raised above a bullock roped at his feet. Spellbound, the people, even the king, joined in the great climactic cry:

With love she will save all from harm.

The dancers collapsed, and a sigh of completion broke like a wave.

The priest's knife arced down to the bullock's throat. Blood spurted high, veering on the breeze, spattering the girls and drenching their leader.

"Eostre! Eostre!" Hild heard the roar. White-faced, she rose and stood, Eostre's maid. The priest handed her a golden bowl. Careful not to spill, she knelt to offer it to the king. He flourished it and drank deep of the blood, pouring the rest onto mother earth. Taking Hild's hand, he led her forward and they stood before the Moormaid in a waiting hush. Handing her a flaming torch, the priest intoned exultantly:

Blossom and bullock, blood of the sacrifice,
Earnest of fruitfulness, Earth Mother's pledge.

He guided her hand and the Moormaid sprang into flame with a loud sucking blast. The offering was accepted.

"Eostre! Eostre!" chanted the crowd. The king beamed at Hild.

"What do they call you, Eostre's maid?"

"Hild, my lord." She sank to her knees.

"Fierce name for a girl. Hild means Battle. Hild, daughter of… who?"

"My father was Hereric, my lord," she gulped, looking up into cold, blue eyes.

"Hereric? My brother's son?" He gripped her hand and raised her. "Hild, Eostre chose you for your name. Battle is the business of kings. You have a royal destiny."

* * *

"Good heavens! What a mess!" Suddenly appearing at her elbow, Hild's mother pulled her out of the crowd. "Let's get you cleaned up. A lick and a promise for now. River dip in the morning." Hild groaned. No eager questions or compliments: that was Ma.

Inside the women's lodging, stripped to the skin, Hild gritted her teeth while Lady Breguswid wielded a coarse rag on her head and neck. The water grew bloodier each time she wrung it out.

"Sit on the chest and do your legs! I'll tackle your back and arms."

Hild bit her lips. Proud of her wounds, she couldn't help wincing as her mother scrubbed and lathered with ointment of thyme. Pain, it seemed, was the price of ecstasy.

"Lady Breguswid!" An elegant lady crashed in, rummaged in a box for a length of braid, dropped the lid and fled. "The queen's left her lodging."

"Let's hope your sister's there," Ma muttered, pulling a fresh tunic over Hild's head and standing back. "You'll do."

She dragged the girl past the sacred bullock, suspended over a firepit, past children leaping to catch lucky black curls of wood ash, past families swigging ale and bawling seasonal greetings, past the mob of hollow-eyed beggars at the hall doors. One look from Lady Breguswid and Forthere, the door thegn, bowed them in.

Edging along the royal side of the Mead Hall, Hild saw firelight reflecting on the wooden wall which had been rubbed smooth by generations of passing shoulders, and sparking on ancient weapons hooked higher up. With a longing glance at her dancers at the far end, she stood with her mother beside the royal dais.

Her eyes stung; smoke from the central fire spiralled to the rafters and turned blue, drifting out through the smokehole in the roof. A cauldron hung bubbling at the end of its long chain. Her guts ached from the smell of broth and roasting beef.

At last King Edwin handed the guest cup to his wife. Spring had reopened the sea roads, bringing a prince from East Anglia, rumoured to be seeking a marriage alliance, a Kentish kinsman of the queen's, a Briton from the far west, and a thegn from Wessex called Eomer. Edwin, it was well known, welcomed all comers to his table. With a slow dignity enhanced by her pregnancy, Queen Ethelburga proffered them the wine of hospitality. As each man drank, he bowed across the fire to Edwin, sealing a mutual pact as binding as kinship.

Immediately, hubbub broke out: men seized jugs to fill their drinking horns; carvers hacked chunks of meat from the bullock and carried them round on trays; servers scuttled from the kitchens with bread, leeks and parsnips; others ladled broth from the cauldron. Quiet fell. Hild tucked in.

When the belching started, the king summoned his minstrel. The song changed each time, for the old scop twined past and present into living history, singing in a rhapsodic monotone punctuated by thrumming on the harp.

The Twister, enemy king of Bernicia, he intoned, killed Edwin's father, snatched his sister, and drove young Edwin from Deira. Edwin wandered to Gwynedd where the king treated him like a son; then to Mercia where he won the princess as wife; then to East Anglia where King Redwald stood his friend. Twanging with excitement, the old man hymned the great victory Edwin won to regain his lands, wreak fair vengeance, and bring peace and justice to his people. More gently he lauded the new young queen and her boy child, ending with a prediction of long life and measureless gold for Edwin, king of kings, Bretwalda of all Britain.

The king sat unmoved. He'd lived more than two score years and ruled for ten. The song was a ritual. Other men called for the harp in the time-honoured way. Hild felt her eyelids droop.

"Lilla's up! A brainteaser!" The gruff cry woke her. Standing at the king's side, Lilla chanted:

The wave, over the wave, a magical thing I saw,
Cleverly crafted, amazing in its beauty.
Wonder on the wave, wave become bone. What am I?

Suggestions flew. "Sea horse? Mermaid?" Guffaws, slapdowns, jokes. All eyes were on Lilla. No one saw the Wessex thegn stir in the gloom, dark hair, dark cloak, dark eyes glittering. Fascinated, Hild watched him creep round the hearthstone.

"Ma!" She nudged her mother.

"Ssh!" Lady Breguswid hissed.

"Remember last winter?" Lilla prompted. "The stranded heifer?"

"Daft, you were," growled someone, raising a laugh.

"Only a short crossing, and we saved the beast!" The memory of their winter dash to an offshore island raised a cheer. "When we landed, remember? Foam on the rocks, waves on the shore. Hard… brittle… solid…"

"Ice!" called a child, to satirical applause; Lilla had almost told them. Only then did Edwin notice the Wessex thegn.

"My lord, I am Eomer, envoy of Prince Cwichelm," he said silkily. "I bring his gift." Lifting a leather purse, he laid it on the table.

"Ah!" Edwin loosed the thong and held up a brooch the size of a man's fist, with engraved creatures interlocked in a great circle. Hild gasped. Their eyes looked bloody with garnets, and their writhing limbs flashed with gold.

"Superb!" Edwin breathed, spinning the piece. "Southern craftsmanship."

"And a message." Eomer's words sounded clipped. "In kingly form, as my lord bade: mind to mind, hidden in words."

"You have the harp," Edwin said absently.

A sneer flickered across Eomer's face. Glancing at the men hedging him in, he breathed deeply, flung his cloak over his left shoulder, propped his left foot on the dais and the harp on his left knee, and caressed the strings with his right hand in a fluid ripple which ended low on the right where his cloak hung down.

Crafted by hands of the fastest and truest,

he sang,

I steal slowly up, my sting lasts for ever;
Honour I bring to the honest and true. What am I?

In a final flourish, he stroked down the strings. From under the hem of his cloak he drew a dagger the length of his forearm. Swinging it up, he leaped onto the dais and lunged at the king.

"Death blow!" Lilla shrieked, solving the riddle, and threw himself across Edwin's body. "To the king! To the…"

"Vengeance!" Eomer stood over Edwin, striking down at his guts. Blood flooded the king's skirts and pooled in the straw. The queen swayed. Hild shrieked. Lilla pinned the king down. Again the blade rose and fell.

"To the king!" Lilla choked on the cry.

"Hreth!" Eomer snarled, wrenching out his weapon to strike again.

"Mine!" Forthere tore a spear from the wall. "Thor, guide me!" he cried, and hurled. The momentum carried him forward, knife outstretched. "Curse you! Apostate! Woden's ravens tear out your eyes!"

The spear thudded into Eomer's back. He crashed to the floor and rolled. Forthere slashed down with his knife. Eomer stabbed upwards. Benches scraped, men collided, weapons clashed, women shrieked. The royal Companions crowded at Hild's feet, jabbing, jabbing down and again.

"Look to the queen!" came a sudden cry.

"Don't stand there gawping, girl!" her mother snapped in her ear. "Ethelburga's collapsed. Give me a hand!"

* * *

Fire crackle was the only sound in the queen's lodging. After her premature labour, Ethelburga slept, pale and exhausted, the child burbled in its cradle, and even Hild's mother dozed upright on a stool against the wall.

Hild had fetched and held and carried all night long, but she couldn't sleep; her mind was spinning: all that blood.

She remembered Ma once saying, *Don't be in a hurry to grow up. You'll know when it's time, from the blood.* The blood of life, she meant, which had come with the child in the night and filled the queen's bed.

But Hild saw only the blood of death: bullock's blood, Edwin's blood, the blood of the assassin. It was everywhere: under her nails, in her hair, on the soles of her sandals, and drenching her hem. The soak bucket was full of bloody clouts.

Her head began to droop. The fire was warm and a gentle clicking came from two small boys, awake and playing knucklebones behind the screen.

"Why?" came a bellow outside the door. "Why hold back?"

Suddenly Hild was wide awake. It was the king, very much alive – praise the gods! – in a rage, and coming here.

"Cwichelm!" she heard. "He was Cwichelm's man!"

"Pa!" Uscrea, Edwin's four-year-old son, burst eagerly round the screen. His curls bounced, his tunic was awry, and he trod on Hild in his rush to the door.

"G-grandp-pa!" Yffi followed. At seven, he was more controlled, the child of Edwin's eldest son by his first marriage. Living in the queen's household since his mother died, he played happily with Uscrea, but stammered in the presence of adults.

"Don't!" Hild scrambled up, grabbing both their tunics. Not a good time to play ambush, with the king raging like a wounded boar. Tough old warlord, he must be coming to inspect his latest offspring. Keeping a firm grip on the boys, Hild nudged her mother.

"King's coming!" she hissed.

"Quick! Those hurdles by the fire." Lady Breguswid leapt into action as if she'd never slept. Seizing the stands of damp washing, she pushed them at her daughter. "And the buckets. Get them out of sight. The boys, too." She glanced round the room, patted the bed covers and stationed herself between the queen and the door. Hild bundled washing and children behind the partition and stood blocking the gap.

"Let go, Bass!" they heard Edwin snap at his Companion. "My legs still work." By now Queen Ethelburga was awake, listening wordless and wide-eyed. Three sharp knocks from the herald's staff, and the plank door swung back to vibrate against the outside wall. The fire leapt, and a swathe of chill morning light flooded the queen's lodging. The baby howled.

Clutching his red cloak tightly around his middle as if he were holding in his guts, Edwin dragged himself inside, Bass at one elbow, and the queen's tall chaplain at the other.

"Enough!" He elbowed them away and staggered to Breguswid's stool, lowering himself with an involuntary groan. His white hair hung lank, his face was gaunt, and Hild thought she could see blood seeping under his fist.

The infant gave a piercing wail. Hild looked for guidance to her mother. Her flash of inattention was all it took. The boys ran past her to the king, expecting him to fling wide his arms and toss them in the air. When he didn't, they drew up, disconcerted. Hild's mother glared.

"Now, my young warriors!" Edwin tousled their heads. "Show me the newborn." They set the cradle rocking. Wincing, Edwin lifted an arm and patted the queen's hand.

"You're well, Tatae?" he asked gently. "No need to ask after the child!"

"She's in good voice," Ethelburga chuckled, relaxing at his endearment. "Her father's daughter."

The mood in the room lightened. Lady Breguswid lifted the swathed bundle and the crying stopped, provoking a titter from the men at the door. She held the child out to the king.

"Fierce warrior princess, eh? Look!" Edwin's finger was trapped in the baby's grip. "Strong enough to breed dynasties. Anfled, I thought we'd call her. Anfled. What do you say, Tatae?"

"Anfled?" Ethelburga wrinkled her nose, but her eyes smiled. "Ani? So be it, my lord."

"Good." Raising her hand to his lips, Edwin leaned wearily back against the wall. "Show her round, lady. Present her to my thegns. Boys, escort!"

Hild watched as her mother, flanked by the two princes, circulated among the king's men at the door. They poked at the bundle, murmuring their pride in a king who could, despite his white locks, beget a second child younger than his grandson, Yffi.

"What a queen you brought me from Kent, Paulinus!" Edwin smiled at the dark-robed chaplain, then turned to his Companion. "Bass, tell Coifi to send out heralds. Sacrifice to the goddess Freyr for her gift of a child."

"My lord!" Paulinus butted in. "It was our prayers and the grace of God, the queen's God, that brought you both safely through. Better a thanksgiving Mass."

"Your bishop is impertinent, Tatae!"

"You would not begrudge us a thanksgiving, my lord?" The queen held out her hand appealingly. "We might have lost the child."

"We did lose two good men: Forthere, and Lilla, my oldest friend," he said bitterly. "And you want to give thanks?"

"Yes," the queen answered steadily. "We have the child… and… you." She tapped his arm at each word. "We owe thanks for Lilla. He saved your life."

"And I shall avenge his."

A ragged cheer broke from the thegns. Whether accepting the princess or approving the king's promise, Hild couldn't tell, but it mellowed Edwin.

"You're cold, Tatae," he said unexpectedly. "Girl, build up the fire."

Hild sprang into action, relieved to have something to do.

"Only a little tired." Ethelburga sighed, long used to living her life in public. "I should like Paulinus to offer a Christian thanksgiving."

How strong she was, Hild thought as she blew on the smouldering ashes; how clever to coax Edwin with her fragility. Everyone knew he'd sworn at his marriage to honour the queen's faith.

"We could hold both together," Edwin said idly, with an impish glance at Paulinus. "Mine to Freyr, yours to Christ."

Paulinus rose to the bait. "Oh, my lord!" he groaned. "Which of your gods has the power of Christ?"

"My gods are the gods of our people," Edwin retorted. "They've proved their power over generations. My victories, my lands and wealth…"

"But Hreth cannot give you a baby," cried Paulinus. "It is not in her power. Freyr cannot deal vengeance to traitors. Not one of your gods can meet all your needs."

"No god can," Edwin snapped, then hissed with pain.

"The true God can," Paulinus roared.

Hild ducked, waiting for an explosion. The thegns muttered. Edwin was their champion, their sworn lord, their sun. Was he to be cowed by this forceful, hawk-nosed priest?

Paulinus pulled himself together. "Forgive me, my lord. But all night we prayed and our God listened. It was he saved your life, he dealt death to the traitor, he watched over your lady's pain and brought this bright new life to birth. Has any one of the old gods such power?"

"Paulinus," Edwin said wearily, "you came to Northumbria to serve the queen, not me. My loyalty is to my people and their traditions…"

"No, my lord!" Paulinus started to pace. "It's mad…"

"Careful!"

"… madness for the most powerful king in the land to worship any but the most powerful king of the heavens. I am God's servant. But I owe it to you, my earthly lord, to offer the best."

From the hearthstone Hild saw his tall figure stop in the doorway, blocking the light. The king, who would in health have outpaced him, crouched on a low stool, weak and shaken. The mood was tense. Not the moment to poke the logs.

"Certainly we need the strongest gods. Don't you think so, Uscrea?" Edwin hugged his son to his side, and flinched. "A bargain! I'll strike a bargain with you, Paulinus."

"My lord?"

"But not till I've avenged Lilla's death." His fighters drew themselves up. Even in weakness, he played on men like a lyre, Hild thought.

"Can I come with you, Pa? To fight?" A warlord in the making, young Uscrea.

"When you can sit your horse," Edwin smiled, "you shall come to the muster."

"Have a heart, my lord," his mother sighed. "He's barely four."

"I'm taking the warband south." Edwin gripped his small son's shoulder and looked him straight in the eye. "You must guard the queen, your mother. At Bamburgh, in the north. Yffi will be your lieutenant."

"My l-lord." His grandson snapped upright, proudly accepting the commission.

"And Yffi's father will be in charge."

"No!" came a sudden cry from Osfrid, Edwin's eldest son and Yffi's father. "My lord, this is unjust!" He was a bluff, weathered man in his thirties. Typically, he stood among the thegns, looking less a prince, more a man of action.

"Osfrid, I need someone to hold Bernicia and guard our backs."

"It's my right as your eldest son to ride with you." Pushing through the crowd and shouldering Paulinus out of the way, Osfrid stopped before the king. "You dishonour me."

There was a gasp. Always forthright, Osfrid stood defiant. Edwin wouldn't stand this, thought Hild. He looked like a wounded stag circled by yapping dogs.

"It's not about honour, Osfrid." Edwin looked up at him mildly. "It's strategy."

"At my age – younger – you were given troops to lead, you won victories. You owe me that chance. When shall I prove myself?" Sympathetic murmuring at the door; there'd been too little fighting lately.

"This is your chance, Osfrid. Be my regent in Bernicia, among the Twister's people, where there is no love for us."

"It brings no peril, carries no glory." Osfrid looked his father's mirror image: long hair, steely eyes, furrows round the mouth, white knuckles and heaving chest. Marooned between them, the boys looked to and fro in consternation.

"No peril?" Edwin mused. "I wonder." He was trying to keep the temperature down, Hild thought. She crept forward and pulled the boys back to the fire. Upset by his father's defiance, Yffi picked up an end of charred wood and started drawing on the hearthstone. Hild fished out a lump for Uscrea.

"What's playing in that devious mind of Cwichelm's?" Edwin continued. "Osfrid, what would you do in his place?"

"Expect an attack. Drill the troops."

"Mm." Edwin seemed to be weighing Osfrid up and – Hild

wasn't sure why she thought this – finding him wanting. Yffi sensed it, too. He'd broken his charcoal, gripping so tightly, while Uscrea drew on unperturbed.

"D'you know what I'd do?" Edwin urged. "Expect an attack, yes. But I'd lay a trap."

"How?" Osfrid flushed. Edwin was hard on him, Hild thought. He'd held the peace for years. What chance had there been for his son?

"Attack's the best defence." Edwin was remorseless. "In Cwichelm's shoes, I'd invade Northumbria."

"Here? You cannot mean…!"

"Not in Deira where we belong," Edwin snapped. "In Bernicia, the Twister's homeland, where we're hated as conquerors."

"Bamburgh Rock is unassailable!"

"I'd lure the garrison out, split the enemy, divert them from the main attack…"

"I shouldn't be diverted!" Osfrid had a soldier's obstinacy.

"You wouldn't! That's precisely why…" Edwin exploded, and stopped short. Osfrid was white. The king shuffled irritably on the stool. Taking a deep breath, he said quietly, "Son, no one's more determined than you. You're the right man to dig in at Bamburgh and trap the fox while I burn out his den."

"It's an insult!" Osfrid stood rigid.

"It's a key command," Edwin snapped.

"Not a prince's command," Osfrid roared. "Anyone could do it."

"It won't be anyone!" Edwin's face was contorted. "It'll be you. With the bulk of the army."

"What?" Osfrid's hand flew to his sword. "The bulk of the army? To guard your new sow and her piglets!"

Yffi yelped. At seven years old, he knew his father had gone too far. Hild gripped him round the shoulders.

The herald shoved the ceremonial mace against Osfrid's chest. Edwin staggered to his feet and, swaying, struck his son hard on the mouth, twice. Osfrid stood glaring, face reddening. His father glared back.

"Unspeakable cur! Out!" Edwin roared, pointing at the door. "You talk of insults! Get out. Now!"

A brittle silence. Osfrid broke it, slamming his sword into its scabbard.

"My father! To steal my honour! In front of my son!" With an anguished glance at Yffi, he swung to the door. "I'll never forgive you!"

* * *

"He thinks you're playing. Let me take him." Hild yanked the puppy to her side and pushed his back end. "Sit, Dog! Sit! Good boy." Gripping the leather thong, she walked forward. "Come, Dog. Heel, heel! See, Uscrea, calm and firm, like this. You try."

She chuckled as Edwin's small son walked ahead, leading his wolfhound like a shoulder-high mount.

"Hild, w-w-what's that?" Yffi skidded up, falcon on wrist. Beyond the buildings a pack of dogs worried a rocky mound.

"Let's look!" Uscrea turned aside.

"No!" Hild yelped; it was the assassin's corpse drying out. Edwin wanted the skull to hurl at the enemy. "Look!" She pointed up. "Is that a sparrowhawk?"

Following her gaze, the boys raced to the stepping stones. Hild's spirits soared; a bright, bracing day and the boys' company which she enjoyed, unlike her sister who preferred the queen's ladies. Women's business bored Hild. She always did her share of chores – well, too; slipshod work earned a beating – but she didn't share her sister's dreams. Four years older, Hereswid loved the weaving shed where the women fashioned robes in Ethelburga's southern style. Hild loathed the floating fibres and gloom. Someone always wanted the door shut against draughts, and the din became unbearable as their gossip shrilled above the clunk of the loom weights.

"How about it?" Hereswid would giggle, posing against the loom with the cloth drawn next to her golden hair. "What d'you think, sis?"

"You'll pull it out of shape!" Hild carped, secretly admiring Heri's style.

"Wilding!" Hereswid taunted Hild. "Hillsprite!" Just because of her unruly dark mop. How could sisters be so unlike?

"Can I paddle, Hild?" Uscrea wobbled on a stepping stone. "Will you take Dog?" Yffi had sprinted across and was scrambling up the wooded ravine, hawk-arm stiff and sturdy legs pumping.

"Wait at the top, Yffi," she shouted, casting in some daisy heads as an offering for the water sprites. She tightened Uscrea's sandals and he splashed about, lifting stones and grasping after fish. No one was in sight. Tucking her skirts in her girdle, Hild waded knee-deep, trailing one hand among the kingcups and gripping the leash with the other. The hound suddenly bolted up the far bank and shook himself in a rainbow of spray. Shrieking with laughter, Hild and Uscrea scattered. She escaped the shower but blundered in up to her thighs.

"Race you up the hill!" Uscrea grabbed the leash and took off. How alike they were! Yffi, Edwin's grandson, had grown taller and leaner with age, while Uscrea was still round and chubby, but they shared the fair hair and scrubbed cheeks of high birth. Scarred over the years, Edwin must once have looked like them.

And he'd acknowledged her as kin. Death dogged royal steps, they said: look at her father, cut down in his youth. Was it treachery, disguised as flattery, that carved furrows down Edwin's cheeks? It must be hard to judge between a wily toad and Osfrid's honest frustration.

"I won!" Uscrea and the hound gambolled in the sunshine above. Hild slithered on leaf mould, hampered by wet skirts.

"Ssh! Listen!" Yffi commanded. Emerging from the trees, Hild squinted at a lonely curlew wheeling in the sun, and listened to the skylarks twittering out of sight. Suddenly Uscrea pounced and the boys collapsed in a wrestling heap.

"Mind your kestrel!" Hild called, struggling to unpin Uscrea's cloak while he squirmed.

"Watch m-me, Uscrea!" Yffi lifted the hood from his kestrel and tossed the bird up. She swooped high, coasting on air currents, soaring in freedom. Yffi swung a long lure round and round above his head.

"Kessy!" he called, whistling in the sharp, high tone his father had taught him. The bird dropped like a dead thing, landing on Yffi's arm to tear at the bait.

"Don't let her eat too much." Hild flopped onto the heather. "She'll only come if she's hungry. Now, here's your food." She unwrapped bread and cheese. "You might find some early bilberries."

"I'm thirsty."

"Look for running water. Clear, mind." They meandered off, chewing as they went, Uscrea tangling with his puppy's leash, and Yffi stroking his kestrel.

Caressed by the breeze, Hild lay back on their discarded cloaks, breathing the scents of peat and furze. Like washday, she thought, when she kept guard while the others bathed. Often some loafer crept up to spy and the daft women splashed and giggled until the last minute before ducking. Last time, no one bathed: the stream was too pink with blood.

She relished the chance to ponder. As Eostre's maid, she'd sprinkle crops and livestock, make offerings for rain and sun, bless the first fruits. Some girls turned into women by the end of their year of service, wed even, left home for a new life. What would happen to her?

"Show him your titbit, Uscrea. Don't give him any yet." Yffi broke into her thoughts, training Uscrea to handle his hound. "Over here, look! Let's try him in this hollow."

"Dog!" Uscrea held out his hand and the wolfhound bounded up for his reward. "Sit!" They tried again and again. Then they rambled round, bringing her small boys' treasures: a pierced stone, a bird's egg, a flint arrowhead.

"Get rid of it," she warned. "It's an elf-bolt. Bad luck."

Everything happened at once. Yffi loosed the hawk's jesses, Uscrea unleashed the hound to walk at heel, Dog nosed a clump of scrub and raised a hare, then bounced in pursuit, barking excitedly.

37

"Dog, here!" Uscrea cried in vain. Yffi was straining upwards, watching his falcon circle. For an instant, she stalled, quivering gently. Then like a stone she dropped, swooped, and rose again. High shriek; echoing silence. With languid strokes the bird flew away, prey dangling from her claws.

"She's gone!" Yffi started to run, lure trailing. "Kessy! Come back!"

"Swing the lure. Whistle. Your special whistle." Hild had little hope. Too many hawks were lost in training. "Stop, Yffi! Whistle!" He was sobbing too much, and set off again. "Yffi, wait!" He carried on running. "Keep to the track," she shouted with all her breath and hoped he heard.

"Where did Dog go, Uscrea? Call him! Louder! Stop crying, or he won't know your voice." Eventually the puppy crashed through the bushes, bowling Uscrea over and licking him enthusiastically. Hild leashed him and rolled up their cloaks. "Now, come on. We must catch Yffi."

He was far ahead, running towards the high tops. They'd never climbed so far. It was where strangers walked the salt road, outlaws lurked, and peat cuttings deepened to swamps.

"Yffi, wait! Y…fi…i!"

But Uscrea couldn't go fast. Red-faced and puffing, he complained of a stitch.

"Piggy-back?" Hild hoisted him up. With his arms round her neck, his legs gripping her waist, the hound tugging at her wrist and their clothing in her arms, she panted hard as she ran uphill along the rough track. Yffi was out of sight.

He would slow down, she hoped. The track was clear. He'd follow it and she'd only to persevere…

Provided he was not diverted into moss or cotton grass. If he fell face down in a quagmire…

But he knew the moor, he could read the landscape, the safe ground. She had only to keep going…

He was young, though. And the kestrel was his pride and joy, the mark of his manhood. If she veered off…

"Gee-up!" Uscrea dug in his heels. Hild laboured.

"Yffi, wait for us!" Her cry sounded thin in the vastness. He might be lying injured, a twisted ankle. Perhaps he was calling, his voice lost on the wind.

"Yffi, where are you?"

"There!" Uscrea pointed. The hills stretched as far as she could see, rounded and bare. "Someone moving!"

"Where? I can't see…" She put him down and peered along the track. He was right. Against the evening sun she saw movement. Men or moor-elves? She shuddered. Oh, Yffi!

Straining her eyes, she saw a gang of men digging and heaving. If they were hard to see, what hope was there of spotting one boy? She toyed with the hound's ears, wondering if she dare approach.

"Can you hear them, Uscrea? I want to get near and listen. Quiet as a tracker. Can we do that? Up you get."

In the growing dusk she picked her way cautiously, each step taking them further from home. If she fell… if Yffi were lost… if he died…

They came to the lip of a gully where a beck rippled pale in the gloom.

"Elves of moor and brook, avert your eyes," she muttered, and slithered down the side, Uscrea spurring her like a warhorse. At the water's brink, she tumbled him off. "Let's drink."

They knelt over the water, slurping from cupped hands. A low growl from Dog alerted her. Hild jumped to her feet, pushed the child behind her, and drew the hound to her side.

"May I be of service?" On the far bank, a young man sat his horse. Eyebrows raised, he looked her up and down.

"Who are you?" Hot, agitated, her face dripping water, she gripped the hound's leash.

"Chilly greeting," he said drily. "Erpwald is my name, and here's my man."

She didn't recognize the name, only the manner. Long hair and a body servant signalled high status: one of her own kind.

"What are you doing here?" Nervousness made her brusque.

"I could ask you the same," he chuckled. "With more reason. A girl and child at dusk in the wilderness?"

He was annoying. She'd thought Uscrea was hidden.

"I heard calling," he continued. "Was that you?" She examined him, aware of her helplessness, nerving herself. "You'll throttle that hound if you screw the leash tighter!" His laugh was like a bark.

"Tell me what you're doing here." She hoped she sounded cool and fearless.

"I've come with Edwin's men to prepare a tomb for one of his Companions who was killed."

"Lilla?"

"So you know?"

"Everyone knows. He gave his life to save the king." Her assurance drew Uscrea forward to put his hand in hers.

"Now you have my credentials, may I be of help?" When he jumped from the horse, he was less awesome. He had the bandy legs of a man who lived in the saddle. The wind streaked hair across his face, revealing a white scar from ear to mouth and a crooked smile. Carefully he led his mount over the stream.

"May I take you home, lady?" With lordly formality he held out a hand. "Let me help you onto my horse. I don't know you, but I recognize this young man." His grin at Uscrea was short of a tooth. "His absence will soon be noted, if it isn't already. He's the king's son."

"Ah!" She felt like a snared bird under the trapper's eye.

"You do right to guard him, but you can trust me. I'm bound to Edwin as his guest. He'll want his son back."

She longed to trust him. She thought she could.

"You still hesitate, lady?"

"Yffi's missing, you see," Uscrea announced importantly. "We can't go home without him. And his kestrel."

"More of you?" Erpwald sighed ruefully, grinning again. "Tell me."

She did, shedding the immense burden and suddenly feeling tired. Briskly, he sent his servant to arrange a search.

"We'll find him for you," he said. "Come, mount." He lifted Uscrea up to sit in front of her. She shivered. The sun that reddened the tops had left the gully chill. "You're cold, lady. Take my cloak." He unpinned his large shoulder brooch and enveloped her and the child. She leaned against him, abandoning herself to his strength and warm leathery smell. She wished she could stay cradled in his arm.

He set off downstream, leading the hound and horse, and chatting to distract her: they'd followed the River Derwent to its source, made offerings to Woden, dug a firepit and built a funeral pyre; Lilla's soul would fly to Valhalla in the flames; his ashes would be buried in the pit and his spirit would guard the land.

"Is he there now?" Uscrea asked sleepily.

"Not yet. The king will lead the cortège." He stopped to listen to a clatter of stones behind them. "Steady, man!" he called over his shoulder. "You'll break the nag's legs!"

"Is this the boy?" His servant approached. "Can't get a word out of him."

"Yffi! Oh, Yffi! You're safe!" Hild's voice wobbled in relief.

He sat the horse, pale and stiff, his kestrel on his wrist. She stretched out her arms.

"L-leave m-me alone!" Yffi rasped, shrinking away. His face was strained and he looked straight ahead. "L-let's g-go home."

* * *

It was the growling that woke her. Reluctantly, Hild reached outside the warm skins to cradle his muzzle. "Ssh, Dog! Too early."

Then she heard it, and crouched, listening. No challenge. No thud of grounded spears. A muttered exchange. Only Edwin came to the queen at night and he usually gave warning. The hound bristled.

Light shifted as the door opened. A soft shuffle. Hild tensed and her pulse throbbed. Grasping Dog's scruff she edged along the partition and twisted her head round the end. Outlined against the dawn a figure groped forward.

With a spring, the hound sank his teeth into the man's shoulder. Stifling an oath, the intruder raised his other arm. A blade gleamed.

"No!" Hild leapt to seize his wrist.

"Thor's guts! Let go, girl. Call the beast off."

"Edi?" she yelped. The king's second son? She hung on tight. "Guards! Lights!"

Edi was revealed, twisted beneath the wolfhound. "Yes, Edi," he said ironically. "Now, call off this cur."

"Not till you put that knife away and I know why you're here."

"King's business!"

"Creeping like a cut-throat?" Sceptical, Hild hung on. "Sneaking into the queen's lodging in the dog-watch? What're you after?"

Shamefaced before the guard, Edi muttered, "Osfrid's boy."

"Yffi?" she gasped.

"Yes, my brother's son," he drawled. From a man splayed at her feet, it was ridiculous. She laughed scornfully.

He growled, "Call off the brute, curse you!"

"Why should the king want Yffi?"

"To join the men."

"Secretly? At this hour?" Some ploy of Edi's, more like.

"Yes," he snapped. "Lilla's funeral. We ride early."

"I'm ready, s-sir." The toneless voice startled them both. Yffi stood by the partition, booted and cloaked. His face was blanched and his hair draggled, but his lips were tight with determination: seven years of age, shouldering a man's burdens. "Come, D-dog! Here, b-boy!"

Releasing Edi, the hound sat at Yffi's feet, tail thumping. Yffi fondled his ears. "I'm ready, Hild. I'll g-go with my uncle to serve my lord the king."

"God go with you, Yffi!" The queen's calm voice jolted them. "Care for him, Edi, for his father's sake."

"For his father's sake? Oh, I will," sneered Edi, massaging his shoulder. "Let's get going, boy."

"My falcon? In the stables…"

"Oh, the famous falcon!" Edfrid gripped the boy's arm. "Leave it. Make your farewell to the queen." He gave an exaggerated bow.

42

"So sorry, lady, to have disturbed you."

Dry-throated, Hild watched Yffi march into the bleak dawn. She didn't trust Edi; he'd inherited the king's cunning, while Osfrid – and his son – had all Edwin's bravery. She shook with fury at Edi's insolence. Failure. On her first lone night duty.

"You were brave, Hild." Ethelburga's face showed no emotion. "Dress now and attend me to prayers."

* * *

The chapel looked like a workshop: plain, bare wood, with monks on either side of a cross on a table. The queen knelt, head in hands, soft skirts fanning out in the straw. In a monotone, one group echoing the other, the men chanted softly. Mesmerized, Hild felt herself relax. So this was Ethelburga's secret. Far from kindred, ill-matched consort of a fierce old warlord, prey to insult and pain, she always shed calm. It came from worshipping her God.

There was no climax, none of Thor's frenzy, no High Priest or sacrifice. The singing simply stopped, leaving an echo in the stillness. Then the monks bustled forward like ordinary men.

"James is back, lady... from Canterbury... he's brought it..." they clamoured.

"Would you like to see it, lady?" said an old monk. Two of them set a heavy package on the table, unfolded its bindings, and displayed a large folio.

"The Gospel book." Ethelburga touched it reverently. "Brother James fetched it? Let him open it."

James blushed, tenderly raising the leather cover to turn the vellum pages. Gasps of wonder greeted the myriad swirling letters and red and blue capitals.

"Will you read a little, brother?" Ethelburga said. Seeing her drawn and sweaty, Hild dabbed her forehead and loosened her cloak.

"*Beati pauperes spiritu...*" he read. Over the queen's shoulder, Hild watched his finger move along the rows. When he stopped, the only sound was a satisfied sigh.

"What does it mean, brother?" asked the queen.

"Like music, the Latin. But alas, my Anglian," James sighed, replacing his finger. "*Favoured are the poor of spirit, for they shall have comfort…*"

"That can't be right!" cried someone. "Favourites have wealth, lands…"

"True," said a deep voice at the door. "But that's not the only kind of favour."

"Paulinus!" They shifted to make room for him.

"Look at my eating knife." He drew it from his belt.

"It's curved!" one old monk exclaimed.

"Mine's worn at the tip!" said another. They held out their knives, bent, stumpy, chipped.

"Once, they were well honed," Paulinus said, "but eating, scribing, whittling," his eyes kindled, "all kinds of use has shaped them."

What did he mean? There was a ferment of murmuring: "My best tool… used all the time… keep them in our belts…"

Hild's mind followed theirs: "Most used? Kept close? Favourite? A favourite knife?"

Paulinus nodded. "Kept close to Our Lord, trusted, *favoured*, is the man who's poor in spirit, not proud." Then he recited the rest in his stilted English. "*Favoured are the kindly… those in grief… those who suffer for what is right.* My lady," he turned to Ethelburga, "see how your gift has powered us, mind and spirit. May God reward you!"

"He already has." She stood up, extending her hand. "Your joy, your teaching…"

"But you're tired. Let me take you back."

"Could you spare James? He'll give me news from home."

Sunrise gilded the treetops and the vill was stirring. Children with kindling, women at hearthfires, slaves carting slops – everyone greeted the queen. She responded to them all. James lost his shyness, gesturing, seeking the right word, as he told her the news from Kent: her brother wed to Emma from Germany and father of a son; the old bishop dead; Honorius to be consecrated by Paulinus who'd brought him to England. Hild listened, intrigued by this wider world.

Few men were about. They'd left for Lilla's howe. Hild tried, but failed, to see the procession among the trees: Edwin leading, slow with pain and grief; behind him, Yffi in his father's place with his uncle Edi; Bass and the other Companions behind. And Erpwald would be… somewhere. Erpwald! A spasm of excitement ran through her.

"Have you taken leave of your senses?" Her mother punctured her daydream. "Wake up, girl, the queen's fainting! Lady, it's too soon for you to be out." Pushing Hild aside, Breguswid took Ethelburga's arm. "Look sharp, brother. Help me carry her indoors."

"Rest, yes," laughed the queen, "but no carrying!"

The day was wearisome. Deprived of men's company, the ladies gossiped and sunned themselves outside the queen's door while she slept. Hereswid tried to amuse Uscrea while Hild walked up and down, jiggling and cooing as Ani thrashed and roared, mouth wide, face blotchy. She was glad to be sent for a wetnurse.

The cattle grazed their shadows. Willows whispered along the river. A horse whickered. *Of every tree the hawthorn bloweth fairest*, Hild hummed, ambling through the meadows, loathe to abandon the sensuous evening.

Returning through the vill, she was brutally driven aside by horsemen racing between the homesteads, vaulting obstacles, leaving a litter of bloody goats, broken thatch and terrified children. Soon Edwin rode past, swaying in the saddle, deadly pale and bolstered by his guards.

In the queen's lodging, he lay on the bed, blood seeping from his groin.

"Hild!" her mother barked, stirring a pot on the hearth and trying to tear a cloth with her teeth. Hild ripped it into strips and took over the stirring. Where were the women now? Never there when needed.

"My sons!" growled Edwin. "Osfrid defies me; Edi – Thor's hammer! Is that poultice going to take all night? A king rides at the front. Whoever overtakes me, supplants me. Edi knows… ah!" He winced as knife and needle bit. "And Edi raced me back!"

"Hild, concentrate!" hissed Ma. Comfrey and white willow were hard to blend. Seizing the mortar, her mother spread the paste on yarrow leaves. "Hold the cloths!"

"Treat it as a boy's frolic," Ethelburga said. "Beneath notice."

"But he damaged beasts and property, injured people! A king defends his people…ah!" He snorted as they lifted him to wrap the bandage round his middle. "Tatae, we must move on. Summon the warband."

"Of course." Ethelburga put a cup to his lips. "When you're better."

"Soon," he muttered. "To the heartland!"

2

DERWENTDALE

Stifled between steep crags and chalk downs, Hild yearned for open skies. She hated the mud, stench, anonymity, the galling mesh of ceremonies and raucous mob amusements. Now she was of age, she frittered long hours with bored, bickering women. In the crowded ginnels of the royal vill, there was no call for the services of Eostre's maid.

Beyond the dripping roofs, she glimpsed watermeadows slashed by the leaden river. Hard to believe it was the same Derwent that burbled up in the moors. Here, it ran sluggish through Edwin's tribal lands, lending its name to the Deirans. And here, worst of all, she had to don female finery.

"Stand still or you'll get speared!" Breguswid fumbled at her cloak, bunching a wad of fabric and piercing it with a gold pin as long as her hand. Round the point she twisted a gold crescent, dented with use. "There. That'll hold. If you go gracefully."

"Where's it from?"

"Your father," she said. "There wasn't much. Hereswid's ring, and this for you. Old-fashioned, but an heirloom of sorts."

Hild twirled experimentally, peering over her shoulder. The soft green wool of her robe swung out from the braided girdle. Somehow the new garments made her feel fluid, beautiful. She ran a finger round the brooch, feeling the discs embossed at either end of the crescent.

"It's yours now. Look after it." Her mother was rummaging in

47

a chest. "Your only inheritance, barring that wretched dark hair. Unruly as its wearer!"

"Oh, Ma!" Swinging round to protest, Hild glimpsed a tear in her mother's eye. Moments alone were rare in the women's lodging and intimacy did not come easily.

"Hereric's words," her mother said crisply. "You're a dark, beady creature, like me. All Briton. Not a hint of his Anglian blood." She tugged out a linen square. "That's why you must wear this."

Hild flinched. Her fair-haired sister could go bareheaded; she could not.

"A beautiful Hild. What a miracle!" she snorted, bending to have the veil fixed.

"Never beautiful." Pragmatic as ever, Ma. "But a miracle, yes." Hild was astounded. She'd only been joking. "You shouldn't be here. Born in a burning byre with killers smoking us out, and your father dead at your side. If you'd been a man-child, they'd have smashed out your brains."

"What!" The brutality was shocking.

"My father was king of Elmet," Breguswid said bleakly. "Edwin arranged our marriage. He had his eye on our rich fields round the Humber."

"Huh, with all his wealth!" Hild plumped down on the chest.

"Not then. He was still establishing himself." Her mother sat beside her. "He wanted my Hereric – his nephew, of course – to bring him tribute." A tinge of bitterness. "Anglians are never fair. Britons don't trust them."

"Even Father?"

"Understandable. He was Edwin's man." Breguswid stared ahead, fingering the corner of her veil. "They couldn't believe he was happy in his marriage, a man of honour."

"They didn't trust Father!" This was all new.

"Edwin was impatient, as always. He wanted my father out and Hereric in his place. The people didn't. They planned to despatch Edwin's man."

"Kill Father?"

"Yes. We fled to a place in the marshes. He went first, I followed with the baby…"

"Heri?"

Breguswid nodded abstractedly. "We didn't know he'd been poisoned. He wasn't where we'd planned. I searched and searched… I couldn't…" Emotion overwhelmed her. Hesitantly Hild put an arm round her.

"I couldn't…!" Breguswid pulled away, struggling against tears. "The baby cried – oh, how she cried! I was nearing my term… So tired." Her face twisted with shame and anger. "I gave up… hid in a byre…"

"You couldn't help it!"

"I wrapped us in my cloak, curled up, and found…" Awe crept into her tone. "I found a jewel. Not mine. Not garnets or mother-of-pearl. Something I'd never seen. Just lying there, in my lap, shining. It lit the whole land. There was singing… unearthly… Then the birth pangs started."

Somewhere outside a trumpet blared. Breguswid didn't hear.

"Heri cried… or perhaps it was me, I don't know… and he heard us." She mopped her face with her veil. Hild hugged her gently. "White he was, sweating, couldn't breathe. Managed to drag the bar across the door. We lay together. Till he died. They'd got dogs, knew we were inside, tried to smoke us out like rats…" Anger sharpened her voice. "Burst the door in. Found a dead man, a crying child, and you. Being born."

"What did they do?"

"I was one of their own. Young enough to be of use," she snorted. "Hereswid – they let me keep her. Even then she could charm with her pretty ways. And you…"

Commotion at the door. Crowds milling past. Hild knew she must go.

"You were safe, lying in my lap." Drained, tranquil, her mother spoke so quietly Hild only just heard. "A jewel from heaven."

"Hild!" Her sister crashed in and stood at the door. "They're asking for you. Come on, you'll be late."

"Coming." Greatly daring, Hild kissed her mother.

"You'll do." Breguswid reverted to her usual caustic tone. "Go gracefully. I'll be watching."

"You've been preening!" Heri crowed. "Never thought I'd see…"

"Look to your laurels!" Hild smirked, ducking under the lintel.

"No, really, you look lovely." Heri gave her an impulsive hug. "Good luck!"

"Race you!" Hild kilted up her skirts and darted away, gaudy as a dragonfly.

"Look out!" Heri's warning came too late. The track was oozy with slops and rainwater cascading from the low eaves. Hild just managed to vault a puddle scattering geese and goats. Venting her energy, outrunning her feelings: it felt good.

* * *

Slithering to a standstill nose-on to the king's herald, Hild wormed through the thegns and horses crowding the door and drew breath in the gloom of the hall, tugging her veil straight and pulling her skirts down over her boots.

"About time!" rasped Edwin, scooping Uscrea up and grunting at a burden which was usually no effort. "Come, lady."

With his boy on his shoulder, Edwin swept the queen to the door. There he stood, outlined in light, rain pearling his hair, nostrils flaring at the roars of acclamation. Close behind, Hild sensed his exultation.

With the instinctive timing of a swordsman, he waited just long enough before lifting Uscrea onto his horse and vaulting up behind. A gasp from Ethelburga, nothing else, hinted at the jarring pain which still dogged him after nearly two months. They rode forward side by side, smiling and serene, a picture of strength and security.

Hild scrambled onto her horse and bent to take the baby. No one else must carry the child to the naming, Edwin said; Hild had the ear of the gods. Tucking Ani under her cloak, Hild set her old hunter nose to tail with the queen's filly and plodded forward at the walking pace of the king's herald.

Crowds surged in the narrow lanes. Shivering in the dank mist, Hild envied the smiths forging spearheads which hissed when tossed onto piles in the rain, and leathercaps grunting over weapon practice between their sagging tents. The queen's horse shied. Her bodyguard staggered into Hild's flank. His eyes flicked nervously at the procession strung out behind. Edwin reined in to watch a cock fight till both birds lay bloody and heaving in the mud.

"Who'll share my supper?" cried the loser, wringing his bird's neck.

"For the winner!" Edwin flicked a gold ring. "Buy yourself a new cock. That one's had its day." Then he spurred on, pursued by ragged cheers.

In open country they climbed through a luminous drizzle which beaded their cloaks.

"Your permission, lady?" A horseman pulled in beside Hild. "Can this be the waif I met on the moors?"

"Erpwald!" With a lurch of delight she smiled at his bronzed grin and missing tooth. "My lord, I'm glad to be able to thank you…"

"So, you're Edwin's kin?" He gave her a glowing look.

"Well," she blushed, "he thinks I've the gods' favour…"

"Have you? The luck?"

"Eostre's." She eased the child on her arm.

"That was you, at the spring festival? What's your name?"

"Hild."

"Just Hild?"

"Hild, daughter of Hereric. His nephew."

"Erpwald!" Edwin had heard him. "Come and ride with me! About the route…"

"Honoured, my lord." He spurred forward: too eagerly for her liking. He was friendly, funny, and she wanted to know him better.

Coifi, the king's priest, awaited them in a hilltop grove, his white robes shining through the trees. His stance, his stillness, made Hild shudder; someone had told her that, before living memory, Eostre's maid was herself the spring sacrifice.

"Name?" With a start she saw Coifi holding out his arms for the child.

"Anfled." Edwin's voice rang out.

"To Woden's shrine," Coifi cried, bearing the baby into the trees. "Follow me!"

The king and queen, with Uscrea and Hild, stood before a dappled wooden altar, a spring purling nearby and thegns fidgeting behind. Coifi deftly slaughtered a pigeon, pronounced the gods well pleased, and named the baby.

It was a shock when the mood changed. Without warning, Coifi waved his staff wildly, drove the women back, and summoned the men.

"Death for death!" he cried. "Raise blades of vengeance to Hreth! Drink the spirit of Thor!"

Whipped to frenzy by his shrieking, men swarmed into the trees, slashing and splashing themselves with blood. Edwin's hearthmates and thegns of the warband, men of field and forest with spike or axe, all stampeded like panicked sheep.

"Oh, no!" Queen Ethelburga breathed.

At the back, isolated from men of rank, stalked a grim-faced Edi wearing no princely insignia, no warrior's sword: to a fighter, worse than death. A living example of how King Edwin punished those who slighted his dignity. A spearman marched beside him: bodyguard, perhaps, or minder. At their heels, pale and haunted, a young boy walked alone.

"Yffi!" Hild gasped.

"Hostage," murmured the queen. "Bearing his father's disgrace."

Wild cries and heavy stamping broke out. A shuddering screech brought momentary silence, then slow and calm came the hollow thud of many spears, interspersed with breathy barks like hounds on scent. Resinous smoke and the flare of torches streaked through the trees. More frenzied the drubbing, harsher the cries, till women were numbed by the thunderous vibration, and children shocked into wide-eyed silence. On and on, ceaselessly deafening, it shredded their nerves.

"What's happening, my lady?"

"I don't know, Hild. No woman is admitted to the sacred rites."

Hild conjured a bristling war line, swollen faces, cold glazed eyes. It was a powerful spell. To drug men to kill. Or to die.

"Uscrea? Will he be all right?"

"He's with the king," Ethelburga said impassively, then, "Listen!" Her lips parted as she strained to see down the hillside. "Hild, can you hear?"

"No… yes, something…" A faint drone beneath the rhythmic pulsing. Humming?

"They're coming!" Ethelburga sagged in relief. Hild saw her sister scramble up and other women take to their feet.

Through the lengthening shadows a dark column wound uphill. Nearer and louder came their long, deep note. The queen's monks, striding loose-limbed at a measured pace, unswerving as a slingshot, straight for the grove. Full and deep they raised their voices, breathing in unison, booming their message:

We pray thee, O Lord, in thy mercy
Turn away thy wrath from this people,
For we are sinners. Alleluia!

The fighters gaped from the trees. Led by Brother James's tenor, the priests advanced, rough robes swinging. At the edge of the grove they filed to each side as if at their altar, leaving the centre to their leader. Paulinus grounded his cross like a spear, crying, "Where is the king? I come to claim my due!"

"Here I am, Paulinus." Edwin leaned nonchalantly against a trunk just beyond the light, with Uscrea perched on his shoulder. Levering himself upright he patted the child towards the queen. "Is this a challenge, priest?" He approached to stand eye to eye with Paulinus.

"Only if you read it so, my lord." Paulinus held his palms up. "You've had your ceremony. It's my turn now, to claim the princess for our God."

"Claim her?" Edwin was stony.

"To baptize her and give thanks to God."

"Baptize her? Yes, I promised the queen. You may baptize the child. And any of her household who choose," Edwin said with deceptive equanimity. It quickly curdled. "You risk my wrath for this?"

"No risk, my lord. My God protects me…"

"Oh?"

"… as he protected you, and restored you to your kingdom."

"Redwald restored me," Edwin bridled. "Redwald of East Anglia. He steered me to victory…"

"With God's might," Paulinus countered. "God was with you at the River Idle. He deserves your homage."

"I pay homage to no one," Edwin snapped.

"Your gratitude, then," Paulinus insisted, "for the greatest kingdom in the land, for ten years of peace, your recovery from the assassin's knife, a brood of children to carry on your name…" His voice rose and he thumped his staff. "These were not your doing!"

A sudden chill. No one stirred. If this powerful priest succeeded, Hild thought, the king would have no voice at the shrine of the gods, and she would have no role as Eostre's maid.

"They were God's gifts," Paulinus continued quietly, "and a lord acknowledges his debts." This went without saying. The Companions nodded. Edwin could not cavil.

"If I honour your God, Paulinus," he said slowly, "will he crush my foes?"

"If your cause is just. My God is a fair God."

"Then we'll give him a fair trial!" Edwin strode forward. "We'll go to war." His men roared in delight. Edwin smiled; he'd got what he wanted. "The Christian God will ride with us. If he rights our wrongs, avenges our friends, then I shall worship him. This," he seized Paulinus's hand and raised it high, "is my word and my bond!"

* * *

Beltane was long past, the day when cattle were driven between fires to their summer grazing. Sun and moon duelled for mastery of the heavens. Edwin was fit again, tracking boar and hunting duck in the dawn marshes. Daily he drilled his troops after the sun had passed its zenith. Anyone could fight in the fresh of the morning; his men must be tougher. Again and again they ran up the slope from the river, banging heavy axes on wicker shields and yelling their pulsating warcry.

"Bitches!" he bawled. "You sound like new-whelped bitches! No more mewling. From the belly. Again!" They loved him for it, guffawing at his insults.

Sometimes they grappled hand-to-hand, showing off to the queen's ladies who wagered on the biggest bruise, and little boys who copied them with sticks. Edwin donned his jewelled helmet and sword, a sight to strike dread into dying eyes, and wrestled with his Companions, gradually inflicting more blows than he suffered.

Fresh thegns joined the muster, bringing fieldmen to add weight to the warband. Used to roaming the hills or weeding crops, they fell prey to thugs in the overcrowded lanes. Quarrels flared.

"Coifi whipped them up!" Edi stood over the king. "We must march, or there'll be trouble."

"Soon," said Edwin coolly.

Edi flushed. "They'll melt away for harvest. Besides, Cutha said the Bernicians think you're scared."

A strained silence. Hild froze; Edi had only recently been restored to Edwin's favour.

"Hear him out, my lord." Ethelburga looked up from her handwork. "Edi's telling you what no one else would dare."

"I know, Tatae. I'm waiting for intelligence from Bass."

Edi may have been snubbed, but he was vindicated. Life in the royal hall became rowdy, violent and squalid. Hild saw a spearman slither down the wall where neighbours kicked him and a server tripped, dousing him in ale. Uscrea giggled.

55

"No place for children," said the queen. "Lady Breguswid, take Uscrea out."

A dozen thegns cajoled and bullied the troops to order. Extra trestles were piled with food and drink. Laughter grew raucous. Bread, bones, cabbage stalks flew across the trestles. Underneath, dogs shied away from kicks, or scrapped for leavings.

Hild was relieved when the queen rose. Her women banded together to go to their lodging. Hild followed Ethelburga. She and her mother were on duty. Breguswid partnered her daughters when the warband was about, and kept a knife up her sleeve. *Giggling girls attract notice*, was one of her sayings; *drunks leave a litter of bastards.*

They settled themselves on the bench outside the royal chamber. Separated from the hall by a simple partition, they couldn't escape the retching and grunts of fighters at pleasure.

"Ignore it, girl." Her mother massaged her knees. "Use the time." She pulled her distaff out of her girdle and Hild copied her with a sigh.

"Which thegns are on duty?" She bent over a tangle in her lap.

"Depends who's left standing. Here, give me that." Deftly, Breguswid sorted the threads to free the spindle whorl. "Grip here. See?"

"It's so thick!"

"You'll need thick cloth in the wilds of Bamburgh." Her mother's fingers flew.

"Wilder than this?" Hild nodded at thuds beyond the partition.

"You won't remember, I suppose. Last time you were only an infant. There's enough fresh air in the old fortress, even for you."

"Windy?" Hild's spirits lifted.

"Cold," Breguswid said repressively. "It's in the middle of the sea, almost."

"Safe, then."

"Quite. The Twister's ancestors held out there for a generation."

"Anglians? Holed up?"

"When they first sailed here. In my grandfather's time. He was with the Britons who tried to push them out. Unsuccessfully,"

Breguswid said drily. "We'll be safe there all right, unless Osfrid gets up to tricks."

Hild chewed her lip. Royal children were rarely close to their parents and Edwin's household was seething with rivalry. She respected her mother's powers of survival and clear-eyed realism. The longer they spent together, the better Hild could read her: her sharp tongue concealed deep feelings, especially for the queen who, like herself, lived among aliens.

"He's coming!" Breguswid hauled herself up and stowed her spinning carefully in her belt. Hild dropped her distaff, unravelling the thread. Nothing for it but to kick the lot under the bench.

"You'll lead the queen's guard, Cutha." Edwin strode up, then stopped dead. "The queen's asleep?"

"Yes, my lord." Lady Breguswid's eyes were politely lowered. Hild stared. A third man came round the partition: the gods were kind tonight.

"Keep your eyes open," Edwin instructed Cutha. "Bernicians may be Anglians, but they're our oldest enemies. You, Erpwald, will lead the diversionary attack" – an eager nod of assent – "while I infiltrate by river. Once Bass gets back with a route." He sighed, turning into the queen's chamber.

The two men raised locked hands in elation. Ill-matched, they looked: Erpwald's stocky vigour beside Cutha's fine features and slender frame.

"It's good to share the watch with friends." Lady Breguswid smiled warmly. "May I introduce my younger daughter?" Hild extended a hand to Cutha and then to Erpwald. He looked intently from her mother to her.

"Now I see where you get those brown eyes. Not a moorland sprite after all!" He groaned with exaggerated disappointment.

"But off to the moors again soon." She tried for a matter-of-fact voice. "Where are you heading? This diversionary attack."

"Ah! You heard."

"Is it dangerous?"

"I hope so!"

She opened her eyes wide.

"Of course!" He laughed. "How else am I to win honour?"

"Ah!" She should have known.

"No risk, no honour," he chanted: the old maxim. "Besides, I need something showy!" He twisted his arms, squinting critically.

"You court risk?" She blushed; she must sound like a dowager.

"Well, sometimes. For myself. I don't expose my men unnecessarily."

"And that's why you're pleased? The risk?"

"Partly, but…" He was taking her seriously. "I welcome the sign of Edwin's trust. It's what I hoped for when I came to Northumbria. Opportunity."

"For what?"

"Leadership. I couldn't expect it at home."

"Couldn't you?" This made no sense. Hild felt stupid.

"There's no campaigning at home," he explained, then saw her confusion. "My father's King Redwald of East Anglia."

"Oh!" She was mortified. "I'd no idea."

"A king-in-waiting's only in the way." He looked amused. "So I'm lucky to be here, studying Edwin."

"Really?" She found it hard to believe.

"He honours his obligations. I'm a living example." He smiled ruefully. "Our nation is Anglian, like yours. Redwald helped Edwin regain his kingdom and my eldest brother was killed in the battle. So Edwin's taken me in."

"And you'll win his battles?"

"I hope so!" he guffawed. "He has a good eye, Edwin, for choosing the right man. So he earns loyalty – look at Lilla – and…" His jerkiness showed it was hard to explain. "And respect. He runs a fair system and has a strong presence."

"Erpwald!" Cutha called in an undertone. "Here!"

"I look up to him." Erpwald was talking to himself as much as to her. "I want to do well by him."

"What does he want of you?"

"Success." He smiled enigmatically. "And so do I."

58

"Has he shown a good eye this time?" she teased. "Chosen the right man?"

Erpwald looked straight into her eyes, weighing his answer. "He's cunning as a fox by a fowl shed. Knows what he wants. I trust his judgment."

"So engrossed!" Cutha slapped him on the shoulder.

"Sorry?" Eyebrows raised, Erpwald turned. His haughty profile, now she knew, was all prince.

"Come and join us." Cutha drew them to her mother. "Lady Breguswid and I think to be baptized with the infant princess. What about you?"

"I'll wait for the king," Erpwald said promptly. "Redwald has an altar to the Christ, but it's never used. I shouldn't like to run counter to my father."

"I could serve the queen better," Cutha said, "as I'm to be her captain."

"You're coming to Bamburgh?" Hild liked the wiry thegn.

"Cutha's leading the northern defence." As her mother spoke, Hild remembered Osfrid rejecting the northern command. Erpwald's words slotted into place: *A king-in-waiting is in the way.* That was why Edwin was hard on his sons. They were a threat.

"What's that?" Cutha froze like a hare in a form.

"Where?" Erpwald tensed. From beyond the partition they heard shuffling. Erpwald put his hand over Hild's mouth, edging her back into the queen's doorway with her mother. Swinging round in a crouch, the men crept forward, knives drawn.

"Who's there?" Erpwald snapped, darting forward.

"King's man," came a broken whisper.

"Ye gods!" Erpwald recoiled as a figure staggered forward, crusted with mud.

"News," he gasped, "for Edwin." Blood matted his hair and streaked his face. His right arm hung swaddled in a cloak which dragged from the brooch at his neck.

"Where from? At this hour? Name?" they rapped out, cold and sceptical. Swaying, the man stretched towards the bench. Before he could reach it, he collapsed on the ground, eyes rolling upwards. Erpwald bent over him.

"Water!" Cutha called. A boy ran in and dashed a jugful over the man. His eyelids fluttered.

"Who are you?" Cutha tried. No reply. "Know him, Erpwald?"

"One of ours." Erpwald looked grim. He was stripping the man of his weapons, turning over a short sword, the curved blade blood-brown and chipped, the handle skewed. "This is locally made."

"Recently used, too." Cutha peered at the weapon. "A tangle with the watch, d'you think? They'd attack in the dark."

"Or another traitor?" Erpwald grasped the man's shoulder and heaved him onto his back. He groaned. Erpwald peered at the face and wrenched away the cloak. The man's left arm was almost severed. Bones poked through, the flesh was green and the fingers stiff. Erpwald recoiled from the stench.

"The river," the man gasped feebly. "Bass. Dying."

* * *

The rancid stench of tallow and sweat was sickening. Backed against the chapel wall behind the queen's seat, Hild leaned over to smell the lavender from her freshly washed hair. She saw her mother's cheeks streaked with tears and Cutha looking solemn, his bleached robes luminous in the candlelight from the table in front of them. The converts' arms, raised in prayer, made wavering, criss-cross shadows in the rafters.

Erpwald stood opposite, behind Edwin. A muscle fluttered above his ear and his scar was white against his weathered skin. She yearned to stroke it, smoothe his brow, touch and be touched. Suddenly he looked her way and she held his glance, smiling.

"Hild!" Ethelburga hissed, stretching for the baby as she rose to stand with Edwin before Paulinus.

"*In nomine Christi…*" He submerged the naked infant in a silver bowl. Ani bawled herself purple. "*Et filii…*" he dunked her again, then again, "*et spiritus sancti.*" Tossing her wrappings round her, he handed her to the queen, who promptly passed her to Hild.

Jiggle her up and down, flick your fingers, hold her to your shoulder, pat her back: none of her mother's nostrums worked. A titter rippled through the crowd as they turned to follow Paulinus to the river.

"Satisfied, Tatae?" Edwin sauntered over. "Our daughter makes her views known!"

Ethelburga laughed as Edwin led her out. He ducked under the thatch of the monks' lodging opposite. Hild settled on the bench by the chapel door, stripping the wet baby, rubbing her dry and wrapping her in her own headcloth.

"Has he spoken?" she heard Edwin ask.

"Not yet." A monk's voice. Then, a harsh groan.

"Bass! My friend!" Edwin was jubilant.

"He's asleep." The monk blocked the door.

"A word. Just a word."

"Not if you value his life, King," the monk persisted. "He lacks a leg and must be stronger before he knows, or he'll…"

"Die? That makes it all the more urgent!" Edwin snapped.

"You must wait."

"There's no time!" Edwin exploded.

"If it matters, God will give you time," came the calm reply.

"My lord," Ethelburga laid her hand on his arm, "they'll send word when he wakes. Come, we're due at the river."

Hild did not follow; the child was quiet at last. She lapsed into reverie. Did it mean anything, Erpwald's look? Did he realize how she felt?

"Hild!" Uscrea towing Hereswid. "You didn't come!"

"No…" She nodded at the baby.

"Wise." Hereswid showed her boots. "Mud's terrible."

"Not for the Christians," Uscrea chirruped. "They had boards. Why does he drown them?" Laughing, the sisters looked at each other.

"To wash them clean?" Heri said.

"Get rid of Woden, I suppose," Hild added.

"She said it wasn't cold…" Uscrea was keen to tell his story.

"Ma," Heri whispered.

"She put on a new robe. *A new dress for a new person*, she said." The sisters grimaced: how they'd toiled over that tunic!

"It was odd, Hild," Heri said. "It was trying to rain…"

"She said the dog-roses were weeping…" Uscrea chipped in.

"Tears of joy, goose! Come on, Hild. Here, let me." Heri took the baby. "Just as Ma emerged, the sun came out, and a rainbow."

They tailed Edwin's white head along the watermeadows, as Heri's rattling tongue evoked the sodden riverside, expectant quiet, ballooning robes, rippling laughter, Paulinus dark and solemn. Who else could have forced Edwin to surrender his child to this alien ceremony?

"Look, they're stuck!" cried Uscrea. A wagon was bogged down in a ring of spectators. The drivers cursed, heaved and lashed the oxen's flanks while their towering load of spear shafts wobbled. They swung the cart: *One, two, three, heave*! Sucking free, the wagon shuddered forward a yard, the bystanders cheered, and the poles collapsed and rolled away. Laughing, the watchers left the gang to salvage their cargo. Uscrea giggled.

"Here!" Unceremoniously, Hereswid dumped the baby in Hild's arms. "A bridal garland." Pulling handfuls of cow parsley, she twined the lacy froth round her head and pirouetted. "*Handsome, noble, rich and strong? Which will he be, my one-day groom?*"

"Old miser, more like," said Hild, "wanting sons before it's too late!"

"Rich, then, and doting, to give me a dappled pony."

"Leaving you a widow with a tiresome brood."

"Oh, you know I'm not the motherly sort." Her crown askew, Heri pulled a face.

"Here's your chance to practise." Hild thrust the baby back, rolling up her sleeves and kilting her skirt. "Or would you rather hew our passage?" Shoulder high in bulrushes, she plunged forward, parting the stems.

"Oh!" Hereswid's gasp halted her. On the bank a bent figure crouched over a huge leather square, forcing his needle through and round the edge, fashioning splayed curls. "Lovely!" Hereswid bent to touch the stitching.

"Don't!" A rough cry stopped her. Hidden by skins strung between the alders, a gang of men worked a large sail. "Keep away from him, lady."

"Why?" Heri looked longingly at the craftsmanship.

"He's a Weird."

"But it's beautiful!" Heri wavered.

"Too good for man's making. He's not human, him!"

"Come on!" Hild crossed her fingers. "We'll lose the queen." She tugged down her skirts and made for the royal couple, letting Uscrea run ahead.

Stranded amid stacks of cloth-wrapped spearheads, water barrels, loaves, leather tents and cheeses, Edwin and Ethelburga watched slaves toss bundles hand to hand in a chain, and stow them inside bouncing ships tied to stakes on the bank. Some sported bright gouges: flat-bottomed boats with copious oars, newly adapted for Edwin's warband to glide through the inland waters. Further along, Hild saw a new ship with a swan neck bobbing gracefully.

"Yours." Edwin drew the queen forward. "And those." Two weathered vessels lay nearby like bodyguards. "To carry you to Bamburgh. Once Bass has spoken."

* * *

The king's feast spread beyond the torchlight into the June evening, but it was subdued. Bass had spoken. The warband faced death.

"Success to our enterprise!" From the dais Edwin poured a wine offering into the rushes. "May Woden grant us victory." Along the crowded trestles, men shuffled. "Let our revenge be sharp," he cried harshly. "Let Wessex groan, their crops shrivel, and their cattle run with their enemy."

The atmosphere changed. Hild saw a flash of distaste cross Ethelburga's face.

"To hurt my people, just two of my people, brings Woden's eagle with the killing claws." Firelight gilded his hair, his gold cup gleamed, his raised arms and sword belt glittered: he looked all gold.

"Edwin! Edwin!" men shouted ecstatically.

"I swear!" He lowered his arms and silence fell. "Their children's children will lament for aeons the terrible anger of Northumbria's king."

"Edwin! Edwin!"

Breathing deeply, he stood narrow-eyed, quaffing adulation, judging the mood.

"Hear now my dispositions." They shifted and settled.

"My dear son, Edi…" He paused. Edi didn't seem to realize what was expected. Eventually, he scrambled up and knelt before the king. "Edi will be my right hand on campaign." Perhaps Edi expected the northern command in Osfrid's place; Edwin had to smile insistently until he touched his sword and bowed in acceptance.

"Erpwald, prince of East Anglia." No delay this time. Erpwald jumped up.

Uscrea seized the opportunity, calling to Yffi across the two empty seats. From Edwin's side, Yffi's face lit up. But Edi returned and the boy sank back like a sack. Loud cheering recalled Hild's attention. Erpwald stood flushing at the ovation from his allocated troop. Hild clapped enthusiastically, sensing his pride, but he didn't look her way.

Cutha followed, to be invested with the northern command, and an old cousin was entrusted with Edwin's homeland. Excited chatter arose. They thought the king had finished. But Edwin spoke again.

"Ethelburga, my most honoured lady and princess." Surprised, the queen moved to kneel before him, but he took her hand and faced her with a courtly bow. Flushing, she stood calmly looking up at him, her hand in his. He waited until the silence was absolute.

"Ethelburga, my lady, your queen," he said, dropping the words slowly. "Courage is her inheritance, loyalty her watchword, and wisdom her nature. To her I entrust my royal powers, my lands and treasury, my people and my justice."

Turning to the herald behind his chair, he took his heavy sceptre and placed it in her hands. Ethelburga sank to her knees, lips moving silently. Edwin raised her and led her round the hall, men bowing before them like wheat in the wind.

"And now to rest," he ordered. "We make an early start."

Disrobing the queen, Hild could see Edwin's exhaustion.

"You've done all you can," Ethelburga reassured him. "The people are with you. The warband will follow you anywhere."

"A prince must die for his people." Edwin's voice was so low that Hild only just caught his words. Ethelburga, she noticed, did not contradict him. "With them and for them. That's the way of the world." He sighed. "It's in the hands of the gods now."

Ethelburga sat on the bed and held out her arms to him.

Hastily, Hild folded the queen's garments and laid them on the chest. As she left the room, she heard Ethelburga murmur, "Yffi? May I take him north?"

"Yffi's pledged," he replied. "Yffi goes with me."

3

BAMBURGH

Where the cliffs jutted into deep water, three ships lolled on the beach, the high tide lapping at their keels. Cutha's men cajoled horses up planks into pens amidships. The queen's vessel sported a fancy leather awning at the stern. Trudging heavily over the soft sand, the royal ladies climbed aboard and settled under it.

Hild, who had paddled along the water's edge, slipped in beside her sister. The crew manhandled the ship into the surf. It drew breath, wavered upright, bucked at the tug of oars, and thrust rhythmically seawards, while barefoot seamen rigged the sail to run before the south-west wind. It was Lithe, the month of fair sailing, nearly midsummer.

The ship rolled gently. Under the awning, Ethelburga swayed with the roll, Ani slept in her lap, Uscrea listened to an old tale of Ma's, Hereswid trailed her fingers over the side, the queen's women chattered, and Hild reflected.

Overnight, Heri had grumbled at the pervasive stink, but Hild, for the first time, saw the bodyguard evicting fisherfolk to accommodate the royal party. She'd watched a homeless widow cooking two small herring between the beached boats and, when the horsemen appeared, throw sand over the flames and slither like an adder under an upturned coracle. Had she been able to relight her fire? Hild wondered. *Life and death both live in fire,* Ma said; *fire to feed, to comfort and to cleanse.* What a scolding she gave Hild the only time she doused the flame! It took hard work to fan it back to life with her veil.

That veil: it dried her tears, cocooned her safely, flapped away bees, draped her cot, and always concealed Breguswid's dark, British hair. Hild sighed, pulling her own veil tight. Never again would she feel her hair stream free in the wind, never again hear Erpwald call her sprite.

She imagined him now, lordly locks flaring as he rode at the enemy, glittering sword aloft, looking death in the face. All for glory…

The cold roused her, and a clap of thunder.

"Thor's chariot," groaned Heri. Bruised clouds tumbled across the sky as the wind whipped from the north. The ship lurched past a low coastline, half hidden by rainsqualls, then canted violently as the crew rushed to haul down the sail.

"In! Out! In! Out!" The master hammered the rhythm, steering inshore against the tide. Hauling against the undertow, the oarsmen heaved in unison, grunting with effort. Hild saw their third ship far away on the roiling waves, tiny figures still scrambling to lower the sail.

"Hild!" Heri clutched her, drenched in spray, spewing into the wind. Hild grabbed her skirts, wiped her face and wrapped a cloak around them both, trying to roll like the queen with the movement of the ship.

The force of the storm grew. Planks heaved, creaked, shuddered and groaned. Horses staggered and squealed. Master and mate lashed themselves to the stern post, putting all their weight against the steering oar to hold course. Bent under their cowls, the queen's priests droned their prayers.

Screech! Crack! Scream of tortured wood. Not the mast, thank the gods! With the sail lowered, it bore no strain. One leg of the queen's awning had snapped.

"Sit still!" bellowed the master, as Hild fought her way out of the smothering leather. Her mother lay white and still.

"I'm all right," she gasped. "See to the queen."

The rest of the awning held firm. Ethelburga sat under a triangular canopy with Uscrea playing military camps. Smiling, Hild turned to face the driving storm. Surging water, swirling movement. She breathed deep, riding fear.

Suddenly, a wrenching shudder, suck of dragging shingle, jarring as the ground drove into the hull. Oars clattered on boards, horses whinnied and kicked, men vaulted over the side and staggered in the seething breakers. They strained to find a handhold on the ship and laboriously heave it forward. Slowly, the fractious vessel crawled up the shingle.

Hild's mother fainted in the arms of the seaman who carried her ashore. He laid her down in the sand. Heri fell to her knees to mop her brow. Hild gazed in horror. Breguswid's shoulderblade jutted sharply, injured by the falling beam.

The strand was a shambles. The second ship beached nearby. Broken spars and dying horses littered the sand. Wet to the armpits and bent against the wind, boatmen and soldiers hauled timber, kindled fires, stuffed wool into leaks and cut up carcasses. Straightening up from despatching a horse, a thegn swung round to peer anxiously out to sea. His eyes passed over the girls, then returned.

"Fighter's curse. Common in battle." He came over briskly. "I'll deal with it. Hold her head." Great eyes drowned in tears, Hereswid jibbed at the bloody axe in his hand. "Buck up, lady!"

"I'll do it." Hild took her mother's head, gusts of sand blinding her.

"Firmly. Both sides. Right!" Laying the axe aside and placing a foot on Breguswid's chest, the man gripped her upper arm.

"Don't move. Ready? Now!" A hard pull. A crack. Hild winced. "Good. She'll do. Keep her warm. Huts over there." He pointed and strode off.

"People live in those?" Hereswid gawped at furze mounds, like half-buried burrows, curving along a pock-marked estuary.

"Salt works." Cutha bustled up. "A good living. You'll be cosy in the hovels. They're used in the gathering season." He turned to two of his men. "Lash those spears and carry Lady Breguswid inside, then bring hot meat from the campfire."

"It's the end of the world," Hereswid moaned.

"Only the end of Deira." He pointed into the icy wind. "That's Bernicia, beyond the estuary."

Standing outside the next hut, cloak drenched and slapping, Ethelburga was straining to look back. "Is that our ship? In those breakers? Can you send men to help?"

"Not without hazard, lady." Cutha's face was drawn. "These sands shift. Men sink…" He gave a slight bow. "I'm sorry."

The priests recited their evening litany and Paulinus, in clumsy Anglian, asked his God to protect the king and gather to himself the souls of those who had died doing their duty.

"The lost ship, d'you suppose?" Hild whispered.

"Much good will it do," Hereswid sneered, "miles from any temple!"

"God is everywhere." Ethelburga had heard. "He listens. Christ promised."

* * *

Cheered by a bright morning, everyone boarded the patched-up ships. Skirting the estuary mouth, the master turned inshore to disembark a search party with the remaining horses. Hild watched them ride parallel, mile after mile, along wind-sculpted dunes and barren scrub. They came to a green island blocking a river like a jar-stopper. The riders made no signal. Hope was fading for the third ship.

"Anything carried by the tide drifts south," sighed the master. "Likely they're back in Deira by now."

"At home, lucky gits," muttered an oarsman.

The day stayed fine and the sun painted the sea deep indigo. They coasted on the power of the sail past rocky headlands frilled with foam. Herring gulls mobbed their wake. The second ship followed close. As the hours passed, the sun swung over the land and started to sink among distant hills. The third vessel never appeared.

Windblown and rosy from two days at sea, Uscrea circled restlessly. Hild tied his girdle tight and held it like a tether.

"Look!" He pointed. "Teeth. A row of teeth!" The seamen chuckled. A chain of jagged rocks barred their way. Beyond them, a towering fortress was bathed in evening glow.

"Bamburgh at last," sighed Lady Breguswid.

"Hold that child," chuckled the master, "or he'll get chewed by them teeth!" He and his mate hauled on the great paddle to align the ship between the overlapping rocks. A shout from behind signalled the second ship in their wake. Looking over the side, Hild saw jagged reefs passing close beneath, and her cheeks were sprayed by the wash of their passage.

Then they were through, landing on the beach, climbing up the dunes, crossing the narrow neck from shore to fortress, and looking back down, down, to the sea and sands far below.

* * *

Hild was to remember the Bamburgh summer as the end of her childhood, a golden time. In the early mornings she would leave by the great gates, circle the wooden walls and lean, watching the distant hills turn rosy, then blue, in the rising sun. If Uscrea came with her, they'd listen to the hamlet wake below, jump down the sandhills, and throw sticks for Dog along the tideline.

Between spells of duty, she would run on her own to the staithe and lie rocking a coracle in the shallows. Or she'd wander field and shore, free in a way she'd never be again.

"Eostre's maid." Word went round. People welcomed her, touched her shyly, pleaded that she stroke their goats, scatter grain for the fowl, touch their fishing nets.

"If you will," they urged, "it'll thicken the fleece… increase the catch." So she stood as they castrated sheep, turned cheeses, or goaded oxen along the furrows. She watered bean rows, soaked willow twigs for hives, and fingered their herbs.

"You choose," they begged. "Which is the best flitch… the best milk for the queen's tribute? You choose. You bring us luck!"

And she loved it all: taste of bean broth, fresh dung-heap smell, warm people and the sense of being useful.

At other times, she lay idling in the sun. Through half-closed eyes she watched the field flowers merge and part in the wind, sparkling like Edwin's jewels. She dreamed of Erpwald, his protecting arms, his leathery smell, his future… and hers?

That, she supposed, lay with her mother. Since the accident, Lady Breguswid moved slowly, resting, even drowsing, in the quiet life of Queen Ethelburga's household. Hild wondered what would happen when the king returned. Ma had never felt secure; it was her husband's family, not her own. Faithful thegns were pensioned off on homesteads where they fed off the land and bred more fighters. An ageing widow must keep on earning her living.

Hers, and her daughters', a task too hard for her now. It was time for Hild – and Hereswid, if she would – to watch, learn, step into her mother's shoes and care for her. Soon. When the king came back.

Bass also was thinking of the king. Still weak from a hard voyage after losing his leg to gangrene, he practised walking with a pair of forked sticks the carpenter made him. The moment he could, he reeled to see the queen.

"Lady, may I speak my thought?"

"My lord Bass, welcome!" Ethelburga rose, hands outstretched. Realizing he could not release his crutches, she left her chair with a sign to Lady Breguswid, and sat on a three-legged stool. While her mother havered, Hild ran to hold the royal chair behind Bass. He folded himself clumsily, leaning on the arms, dropping his crutches.

"Hrumph, thank you, thank you," he muttered grumpily as she rescued them. "Now, lady." He faced the queen. "A duty. You won't like it."

"Your duty's to regain your strength, my friend." Ethelburga leaned as if to pat his knee, then pulled sharply back. "Give yourself time."

"Lady, listen!" he snapped, shocking himself to silence. "Pardon. Don't mean to be rude." He was struggling in mind and body. Ethelburga smiled reassurance.

"What if the king does not return?" he blurted.

"Not return? Bass!"

"If he's killed. In battle. I said you wouldn't like it." He hunched his shoulders.

"Hild!" The queen sat up straight. "Close the door, and tell the herald to stop anyone entering. Now, Bass, what is it? What have you heard?"

"Nothing, lady. It's just… I've had time to think. If anything happened to the king, you could be in danger."

"The Twister's sons? Are they marching? That's why Edwin sent you and Cutha…"

"The children as well." He carried on as if she hadn't spoken. With heavy significance, he said, "Whoever steps into Edwin's shoes… and I mean 'whoever'…"

"Whoever…" Ethelburga repeated slowly, eyes widening. Hild felt cold. If Bass wasn't thinking of the Bernician princes, then who?

"I mean no treason, lady," he said nervously, "but new kings tolerate no rivals."

"Of course. It's the way." Ethelburga's flat acceptance made Hild shiver.

"And… forgive me, lady…" Bass's voice wavered. "Nor do new kings tolerate a queen who could breed rivals… especially if her brother is king of Kent."

"Ah!"

"You need a plan of escape. For you, and the children."

"Kingship before kinship," she nodded and sat thinking. Then she switched to a purposeful tone. "You're a loyal friend, Bass. You've been thinking hard, you say. What do you suggest?"

"Your ship. Is it still at hand?"

"I imagine so…"

"Get it hidden!" he barked. "Let me speak to Cutha. Somewhere you can reach it quickly. Unobserved. We'll pick a crew, loyal, good fighters…"

"So be it."

Bass sagged back, job done. Struggling to the edge of the seat, he tried to kneel. Ethelburga forestalled him by standing and offering her hand. He folded it in his.

"Lady, my lord's queen," he breathed, "I swear by Woden's spear to wield your sword while I live."

"I accept your service, my lord," the queen answered formally, "and trust you unto death. Now, we shall speak of this no more. Open the door. Let the people in."

A queen's lady heard much and said nothing. Hild found it hard. She couldn't discuss Bass's warning, even with her mother. She began to make mistakes: dropped a glazed bowl, ripped her robe on a fence stake, loosed the hound near the cattle pen.

"Pesky nuisance!" Lady Breguswid scolded. "What's the matter with you?"

"Nothing," she muttered, and sloped off to brood. How could the queen carry on as if nothing had changed? All princes met a bloody end: fact of life. But little Uscrea? Ani? Yffi? Who would harm them? It brought back her father's murder. Had that been kinship rivalry? Jealousy because he was close to Edwin?

She started to imagine that the sentries watched her down the causeway. Hunting parties seemed like cavalry patrols. The atmosphere was thick with insinuations. She could gain no relief; the secret was not hers to share. She lay among the dunes, beating the sand in frustration.

"Hello. You again?"

"Brother James!" She'd seen him before. He came here to read aloud from his book of words, every day the same.

"What're you up to?"

She sat up, and pulled at the marram grass. "Just thinking."

"What about?" He shunted nearer.

"Oh, I don't know… the future, I suppose."

"Ah." He waited, clasping his robe round his knees. "Why the frown?"

"It's depressing."

"Really? Many would envy you. Security, luxury…"

"Luxury!" she spat. "I mean… I like it here because I help people. As Eostre's maid."

He looked blank.

"You know – the goddess of fertility…" She shrugged. "But it won't last. There'll be a new maid next year, and then…" She tailed off, contemplating the void.

He sat watching the waves, but she sensed his sympathy.

"You need something to get your teeth into," he pronounced. "I can't do much about next year, but I can offer something to take your mind off it. If you'd like to learn?"

"Learn what?"

"Here, look." He wriggled close and started on the familiar words, running his finger along the page and pausing at intervals to explain. She was intrigued. "This is my daily task. You could join in, if you like."

She remembered James bringing news from Canterbury, leading the chant at Woden's grove, praying in the storm-tossed ship. Was he offering her serenity?

"All right," she said, uncertainly.

* * *

Whenever they met, he crouched beside her, folded in his dark robes, laid his book on the sand between them, and ran his finger along the lines, helping her read the familiar words, a little at a time. It was fascinating how the little marks meant speech. Slowly she recognized Latin words, learned their meaning, and began to read them aloud. Then he tried a story: servants left in trust by their lord, like Cutha by the king, and how he discovered the kind of servants they were by the use they made of their gifts.

Then James chose another story. She picked out words she knew, guessed others from the sense, accepted help when necessary, and worked out the whole, glowing with achievement.

The stories stuck in her mind, coming to life inside her as she performed her daily tasks. The rebel son reminded her of Osfrid, and she hoped Edwin would be like the father in the story and

welcome him back. The lord who chose fishermen as Companions
– well, that sounded too far-fetched.

"You know," she confided one day, twisting towards him,
holding her windblown hair flat against her ears, "these dull marks
are magic. They make pictures in my head."

"Powerful things, words." James chuckled. "They set your mind
alight. Talk across time and space, carry ideas."

"What ideas?"

But his gaze was fixed on something inland: a plume of white
smoke against the purple hills. It turned black.

"Fire! They're firing the crops. Quick! We must raise the alarm!"

* * *

They panted up the causeway amid fugitives from the fields with
ducks, pigs and goats. A grim posse of horsemen, spears balanced,
scattered men and beasts as they swept in the opposite direction,
kneeing their mounts and whooping wildly.

"Did I see… could that be…?" Hild gasped, turning to look.

"In!" James pushed her. "They're barring the gate." A loud thud
shook the ground.

She was engulfed by crowds. Cattle stared or rushed blindly,
baulked here by a barrier, there by a dog; a bull lashed its tail and
lowered its horns. Bass perched on a cart, directing men with
swinging crutches. Hild wormed her way to the queen's lodging.

"Take that beast outside!" A familiar wail met her. "Oh, Hild, look.
That dratted hound." Hild saw upturned baskets with Dog frolicking
in the fabrics. She grabbed him and Uscrea dragged him outside.

"She's out, the queen, calming people." In confusion, Ma stowed
cups, robes, jewels and hangings. "Give me a hand."

Eventually, a shocked silence distracted them. Outside, a troop of
riders dragged at rope's end a staggering wretch matted with blood.
Winding in the captive, the captain tossed him at the queen's feet.

"Cutha's prisoners, my lady." He jerked his head to the rearguard
with a writhing boy between them. "This one," he tweaked the rope,
"was caught red-handed. The boy looked shifty. Won't speak."

"Take the lad away. I'll see him later. Treat him well." Ethelburga turned to the man at her feet. "Now, you. Who are you?"

"He won't say. We saw him grab a woman's hair and slit her throat." The crowd gasped.

"Is this true?" Ethelburga stood like avenging Hreth. The prisoner was silent.

"Lady, he used a knife. But…" Reaching over his shoulder, the captain pulled a heavy sword from behind his back. "He was wearing this." He handed it to the queen, hilt first.

"A lord, then?" She twirled it on the point, watching inlay glint down the blade. "You hope for ransom?" No reply.

"Raiders," said the captain. "Crops and farmstead fired. Cattle gone. Everyone put to fire or axe. The woman he killed…"

"Hamstrung my horse," the prisoner snarled.

"The boy: found hanging in a tree kicking and shitting. Brought him round. But whether he's theirs or ours…"

"Murder," Ethelburga rasped at the prisoner. "Is it true?"

"He won't speak, my lady."

"He will. In time." Surprise flashed across the prisoner's face and rippled through the crowd. "We already know he's a woman-killer, a horse-riding, sword-bearing lord, serving a master who lives by theft. Should be easy to uncover."

Hild had never seen the queen like this, white with fury, holding a crowd to her will. At a nod, they'd lynch him. He knew it, too.

Ethelburga had him hauled upright. "He understands our tongue," she went on, looking him in the eye. "And speaks it – in a way." Laughter met her scathing tone. "He's easily provoked – anger stronger than judgment. Perhaps…" She paused, looking him up and down. "Perhaps he's a liability to his lord. We'll see." She turned away. "Secure him well. All this damage. He'll pay for it."

* * *

In her lodging, the queen looked round in surprise.

"I thought we may need to flee," Lady Breguswid muttered.

"Ah!" Ethelburga frowned, dismissing her ladies. "You're not to torment the prisoner," she turned to Bass, limping in belatedly. "It's a foul practice."

"He's earned it, Hreth knows. And he'll see it as weak, lady."

"Did you think me weak, Bass, just now?"

He shuffled awkwardly. "He took a life," he grunted, "and should pay with his."

"He will pay. But if we kill him, we'll provoke kin vengeance. If we don't, he could bring a ransom. Gold may be more use than his death. Which do you think Edwin would prefer?"

"Gold," answered a new voice from the doorway.

"Osfrid!" Ethelburga broke into a smile at sight of Edwin's eldest son.

"So long as we can subdue him." Osfrid was as forthright as ever. "Father likes gold, with fealty."

"I'd feel easier if we knew who he is," Bass growled.

"You're a loyal bloodhound, Bass." Osfrid clapped him on the shoulder. "I'm glad Woden preserved you."

"What of your sortie, Osfrid?" Ethelburga asked. "Where's Cutha?"

"Gathering intelligence. Won't be long. I came to ask permission to camp my men below the causeway."

"You'll set guards?" barked Bass.

"Yes, double-watch. But I doubt there'll be more trouble. Cutha caught them and retrieved the cattle. Looks like the Gododdin along the Firth."

For the first time in Bamburgh, they feasted ceremonially in the mead hall. Waiting on the queen, Hild watched Osfrid leaning across to talk to her, drawing Bass in from his other side. The hall gusted with good will. Only at the far end, the boy prisoner sat with bent head, eating nothing.

"My friends," the queen rose, "raise a cup to my lord, the king." A rattling of benches and drinking horns. "Now to the lord Cutha, and you his fighting men." With both hands she raised the heavy cup, touching it to her lips and passing it to Cutha, who stood to drink, a slight figure, bowing in acknowledgment.

"As a memento of today's triumph," continued the queen, "I present your captain with this honour gift." She held out a gold armband, heavy with moulding.

"Cuth-a! Cuth-a!" The men stamped their rhythmic warcry.

At that moment the far doors were flung open for two guards with the nameless prisoner. He looked round like a trapped bear, blinking and deafened. The cheering turned to curses. They pelted him with bones and soggy bread as he stumbled across the floor unprotected, elbows bound and ankles hobbled, until he stood, caked with slops and blackened blood, hearing the hatred, bowing his head.

"Cerdic, fief of Gwylget, my prisoner!" The queen's pure tones cut through the disorder. Her gold circlet shone in the lamplight and her jewelled robe flowed over the lip of the dais, making her taller than life. Surely, Hild thought, he must be awed.

"Cerdic, I call on you to yield." Ethelburga looked down at him. "Pay you must, in law and justice. Yet as a lord, you may live in dignity as my prisoner-on-oath until the debt is paid."

"I'd rather die!" he muttered.

"Die?" The queen's icy tone made Hild shiver.

"I'll kill him for you, lady." The crude voice raised guffaws.

The queen stood impassive. "We all must die," she said. "Living is the harder way of paying." An indrawn breath hissed along the tables. *Death before dishonour* was any fighter's dictum. What must the man be feeling?

"My men?" Hild heard him mutter.

"Fell in fair fight. Those who ran were killed," said the queen. He ducked as if struck. "Your estates I claim. I have sent to your Gododdin chief to demand submission to King Edwin." He strained wordlessly against his bonds. "He may ransom you, if he will. Or," she finished lightly, "he may disown you."

The waiting began. There was nothing he could do, humiliated and ridiculed in his enemy's hall. Bleak was the future for any thegn who sullied his lord's name. Slowly, clumsily, he knelt.

* * *

Ethelburga looked round, subsiding into her chair. "This is comfortable, ladies," she said to the women stacking baskets away and rehanging the last tapestry. "Could you bring a bowl with bread and milk? Then you can leave. Hild will stay."

Cutha brought the boy captive in. Hild settled herself with needle and thread to repair the puppy's depredations. Ethelburga stood the boy in front of her, turning him gently to examine the weal round his neck. She held his arms to his sides and looked upwards into his face.

"You've nothing to fear," she said quietly. "Tell me your name." He stared, jaw muscles working, tears brimming.

"Sit there."

He crouched on the hearthstone, looking up like a heel-hound.

"Good. Now, eat this." She gave him the bowl and watched as his fingers clumsily pushed sops into his mouth. "He can barely swallow, Cutha. His throat's sore."

"He'll need time, my lady. He was all but dead."

"I wonder what he does," she pondered, watching him closely. "Woodsman? Baskets? Ploughing?"

"No!" Cumbered by needlework, Hild failed to stop the hound bounding in. She lurched towards him, and he jumped back, barking at the game. "Oh… my lady!"

"Try standing still," the queen said. At once, Dog found another attraction, sniffing a path through the rushes to the prisoner's bare feet. The boy bent and stroked the puppy's head, pressing his tail end until he sat at heel.

"Where is he?" Uscrea skidded in. "Naughty Dog!" He raised his hand. "Ow!" The prisoner had his wrist in a firm grip, turning over Uscrea's hand and uncurling his fingers.

"My lady, is…?" Osfrid careered in anxiously.

"Ssh! Watch!" The prisoner guided Uscrea's hand to the hound's ears and helped him fondle them. "He's showing Uscrea how to handle Dog."

"You've discovered him, my lady!" cried Cutha. "He's good with beasts."

"Give me your hand, boy," said Ethelburga. "You shall stay with me and work with stock. Your first task: help Uscrea train that hound. Would that please you?"

The boy's mouth worked again. No sound came. Shrugging, he twisted his hand in the queen's and half bent at the knee in a caricature of a thegn's swearing.

"I accept your service," said the queen, as formally as to Bass. "You will stay with me. Unless you claim your old name, I shall call you after a goatherd we had when I was a girl. Caedmon, his name, and Caedmon you shall be."

Caedmon walked to the door, his hand resting lightly on the hound's head. At the threshold, he replaced his hand with that of the little boy, and they went out together.

"I'll arrange a bed in the stables, my lady." Cutha followed.

"And I'll… unless…" Osfrid hovered. "Could you spare a moment, my lady?"

"I wanted a talk with you, Osfrid," smiled Ethelburga. "Draw up a stool."

"Lady Ethelburga," Osfrid did not sit, but knelt before her. "I come, with the king's knowledge, to ask your pardon."

"My friend," Ethelburga leaned down to him, "you have it."

"I once spoke hot and insulting words about you." Shame burned in Osfrid's cheeks. "Bitterly do I regret them, for I wronged you and dishonoured myself."

She stood, took his hand without coyness, and raised him to face her.

"I knew you, Osfrid, and loved you as my lord's firstborn, the day he brought me to your home." Her words came slowly, answering his hidden need. "I love your child, Yffi, as my son's companion. I shall not dispute your right, when the time comes, if the elders elect you king. You've nothing to fear from me, or mine, I promise you."

"Nor you from me, I swear!"

"The kiss of peace." Standing on the tips of her toes, the queen raised her lips to his furrowed brow. "Let us be friends, and work for Edwin's good."

"Ethelburga!" His voice quivered and he paused, holding her hands in an iron grip and looking deep into her eyes. "Queen of queens!"

A log crumbled and a spark flared, glancing off a glitter on his cheek.

"Those boys!" he exclaimed. "Lady!" Sketching a bow, he swung out.

"Go with God, my friend," she said quietly. "Hild, could you find a drink?"

"Your poor fingers." Setting down a cup of wine, Hild gently chafed the queen's hands.

"Doesn't know his own strength," Ethelburga smiled, "like Dog!" She spread out her fingers for inspection. "Much better. No, don't go." She nibbled an oatcake. "The trees are turning. I ride to Catterick to meet the king in time for Blodmonath."

"I hear he's sent good news? Praise be!"

Ethelburga smiled, sipping her wine. "I'll travel with Cutha, showing the royal presence, a few nights here, a few nights there. The sort of journey that's hard for your mother."

Hild's heart sank. "I can help her, my lady," she urged.

"I know, Hild. But she takes things to heart." Was it the beginning of the end? So soon? "I want you to take the sea route with your mother. Hereswid will come with me."

"Heri?" Her scatterbrained sister! Ma would die of worry.

"The other women will help. Bass will go with you, supervise your bodyguard. We'll be riding a month or more, too much for them both. You'll arrive in seven days at most: sail to the Tees, then upstream, just the last stretch by road; say, a slow day's ride."

Hild couldn't speak. It would destroy her mother. She'd eased the young queen into Edwin's court, guarded her dignity, lavished on her the love she couldn't show her daughters. Ethelburga was the centre of her life.

"Hild, what's troubling you?"

"Does this mean my mother's usefulness is over, my lady?"

"Never!" Ethelburga reddened. "Her experience, her knowledge of cures, her companionship – all irreplaceable." She took a deep breath. "As long as I live, Hild, there will be a place for your mother in my home."

"My lady!" Hild's voice broke. Relief warmed her like mulled wine. "You could give no better gift."

"Besides," Ethelburga's eyes twinkled, "there'll be a lot to prepare at Catterick."

Hild smiled conspiratorially; her mother would have work after all. "Tell me, lady, what you need."

4

GOING SOUTH

Blodmonath, the Month of Blood, fell as winter set in. Beasts which could no longer browse were killed and put to use. The steward ordered the cattle to be corralled for sacrifice or feasting. The herdsmen swilled out the byres to winter a bull and the best heifers, stacking the roofspace with oats to last the winter. Hild watched swine slaughtered, blood puddings shelved, flitches hung over hearthfires or steeped in brine and honey, and next season's breeding sows driven to forage among the beech trees.

Catraeth, boasted the steward, using the old name, was the greatest vill in the kingdom; it had been the British capital. Biased, thought Hild; Catterick was important, but that wasn't why. It stood on the old road to the Tees, the river where Edwin's Deira faced the Bernicia he'd captured when he killed the Twister.

She was gratified that the steward took her seriously. He showed her round the curious round houses, fragrant with fresh thatch, flowery straw and herbs in the rafters. Their traditional arrangement of alcoves round the edge was, she thought, versatile with a judicious use of hangings.

"If the king's had a victory," he commented sourly, "we'll need to build for the extra lords. He won't want them dossing with the warband." Practical, if acid, this British steward.

He must have spread the word the king was due; everywhere, Hild saw preparations for feasting: barley threshed to seed and straw; cheeses propped like moons, leaking through their cloths; ale and mead in stoppered jars; eggs cradled in ash pits; firewood stripped and piled near the Mead Hall.

"Are you the lady queen?" A scrawny girl sat on a fence, kicking at a pile of leaves. Rags stretched tight across her growing body made Hild feel like a queen in her tough boots and thick veil.

"Get down!" The steward cuffed the child.

"Don't!" Hild cried.

"She knows this fence is for poultry, not idlers."

"What does she do?"

"I keep food fresh for the lady queen." The girl nudged the piglets snorting round her feet.

"I serve the queen, too," Hild smiled. "We'll meet again." The girl cast her a dull look. *Not enough fuel to light her lamps*, Ma would say.

Lady Breguswid busied herself helping Bass. *His legs*, she dubbed herself. He stored Edwin's booty as it arrived by packhorse: goblets of glass and gold, filigree neck chains, strings of Tyne pearls, jewelled swords, West Saxon treasures from overseas. At day's end, they sat companionably in the sun's last rays, listening to the river roar through its cavernous cleft.

Hild ambled along to the shallows, dreaming she'd meet Erpwald riding across the ford. Once, seeing riders, she waited breathlessly, but it was only a group of leathercaps, bringing captured horses. In the end, Brother James arrived, picking his slow way on an overfed nag.

"Hild!" Clumsily he tumbled over his panniers and riffled inside. "A small gift."

She looked hard at it, a parchment scrap with writing on both sides, crammed in tight rows down the middle and meandering round the margins. "You wrote this?"

"I practise," he said in his stilted way. "Fat round bookhand. Not like at home."

"What is it?"

"Snippets, I think you say."

Her eyes lit up. "Where do I start?"

"There," he said mischievously, turning it over and round, "there, and there."

"Hild!" A shrill cry. "Hild, where are you?"

"Ma!" Stuffing the page in her waist pouch, she ran off calling, "Thank you… for remembering."

Hubbub greeted her: cries of greeting, warnings, bundles thrown and dropped, horses stamping and neighing.

"My legs!" Her sister sagged on a bench, rubbing her thighs. "Cursed frisky horse. I'm sore. Scarred for life."

"Cheer up – no one will see it there!" Hild laughed, and gave her a hug. "You look radiant – all that air and exercise."

"Don't!" A sharp cry from Lady Breguswid, pushing through the crowd towards Bass. "No, don't!"

"Stand clear!" He was lurching on his crutches towards a riderless horse bucking dangerously in the maelstrom.

"Bass!" Breguswid screamed. "No! You can't!"

"Heri, is that yours?" Hild's hug turned into a shake. "That horse. Is it?"

"Bass must be in Ma's favour," Hereswid drawled. "She only nags people she's fond of."

"It is yours!" Heri never heard anything inconvenient. "Get hold of it, Heri! There'll be a disaster." Hereswid ignored her. Hild ran towards the panicking beast. One of Bass's men caught its rein.

"I'm quite exhausted," Hereswid announced while the rest of the company unloaded, subdued by the alarm. "That's the trouble with being sensitive. I don't have stamina."

"Sensitive, my foot!" Her mother stood over her. "You've a skin as thick as a mule. On your feet." She stood waiting. "Right, you've a job to finish, girl. So have I. We'll talk when the work's done."

After their simple supper in the queen's roundhouse, the women fluttered out like chickens in a new roost, leaving Hild to clear up. Ethelburga took Lady Breguswid's arm and they stood at the door looking out. Beyond the black bulk of the hall, flames rose from a bullock roast. The shadows of the bodyguard reared monstrous as they jostled round the carcass.

"Here at last!" Ethelburga sighed. "I hope you've not tired yourself."

"The stars are bright as glass, my lady." Breguswid's crisp tone concealed her pleasure. "It's frosty. Come in or you'll catch your death."

"It's been a golden day." Ethelburga turned meekly to the recess where the planks of her bed were cushioned with sacks of fragrant grasses and Hild was spreading sheepskins warmed at the fireside. "But a long one. This looks welcome."

"You'll be cosier when the king comes." Breguswid lifted the queen's robe over her head, draped it on a chest and wrapped her in a thick woollen cloak. "Quick! In with you while the skins are warm."

"Don't be too hard on Hereswid," Ethelburga murmured as she snuggled down. "It's affectation, put on to tease you. She did better than you think."

Grunting, Breguswid patted the covers. Hild piled peats on the fire, and left.

* * *

"The king may come today." Lady Breguswid stirred early. The women heated water with dried flower petals for the queen to bathe. She sat on a low stool by the fire while Breguswid combed dry her long, fair hair. She nursed Ani and told Uscrea stories, but the king did not come.

"The king may come today," Breguswid said again the next morning, and the next, and the next, making a daily round of the queen's ladies, the steward, the slaves. Those who dared laughed, but Hild noticed they worked with more vigour.

"I've been thinking about Begu." Her mother was helping Hild fill flagons in the mead store, door shut against the cold.

"Who's Begu?" Hild said absently, trying not to spill in the gloom.

"The pig girl. Bright child. Wove them a shelter of hazel twigs. Sleeps there for warmth."

"But we've nearly eaten them!"

"Exactly. Not enough to keep her warm. We should bring her in."

Hild cocked an ear. "Hear that? A bull at large? Or a roadhorn?"

"An outrider's trumpet? The king?" Breguswid dropped the ladle and sped to the queen's lodging. Ladies blocked the door, craning towards the ford.

"It's him. It's the king… Wouldn't blow his own horn, silly… But the red cloak, the royal colour!"

"Inside!" Breguswid drove them like a sheephound. "You'll soon know."

With a brief knock, two slaves entered and unfurled on the floor an enormous pelt. Dog froze, growling at the scent. Uscrea tumbled onto the rusty brown fur, and lay stretching arms and legs towards the monster claws.

"You'll have to grow!" A thin form stood outlined in the doorway.

"Yffi!" Uscrea, the only one to recognize him, hurled himself at his playmate.

"Hey, all right!" Yffi said gruffly, giving him an affectionate punch. "Let me in!"

"Touching scene." The mocking voice made Yffi fall back. Edi, his uncle, the king's second son; Hild shivered. He bowed with cold formality. "My lady," he said, "my lord the king sends you this trophy of the royal chase as a sign of his regard."

"A bearskin? From the king?" Ethelburga exclaimed. "My thanks to my lord, and to you for acting as messenger. May we expect him soon?"

"He's enjoying the forest hunts, lady." A thin smile flitted across Edi's sharp features. "Yffi did, too. Tell the queen of your prize, Yffi."

"I took a boar, quite a big boar…" Yffi's gruff voice squeaked, and he stopped in embarrassment, standing stiff as a spear at his uncle's shoulder.

"A prime specimen, Yffi. Tusks sharp as a sword," said Edi. "And who speared it? Go on."

"I did. Well, kind of."

"You did, Yffi. You stood firm when it charged, held your point to the throat." Edi sounded ironic, bewildering the boy who could not see his face. "You leaned into its weight so that it couldn't side-step and savage us. Everything correct, Yffi. Just as you were taught."

"But I wouldn't have been able to hold firm if you hadn't pushed from behind, my lord." Why on earth, wondered Hild, was Edi behind Yffi? And pushing? Never had a lad looked so wan describing his first blood. He must have been scared stiff.

"Yffi, that's wonderful!" Ethelburga knew what his first kill meant to a boy. But Yffi did not respond.

"The tusks! Where are the tusks?" Uscrea was dancing round him.

"Come along, Yffi," said Edi thinly. "Killer's prerogative, to bestow the spoil. Tell your little friend your plan."

"Well, I thought to give one to Grandfather."

"I'm sure the king will be thrilled," Edi sneered. "And?"

"And the other…" Yffi swallowed, and lifted his chin defiantly. "I'm going to save it for Father when he comes back from exile."

"Exile!" Ethelburga was shocked. "Whatever gave you that idea?"

"He angered the king and had to run away," Yffi answered tonelessly.

"Yffi, that's nonsense! Come here," Ethelburga said firmly. Annoyance crossed Edi's face. Yffi stood downcast before the queen, and Ethelburga peered up at him, in that way she had, obliging him to look her in the eye.

"Yffi, it's true your father quarrelled with the king, but it's not true he's in exile." Ethelburga made her tone unemphatic, treating him like a man. Yffi remained impassive. Taking a deep breath, she went on, "Osfrid was hurt and went to lick his wounds on the moors. My belief is you met him there." Yffi blushed. "I don't know what he said but it alarmed you." Reluctantly, Yffi nodded. She waited.

"He said no king can brook defiance, especially from a kinsman who could be after the throne for himself." Hild could hear Osfrid in Yffi's words. The poor child must have rerun them endlessly. "He said Grandfather would have to punish him, perhaps kill him." Yffi was stiff with misery. "And it might rub off on me."

"Osfrid hadn't thought up his plan at that stage, I suppose," Ethelburga said easily. "He had no wish to harm the king or the kingdom…"

"That's what he said!" The boy's eyes filled. It must have been the first time he'd heard anyone speak up for his father. Hild looked from him to Edi.

"He had to find a way to prove his loyalty," Ethelburga continued. "And he did."

Edi could not hide his feelings. Contempt, then annoyance, gave way to surprise.

"The king was angry that the Wrekin men had not joined the muster. Your father rode to fetch them. Either they were traitors and he'd die in the attempt, or he'd spur them on. They followed him, fought well, and the king was grateful. Osfrid accepted the command of the north. He was sworn in on the battlefield, I hear, while they were sorting out the dead. You may have seen him?"

"I watched the battle…" With an uncomfortable glance at Edi, Yffi continued, "We watched from the top of a ridge. I saw the king send my father away."

Edi's eyes glinted. Humiliation: at being denied the battlefield, Hild wondered, or at Yffi letting it slip? Vexation, too: that Osfrid's exile was a myth and he'd been caught fostering it. She shivered as she recalled Bass warning the queen that new kings tolerated no rivals. Edi could be dangerous.

"Your father's at Bamburgh, Yffi." Ethelburga allowed herself to smile and take his hand. "Keep the tusk safe for him."

"Our gratitude, my lady." Edi stepped lightly forward, taking possession of Yffi's arm. "We welcome the news of my brother's rehabilitation." His voice was cold. "Now, we've done as instructed, Yffi, and other duties await."

"Join us in the Mead Hall tonight, my lord." Formally the queen gave Edi her hand. "And you, my lord Yffi."

* * *

Against all precedent the king arrived unheralded in the small hours. The hound's welcoming yelp roused Hild.

"Don't disturb the queen." Edwin was poking the fire ineptly. "Or all those women. Draw me some mead, and I'll stretch out on this bearskin by the fire."

Hild let Begu, tongue protruding, carry in the heavy jug. While the king wolfed chicken joints and barley bread, Hild answered his questions about the queen's ship, harvests in Bernicia, and the cattle raid.

"You've got a head on you, girl," Edwin grunted, as he lay down in his boots like a thegn, pulling the bearskin round him. "Know what a man wants to hear. See anything of the lord Osfrid?" Relaxing at her nod, he rolled onto his back and was snoring before she finished her sentence.

When Hild brought the water basin in the morning, Edwin was sprawled on the queen's bed in his boots. Both were talking at once. Leaning over her, he doused himself with a snort and dried on her shift. They laughed, paying Hild no more attention than a spider.

"Cutha can have the land," he said. "He's earned it."

"How will the hostage take it?" asked Ethelburga.

"As he must. The Gododdin may pay up and give him new lands. If not, he'll stay, and learn to be civilized."

Ethelburga extricated herself and sat on the stool. Hild eased over her head a braided crimson robe and stood back, trying to see with her mother's eyes; she must do the king honour.

"Besides…" Edwin lay back, legs crossed, hands behind his head. "Cutha works well with Osfrid."

"Edwin, are you sure of Osfrid now?" Ethelburga fixed her emerald eardrops, a gift from her Frankish mother. Hild handed her the jewelled cross she wore as a talisman. Ma said it came from her grandmother.

"I've made him lord of the north. That good enough?"

"Will Yffi join him, then?" She sounded casual but, brushing her hair, Hild noticed her temple throb. "Now he's riding with the men, he's left Uscrea behind. His father's his natural model."

"Better than Edi, you mean?" Edwin's face was blank and his voice cold. Hild held her breath as she drew the queen's hair into a golden fall and picked up the diadem. It would dazzle the tribute lords like moonglow. "Did Edi bring my message, Tatae, as to why I was delayed?"

"Of course. He brought the bearskin and said you were hunting."

"And?"

"The saga of Yffi's boar. He's kept a tusk for you, by the way." She stood so that Hild could drape her in a fur-lined mantle fastened with a massive gold brooch.

"Nothing of Erpwald, then?" Edwin asked casually.

"Ow! Careful, Hild!" Ethelburga took the brooch to pin herself. "No, what should I know about Erpwald?"

"Too much to tell you now." Swinging off the bed, he put his hands on her shoulders and kissed her brow. "You're beautiful, Tatae. I must tidy up to match your splendour."

* * *

Lady Breguswid seemed to give up once the king was back. That morning she lay still when the others rose.

"Ma's worn out!" Hereswid, skirts bunched, was dancing with impatience. The tribute was the royal event of the year, the chance to see and be seen. "What shall we do?"

"I'll stay," said Hild. "Let the queen know – but only if she asks."

Heri joined the women picking an erratic path to the hall, iridescent as starlings, bowing from side to side. The entrance was blocked by thegns, handing in weapons under the new rule and wrangling over precedence. Enveloped in her chattering flock, Ethelburga made for the royal door.

A stink of manure and male sweat assaulted Hild, and the jingle of harness. The tribute lords thudded by, pressing closely on each other, their horses bucking and swishing their plaited tails. Those from Gwynnedd and Anglesey were familiar, but new lords came from Wash, Wight and Wessex. No Erpwald. Why not?

Heavy with disappointment, Hild returned to the stuffy women's lodging. Among the empty pallets, her mother slept, face sagging. Days – years – of chivvying them all had taken their toll. Hild stood the door open and sat beside her.

A weak sun streaked across the floor. A late bee buzzed in the roofbeams and a starling foraged noisily in the rushes. Occasional roars drifted from the hall. When the sun shifted to the bed, Hild dug out James's parchment and began to decipher the words. As dusk fell she shut out the chill and sat in the dark with her thoughts.

Ma was going to need care. Hild and Heri could take turns, perhaps, but her duties must be performed in full, or she'd fret. How could they manage?

The pig girl!

"Begu, have you any kin?" Hild had asked, and heard about a dead mother, a father too feckless to string his fish traps, a winter of starvation, and adoption by the cheesewoman.

"You're her slave?" Hild had asked.

"Dunno. I help wi' the cheese, is all. And get the buttermilk – lov-e-ly!" Begu rolled her eyes in ecstasy.

She was tough: the way she stood up to the steward, her knack of killing chickens. Someone after Ma's heart. Could it work?

The township was quiet. Nothing to lose by trying.

The steward was in the slaughter yard, counting the day's carcasses.

"All these lords eating their heads off," he grumbled. "What if we run out?"

"Weren't there cattle with the booty?" Hild said briskly. But she understood his fear; she'd seen Paulinus write fifteen more provinces into Edwin's tribute list. "How long does the feasting last?"

"A month, at least. All day, if the weather turns bad. And that's only the half. Look at those useless mouths." He pointed to a pen of forlorn women and children.

"West Saxons? Surely they'll earn their keep?"

"Not till next spring, they won't. After a deal of food and training. The best were sold. These're the leftovers."

"Talking of slaves…" Hild seized the moment. "What of the pig girl? Begu, they call her. Helps with the cheese."

"Her!" he groaned. "I got saddled with her. For debt."

"She's a worker," Hild countered.

"Worth more than the father," he admitted, "but so sharp she'll cut herself."

"Bright and nimble. Just what I need. Can I have her for the queen's household?"

"Hope you know what you're doing!" Sour as usual, but he didn't say no.

Turning to sprint back, Hild found her route blocked by fighters. Scarred, half-naked roisterers sprawled round campfires slurping ale and mauling women. Some had purple sores and blackened stumps, some clenched themselves over internal injuries. Others looked blank, dazed by what they'd done and seen. Hild shrank from them, edging past. Already she could see lords scrimmaging at the hall doors and the queen sweeping out in a knot of women.

"How's Ma?" Heri had Uscrea by the belt.

"Dead to the world," Hild said. "I've a scheme. Tell you later."

"I'll go to her now. You take his nibs."

In the queen's lodging, Ethelburga threw off her cloak and diadem, stretched her arms, and tossed back her hair. A hubbub of male voices signalled the king's approach. Hild dumped Uscrea on the bearskin and rushed round lighting candles, tidying clothes and pouring wine.

"I'll see Paulinus first." Edwin swept in. "Well, son." He tossed Uscrea up, and dropped him safely back. "What d'you think? Good, wasn't it?"

"My lord!" Paulinus darkened the doorway. Even his formal words, Hild thought, seemed a challenge to Edwin.

"I know, you old terrier!" Edwin chuckled, settling beside his wife. "Always after me about my oath."

"My lord…"

"You wondered if I'd forgotten or..." Edwin lowered his voice in mock horror, "even reneged!" He rumpled Uscrea's hair and stretched his legs. "It was a splendid tribute. You know better than anyone. You kept tally."

"Yes, but..."

"Bretwalda, they call me: overlord. I've taken your father's place, Tatae, and Redwald's. Princes bow to me, even southerners." He gave Uscrea a gentle punch on the arm. "New provinces, son, new warbands, more riches!" Exultant, voice rising, he turned again to Paulinus. "Your question is not whether I shall keep my vow, old watchdog – never have I broken my word. Your question is..." he lowered his voice dramatically, "how."

"Wh...?" The priest floundered before Edwin's jocularity as he never had before his anger. Ethelburga intervened.

"Paulinus, you remember my cousin Sabert, king in Essex?"

"He built the church by the Thames."

"Remember what happened?"

"I dedicated it to Saint Paul..." Paulinus glowed.

"After Sabert died, I mean," she cut in. "His sons reverted to Woden."

"Apostates!" The priest's eyes flashed.

"Yes, of course, but..." she paused, "it was too sudden, the change. His people weren't with him. My lord doesn't want that to happen here."

A whimpering in the shadows. Gliding to the cradle, Hild picked Ani up. The whimper became a roar.

"Listen, Paulinus!" Ethelburga chuckled. "Our daughter Anfled makes sure Edwin never forgets his oath."

He nodded; the matter was too serious for joking.

"My kingdom's the widest ever," Edwin explained. "I've to win the people over, not compel them. You see?"

"Is that the evening hymn?" Ethelburga had sharp ears. Paulinus left.

"Oh, Tatae!" said Edwin. "How can I bind them to me, all these new peoples who are too far away to know me?"

The weeks passed. Edwin made no move. Perhaps someone complained to the Pope; Paulinus, or Bishop Honorius of Canterbury. A letter arrived. Edwin fingered the lead seal, sliced through the ribbon, and sent for Paulinus while Ethelburga and Hild cut open the hemp bundle, and unrolled a purple silk cloak, crusted with gold stitching. Draping it over a high beam, Hild stroked it, marvelling at the smoothness.

"Not from Canterbury," Paulinus said, flattening the parchment and translating: "*To the illustrious Edwin, king of the Angles: Boniface, Bishop, servant of the servants of God.*"

"The Pope!" Ethelburga breathed.

"*The words of man,*" Paulinus ran his finger along the line, "*can never express the power of the most high God. No human mind can understand it. Yet God of his goodness has opened man's heart.*" He paused to unfurl an edge.

"*We bring you knowledge of the Gospel of Christ. We offer you salvation.*" He hesitated. Was the script blurred, Hild wondered, or was he nervous of Edwin's reaction?

"*Our Redeemer has granted light to Edbald of Kent and his people. Your gracious queen already has the gift of eternal life through holy baptism.*" Far from being angry, Edwin was smiling.

"*We affectionately urge you to renounce the worship of idols. You owe nothing to their power.*" Paulinus's voice began to swell; he couldn't help himself. "*For God has given you life. Born again by water and the Holy Spirit, you will abide in eternal glory with him.*" He straightened, letting the parchment roll up again.

"He sends you the blessing of the apostle Peter and some gifts, my lord. A cloak from the silklands of the east – that must be it – and a tunic."

"It's woven gold!" Edwin fingered the gossamer threads.

"Let Hild do it." Ethelburga caught his rough hand.

"There's more," said Paulinus. "A letter and gifts for you, my lady."

"For me?" Ethelburga stared.

Later, Hild told her mother, "It was a dainty ivory comb for the queen."

"Embossed," Heri added, "inlaid with gold. Better than her old bone one."

They all laughed. Lady Breguswid was settled in a small lodging near the women's quarters with Begu to do her bidding. She sat uncharacteristically idle, a bowl of apples beside her. Visitors called as they passed, Ethelburga on her way from chapel, and Bass showing off the new wooden leg fitted to his stump by the carpenter. The sisters ran in with queries, making her feel useful.

"A mirror too," Hild continued, "like a pool of still water."

"I could see the whole of my head."

"You, Heri?" Breguswid pounced.

Heri blushed. "Even you would've tried it. I don't think she'd mind."

"Tch!" Ma smiled. Was it the accident, or Bass's attentions, bringing out her gentler side? "Tell me, the letter, what did the Pope say?"

"Oh, I can't remember all that stuff," Heri flapped dismissively.

"I can, some of it," said Hild. "He was glad she and her brother are Christians and will influence Edwin. Pray, and so on."

"Doubtless she's doing that already," Ma chuckled.

"*Melt the coldness of his heart*," Hild quoted. "Not that Edwin's cold, exactly! *You can only truly be one if united in belief*."

"And then everyone will copy Edwin," Heri said with a final flourish. "D'you think they will? Give up on Woden? I mean, he's the men's pattern."

"Woden! Woden!" Balancing on her left foot, Hild rhythmically stamped forward with the right, arms braced like a front-liner in the face of the enemy. You couldn't always take seriously the ritual antics of grown men.

"Hreth's vengeance." Giggling, Hereswid leered maliciously.

A sudden silence fell. It was this, after all, that led men to die, or end up stunted wraiths.

"They will." Breguswid twinkled at their frolics but spoke seriously. "It happened in Kent, the queen says. The thegns took to Christ and fighting stopped."

"There's hope, then," Hild sighed. "Edwin's reluctant in case he splits the kingdom."

"True," said Ma. "But he has a plan. Have you noticed how often you're on duty these days?" The girls looked at each other.

"Because we're his kin?" Hild ventured.

"Exactly. Training you up. One prince has asked for a marriage alliance. That's how Edwin can bind distant peoples to him."

"Oh!" Hild was shocked. "Edwin married Ethelburga to get support from Kent, and now he wants…?"

"But Ethelburga was a king's daughter!" exploded Hereswid.

"You're the daughters of a prince, Edwin's closest marriageable kin," said Breguswid. "*Peace-Weavers*, they call them. Brides who gather broken threads and weave them together to mend the hurt men cause."

"You first, Heri," teased Hild.

"Yes," said her mother. "Heri's older, and she looks the part."

"Father's hair." Hereswid tugged viciously at her plait. "Lucky old Hild!"

"Her turn will come," said their mother.

"Who? Who's asked? Oh, Ma!" Hereswid collapsed at her feet.

"He'll tell you when he's ready." Breguswid stroked her head. "Watch the queen. Ethelburga has more power than she shows. Watch her and learn."

* * *

They were on the move again, poling down the Swale in the royal barge to celebrate the Mothers' Night in the king's heartland. Ethelburga sat muffled against the east wind with Ani tucked close. Lady Breguswid lay beside her, wincing at each surge forward. Out in the drizzle, Hild saw the treasure ship following close, riding low in the water, fenced by bristling guard boats.

She had her hands full, so excited was Uscrea by the braying of the riders' roadhorns. Edwin and Edi, with their Companions, rode parallel to the boats, beating the undergrowth, aiming at any game they raised. What a curiosity Edwin was, thought Hild: a hoary old

97

man frolicking like a youngster, crowing over victories but worried by his vast lordship, proclaiming tradition while planning change, demanding advice while set on his own way. Irked by the slow progress of his barges, he stood his horse in the shallows, waiting ostentatiously.

At the confluence with the Ouse, brown eddies jostled them and the oarsmen leaned out to fend off converging craft. Gradually woods and scrub gave way to an open landscape dotted with farmsteads. Hild sighed with relief. At long last, Edwin would need to ride among the people. They'd have a few days' rest.

"Ouse, did he say?" Ma clawed at Hild's arm. "Hild, I know this place!"

Hild was too breathless to reply, trying to keep pace with Bass's spearmen as they carried Ma's stretcher up the steep bank. Bass had arranged a separate lodging for her. Hild found the fire burning, fleeces warming, and Begu poised to drip honey into a bowl of hot gruel.

She stayed at her mother's side. Lady Breguswid knew she was failing. She talked dreamily of brisk autumn mornings when she hunted with her father, the old king of Elmet; his lovely sleek horse, and how she cried when it died and he caught her a squirrel; harvest revels when the mead went to her head; sunny afternoons by the river with Hereric in their early days, watching the fish jump; her wonder, and his, at Heri's birth, the tiny baby who amazed the British household with her startled blue eyes and golden fuzz. And she chuckled at a memory she wouldn't share, something about youthful frolics round a celebration bonfire. Day by day, in disconnected instalments, she relived her past.

"You know why, don't you?" Bass seemed always underfoot. "It's this place, bringing back memories. She's ending where she began."

"Don't say that!"

"It's true, child," Breguswid whispered. "Bass understands. I've come home." Only then did Hild realize how close he was to her. "What's that you've got?"

For the umpteenth time, as she bent over the bed, the pouch attached to Hild's girdle swung over Breguswid's face.

"You don't miss a thing," she chaffed, tucking the skins round her mother. "A parchment from Brother James. Scraps of Gospel, for me to work out."

"Gospel! Have you? Worked it out?"

"I think so."

"D'you hear that, Bass? She can read like a priest!" After a minute she roused again. "Read me some."

"*Come to me…*" Hild knew the first line, having so often started from the beginning. "*Come to me, you who labour and are burdened. I will give you rest…*" Strong words, powerfully caring, she thought. No wonder they gave Ma joy.

"*Come, I will give you rest,*" Breguswid murmured, her eyes shining. "Hear that, Bass? Christ speaking to my need." She held out a hand and he took it. "Go on, Hild."

"*For I am gentle and kind and…*" Hild's reading was more hesitant.

"*And you shall find rest for your soul,*" James finished for her from the doorway. "I've come to see if we can help." He laid a hand on Bass's shoulder and smiled down at her mother. Suddenly frowning, he leaned forward and touched her hand. Bending closer, he laid a finger on her neck.

"What is it?" Hild whispered.

James marked a cross on Lady Breguswid's forehead and took Hild's hands in his own. "She's gone, Hild. *Come unto me*, he said. Your mother has answered his call."

* * *

With Begu's help, Hild washed and dressed her mother in her finest, and scattered autumn leaves on her breast. Begu found hips and a fallen branch to adorn the bed. Bass sat miserably outside the door.

"We must have the best for her," he said. "A great fire to free her spirit. Up on the old barrow."

"But Bass, she's Christian." James hauled his thick skirts forward and crouched beside the old thegn. "She's going to new life. She'll need her body. We must bury her."

He waited.

"*Cattle die, men die. One thing never dies: the name you leave behind.*" Bass muttered the old saying. "She leaves a good one."

"So we may bury her?"

Bass heaved a sigh that was like a sob. "Soon, then," he growled. "Before the Mothers' Night, so we don't defile the earth. She loved it so."

"Up on the old barrow," James nodded. "She'll rest quietly there."

In later years, the scent of winter burning, or stars on a frosty night, would bring it all back to Hild: the column of flaring torches winding up the slope, raucous horns to drive away spirits, women keening like wolves in the moonlight, and Heri choking on her sobs.

She remembered walking, dazed and dry-eyed, beside the wooden bier, her mother's face upturned to the sky; feeling the comfort of her rough woollen cloak, the weight of her father's old brooch, and the prick of the holly garland, tree of death, bright as blood; hearing the chink of goods for the afterlife – spindle, inseparable from her mother, waist-keys and knife – and the thud of the lid being sealed. And she remembered how cold, how alone she felt as the crusty earth fell.

Always there followed the calming words, *Lord, now let your servant depart in peace*; Paulinus blessing her resting place with his silver cross which glinted in the moonlight; and the queen's quiet words: *Hail, sister! May you rest in God.*

* * *

She still felt raw the day she met a gnarled old Briton casting for fish.

"You'll be with them, I guess," he muttered, eyeing her boots, "the king and his crowd." He peered at her with marbled eyes. "You been here before?"

"No."

"I'd an idea I'd met you." He shrugged, winding in his twine. "Name?"

"Hild."

"Father?"

"Dead." The old man waited. "Hereric, he was called."

"Hereric the Anglian?" He slapped his knee. "Wed our lass?"

"You knew her?"

"You've got the look of her. Those dark curls bubbling all ways out, the same beady eyes, full of life. Strong-willed young thing, she was. What's the matter?" He peered closer.

"Nothing." Tears streamed down her face, tears of release, and delight at his picture. "Tell me more."

He paused to cast his line. "She liked it here, by the Ouse. Came with her pa. Wrapped him round her finger, she did." He gazed at the water. "Came on her own once. Some lads cut off a dog's leg. They were drowning it. Up comes the little maid and gives them a right scolding. Great gangling boys, and they just skulked off!" He chuckled. "Saved the dog, too. It followed her everywhere on its three legs. She was a dab hand at the healing."

"She was." Hild pictured her at Ani's birthing, and binding up Edwin's guts.

"Came every year. Oftener. Till they married her off," he sighed, "and disaster struck."

"Who was it killed him? D'you know? Why?" she pressed.

"Never knew who. Edwin blamed us, Elmet. Terrible revenge he took." The old man scowled. "But it wasn't any of us. It was strangers drove him out of Elmet. We never saw him again. Or her. Have a bite?"

He broke off a lump of cheese. They munched in silence. Eventually, she told him of her mother's delight to be here, and of her funeral.

"It's fitting she lie there," he grunted, "near the old king and queen. Together, like." Side by side they waited for a fish to bite, listening to the water ripple and willow fronds drop.

"I'm glad you happened here," he said. "Like her, you are. It's good to know she reared a family and completed her life's work."

* * *

The year turned at the darkest day, which was sacred to the Earth Mothers: Yule log and merrymaking were burned out, and the light gradually strangled the dark once more. Soon they would abandon stuffy conviviality and rise in the frosty dawn to hunt in the gulleys and hawk over the chalk downs.

This was the moment Edwin chose to sit with his elders in the time-honoured way. They were his most trusted advisers, with nothing to gain by deference, and nothing to lose by crossing his will. Grounded in the land, knowing his lordship from years of service, they'd weigh up his proposals and decide on the people's good.

They were in Deira's oldest royal hall, set below the high ridge where Edwin's guards watched over Humberwater. The thatch hung thick and low against the cold. With the door latched against the east wind, the only light filtered through the smoke gaps at the gable ends. Edwin sat facing the door, nearest the fire, his men as close as they could huddle, with the queen and her women at one end, and the young lords at the other. Hild was tense. If these old men agreed to change, there'd be no more Woden worship, no more Eostre's maid.

The new god, Christ, had worked well for Kent, Edwin said. Their southern neighbour in East Anglia planned to adopt him. Now that he'd helped avenge Lilla and Forthere, should Northumbria keep Edwin's bargain with the queen's priest? The Twister's sons were being raised by monks in their Strathclyde exile. Could Edwin afford not to seize any advantage those young dogs had?

A weighty silence fell. There was no rush. Time and drink would stir their thoughts. The fire crackled, the latch rattled, Uscrea clicked his knucklebones, Ani burbled in Hild's arms, the young lords fidgeted, and the women rustled quietly with their spindles.

"Asa?" Edwin always consulted in order of seniority.

"The assassin wasn't the only threat," Asa grunted fiercely. "Remember Redwald? Before these puppies were born." He jerked his head in irritation at Edi and his cronies. "Redwald plotted your death."

"But his wife stopped him," shrilled Edwin's priest. "Told him not to stain a fighter's honour."

"Coifi!" Edwin barked. "Wait your turn."

At precisely the same moment, Paulinus jumped in with, "It was an angel of God, not her!"

Chatter broke out, surprise, anger, argument. Shivering next to Ethelburga, who was cocooned in a fur cloak, Hild spotted a sparrow blown in at the smoke hole above her head. It settled on a beam to preen. Edi aimed an apple core and it fluttered up to the rafters. Cerdic, the hostage, keen to keep in with Edi, shied a bone. The little bird panicked, launching itself from side to side, dropping involuntary missiles, until it found escape through the gap at the far end. Hild relaxed. Edi sneered.

"Redwald had an altar to the Christ," Edwin snapped over the disorder. "Anyway, he's dead now. Erpwald is king, and he owes allegiance to me."

Hild froze. So that was why Erpwald never came back. He was king in East Anglia, meeting his people, gifting his lords. And his queen? Her stomach lurched. Was it Erpwald who'd asked for a marriage alliance?

"My God melted her mind." Paulinus was still chuntering about Redwald.

"Elders first, Paulinus!" Edwin scratched irritably at his shoulder.

"Let's look at this practically." A scarred old warrior rose to his feet: Oswine, the king's cousin. "Your lady's father," he bowed towards Ethelburga, "lord of the south with friends beyond the seas and gold beyond measure – he worshipped this Christ. So does your lady's brother. Isn't that good enough?"

"What about our crops and cattle?" came a gruff cry from a man with his head in his hands. "Will he keep Eostre sweet?" At last, Hild thought, the heart of the matter.

"Ay, what can he do?" Coifi bounced up and this time Edwin let him have his say. "No one can say I don't honour the gods. But other men always get the rewards. If Woden had real power, I'd get something."

There was a gasp of horror; this was heresy.

"Power?" Paulinus boomed. "Christ can throw down the mighty. Look what he did to the king's enemies."

"My lord Edwin." Speaking conversationally, Edwin's bent old kinsman, Osric, struggled to rise. The room quietened. Ethelburga leaned forward. *A man of few words but worth hearing*, she'd once said of Osric. "All good things pass too soon. It seems only yesterday I was a lad in your father's hall. Now nothing's left to hope for but a good death." He shifted his weight to stay upright.

A good death, Hild thought. Erpwald's dream: to go down fighting.

"Go on, Osric," Edwin urged.

"That sparrow. Did you see it? Blundered in just now. One brief moment of warmth and light, then out again to the dark unknown. Just like life." He shrugged. "If this Christ knows where we come from and where we're going, let's hear about it." Shaking with effort, he sank back amid respectful nods.

"Good thinking." Edwin looked at the queen with a thin smile. He'd planned for this moment, Hild realized. He was as slippery as Edi. "Paulinus," he cried, "what follows death?"

"Life!" Paulinus sprang up eagerly. "Life transformed, for all who believe and serve Christ."

"What do you mean, 'transformed'?" Osric's question took him by surprise. Hild saw him hesitate and wondered if he was put off. Then he started to intone:

A spotted, wriggling grub
I die on the summer leaf,
Feast on my inner tomb,
Burst into radiant life —
What am I?

"Fair warms you, to think of summertime!" Shrunken old Asa raised a laugh.

"Egg… fountain…" The old men mulled over the riddle. "Caterpillar…"

"Yes!" Ethelburga breathed.

"Ah!" Osric had heard her. "Radiant creature, fluttering among the flowerheads…"

"Butterfly… butterfly!" echoed round the room. Paulinus was triumphant. Hild smiled. His preaching confused them; his riddle was winning the day.

"Life transformed," Osric challenged again. "How do you know that's what it will be like?"

"Because Christ promised, and he was a man of honour." They waited. "He died, and proved death is not the end by coming back to feast with his Companions."

"Were you there?"

"No. Before my time. But word spread like wind-blown fire and it was written down." He held up his Gospel book. "This is the volume of his life and teachings."

"Why didn't his Companions die with him?" It was the gruff voice that had asked about Eostre. Hild could see his point. No Companion would abandon his lord. They were bound by oath. All the scop's songs lauded their values. *It's honour to serve, and honour to die in serving.* With a pang, she thought of Erpwald.

"He ordered them to stay, tell everyone about it." Paulinus was still on his feet. "When their time came, he said, it would be like going home to their father's house."

"You see?" Coifi scrambled to his feet. "This is a better god. The old gods don't care about us." Holding up his skirts, he stretched a spindly leg over the bench and stood outside the circle. "Find me a horse!"

"You can't ride… You're a priest!" Horrified cries rose from the elders, cheers and guffaws from Edi and his crew. Coifi ignored them all.

"Paulinus, do you ride a horse?" he called above the din.

"Not often."

"But you can?" He waited for the priest's nod. "If you can, I can." He strode to the door and flung it open. "A horse, you there!" he called, and then leaned back into the room. "I'll be the first. Show the old ways are dead." He turned to the guard and seized his spear. "Here, lend me that… and bring a horse. Quick!"

The queen was on her feet. The baby squalled and Hild had to grab Uscrea one-handed. There was turmoil. Coifi had only ever ridden a donkey, like his father, like his grandfather. It was what priests did. And he was calling for a horse!

"God keep him," murmured Ethelburga. Hild clutched Ani in her shawls and, like the young lords, ran to the door to watch.

Unsteadily at first, skirts tucked round his scrawny thighs, Coifi sat the horse, pressed with his knees and pulled the head round. Skittering over the icy ground, he scrambled through the hamlet and turned up the hill, followed by hoots and cheers. Roused from their stupor, Edwin's Companions stumbled out, breath steaming, donning cloaks and arms, scattering to their mounts and streaming after him. Away up the hill, Hild saw Edi and his gang outstrip Coifi and speed ahead, hotly pursued by the king, bent on keeping order.

"He had quite a welcome party," Edwin reported later, taking a cup of honeyed mead from Hild and sinking onto the bed.

"Ssh!" Ethelburga pointed to the cradle, but Hild knew she was conscious of listening ears beyond the screen.

"I thought his spear would tangle in the horse's legs and upset him," chuckled Edwin, rubbing a hand across his face. "He kept going, the gods know how. Quite something for an old priest." He swallowed a long draught. "Everyone overtook him, but they waited to see what he'd do." He held out his cup for Hild to refill.

"And?" Ethelburga prodded.

"His face was fixed forward. He rode without pause straight into the trees and hurled the spear at Woden's shrine." Hild gasped. It was the altar where he'd given Anfled her name.

"It stuck there quivering, then fell to the ground. Not a good throw – he doesn't get much practice." Smiling ironically, he leaned on his elbow. "So he rolled off the horse, picked up the spear, and jabbed it hard into the wood. Someone held up a pitch torch. It looked like a golden lance piercing the shrine." Edwin was white with fatigue. Or was it emotion? Ethelburga took his hand. "We all stood waiting. Waiting for Thor's thunderbolt. Nothing. Just... nothing."

"*You made your gods; you are nobler than they.*" Ethelburga squeezed his hand as she quoted the Pope's words. Edwin gave no sign of hearing.

"Coifi seized the torch," he continued, "and hurled it at the shrine. There was a whoosh like a sneeze, and the flames took hold. Paulinus stuck his cross in the ground and claimed the place for Christ."

"Where is he now, Coifi?"

"He stayed there, looking a bit crazed. Paulinus stayed with him. He'll baptize him first. We'll get everyone done straight away."

"There are special days, you know," Ethelburga laughed. "And training."

"Eh?"

"Would you lead men into battle without training?"

"But we didn't need training to worship Woden!"

"Because you were brought up to it. Christ is different. You'll soon find that out. Paulinus will help. And so will I."

* * *

The high slopes of the wolds were slick with frost but Edwin said they must move on, and so they left the hamlet near the sacred grove which had stood for generations as the beating heart of Deira. Good Man's Hamlet, they called it now, to signify the transformation effected by High Priest Coifi.

He never left Paulinus's side. Perhaps Paulinus was teaching him about the new god, Hild thought, or making sure he didn't change his mind. Not that this seemed likely; the High Priest talked exuberantly of the new god while riding erratically.

"You can tell he's not a horseman," muttered the Companions when he dropped the reins to wave his arms. They may have muttered other things, too – Hild wasn't sure – but Edwin's decision was final and they'd follow his wishes to the last. They seated Coifi on the steadiest nag and rode close, in case he tumbled.

Hild was in her element, flushed and excited as she galloped about on a spirited mare like the young men, though she was not coursing hares. Heri was confined with Ethelburga, Uscrea and the infant Ani behind the close-drawn curtains of the royal litter, proceeding at the slow pace set by the herald to suit the baggage wagons. Circling away and back, Hild glimpsed sea to her right, bright blue in the winter sun, and brown moors rising sharply across the River Derwent. The north wind scoured her face, her hair flew out behind, and her body swayed to the rhythm of her mount. Leaning forward, she gripped the mane and crooned in its ear.

Eostre was happy, judging by the valley below. The frosts had readied the soil for harrowing. The water meadows stood in meltwater and would sprout bright grass for the cattle. Curls of smoke rose from the trees where the woodsmen's axes thudded. Everywhere, the promise of the new year.

But how long would it last? Would the new god care about the cycle of birth and death in the land? How could she, with Eostre abandoned, persuade the goddess to swell the seeds or curb rats and mould in the food stores? Why should Eostre cherish the people through the hungry months ahead?

Hild knew no one to advise her. Coifi was a different man; Paulinus was unapproachable; the queen had never understood; Osfrid, whom she could consult, was in the far north; Edi would merely laugh. What should she do?

Deep in her thoughts, she'd ridden off course. On the horizon, against the setting sun, she saw the last of the wagons plunge over the brow. Wheeling, she raced to rejoin the party, hoofbeats thundering as she cut diagonally down the slope. Edwin planned to stay the night at a modest homestead before fording the river.

Riding at full tilt, she recognized the pandemonium of arrival.

The king was nowhere to be seen. The queen, with her ladies, was being helped to the houseplace and would now be looking round for Hild. Labourers unloaded panniers and led away horses. Companions quaffed ale, stretched their legs, and bandied hunting trophies. Spearmen started to erect tents. Shrieking children raced between the different groups. Meat spat and sizzled over a huge fire outside the farm. She would be just in time.

She was hauling on the reins when, with a cry of *Hild!* a child shot across the horse's legs. She screamed. The mare reared. She struggled to dominate, stay on its back. Edi roared after the child. Hands stretched out to grab the reins. The mare panicked, reared again, and fell. Hild felt a blow to her head. A flash. Blackness.

5

YORK AND AFTER

She woke to a cold shower as Heri shook off her wet cloak and plomped down on the bed. "Welcome back to the world. Feeling better?"

"Think so." Hild levered herself up.

"Your hair's growing back." Heri parted it and peered. "Lump's gone."

"Heri, what happened? I remember... think I remember... a mare?"

"Yes, you fell off!" Heri guffawed. "Not your fault. Uscrea – of all the things! Rattling around, as he does, silly kid. Ran right in front of you. He's in a state. Edi keeps telling him he'll have to pay the murder fine if you die. You certainly looked like it at one stage."

"Did I?"

"Edi's not fair. He made things worse himself. And Cerdic turned up. You know, that Gododdin hostage, the slimy toad who's always hanging round Edi. I don't trust him. Didn't raise a finger to help. Just sniggered while Edi yelled."

Hild was confused. "How long have I been here?"

"All through February Fill-Dyke. We're in Hreth's month now, though you wouldn't think it. No wind, endless rain."

"Have you been looking after me? Only..." Hild frowned. "I dreamt I heard Ma."

"Begu!" Heri exploded into laughter. "She's got Ma's no-nonsense manner to the life!"

"The pig girl?"

"As you were bad, the queen let her stay." Heri stood up. "Must dash. Trying on robes. I'll tell Begu you're in the land of the living. She'll give you a wash and all that." Heri held her nose as if at a bad smell, pealed with laughter, scooped up her cloak, and danced out. Then she stuck her head back round the door. "You know we're in York, don't you? You travelled in the queen's litter."

"Sorry I missed the thrill," Hild smiled wanly. She lay back, listening to rain plopping off the thatch and thinking longingly of Ma. At least she'd seen Elmet at the end; it had comforted her, almost as if Hereric were there.

The men of Elmet didn't kill him, the old man said. What Ma believed wasn't true. So, who could have done it? After all, he was a prince – not easy to murder without power, or money, or cunning. Oswine drifted into her mind, and Osric, the two old cousins at the winter council. They must once have been ambitious. But there was no sign they'd gained anything by his death. So, who?

Next time Heri came, she helped Hild to a stool by the fire and wrapped her in a thick fleece.

"He's young," she muttered, kneeling at Hild's side. "Lord of a rich land. I could do worse."

Hild stared, her mind working. "He? Who? Heri, has Edwin arranged…?"

"Wish you could come with me, but Ethelburga says Edwin can't spare you."

"Where are you going? To be wed?"

"East Anglia."

"Erpwald!"

Hild's Erpwald, her dream, the prince who struck sparks off her. The man who made her melt. Heri was to have him. And Heri didn't want him. Oh, the irony! She throbbed with longing.

Heri beat the embers. "The queen says I'm of age, and I've to make his people love me."

"Like she does." Hild pulled up the fleece to hide her quivering lips. Would Heri have Ethelburga's determination and patience? Heri, her mercurial sister? *Stronger than she looks*, Ethelburga said. Thank the gods she was blind to any feelings but her own!

"The ladies are making me robes in the southern fashion. Long sleeves and fastening up the front. Think they'll suit me?" There was a pause and then Heri suddenly flung herself into Hild's lap. "Hild, I'm scared."

Hild stroked her hair, as Ma used to do. "When's it to be?"

"They're building a chapel in the Roman ruins." Heri's words came muffled. "Paulinus ordered it for the king's baptism." She unfolded herself and crouched on the hearthstone. Hild waited, thinking of Ma's Peace-Weavers.

"Pity Ma isn't here to see the end of Woden," she said.

"It looks as if you'll be better in time for our baptisms."

"You?"

"Everyone. You too. King's command. Vassals as well. Erpwald."

Hild bit her lip.

"Paulinus says he'll marry us there, in the Christian way."

Hild froze. She must endure.

Eostre's feast day came and went. Last year, she'd danced at the festival and met Erpwald on the moors. This year, nothing. The end for the spring goddess.

The beginning for the new god, Christ.

* * *

Hild followed Heri as the line shuffled along the riverbank.

> *Bridle of wild horses, Wing of unerring birds,*
> *Firm helm of ships, Shepherd of royal lambs,*
> *Guide us in the footsteps of Christ…*

The old hymn rang in her ears as she stepped waist-deep into the chilly water.

"In the name of the Father… Son… and Holy Spirit," intoned

Paulinus, at each invocation pushing her under the water. Rainbows sprayed round her and she gasped. Finding her footing, she dragged herself up, wiped her face, pushed her hair behind her ears and glared. She did not want bathing. It was Eostre's festival; she should be handing over to a new maid. She shivered in the April breeze. Paulinus printed a wet cross on her brow.

"Welcome, sister, to your new life in Christ." He turned her towards the opposite bank. When she looked back, he was already busy with the next in line.

The queue roared amiably at each submersion. Was it mob fervour or some special joy? She'd missed all Paulinus's teaching and had no idea what she should feel.

"Come on!" Heri struggled to wring out her hair behind the wattle screen set up for them. Towelling herself, Hild hastily pulled on a green woollen robe. Lifting Heri's hank of hair, she squeezed it between wads of wool, combed it up, pulled it tight on the crown of her head and knotted it so that it would fan out to dry in the air.

They stood watching the scene for a while, reluctant to take the next step.

"Ah, well!" Heri moved first. Her gold wedding tunic was crusted with embroidery, and the jewels scratched as she burrowed through the stiff garment. Emerging flushed, she pirouetted on tiptoe, admiring the flash of garnets and the swirls of mother-of-pearl down her front.

"I feel like Ethelburga," she crowed.

"Keep still!" Hild said. Ironic; just like her mother. She pinned on her sister's new cloak. Fixing the traditional chain from shoulder to shoulder, she stood back. "You look like her, you know. You'll have to be like her now."

Heri was pale. "I'm not a calm person."

"I suspect she isn't always, inside." Hild's voice was muffled as she bent to ease on her sister's stiff new sandals. "Just puts on a good show." Impulsively she hugged Hereswid. "And so will you!"

113

Twisting into her own shoes, she smoothed her hair, grabbed their veils and chivvied her sister along the bank to where the queen was watching the baptisms from her chair of state.

"Welcome to your new life in Christ." Ethelburga held out an affectionate hand to each and drew Heri to her side. Standing behind in her usual place, Hild saw Edwin stroll up, fresh-faced and robed in the exotic cream and purple sent by the Pope. He had Uscrea by the hand and was talking over his head to Edi: something about the summer campaign. No transformation there, then.

She caught her breath. Brows furrowed in the old manner, stiff in an embroidered red robe, trailed by his East Anglian thegns, Erpwald was making a stately approach. Why the frown, Hild wondered: baptism, marriage, his nation's business? Taking up position near the king, he looked shyly across at Heri, whose fair hair streamed in the breeze. He must have felt Hild's gaze.

"Welcome, sister," he said, "to your..."

"... new life in Christ." They ended together and laughed; Hild was surprised how naturally.

"Catching, isn't it?" she said. He'd been baptized with Edwin.

"Sister in more ways than one." His eyes slid to Heri and back to Hild. Then he said with a grin, "To be kin to a moorland sprite!"

"My hair again!" she groaned. With hands full of veil, she tried to smoothe it.

"I've seen worse. A certain day on the moor..."

"Unfair!"

"Like a polecat with cubs..."

"You rescued us."

A breathless pause, and an easy chuckle at their past discomfiture.

"How is it to be king?" She had to wait for his answer. He looked behind, and spoke in an undertone.

"Too soon to say. Only five months. Winter, too. No campaigning, no riding the land, no booty. And to succeed Redwald..." He looked bleak, the pulse throbbing near his ear, his scar a white streak. She yearned to stroke it. Even Edwin leaned on Ethelburga. If only she could be his Ethelburga!

She never forgot the moment, the light wind stirring his hair, sunlight etching his frown, the furrow down to his crooked mouth, the muscles like cords in his neck.

"You see it, don't you?" he sighed. "Edwin's support is crucial, and this marriage… your sister is so delicate."

"Tougher than she looks," she said wryly. "Give her time."

"Oh, I will!" he said fervently.

She knew her moment was over.

"May the gods bless you, my lord," she bowed formally, "give you fruitfulness in your home and kingdom. And for yourself… a fighter's blessings." Wordlessly he took her hand. She knew she had touched his heart's desire.

The rest of the day passed in a blur: the procession to the chapel in the ruins, the marriage vows sworn round the wooden cross at the door, Paulinus declaring they were joined *till death them do part*. She shivered at the words of bad omen.

There was a stampede to the feast, with Heri and Erpwald mobbed in the traditional way. Hand in hand and laughing, they ducked and wove between showers of flowerbuds and nuts, easy prey since they must not overtake the king.

In the hall, Ethelburga yielded the welcome cup to Heri, who offered it prettily to Edwin, then to her new lord and the thegns in his train. She sat between Edwin and Erpwald, picking abstractedly at her food while her groom talked seriously with Ethelburga. Hild could not hear past Edi bandying bawdy jokes with the odious hostage. Waves of raucous laughter surged. No one listened to the scop's twanging.

At last, men drooped in torpor and hounds gnawed quietly in the straw. Edwin rose for the gift-giving: matched gold rings for the bride and groom, and two chests full of riches for Heri. To buy the loyalty of her new ladies, Hild supposed. And he endowed her with two big farmsteads in Northumbria.

"These her lands, to hold as she will for the term of her life," he cried. Hild shivered. Not a gift of love, but a safeguard. If fate turned against her, Heri could always return.

"Phew!" In the bridal chamber, Hereswid made straight for the bed and sank down, blowing up into her heated face, and gobbling honeycake. "Couldn't eat a thing – all those people watching." As she munched and swigged, Hild performed the duties she carried out for the queen, loosing her heavy robes and veil and combing her hair in long, slow strokes.

"That's soothing. Hild, I just want to curl up and go to sleep."

"Into bed, then. I'll bathe you." Hild sponged her with rosewater and smoothed the covers. "Joy be yours," she whispered as she bent to give her a parting hug. Heri clung to her fiercely, then flopped back in resignation.

"I feel like a breeding cow," she groaned. "If only he were good-looking!"

Hild sighed deeply as she stole away.

Ethelburga was already disrobed, with a fur wrap round her shoulders.

"How is your sister?" she asked. "Happy, you think?"

"Ready to be a good wife to her lord," Hild said shortly, picking up the comb, tired beyond bearing.

"God give them peace and protection."

"Protection?" Hild croaked. "Is there danger?"

"There's a brother in Gaul, his mother's son but not his father's. He's got an eye on the kingdom. But Erpwald was elected by the lords in council. Edwin witnessed it. He must just show his paces and Hereswid her charm."

"She never said. Does she realize?" Hild was combing the queen's hair.

"It's always the same. It was like that for me, and for your mother. I talked with Hereswid about it." *Peace-Weaver*: that word again.

Hild yearned to be alone. Shrugging on a cloak, she picked a way through the flickering torches and gusts of carousing to the chapel. Sinking onto a bench under the overhang, she leaned back, breathed in the scent of new wood, and let her mind float: first, Paulinus's ominous words, then Erpwald's danger and Heri's future as his Peace-Weaver. She recalled Ma's failure at peaceweaving. Was she to blame? Legend said the people of Elmet rose against the Anglians. The old man said not. Who, then? Who had Breguswid failed to charm?

She sighed. She was the real failure. She'd lost everything, man and sister, happiness and companionship. Pain sliced through her. Tears began to roll down her cheeks. Unaware, then uncaring, she let them fall. Better to void the pain. No one could see. Sobs welled up and shook her. She curled on the bench, burrowing into her old felt cloak, and let her anguish flow.

She must have slept. A snuffling roused her, and a wet nose pushing her hand.

"Dog?"

"Begu, lady."

"Begu?" Hild scrubbed her eyes and lowered her legs. Then panic seized her. "Is something wrong?"

"No, lady. All's well."

"Ah!" She relaxed. "But you shouldn't be out at night."

"What's safe for you is safe for me, lady." That wasn't true, Hild knew, because of Begu's menial status. "And I brought the hound. Or he brought me!" Begu was squirting from a small bladder into a wooden cup. "Here's milk and honey. It was warm when I set out. And some oatcake."

"You're a loyal friend." The drink was tepid but Hild gladly nibbled the biscuit. They sat in silence, Dog pushing between them. To their left, a thin strip of sky lightened, sculpting leafless trees against the spreading dawn.

Still they sat, without a word. Hild felt oddly comforted, watching the glow spill over the watermeadows, the yellow thatch, the grey catkins, the green fuzz on the willows. Through the prism of spent tears, she saw everything fresh-washed, sharper.

Dog moved first, dabbing an exploratory paw.

"He's hungry!" Hild sighed. "We'd better go."

* * *

Northwards again, stopping along the route for Paulinus to

117

preach and baptize till he judged Deira to be Christian. Beyond Teeswater, the journey was no quicker as their wagons trailed sluggishly and crowds flocked to the bray of the herald's trumpet.

"His plough trespassed on my strip… your goat ate my beans… they cut switches in my coppice… he battered my slave… my brother's ear was sliced off."

"Remember Edwin's justice!" the king said as he levied a fine, ordered a beating or issued a reprieve. Threat or boast, Hild wasn't sure, but she knew they'd never forget.

Where the crowds gathered, the priests mingled and Paulinus preached.

"Look at your wickedness!" he cried. "Repent! Seek God's forgiveness before it's too late. Death without pardon is grimmer than your worst nightmares." If only, thought Hild, the new god were not so fixed on sin. At least Woden punished you straight away. This god prolonged the agony!

She remembered the folk who'd mobbed her as Eostre's maid. They were comfortable with the gods they knew and grateful for the magic that touched their lives: branches bowed with fruit, rivers glinting with fish, lambs leaping, clouds shifting, and pastel tints on the protecting mountains. Their king spoke for them and kept the gods happy. They knew where they stood. Now, Paulinus thundered, his priests cajoled, the king was silent and the people queued to be washed clean for this new god who did nothing for them.

"Filching, quarrelling, violence – aren't they wrong?" Brother James asked, when she challenged him.

"Just part of life, seems to me," Hild answered. "The gods do it."

"Not Christ." James's eyes gleamed. "He came to free us from evil. He gave his life – you remember, no?"

"*A prince must die for his people,*" Hild quoted Edwin.

"In a way," James said doubtfully. "It's hard to understand, yes? For us, too."

She sighed. At least James was easy to talk to. Paulinus pierced you with his eyes and never lowered his voice.

They followed the valleys to the heart of Bernicia, untamed, rugged, the Twister's country, living with the fear that his sons, now men, would claw it back and assault Deira. The further they travelled, the nearer the threat.

It was the month when elders drooped with blossom, crops stood tall, bearing cattle must be milked three times a day, and bearing women grew faint with the heat. The "June drop", Ethelburga called it wryly; the month when small apples fell hard and unripe, and women who'd embraced their men too eagerly last Bloodmonth waited wearily to give birth. Heavily, the queen balanced with Ani on the baggage in her cart.

"For luck!" cried women who saw and sympathized, darting up and tossing her straw dollies and meadow posies.

At last the hills opened on Yeavering, the ancient Bernician vill which Edwin had modernized. Hild gasped at his new structures: the biggest hall she'd ever seen, a pillar reaching to the skies to proclaim his closeness to the gods, and lodgings with hinged doors and windows to vent the hearth smoke. Within the old earth walls, Paulinus baptized in the River Glen, and Edwin chafed till the warbands massed.

Osfrid rode in, his son beside him and a boar's tusk on a thong round his neck. Turning to Yffi, Edi bowed to "my young lord of the northlands". Jibing at his brother was an old pastime; bullying his nephew, a motherless child not yet twelve, made Hild shiver. Then, in a flash, she saw. Yffi was Osfrid's successor. He was in Edi's way.

Later, Hild took Uscrea and Yffi up the nearby hill. They recaptured their easy rivalry, rolling each other down slopes, giggling, and stopping earnestly to distinguish the spoor of deer and goat droppings.

"Smashing spy place, isn't it?" Uscrea looked anxiously at Yffi, then back to the sweeping view over the vill where men toiled, coracles butted down the stream, and cattle jostled in the pen. "They look like ants."

"Mm," grunted Yffi laconically.

"Don't tell anyone." Emboldened by Yffi's approval, Uscrea knocked him over.

"Hey!" Yffi cried, as Uscrea reached for his sword. "It'll c-cut you!"

"Show me."

Hild sat on the breezy hilltop, the sun warming her back, while Yffi displayed his half-size sword with a fishbone design welded into the blade.

"My p-pattern, see? Special to me." He slashed gently and the tops came off the grasses.

"Oh! Can I?" Uscrea bounced up and down. "Please! Let me!"

"Well… It's sharp as a man's, Pa says. So, only if you d-do exactly as I say."

Uscrea nodded, speechless with excitement.

"Right, hold it like your wooden one. G-good. C-come over here, away from Hild. Now, a gentle swing." With unusual solemnity Uscrea followed his instructions again and again, until he tired.

Hild noticed their fair heads close together, Uscrea whispering his misery. "Edi said I'd have to pay a murder fine. He keeps on telling me. Is it true?" Typical! All this time Edi had stoked a small boy's worry.

"Well… every man has his p-price," Yffi explained judiciously. He was learning fast, riding with his father, but his stammer was worse. "Every woman, too. All k-killings, however accidental, must be paid for. With life. Or m-money."

"But I'm alive and here!" Hild expostulated. "Come on, you two sobersides! Let's try and see the sea." She jumped up.

"What's h-happening down there?" Yffi pointed. Tiny figures swarmed out of a tiered structure shaped like a wedge of cheese. Paulinus had preached in the king's auditorium. Now, like a mother goose, he led the people in a line to be baptized.

"That's Paulinus, in black," Uscrea proclaimed, proud to be able to tell Yffi something. "He talks all the time."

"What about?"

"The new god."

He sounded dismissive. They watched the ceremony in the stream and people dispersing to their farms as soon as they could.

Hild sighed. It had been such a big step for Edwin and taken so long, but it had no meaning. Thegns still fought, men harassed girls, the queen's women flirted, masters whipped their slaves. It felt like walking breast-deep through a river, straining all your muscles, and looking back to see the water close up behind you.

Her days were like that – ceaseless work, then all to do again: liaising with stewards, managing the lodgings, preparing for Ethelburga's next birthing, keeping Ani and Uscrea occupied. She was surprised how naturally the women looked to her and even thegns did her bidding. Was she growing fierce, like her mother? No, it wasn't what she did, but what she was: the king's niece and sister to a queen.

Heri's skittishness, Lady Breguswid's tartness – how often she'd wished them away. Now, with no one to tease or nag, no undemanding silences, even her dead dreams of Erpwald left her hollow. Always in a crowd, always on duty, she felt always alone.

* * *

"Something bad's on the way," Bass said miserably, pointing. "Those are Woden's black birds. They've followed us ever since we turned our backs on our own gods."

"They're crows, not ravens, Bass." Hild watched Anfled galloping on Uscrea's old wooden horse, while she rocked the latest infant outside the queen's lodging.

"Black, though," Bass insisted.

"God is stronger than Woden," said Brother James. He and Bass were old sparring partners. "Cadwallon fled, yes? Not a blow."

"That only means he's alive to fight again."

"At least the north's quiet," said Hild. "No sign of the Twister's brood."

"Keep your ears skinned," Bass snapped. "Bernicia is their heritage, but they can claim Deira through their mother, Edwin's sister, Acha." Hild gasped. How often the scop sang of the Twister raping Edwin's sister! She'd never realized the implications.

There was no booty when Cadwallon was beaten back to Gwynedd, but the scop sang even longer about Edwin's valour, and the king conducted an ostentatious gift-giving. Osfrid was honoured, as was Cerdic the hostage. Hild froze in horror when he knelt to have a heavy gold clasp pinned at his shoulder. *I don't trust that man.* Cerdic stayed too close to Edi, looked too darkly at the queen.

Despite the pageantry in the mead hall, Edwin was nervy.

"I've sent Edi west," he told Osfrid, who had come at his summons. "Pirates are raiding the coast. Cadwallon's behind it, I'm sure."

"Cadwallon? Didn't know he was still going!" said Osfrid easily.

"He's been in Ireland ever since we captured his fortress." Edwin jabbed the chart. "There! Anglesey! That's his centre." His knife vibrated in the table.

"In your first campaign? Years ago?"

"Yes. He's never forgiven me. Stayed quiet till now. After all, I know his lands as well as he does, having fought for his father."

"D'you want me in the north?" Osfrid asked carefully.

"No, Cutha'll do that. He managed last time and, now he holds Cerdic's lands, he knows the people. I want you with me. And Cerdic."

"The hostage!"

"He's too near home to leave behind. Cutha has to watch him like a heel hound. Besides, he'll fight for his keep. There's no ransom forthcoming, and the queen thinks he's bad for Edi."

"Ah!"

"And I want Edi to guard Deira against Penda, while you and I deal with Cadwallon."

Time passed. Hild lost count of the years. Before Penda, neighbouring Mercia had been Edwin's ally; he'd wed a Mercian princess, Osfrid and Edi's mother. Once he conquered Wessex, on Mercia's southern flank, Edwin had Penda in a vice. But, like all new kings, Penda was testing his muscle. His alliance with Cadwallon of Gwynedd was unprecedented; Anglians had always fought against Britons, Penda was ganging up with Britons against his own kind.

Every campaigning season, Penda and Cadwallon came closer. They forded the River Don, nibbled into Lindsey, slunk up through Wirral, crossed the Pennines, marched the old road to Elmet. The Twister's eldest son wed among the Picts and his two younger brothers rode with the king of Strathclyde, fighting his battles, learning their trade. And Strathclyde had links with Britons in Ireland and Wales. With Cadwallon.

The ever-present warbands were a nuisance. One day Hild found Begu scratching and kicking in the arms of a spearman.

"Bit of a wildcat, eh?" he smirked, assuming Hild's complicity. Back from campaign, Edwin's fighters had an unspoken right to women and food.

"Let her go! She's the king's." Hild rounded on him furiously, blaming her blindness. Begu was maturing. Her glossy dark plait, melting hazel eyes and low status made her easy prey.

"Keep this," she said later, giving the girl a knife. "Never go without it. And remember, fingers probe eyes, feet hook ankles, and knees…" Begu's eyes opened wide as Hild demonstrated the technique of a knee in the groin. "Don't hold back, Begu. Edwin supports his own."

As she walked away, she remembered with satisfaction her first successful skirmish, soon after Ma died. Probably word went round; she had no further bother.

An old king is a weak king, Edwin used to say. These days his hair lacked lustre and his bony body had not the stamina to run and drill. Was Bass right? Was it this new Christianity? He'd lost his royal privilege of representing his people to the gods. Less power, more fear. His enemies were closing in.

* * *

Woden's ravens struck. Hild never forgot the day. Crouched in the summer sun, she was rolling pine cones between Ani and the baby, when James bounded up and pushed her inside the queen's lodging, staying with the children.

The queen held a letter brought by a Canterbury priest. His ship had called in at East Anglia for water, and been assailed by volleys of spears.

"We were boarded. Axes, spears, clubs… and when they saw me…" He shook in horror. "Some traitor has seized the throne, restored the old gods and is massacring Christians. He's killed the young king."

Hild gave a sharp cry.

"What of Hereswid, the queen?" asked Ethelburga.

"I don't know, lady."

Hild fainted.

"Wrap her in this," she heard someone say. Rough wool enfolded her, strong arms placed her in a chair. Behind closed eyes, she saw Erpwald, his windblown hair, the scar down his cheek, his crooked smile.

And Heri dancing through the cow parsley, fingering silks and leather, collapsing in giggles. Beautiful, frivolous Heri, flighty as a butterfly.

And Erpwald.

Dead.

The queen should have kept her working. Ethelburga meant it for the best, but Hild had too much time to brood.

Where did it all go wrong? she wondered. Erpwald had done everything princes did, lived with Edwin, watched and served him, learned from him. Erpwald's fighters applauded him. All the signs were good.

Had Heri anything to do with it? The idea frightened her, but no one knew better how irritating and insensitive Heri could be. Had she turned the courtiers against her lord? Would Hild have done any better?

Distraught, Hild stamped along the riverbank, galloped across the moors. When she sat gnawing her knuckles, Ani curled up close. None of it stopped Hild's mind. How had Erpwald's half-brother stolen his kingdom? Why so soon?

Erpwald was not too young; Edwin had been younger. Had he failed to win booty to lavish on his thegns? Did his warband resent becoming Northumbria's subjects? Perhaps they objected to the new god. Even Ethelburga's brother was challenged when he first took the crown of Kent. But he'd come through.

And Edwin had guided Erpwald. Edwin was with him at Redwald's funeral, saw him acclaimed king. Had Edwin forced the issue? Peace, good living, religion, kinship: nothing outweighed holding on to his power. Even as overlord of kings, he was fiercely jealous. He would tolerate no threat to his rule.

And even he had struggled at the start, when he crushed Elmet. *It wasn't any of us,* said the old Briton by the river. *Terrible revenge Edwin took.*

To see him in his youth, she had only to look at Edi bullying Yffi; an uncle bullying a young boy, threatened by his closeness to power. Edi was uncle to Uscrea. Edwin was uncle to Hereric.

Edwin.

Hild gasped. Her questions dissolved like mist in sun. It was so obvious.

Edwin. She must think. She must be sure.

It had to be him. His deeds ran through her memory, she saw his secret ways. He wanted Elmet. He took Ma into his household to prevent her causing trouble. He posed before the people, firing their fervour. He steered his council with a subtle smile. The pictures flashed through her mind. They made her sick, but they made sense.

But the risk, if she challenged him! Could she, scarcely seventeen years old, challenge the Bretwalda? To lose home, livelihood, maybe life itself. Had she the daring?

It was for her father. No one else was left to act.

She stood up, squared her shoulders, and strode to confront her father's murderer.

Shaking, determined, she stalked to the hall. Edwin was not there.

Breathlessly, she made for the queen's lodging. Ani chirruped merrily on the threshold. Ethelburga sat by the fire, nursing her youngest. Edwin sprawled on the bearskin at her feet, play-wrestling with Uscrea. Hild had eyes for nothing but the king.

"You!" she burst out. "It was you."

"Hild!" cried the queen.

"You!" Hild pointed at Edwin. "It was you killed my father!"

Languidly, the king unfurled. Silently he took to his feet. At full height, he stood facing her, his cold eyes raking her flushed face, wild hair and heaving chest.

"Clearly, you're recovered, lady," he said impassively. "I think it's time you wed."

PART 2

6

DOON HILL

"God prosper you, Hild." Cutha leaned across, patting her shoulder. His was the last home to offer hospitality on their marriage procession through Bernicia, and his was the final greeting. He lived beyond the River Tweed, the Northumbrian border, in Gododdin land. He held a lordship there, conferred on him by King Edwin as reward for capturing the raider: her new husband.

Night after night on their progress, they'd been feted as a royal couple. Day after day Hild was forced to tail her man: Cerdic, the hostage; Cerdic, the sneering accomplice in Edi's bullying; Cerdic, who resented her as Edwin's pawn, and hated her presence at his homecoming from six years' disgrace; Cerdic, her unwanted lord.

Cutha wheeled to ride back, waving.

"Thank you," she called, "for everything." Sitting her horse on the hilltop, she looked down into the dark woodland where her married future lay. Skylarks chittered, goats bleated and branches creaked, but the familiar sounds gave Hild no comfort; she was entering enemy territory.

"On!" Cerdic barked. "On, Satan!" His black stallion, Edwin's marriage gift, sprang forward, tail lashing. Hild's mare lurched behind, trailing her braided skirts: not the best riding gear, but suited to his needs; she must look the part of a royal bride.

The track narrowed as they dropped into a ravine. Her Anglian guards rode close, spears unstrapped, listening intently as their own rhythmic clopping hammered back from the cliffs on either side.

When darkness threatened the horses' legs, they camped in the trees. Cerdic took a swig from his flask and handed it to her wordlessly. The wine was thin, tepid from his body and slightly sour. She swallowed some and stamped her feet warm.

"One night in the open," he said gruffly to the escort. "Then you return."

"My lord," their leader half rose, "my order is to see your lady home."

"Two men," Cerdic snapped, "to ride the baggage to my homestead. I take my lady first to greet my chief."

They muttered resentfully. "How far, then?" asked the leader.

"This track leads to the Firth," he answered. "A half-day's ride, too far for tonight. From there, Din Edin's west, my homestead east. One day at most. Sort out the men and I'll brief them in the morning."

"How will they receive Northumbrians, your household?"

"Peaceably. You can take this to show. It's an old arm-clasp of my father's." He twisted it self-consciously. Hild remembered Edwin returning it as he presented gold armlets for Cerdic's war service.

She couldn't sleep. Through the flaps of her leather tent she saw the camp fire glow and the bushes glitter with frost. She wished they'd made offerings to the night elves. Owls hooted, sentries chinked, the ground felt lumpy, her bones ached. Before marriage she'd never slept alone, always with the women or in the queen's lodging.

Edwin's words beat in her brain: *A prince must die for his people.* Death in battle, he'd meant, but this was a kind of death. He'd stolen her life, stripped her of affection and self-respect. *Consort to a captive Briton*, she mouthed angrily. Brides should be carried home amid flowers and singing, *My love she'll be, My love she'll be, The hawthorn bloweth fairest.* The old song soothed her and she relaxed, rolling onto her side. Almost at once a warbler trumpeted dawn. She gave up.

* * *

The sun was setting when they broached the sharp incline to the Gododdin fortress of Din Edin. Cerdic led his horse between high earth banks which curved sharply and cut out the light. He vanished ahead. Two of her guards levelled with her and, bunching, advanced cautiously up the narrow gulley. A stone dropped beside them. Looking up they saw a row of heads peering down. She shuddered. Rocks, spears, slops, anything might fall.

"Come, lady!" Cerdic sent loose stones skittering as he strode back, hand outstretched. A swarm of small boys bounced and hallooed around him, leaving the bank-top bare. "Couch your spears, men, and give the boys your horses. Follow me. You're among friends." He gripped Hild's elbow, leading her along a narrow turf bank between deep pits brimming with brushwood. "Keep close. These are man traps."

She found herself on a plateau among homesteads and felt, rather than saw, the land drop steeply around. Grey hills folded into the distance, and water shone luminous below.

"Lady, you must join our feast." A white-haired woman took her arm, drawing her to a circle of felled trunks around an open fire where a pig was spitted. Hild felt herself pushed onto a seat with a back and sank down gratefully, her stomach rumbling.

"Food!" a man chuckled to her right, patting her knee. "Not long now. Welcome to Din Edin, lady. My wife, Gerda, will make you comfortable." The old man wore silver rings and neck-chain. Cerdic knelt formally before him.

"My lord Gwylget!" His voice cracked. "This is my wife, the lady Hild, kin to Edwin of Northumbria."

"So!" Shrewd eyes peered from Cerdic to her. "Welcome, lady Hild. And Cerdic." The Gododdin chief raised him. "At last you return to my service. Sit by me and we can talk."

"'Tis well you come tonight, lady," Gerda whispered to Hild.

131

"We've killed a pig to last till the new crops." Hild tried to surrender the seat. "No, my dear, sit. Share what we have, you and your people. The bread is hard, but the meat is fresh." She indicated a wooden tray heaped with the best cuts which the servers had placed on an upturned log before Gwylget. Hild speared chunks of pork with her knife, chewing them with the tough bread. Offered a small beaker, she scooped from a large silver bowl and drank a wine as fragrant as any she had ever tasted.

"Comes from France, up the western seaboard," said her hostess.

Glowing with warmth, Hild saw through the smoke her guards back-slapping and guffawing as they tried to communicate with the Britons. Young boys crouched round them, fingering their fighting gear. Beyond the light, small children shrieked in a chasing game. Someone lined up the girls to sing a welcome chorus. Hild felt herself slipping towards sleep.

Drowsily she heard Gwylget giving Cerdic the news: poor crops last year, winter storm damage, the Pictish king threatening, good fighters killed on the border, a boat lost on the Firth. Cerdic drank steadily.

"So you've brought home a princess?" Gwylget tried to draw him out. "A bonny one, too. What honour they've shown you."

"More than you!"

"Eh?" The old chief unbent abruptly.

"Why didn't you ransom me?" Cerdic wailed. "That's what I don't understand."

"You're too valuable!" the old man chuckled, putting a hand on his arm.

"You find it amusing?" Cerdic stiffened. "That I spent six years a laughing stock to Northumbrians while you forgot about me? If you'd really valued me…"

"Value you? Oh, I do, my boy." Gwylget's tone was earnest.

"I'm not your boy!" Cerdic rasped.

"What I mean is, they set your value too high. We tried…"

"If I had been your boy, you'd have found it, sold everything…"

"I tried, Cerdic. Your weight in gold. That was Edwin's price.

More than our small kingdom holds." The chief looked sadly at him. "And we had no one of his to exchange. Nothing to bargain with."

Cerdic slumped.

"He wanted you," the quiet voice continued. "My best man…"

"Your best man? Huh! Downed by a woman…" He choked on his bitterness. Hild had always known his deepest scar was being mastered by Ethelburga.

"My best fighter," the old man repeated firmly. "He set your price too high so he could keep you where he wanted you."

"Wanted me? No. Gold's what Edwin craves. Gold to buy loyalty where it does not spring, gold to flaunt and dazzle…"

"We sent an offer, you know. It wasn't enough. The envoy came back and said you were being well treated…"

"Huh!"

"… tenting with Edwin's sons, and the younger was your friend." There was a pause. "You fought for him, didn't you? For Edwin."

"I fought for him," Cerdic said in a flat tone, hunched in misery. "In the end."

"And fought well. Well enough to have earned your freedom."

"You know why, don't you?" Cerdic jerked back his head, his eyes black pools of fury. "Why he's sent me back? It pays him. It's to buy something he wants. Safety on his border. He's even sent his minion to make sure I do what he wants."

"What do you mean?" The old man was confused.

"Her!" Cerdic spat, jerking his head in Hild's direction. "She'll tell him if I don't do his bidding. A spy in my own home!"

"That's not true!" Hild leapt to her feet. With a rattle of arms her escort scrambled up. The old chief blanched. Not, she realized, with alarm; he'd not expected her to understand their British talk.

Ashamed of her temper, keen to restore calm, Hild waved the guards down and made a formal bow to the chief.

"My lord, you've extended a kind welcome and I thank you. Will you permit me to withdraw?"

Gerda led her to a tiny lodging, almost filled with a pallet covered in skins.

"God give you rest," she said, then took Hild's hand and squeezed it hard. "Give him time, my dear. Cerdic will heal, now he's home."

* * *

Next day, they rode hard along the water towards the rising sun. As it sank behind them, they turned inland to climb a rough track by a stream and follow a sturdy palisade of split trunks sharpened at the top, some recently renewed. Cerdic dismounted. Hild waited and the escort hung back.

"This is all the kin I have now," he murmured harshly, looking at shallow mounds near the gateway. Hesitantly, she moved to his side.

"Tell me," she said quietly.

"They lived, they farmed, they fought, they died. That's all. Except…" his voice was sour, "my young brothers, here. Killed before they knew life. Brawls over the water. Picts!"

He swung abruptly and strode in through the gate, looping his reins over a bar. Hild copied him, then shook out her skirt, swept her veil behind her shoulders, took a deep breath and looked ahead. Deep sloping rush thatch, mud walls curving under the overhang, and a family bunched in the open doorway: her new home.

"Rohan, my steward," Cerdic flung back. A stocky, weathered man stepped out to grip him fiercely by the elbow. They stood silent, arms locked, both faces twisted. Eventually Cerdic slapped Rohan's arm and pulled away.

"Your new mistress," he pronounced. "The lady Hild, princess of Northumbria. See you attend her in a fitting manner."

Hild saw a willowy woman bob nervously. Stroking the child at her skirts, she eyed Hild silently.

"Let's ride out, you and I." Cerdic nudged Rohan. "See the land. There's just light enough." He laughed at the absurdity. Roused from their torpor, the boys saddled fresh horses while Cerdic called to Hild, "Feed your guards tonight, lady. I'll see them to the border in the morning."

"Well," she said to herself, "that's a task that won't defeat me." Moving to the door, she said, "What's your name?" The woman's cloudy blue eyes opened wide.

"Brigit, lady," she gasped, astonished to hear her own tongue. Hild smiled at the memory of Ma beating the language out of her for the sake of her future at the Anglian court. The memory stiffened her. She would make this marriage work.

"Will you show me round, Brigit? Before we organize the food? Outside first."

Beyond the doorway, the walls were breached and the thatch sagged. Round the back, they entered by another door which led into a passage across the middle of the house. A fetid stench made Hild gag. Clapping her veil to nose and mouth, she peered past a broken plank to her right and saw dung piled deep, and wads of straw dangling from the rotten thatch.

"We drove them to the hill last night," muttered Brigit, "when we heard you were coming."

"Cattle?" Conscious of the woman's misery, Hild walked the other way into an airy space with shutters thrown back and the door open to the setting sun. In one alcove cots, pots, tools and stores were ordered. Hild's chest was set in another. She breathed in the yeasty smell from a crock of fresh bread sitting on the hearthstone, and saw a ham dangling in the smoke above. Dried herbs hung over a cooking table.

"A well-tended homeplace," Hild smiled.

"Oh, lady!" Brigit swayed and went white. Her fingertips were blue from twisting her veil. "We didn't know… know if… if he would come back."

"Of course you didn't. But you've kept the place secure…" Hild nodded to the palisade, "and maintained food stocks. The rest will come right in time."

"Oh, lady!" Brigit crumpled in relief.

"Now, food for tonight." Hild knew the woman needed action. "We've to feed six extra men."

"Rohan killed a sheep when we heard." Brigit's voice grew

firmer. "It's spitted over the fire outdoors. And…" she pointed to a large iron cauldron hanging on a long chain over the fire, "that's a bean broth."

"And here's bread. Good. I was given some cheese and a few of last year's apples. Now…" Hild kept the pace up, "sleeping quarters?"

"We sleep round the fire."

"My lord should have a bed, even if he chooses not to use it," Hild said firmly. Brigit showed her a dark corner where a bare wooden frame, lashed side-to-side with leather thongs, held a grubby heap of skins.

"You'll need those." Hild crossed to her chest. "Here's some more for the bed, and we could fashion a mattress of sorts. Send the children to gather beechmast, leaves, grasses, scraps of sheep's wool, anything soft and dry. We'll fold it into this old cloak for now. And this…" she flushed with burrowing to the bottom, "we'll drape across here." She stretched a light cloak between two beams to afford some privacy. "That'll do for the present."

"The spearmen?" Brigit asked.

"Outside. They're used to it, and you say there's a fire? Let's bustle!"

Fishing in the pouch at her waist, she drew out a large bodkin and rummaged for strands of wool in a basket near the loom. Perched on the bedframe, she stitched her summer cloak into a bag.

"Who'll find the most?" she cried as the children ran in with armfuls of foliage, tossing it into the opening when she held out her arms. They chased in and out, bumping each other aside, and crowing in excitement.

"Winner tests the mattress," Hild cried, tying off the stitching and fluffing the bag out over the bedframe.

"Me!" cried the youngest. Clambering up, he threw himself backwards, shrieking as he bounced back into the air.

"That's enough." Brigit ran in, alarmed by the noise, and hauled him off. "The leather won't stand that!"

"I started it," Hild admitted. "Don't blame him."

"Lady, you're a marvel!" Brigit wiped her hands on her skirts. "You've kept them from under my feet and we're nearly finished."

"Anything more to be done?"

"The lads have brought some fresh flooring, if you don't mind." She motioned Hild aside. Two boys brushed and kicked the worn rushes out of the door. Another staggered in, dropped a towering bundle, and went out for more. They spread out the fresh stems, beating up a sweet, summery smell.

"Now, boys, set the board for mead. I've drawn it into jugs and found some extra cups." Brigit sounded in control again.

"Have we a guest cup?" asked Hild.

"We've never…"

"May I?" Hild drew from her chest a chased silver goblet. "A bridal gift."

"It's lovely!" Brigit fingered the surface. "Will you hold it steady, lady, if I pour?" She carried the brimming goblet to the makeshift table. Hild flipped her hair back and held her palms to her flushed cheeks, surveying the room.

"Looks good, Brigit. Now, let's send the lads to the gate. They can warn us when the men arrive, and they won't upset the trestle. I'll dress to greet my lord. Have you a little water?"

Washing freshened her weary body. Donning a clean shift, she stepped into a favourite brown tunic, easy to wear, fastened down the front in the Kentish style with a woven cream edge. Sitting on her chest, she combed her tangled hair and folded it into one dark plait which swung heavy against her back. Flinging on a linen veil and fixing it with braid, she stood to tie her waistbag on to her girdle.

She dug into her chest to find a silver disc and examined her reflection. A solemn face confronted her, as strained as Ethelburga's, with blue shadows under dark eyes. It was Ethelburga's gift, the mirror from the Pope which she and Heri had brandished the day their mother warned them what marriage really involved. Sudden longing swept her for Heri and her mother. Was this how they'd felt, wed to foreign princes?

"They're here!" came the cry outside. "Lady, he's coming."

With a deep breath Hild rose, slipped her knife in her girdle, and walked to the door to meet her lord.

* * *

At the bottom of the home slope, Hild clapped a hand to her back and eased upright. Throwing back her veil, she walked away from the hives. In the shade of a bush, she drank from her flask and watched the field workers. Yoked oxen strained along the furrows, then stopped patiently, flicking their tails. Balancing on the flat cart, Rohan hefted forkfuls of dung over the side for two lads to turn into the soil while a boy followed, raking it smooth. The plan was to plant cabbages and beans.

"Should make for a good crop," Hild called. Perhaps they didn't hear. More probably, Rohan was standing on his dignity. Riding with Cerdic, he was the man in charge. Left to himself, he felt as good as his lord. But to owe duty to a woman!

She'd had to wait till Cerdic was away for the dung to be cleared. Rohan had no reason to refuse her, but he had plenty of excuses: they needed a byre away from the house; a shed, too, for stabling the horses; repairs to the barn roof; a platform to store the grain off the ground; and some racks for the honeyed mead.

Honey. That brought her back to the bees. Clamping the lids on the hives, she flapped away the strays, admired the gorse-gilded slope beyond the stream, and turned uphill to the homestead.

Hearing shrieks, she peered round the gateway. Brigit, in a flurry of skirts, was trying to milk a frisky goat, with the old billy nibbling at her hair.

"Daft animal! Move it, for pity's sake," she yelled to the children. They danced round, laughing. Hild chuckled as she climbed further up the slope to the hawthorn tree she'd discovered her first morning.

Cerdic had ignored their efforts with his homecoming meal and, when her escort bade farewell, stood stiff and silent as a gatepost. Such rudeness was infuriating. She stamped away, hands clenched, head down, snorting with anger, and almost hurtled over the escarpment behind the house.

Pulling up short, she grabbed a branch and, despite the thorns drawing blood, clung on. The Firth glittering below the cliff made her gasp in wonder. A sacred place, this must be, haunt of kindly gods. She would bring an offering to Eostre.

Since then, she had returned to her hawthorn tree whenever feelings overwhelmed her, usually annoyance at Cerdic or Rohan; in this new life, nothing happened without a struggle. The ribbons she'd hung may fade in the branches, but Eostre's peace never failed. Blue water stretched below, stippled by the breeze. Black, conical islets reared up, fringed with breaking waves. Gannets swooped and dived. Golden sand dunes framed the water, and blue hills folded, layer on layer, as far as the eye could see.

This time, she dug from her waistbag the tattered page James had given her. *Create in me a clean heart, O God; renew a right spirit in me.* Reading was easier now, but disconnected fragments were harder than stories. This, if she remembered, was part of a very old song, good for calming down. She wondered about the poet who'd written it, and why.

"Lady!" The cry made her turn. "Ma says, come. If you like."

Anxiously, Hild ran downhill. "What's the matter?" she called from the gate.

"Oh, lady, nothing." Brigit was pushing the door shut behind the children. "I didn't want you to miss him."

"Who?" Hild doubled over to recover her breath.

"The preacher."

"Preacher?"

"He's set up the cross. They come from the sunset. Monks. They tell stories, heal people. Do come."

With the children scampering ahead, they walked down the stony path by the stream. A crowd was massing at the waterside, sitting on shingle, squatting on boats, standing on boulders, all facing a round-headed cross, fixed upright in a socket.

One hand on the shaft, an old, bald-headed man with streaming beard stood bent, listening to a small boy who was prattling earnestly, scuffing his feet. When the man looked up, Hild saw he wasn't old at all. His beard and the hair trailing down his back were not white but fair, and he wore plain homespun, like Rohan. Paulinus and his men had cropped round heads, not hair streaming down their backs. So, who was this?

Beaming, the man found a perch on the rim of a boat and beckoned another boy. The three heads bent close.

"He mends quarrels," Brigit whispered. "Grown-up ones, too. Come and sit on this basket, lady."

Hild saw the boys join hands. The man sketched a blessing over their heads before they burrowed back into the crowd.

"Me, too!" cried Brigit's youngest, and the whole brood pushed forward, crying, "Brother, brother!" Others followed. They tugged at his skirts, clambered on the boat, his lap, anywhere to be near; pulled his leg, his satchel, his arm, to gain his attention. Their shrill voices carried over the crowd. The man listened, nodded and, when they quietened, swept them all into his arms for a blessing.

As they pelted away, he rose and scanned the crowd. The same piercing gaze as Paulinus, Hild thought, but his eyes were different; not dark and deep-set but a radiant, all-embracing blue.

"Children first!" he tutted indignantly. "To leave the pot on the fire, the boat on the stocks, the plough in the furrow, and have to wait for children!" Hild saw wry glances and some vigorous nods and broad grins. This was nothing like Paulinus.

"You, and you, and you…" he pointed at three nodding heads, "you're just like Jesus' Companions." They looked uncertain, but he had them gripped. His light voice rang over the restless pebbles as he told of Jesus welcoming the children when his men drove them off to give him rest. It was a story Hild knew, so it must be the same God as Paulinus's. She waited for the familiar ending.

"To enter God's presence, you must be like a child."

"Noisy brat, you mean?" a man called and the crowd laughed.

"No problem with a bit of noise." The monk laughed too. Then he dropped his voice and they had to listen hard.

"But children have other qualities. What about trust? Love? Obedience? And have you noticed how welcoming children are?" He paused. They waited. Not in awe, Hild thought, but in anticipation. "If you want to meet God, what must you be like? That's the question. What do you think?" He waited, looking round, grinning. Hild thought he smiled at her. "Well, there are several answers. I'm leaving the question for you to talk over, till next time."

An affectionate, exasperated groan swept the crowd. "He's done it again!"

"Now, shall we pray?" Stretching out his arms and cupping his hands upward, he spoke for the people to his God: praise for the good things around them, thanks for their livelihoods, a plea for strength to bear whatever life dealt. Not ceremonial or ponderous, Hild noticed, but conversational, like old friends meeting after an absence.

"D'you know about Saint Kevin?" Brigit's small daughter, who was holding Hild's hand as they walked home, suddenly pulled away and stood in front of her, arms outstretched and hands cupped like the priest. "He stood praying so long, a blackbird nested in his palm." The children giggled.

"Yes," her brother took over, "and he had to keep standing like that until the eggs hatched."

"Eggs – anyone searched today?" called Brigit, and the children tumbled up the hill out of sight.

"What does he do now, the monk?" Hild asked as they rounded the bend.

"Oh, he'll travel on, lady, unless someone needs him. Then he stays with whoever has room. Fishermen, usually." She swung round at the sound of a small avalanche behind. "Whatever have you got there?"

"Look, Ma," her eldest boy puffed up to them. He held a stick bent under the weight of a row of dangling fish. "Fisher Daigh gave me these."

"Herring!" Brigit stopped to examine them. "Fresh, too, by the eyes. You'd better take him some cheese when you next go down."

"He'd rather have mead, Ma. He said he'd run out, and if you could spare it…"

141

"He did, did he?" Brigit laughed. "Well, hang them on the drying rack. They'll be good tack when the men ride out."

"Oh, Ma!"

"You'll soon be one of the men," she jollied. "Oh, all right. Just one."

When they reached the yard, Hild watched him lay his stick between crossed branches jammed on either side of a pile of dead embers. Fixing the ends tight against the wind, he tied on the fish by their tails, counting them ceremoniously.

"Seven," he called to his mother.

"With or without yours?" Brigit was inside, clattering a ladle.

"Without." Carefully, he detached the largest fish and ran in with it, leaving someone else to kindle the embers.

"Here, lady!" Little lame Caitlin, as usual, trotted out with Hild's spindle.

"You're as stern as my mother," Hild chuckled, lifting her onto the bench and unrolling the hank of wool with a sigh; she'd never become adept at tucking it in her girdle and twiddling all day.

"Horsemen heading here, lady." Rohan arrived in a miasma of dung. Back from the field, the men doused their hot faces, stripped off their cloth leggings and dropped them in the soak bucket. "It's the wrong direction, that's the thing. From the south. Friends of yours?"

"None that I'm expecting."

"Don't like it," he grunted. "We're off the main track. But…"

Hild's heart thudded: a remote hillside farm, a handful of women and children, and Rohan watching her suspiciously. They hauled the heavy gate closed, four lads staggering under the weight of the crossbeam while Rohan laboriously hammered its ends into sockets.

"Axes at the ready," he barked, "tools indoors!" They went to supper.

A livid red stripe slashed the darkening sky. Hild couldn't see past the palisade; no one could see in. She stayed by the door, growing calmer as she listened to the gentle clucking of the hens and the wind stirring the trees.

"Tipped the dung at the bottom," she heard Rohan say.

"And the endplace? When will you get round to that?" Brigit nagged.

But Hild existed in a kind of bubble, unneeded, unnoticed. If only she didn't feel sick so often. With the thought, a shudder ran through her. Couldn't be, given Cerdic's coldness, yet... Those Yuletide nights after the marriage, when they were bedded in the guest house and Cerdic drank his fill...

Heavy thuds rattled the gate. "Gate, hey! Cerdic, let us in!" What friend of Cerdic's would come unannounced at night? Rohan came to the door.

"Cerdic, you old devil! Is this how you welcome a friend?"

Hild gasped.

"That voice!" she whispered. The last person she expected, or wanted, especially with Cerdic away. But her duty was plain. "Open the gates, Rohan. I know who it is."

His lads hammered and hauled at the beam, sweat dripping off their noses. Jeers and guffaws outside were answered by grunts and oaths within. Suddenly, with a wrenching creak, the beam shot up and the massive gate sprang back, flinging the lads against the palisade.

"We were not expecting guests." Hild stood in the gap, torch high above her head. "Welcome to Cerdic's homestead, my lord Edi." She bowed with dignity and stood aside. "Welcome to Doon Hill!"

* * *

"How soon will he be back?" Edi stood by his horse's head, sniffing in the morning mist and slapping a switch against his boot.

"When the council finishes," Hild replied.

"What're they dealing with?"

She shrugged. "Men's talk."

"Not another Ethelburga, then, meddling in men's affairs?"

She sighed. His bitterness towards his stepmother meant she couldn't ask for news.

"Well, I'll give it one more day." He squinted at the clouds. "Hunt your hills, if you can spare your man."

Cerdic came home late that night, wet and tired. He stopped dead at the sight of Edi feasting round the fire with his men, then twisted off his sodden cloak and draped it over a nail.

"Budge up, friend!" Hoisting his leg over the bench, he slapped Edi on the back. "What brings you here?" He held up a goblet to be filled.

Heads together, they ate without seeing, drank without pausing, and talked urgently in undertones. One by one, Edi's men dropped down to sleep. The fire burned low. Hild sat yawning on the bed, shivering in the dank room.

"I'll ask," Cerdic snapped, and she jerked awake, the spindle rolling off her lap. He leaned back, stretching, and she heard him say, "Holding the frontier's in our interests, but as for fighting abroad…"

"The Gododdin swore allegiance," Edi pressed.

"Show sense, Edi! We haven't the manpower to wall off the Picts and traipse south with you."

"At least give the Gododdin Edwin's gifts."

"Take them yourself. You'd make a better case."

Edi bit his lip. "Keep the gifts," he hissed. "You're the warleader."

"That's why I must be straight. I can't advise him to leave his lands exposed."

"Our lands," Edi corrected sharply. "Part of Northumbria."

Both men glared.

"The thing is," Edi tried to recover, "it's not just Penda. Cadwallon's rousing Gwynedd…"

"Again!" sighed Cerdic. "So Edwin's in a sticky spot."

"He's never been beaten," Edi said indignantly. "But he can't move against Penda without diverting Cadwallon, and that's where you…"

"… where we come in," Cerdic finished. Thoughtfully he drifted outside to relieve himself. A damp blast cut across the room. One of the men coughed in his sleep. Hild pulled her cloak tight.

"Nippy, out there." Cerdic strolled back. "I'll put it to the old man, Edi, with your bribes. But I can't advise leaving here. The Firth's a leaky boundary."

"Just tell him we need you. He'd win rewards, and you… honour and glory."

With a sceptical grunt, Cerdic kicked the embers to a flame, rolled to the floor, bunched the rushes under him and slept.

Dawn was not far off. Hild lay fully clothed, mind racing. She hoped Edi wasn't weaving some ploy of his own: claiming Penda's throne through his mother, conspiring against his brother, ousting his father. He'd always been dodgy in his loyalty and, she had to admit, Edwin had never had much time for him.

For all her anger and distrust of Edwin, she didn't like to think of him encircled like an old bear. But he'd look death in the eye, if his time had come. He'd always said, *A prince must die for his people.* Would her marriage safeguard him as he hoped? Cerdic's firmness under Edi's pressure was impressive, and his shrewdness against the barrage of midnight argument reassured her.

She must have drifted off. Coming to as weapons clattered and harness jingled, she felt seedy and sick.

"Wife!" Cerdic shouted. "Lady, where are you?" Groggily she straightened her skirts and jabbed pins in her veil as she walked to the door.

"God's teeth, woman, you look like death," he snarled. "Where's the farewell cup for Lord Edi?"

Brigit thrust it into her hand.

"My thanks for your princely hospitality." Edi, who was already mounted, sketched a derisive bow. Draining the cup, he hurled it over his shoulder, then galloped down the open slope, Cerdic and the men in hot pursuit.

Cerdic must be squiring him to the border. He might have told her. She'd done her best: unskilled pig killing in the rain while Rohan rode with the prince, messy butchering of joints, garnering and cooking for the feast, dressing finely for his sake.

And he didn't say a word to her. Tears of exasperation came to her eyes. *Give him time*, Ethelburga said. *Give him time*, said the old chief's wife. How much time?

"Well, they've gone!" Brigit held out a cup. "Drink this, lady. Honeyed mead."

"To wake me up?" Hild said ironically, but she drank. "Well done, Brigit. All those unexpected meals."

Brigit bobbed. "Truth to tell, we're out of practice. Nothing like it since his father's day. We must get better prepared. I was saying to Rohan…"

"He's gone to the border too?"

"Yes. He says this has brought home what needs doing. Left orders for the men to dig out the far end of the house. Properly, this time. When troops are wished on us again, you'll be able to sleep decently, lady. I'll go get them started."

Hild sat on the bench, deafened by the clatter. Brigit shrilled her orders, men hacked out wattle, hurled lathes, swung spadefuls of dung erratically at the cart. The sun grew warmer, the stench thickened, children shrieked and her head rang.

"Ye gods!" Cerdic pulled up in the gateway, his mount rearing. "What is it, old Satan? Battle sounds, eh?" Slipping down, he gripped the harness, soothing the horse. "Mead, hey!"

"They won't hear. I'll go." Hild took his spear and cloak, while he tethered the horse. Returning, she fondled Satan's ears while Cerdic rubbed him down.

"What a stink! We'll escape this, lady. I need to see the chief about Edi, and it's nearly Easter. Prepare the bags and we'll go to Din Edin."

A familiar task; she found herself humming. A change of clothing, undershifts, combs, brooches. Pausing, she fingered her father's battered cloakpin, rarely worn but never left behind. Was she right? Did Edwin have him killed? After all that, she still didn't know. Heaving a sigh, she carried on. Woollen stockings, her old plaid, tallow, and sewing kit, agrimony for wounds and sore stomachs.

"Spindle, of course." She wrinkled her nose. Ah, crushed rosemary for the fusty smell that tainted used clothes.

146

"Pack this, lady." Cerdic held out a glass decorated with fragile blue trails. "One of Edwin's gifts. I think it'll please Gwylget." Hild folded it in a length of purple silk and added guest gifts, spices, a strip of gold metal curiously beaten. By the time she'd finished, she no longer felt sick.

* * *

The journey became one of Hild's good memories. Cerdic was not given to chatter but he seemed at peace as they trotted through the spring. The Firth lapped blue, the ploughland bristled green, and blackthorn buds gleamed like Tyne pearls in the bare branches. When the sun sank, they stopped in the dunes, and Cerdic lit a small fire, laying some feathered scraps in the embers.

"A bird?" Hild asked.

"A meal," he replied drily, handing her the flask and a wrinkled apple. She lay back in the sand, lulled by the sighing of waves on shingle. Other Easters drifted through her mind: the attack on Edwin, the baptisms, and the night on the hill with the Moormaid. Could Edwin's troubles have stemmed from abandoning the old gods? She was glad she'd run to her hawthorn to offer catkins and bread before they left.

Easter was different at Din Edin. At the heart of the settlement a preaching cross stood like a man at prayer, arms curving upwards, fingertips fusing into a circle of perfection. People gathered in the open, like Woden worshippers, lifting hands and voices to the open skies. Together they chanted the Lord's Prayer and the Creed: Hild, too, for she knew them from Paulinus's ritual.

They shared supper in remembrance of Christ's last meal. Monks, with the flowing hair and homespun robes of the preacher by the shore, broke the bread, laying the pieces out in the shape of the cross before gathering them up in baskets and circling the hall to share them out. *Renewed through the body of Christ, we praise you, O Lord*, they chanted.

After that, they fasted through the black day of Christ's death, and ate barely a mouthful during the blank day when his body

147

lay in the tomb. As if they must feel his suffering in their own bodies, Hild thought. And afterwards, however old or young or tired, they kept themselves awake through the night hours.

"Christ is risen!" came a sudden cry. "The light has returned!"

At once Gerda, who'd been nodding in her chair, prodded the chief, grabbed Hild's hand and pulled her to the cross where they gazed at a silver thread streaking the dark sky.

"He's alive. He's conquered death!" cried a monk, torch flaring and beard streaming. He touched his flame to others and the light spread. "The Light of the World! He is risen! It's Easter Day!" A glorious, jumbled roar of joy spread through the massed crowd. Hild was borne along on the tide, hugged by Gerda, by Gwylget, by Cerdic, by complete strangers. She felt their excitement. "He is risen!" they cried.

There was plenty for everyone at the feast, though not all Din Edin could cram into the hall. Joints and jugs passed perilously overhead, and baskets of nuts and berries. Hunger sated, they exploded like river-bubbles. Men and boys raced down the side of the rock to the surrounding hills, where they boxed and wrestled, climbed trees and kicked bladders till their bones ached. Cerdic and others vanished to replenish the stores by a hunting trip.

Mothers took their youngest to the lake below the crag where they paddled, swam, fed birds, and gathered flowers for the Easter cross, and laughed. Shyly Hild watched. She had never seen Easter celebrated with such joy: Christ conquering death, light returning to the world, life renewed like Paulinus's butterfly breaking out from its bonds. Like new shoots bursting from the dark earth: Eostre's festival.

At the end of the day, with babies asleep, the women relaxed round the fire in their lodging, shedding all reserve.

"A miracle he's back," said a round matron, hitching up her skirts to toast her legs. "We feared the worst."

"Gwylget was lost without him," agreed a granny combing wool.

"You're lucky to have him." The wistful sigh from a girl of Hild's age, still unwed, made everyone chuckle.

"Don't be offended," Hild's neighbour whispered. "We share everything here. Nothing goes outside. And we did so miss him."

Hild was stunned. Could it be Cerdic they were discussing?

"Canny lad. Knows when to fight and when not." The toaster lowered her skirts.

"Mebbe. Now…" muttered the wool comber darkly.

This silenced them. Everyone knew Cerdic's exile came from his own foolhardiness. Then a rush of voices spoke together:

"You'd go wild, losing all your brothers… No more than custom, cattle-raiding… A warleader has to prove himself… He just had bad luck."

"Does he know about the bairn?" Granny asked sharply over her wool.

Hild jumped. "How did you know?"

"Your walk, shape, everything. Can't hide from the eye of experience."

"Oh!"

Everyone laughed.

"It'll be a fine thing, a child of his line, something to steady him."

After this, Hild looked at Cerdic anew. She saw him listening attentively to the men, responding thoughtfully, devoid of Edi's sarcasm. Small boys followed him, copying his mannerisms, like the way he tucked his hand in his belt to check his knife, especially one perky-looking lad with bubbly red hair. With Cerdic it was unconscious; with the lad it was a swagger. For the first time she saw in him not surly pride but natural reserve and determination. If only he would trust her!

"You fit in, my dear." Gerda slipped her hand under Hild's arm as they watched the children twist fresh flowers round the cross. "And Cerdic's healing." She bent to pick up a strand of columbine. "Thanks to you."

"Me?" Stupidly, Hild's eyes filled with tears. "There's nothing I can do."

"Do?" The little woman hugged her arm tightly. "It's not what you do, it's what you are. Quiet, patient, giving him space. That's what heals a man's spirit."

In the morning, a large group of families rode eastwards together, the women plodding behind the men, while the girls hung back to whisper secrets. One by one, families turned aside to farmsteads hidden behind the woods and dunes.

"Safe birthing," they whispered to Hild.

Cerdic was waiting at the mouth of their stream. He pointed to the lad who was climbing ahead on a pony, slewed to the side by an over-long spear. "That's Eata, my new spear-bearer."

"Spear-bearer?"

"You have the same custom in Northumbria."

"So he'll live with us and learn to be a noble thegn?"

"A challenge, I admit." He gave a crooked smile. "But he's an imp of Satan and his father's dead – a Bernician, by the way. His mother thinks I could train him as a fighter."

"I'll do my best to keep him out of mischief."Hild had known boys fostered at Edwin's court: the toughest turned out well; some wasted into nervousness. "But your spear's too long for him."

The lad was far ahead and out of sight as they rounded the palisade. At the gateway Cerdic stopped, as usual, by the little clutch of graves.

"Rohan, we're home," he shouted, turning in. "Help my lady, will you?" He tethered his horse and strode towards the house. "Holy angels!" he cried from inside. "What a difference! Lady, come and see."

Hild was explaining the various panniers.

"What's keeping you?" Cerdic erupted. "Leave that, Hild. Come and look." He seized her arm, then suddenly stopped.

"What's happened to the boy? Rohan, the boy. Where is he? What have you done with him?"

"What boy, my lord? There's no boy here!"

* * *

Never had Hild returned anywhere so soon. Even so, there were changes: trees in full leaf, crops sprouting, newborn kids and a brood of goslings. That, she supposed, was homecoming.

Indoors there was twice the room. A screen blocked draughts from the back door. A wooden partition concealed a small room at the end, where she saw nails for hanging clothes, a new wide bed, a stool and her marriage chest. Fresh straw, not dung, was the predominant smell, overlaid by appetizing aromas from the iron pot over the hearth.

"Good work, Rohan!" she called. There was no reply.

"They've gone to search for the boy." Brigit held up the welcome cup.

"What a lot you've done, Brigit." She smiled her thanks and drank gratefully.

"Will you eat? They may be some time."

When the horses finally straggled in, the moon hung low, casting grotesque shadows on the palisade. Cerdic held the boy across his horse, half conscious, lips tight with pain. Hild lifted up her arms.

"No! Let Rohan," snapped Cerdic.

Hild bunched goatskins by the fire. "Here. Gently." Eata's face was an angry red, despite the shivering. "Feverish. Let's remove his sodden clothes."

The boy clenched his fist, whimpering. Hild stroked the hand, unable to prise open his fingers. "What's this?"

"My spear – what's left of it," Cerdic said wryly.

"What happened?"

"He fell in the stream. Couldn't move. His foot, I think."

"We must get him dry. Lend me your knife." Slitting the boy's tunic, she pulled it off and wrapped him in a warm blanket, then rubbed the clammy body. Swathing him in a soft sheepskin, she murmured, "Hold his leg while I look at the foot."

"Is it the bone?" Cerdic peered in the flickering firelight.

"No. Fighter's curse, I think you'd call it. The ankle."

"If you know the name, you know the cure. I'll do it while he's unconscious. Hold the leg firm." A quick wrench, a twist, a sharp cry from the boy, and a cradle of sticks and bandage to immobilize the joint.

"All over! Brave boy." Hild cuddled him, putting a cup to his lips. So slight he felt in his swaddling, she gave him a kiss. "You'll be good as new in the morning."

"She did all right for a woman, eh?" Cerdic grinned, extracting a wan smile.

"Good teamwork, say I," Hild retorted, flushing at the compliment.

"What did you give him?" Cerdic whispered.

"French wine from my chest."

"Any left? I need to sleep too." He reached for Eata's cup. She laughed. "Come, wife, we must try the new bed."

* * *

"Stu–pid!" Eata's forlorn wail woke her. Peering round the screen, she saw Cerdic crouched in a streak of morning sun, absently feeding the fire and listening. Eata swung between childish piping and gruff croak. "… just following the stream. The path was clear."

"And you kept ahead? Like an outrider?"

The boy nodded. "It would be better, you know, if you had a sceptre."

"Eata!" Cerdic guffawed, "I'm not a king. Anyway…"

"Jezebel bolted. Something startled her and she bolted under the trees. I got hooked up, she slewed round and – well, I suppose… anyway – I ended up in the water. Couldn't move. Must have… think I passed out."

"You did. Lucky we found you when we did." Cerdic was solemn. "It was the spear got jammed, I suppose?"

"Oh no, not the spear!" Eata was indignant. "Can't be. I mean – no, I wouldn't let the spear go."

"A-ah!" Thoughtfully Cerdic tapped his teeth with a stick before shoving it in the embers. Abruptly, he sat back, looking sternly at Eata. "Here's your first lesson, young 'un."

Eata looked nervous.

"What is most precious to a good thegn?"

"His lord's honour."

"Uh-huh! What about an injured thegn?"

"Well…" Eata hesitated, "better dead than incapable."

"Exactly."

Eata swallowed hard and went white.

"So how do you avoid it, this fate worse than death?" There was a long pause. "How could you have avoided this injury?"

Eata wrinkled his brow. Cerdic waited. Eata lowered his head. "I don't know, my lord," he whispered.

"First." Cerdic's brisk response made the boy look up. "Good advance planning: know your terrain and equip yourself suitably. Second." Cerdic held up his hand, counting the fingers off. "Keep within sight of your troop at all times – unless ordered."

Eata pondered. Hild saw his auburn curls glint when he slowly nodded.

"Third. I suspect – I don't actually know, mind – I suspect that what tangled you was my rather long spear." Cerdic waited, but there was no response. "Look at me, boy. Was it?"

"I'm not sure." Eata twisted and went red.

"Hm. I'll accept your word for it. But tell the truth if you want to be trusted." Eata fixed solemn eyes on Cerdic's face, eventually finding something there which let him smile sheepishly. "Right," Cerdic continued magisterially. "Let's assume, for the sake of argument, that it was the spear. How could you have avoided injury?"

"Well, I couldn't let it go…"

"Why not?" Cerdic jumped in sharply.

"A spear-bearer can't let go of his spear…" Eata shrilled miserably.

"Disgrace?" Eata frowned. "Dishonour?" Eata looked down at his lap. "Failure?" Unsettled, Eata nodded ever so slightly. "Whose failure?"

"Mine." Eata looked squarely at his mentor, ready to take the blame.

"And whose honour are you pledged to uphold?"

"Yours, my lord." His voice rang.

"So you clung to a spear that was tangling you like a birding net?"

Eata smiled faintly. "Was it worth it? For a spear that's replaceable? That you're going to replace?"

"Oh, my lord, can I? Can I make you a new one?"

"I'd be peeved if you didn't. The yard boys'll help. When you're dressed." Chuckling, Cerdic got to his feet and stretched. From his full height, he spoke earnestly. "Do you get the point, Eata? You can't preserve your lord's honour by letting your own pride put you – and perhaps him – in danger."

Hild was impressed. Men, very young men, had such delicate sensibilities in matters of honour. But Eata's chin was high and his face glowed. Suddenly Cerdic said, very quietly, "Eata, remember this. I once made the same mistake. The result was dire." He turned on his heel and swept out. She knew he had bared his soul.

For days Eata languished outside, bandaged ankle propped up. One day, Hild found him with a pile of wood shavings below his bench.

"I'm making Cerdic's new spearshaft," Eata explained. "When the smith brings the head, we have to fix it round here, see, and here." Injury forgotten, he explained exhaustively. "He says we'll make one for me if there's enough iron. If not, I'll make do with sharpened ash-wood. I don't suppose…?"

"No!" Hild laughed, beating a speedy retreat. "Ask the lads."

Cerdic was riding the land from dawn till late, like a cadet on probation. He ate silently, slept on the nod, and left before she woke.

"Met Cutha on the border today," he informed her one night, "riding fields that used to be mine. We couldn't help but laugh. He sends regards." Hild was surprised. Laugh? Together? He used only to laugh with Edi, usually at someone's expense.

"He's raising troops like you?" she asked, pouring broth into a bowl. Brigit had long since gone to the new steward's lodging.

"He says Edwin's sent Ethelburga to her vill on the Deiran coast during his campaign." He seized a loaf. "Any ale?"

"Who's with her if Cutha's up here? Bass can't fight."

"No, but his men can," Cerdic said, mouth full of bread. "I gather they've some plan which Cutha didn't explain. Osfrid's boy's with them, too." Yffi? He'd be marching with the men in another year. She remembered Bass's old escape plan. "You all right?" Cerdic asked absently as she strained to lower the heavy jug. "We're going to muster. Damned Picts!"

"Just when Edwin's in the west?"

"Because Edwin's in the west," he emphasized. "It's why he sent Edi to ask for help. We're to hold back the Picts. If we can."

Hild felt his tension: his first proper campaign as warleader, and against his old foe. Would it help him to know her news? The fire cast her reflection on the wall, a bulging outline bouncing on the plaster. Could he really not have noticed?

"I've news for you," she said quietly.

"Good?"

"I think so." He was puzzled, curious. Suddenly his eyes lit up. "A child?"

She nodded. "In the autumn."

"Will you be all right while I'm away?"

She giggled. "Brigit'll be more use than you. Oh!" Her breath exploded as he clasped her. Just as suddenly he released her, looking abashed.

"Now I shall truly be fighting for my own," he reflected. No diplomat would have given himself away so impulsively. Cerdic may be grumpy but she was learning he was as straight as a spear.

The farmhands sharpened their axes, wadded their jackets, and wrestled with each other, helped or hindered by Eata. He was ecstatic when Cerdic allowed him on horseback and galloped the scrubland, practising the warcry and charge.

"Will he go with you?" Hild asked as they watched.

"Yes." Cerdic nodded. "If we fight, he'll stay at the rear with the horses."

"He'll see and hear horrors, though. Is he ready for that?"

"Not something I can ask a man."

The boy showed no sign of nerves. He wrestled and boxed with the farm boys, hurled his spear at shadows, and toyed with his bow, eventually stitching together a clutch of fish by aiming along the drying rack.

"You call that good?" Hild berated him.

"Skilful," he grinned. "Only a few fish. Nothing to fuss about!"

"Fine," Hild snapped. "Two days of scaring crows for you."

"Oh-oh," he moaned. Everyone hated warding off the black predators.

"Don't whine. You know the law about making good."

"But crow watching!" He looked mutinous. "For a spear-bearer!"

"All right. This…" Hild was unravelling the fish, "is a man's tack for two, no, three days." She laid them out. "You can fast for three days."

"Oh!"

"Or replace them."

He was gone like a shot from his own bow. Hild was not surprised when he was missing at mealtime. At bedtime she began to fret.

"He'll be fine." Cerdic was amused. "He's got to learn."

But they were both relieved when Eata appeared next evening with a marked limp, bloody face and two fish drooping from a string.

"Caught nine," he muttered defiantly through swollen lips. "Got stolen."

"Go and wash!" Cerdic barked. "And use a bucket. Don't taint the barrel."

"So?" he huffed when the boy returned.

"No one'd swap for my belt." Eata twanged disparagingly at the scuffed leather. "Couldn't part with my knife. Fisher Daigh lent me his coracle."

"Did you capsize?" Hild looked at his black eye and decidedly crooked nose.

"No, but… it kind of bounces and you have to sit to weigh it down. Weird!"

"Easy to step through the bottom." Hild remembered the feeling.

"Anyway, I caught one and dangled it overboard and, in a flash, millions! Wouldn't mind going again."

Up to this point, the boy had looked straight at them, narrating like a bard. When they asked what went wrong, he turned to step over the bench.

"Village boys. On the way back." His tore at his bread and glowered, finishing unnaturally brightly, "But I gave them something to remember."

"Oh, dear!" Hild looked at Cerdic, wondering if he'd noticed the gap in the story. "Will you need to intervene?"

"Doubt it. All boys are animals. And a fighter must follow his instincts." Cerdic turned cheerfully to Eata. "So you reckon you've earned your food?"

"I think I've paid." Eata grinned, touching his nose gingerly.

"You'll mend," Hild said briskly. "Though that'll stay crooked. Can't splint it like an ankle."

"Badge of a fighter!" Cerdic laughed.

Hild said nothing. She wondered what Eata was not telling. Several days later she found him by her tree.

"All right?" she asked. "Homesick?"

"No. You talk to me more than my mother did with all those babies," he said disparagingly. "Just thinking."

"What about?" Hild asked. "Going to war?" He shook his head. "The village boys?" He did not move. "You didn't fight over fish, did you? It was something else."

"Don't ask me!" Eata looked at her pleadingly. "I can't tell. Ever. It would be treachery."

"Treachery to your lord? To Cerdic?" His crumpling face told her she was right. "They said something about Cerdic and you went for them?"

"Don't tell! He must never, ever know."

"He doesn't need to know. But I think you should share it. No fighter goes into battle carrying an extra burden."

"Promise you won't tell?" His mixture of childish insistence and adult reticence convinced her it was a damaging secret.

"I promise."

"They said Cerdic's bad luck, not to be trusted. He lost last time and he'll lose again. That's what they're saying. He's death to victory."

Eata's ill-omened words nagged at her as she walked the summer fields, fingering the dangling oat heads.

"Not yet!" Rohan glowered.

"Just feeling, Rohan." Of course it wasn't time; of course he was in charge. He'd tilled the land as his own for six years and knew his job. How could he understand her gratitude to Eostre? Or her new delight in the ripening? But the waiting was hard, with harvest a long time off, and the baby not due till after that.

"No workers worth the ale," Rohan groused when the warband did not return in time. But the greybeards rallied round and made light of scything: oats first, then barley and rye; they'd perfected the rhythm years ago. Winnowing was a simpler affair: eyes streaming, noses caked with dust, deafened by the crack of the flails, young and old sweated it out together, as long as the ale flowed.

Sacks mounted in the storehouse alongside beans and fleeces. Brigit steeped barley heads, folded eggs in woodash, and smoked the hives.

"Curl of honey," she yelled, "for anyone who'll hold these skeps to drip." The children raced to the storehouse door, flapping at stray bees. In no time, Brigit held her spoon to a row of open mouths.

"Come and look, lady," she called. "All these jars. Just need the fat to stopper them when we kill the stock." Hild heaved herself up from the retting pond where she'd been watching women soften the flax, and breathed in the heady scents of the storehouse: grains and soaking barley; bunches of marjoram, lavender, sage and agrimony; pots of thyme and tansy; orange marigolds tossed with greying peas; baskets of hard cherries and hazelnuts.

"A wonderful store, Brigit!" said Hild.

"Ready to face anything this year." Brigit glowed with pride.

Before they drove the hogs to the woods, two monks came up the track.

"Everyone in line!" Rohan barked. "Ready?"

Unable to walk far in her bulky condition, Hild sat with little lame Caitlin on a log by the gate, and watched the children lead the way, dancing and singing, while the boys followed the men, shouldering spades and axes. They were blessing the bounds. Astonishing: Eostre's rituals, but for a different god.

She and Caitlin chuckled as they watched. At every plough-turn and field-edge, the household bunched while the old monk lifted his arms in prayer, and the younger sprinkled holy water. At streams or ditches, they girded their skirts and waded across, Rohan or the young monk carrying Brigit with much joking. It was a raucous party that meandered from the fields to the byre, the store, the ox cart, even the water barrel.

"What about these imps, brother?" Brigit lined up the youngest in the doorway. "They're in sore need of cleansing!"

"Oh, Ma!" They wriggled, twisting their toes in the rushes. Hild wished her new baby was with them to be sprinkled like seeds in the plot. They had humanity, these northern monks, and a humour she'd never met in old Coifi or Paulinus. Why, she wondered, if their God was the same, were they so different?

In the end, the baby caught her by surprise when she was strolling along the stream at the field bottom, watching poplar leaves break off and spiral onto the water. Suddenly bathed in sweat, sick and faint, she clutched herself and waited. The pain flared. Was it always like this? She remembered Ethelburga's gritted teeth and wet, white face. Gasping, she froze. Stabbing, wrenching, twisting: cruel agony.

Cautiously she unbent, wishing she'd chosen to walk up to her hawthorn today. Think of the tree, the dancing water, the blue hills. Think of the hills. Where the warband was. Where Cerdic was.

She gasped. Another spasm. A few steps. Again, torture. Head swimming, she crept forward, her dry throat mocked by the burbling stream. *Breathe deep, count ten*: she heard her mother. Whimpering, bending, swaying, slowly she dragged herself up through the stubble and clung to the gatepost, sliding down, calling feebly.

It was a long, hard night.

"Nearly there," she heard through a haze of agony. "One last push!"

"Freyr!" The scream burst from her. She heaved and thrust, "Fre-e-eyr!"

A tiny, thin cry.

"A boy, lady; a son!" She felt Brigit wipe her face. "A nose like his father's, look!" She didn't want to look. She'd done enough. She wanted to be left alone. To sleep.

"Give him a drink." Brigit held the child to her breast. Silence fell and the first milk flowed. Deep within her, tenderness welled up, a fiercer pull than she had ever known. Dazed, she cradled the tiny red frog and smiled at his old man's wrinkles.

"A born mother. See how easily…"

"Without you…" She looked at Brigit through moist eyes.

"Just rest, lady. Rest is what you need."

Later, roused to a wash and fresh shift, Hild looked with awe at the bedside cradle.

"Never known a firstborn so quick." Brigit held a cup to her lips.

"Quick!" Hild snorted.

"Impatient as his father."

As summer faded into autumn, the growing infant brought her new delights. Sitting in the sunlight, she watched his eyes, looking deep and wise. He turned at the cockerel's squawk, laughed at a squirt of water, crumpled at the rumbling of the quern, grasped for twigs twirled over his head. Hild sang to him, her Moormaid song, or her mother's old, old lullabies.

The days sped by. Hild slung him in front of her in an old veil and walked, children leaping round her, rolling and somersaulting through the fields till Rohan ordered the oxen out. Then they gathered hips, brambles, roots, anything that might be useful when the men came home. Edwin had always returned by Blodmonath and the girls had already penned the geese to fatten. Surely Cerdic must come soon. *He lost last time and he'll lose again.* She slapped the words away like midges.

The monks called on their homeward trek, accepting a night's lodging.

"Any news of the warband?" Rohan asked.

"Nothing. Everyone's asking. We'll keep a lookout. But we're crossing the mountains to Melrose, then by sea to Iona."

"Don't forget Cutha," prompted the young monk. "We always call at Cutha's."

"Edwin's thegn?" Hild gasped.

"A good man," the elder nodded. "He didn't steal or destroy Cerdic's homeplace, he guards the hills, keeps the tracks safe, and cares for the people."

"I knew him once. Please greet him for me, and tell him about my baby."

"May we bless your baby?" the young man asked.

"I should like that."

"Has he a name?"

"Not till his father comes home."

But they blessed him all the same. Leaving at dawn, they would only take bread and cheese. "God will provide."

"Aren't you ever fearful?" Hild looked to the dark woods beyond the stream. "Beasts, outlaws, wood elves?"

"God made the wilderness, sister." The older man patted her arm. "His spirit is there. He's with us wherever we go." Staff in hand, he strode off purposefully. She heard their bell clanging as they entered the trees. "God be with you… with you… with you," it rang, blessing all who heard.

Cerdic arrived alone, before his men, in the mist of early morning.

"Rohan!" he called at the gate. "Wife!"

Wrapped in her night fleece, carrying the child she had just been feeding, Hild ran to the door. Gaunt he looked, with a scar at the neck, an angry gash on his sword arm and one leg hanging straight.

"You're wounded," she stated as he slithered off his horse.

"Nothing that won't heal. Let me look at you." Reaching out, he was baulked by the bundle in her arms.

"Your son," she said and the baby sneezed. Cerdic eyed him solemnly. He opened his mouth in a howl.

Cerdic chuckled. "What's his name?"

"He's waiting for you to tell him," said Hild, shivering in the cold.

"Me?" He stood stroking the bundle, looking. "They're your brown eyes."

"But your nose." Hild blushed; she didn't know he'd noticed her eyes. "Brigit said that, the moment he was born. You should name him."

"Golistan, after my father. No…" he hesitated. "Wulfstan. That's Golistan in Anglian. A bit of us both. What d'you think?"

"Wulfstan," she whispered, nodding. "Wolf Stone. Oh! Look to your horse."

"Wulfstan," Cerdic eyed the baby sternly, "you're getting twixt me and my wits!"

"I'll do it, my lord." A breathless Eata skidded up. "Come on, old Satan. You've earned your fodder. Hope I have too."

"Eata, you've grown," Hild groaned dramatically. "An even bigger hole to fill!" Scraggy he looked, pale and pimply as a plucked chicken, but mercifully unwounded.

"Your nose may be crooked, Eata," grunted Cerdic, "but it can still sniff food a mile off!"

"Hollow as a monster's maw," Eata agreed enthusiastically. "And this monster?"

"Wulfstan," said Hild faintly.

"Hello, Wulfi!"

* * *

Cerdic ended his speech and sat down with a relieved grunt; he wasn't given to oratory. His fighters, crammed round the walls, cheered and stamped approval. Hild hoped Wulfstan was sleeping through it; she wouldn't hear if he cried. Sodden bread, rind, bones and cherry stones littered the floor reeds: signs of a merry feast, except for the memory of two of the troop who hadn't come home. Fisher Daigh's son had slipped over a cliff and couldn't even be buried. And Vin, the deaf old smith.

"He said my father'd never dare leave him behind, and I'd better not try," Cerdic explained wryly. "Gashed himself skinning a deer, and it festered. Slow agonizing death." She knew he felt to blame.

The gift-giving was over. Men flashed silver brooches and armbands in the firelight. Now was the time for drinking. The lads staggered in with jugs. Women gathered up cloaks and food parcels, leaving the men to their orgy. Hild stood at the door, thanking them for what they'd brought: cheese and eggs, fish and honey cakes. Baby gifts, too: the shepherd's wife had sewn a fleecy ball, Fisher Daigh had carved a floating fish, and the cowman's girl thrust a horn spoon into Hild's hand.

Suddenly, Hild heard shrieks and blows. She sped round the outside of the house. Eata and young Rohan were locked in combat, ringed by bellowing youths.

"Stop this!" she cried. "Stop! Stop!" To disturb a lord's peace was serious. Young fools! If only she could make them hear. Elbowing forward, she was knocked breathless by a blow from behind. Skirts trapped, veil torn, she was just in time to see Rohan lay his son flat with a hefty punch.

"Stand there!" Cerdic, with a mighty roar, wrenched Eata aside. "Don't move!" Silence fell. Panting, Cerdic looked fiercely round.

"My lord, I beg pardon." Rohan glared at his prostrate son, but spoke abjectly to Cerdic; his livelihood was at stake. "Too much ale."

"Wait!" Cerdic bawled as the other youths melted away. "Witnesses, all of you. Face me!" Warily they turned. "Who started it?"

They shuffled their feet.

"You," he glowered at Eata. "Have you anything to say?" Bruised, dishevelled, blood pouring from a cut above his lip, Eata stood pale and defiant.

"Right," said Cerdic. "Banishment. That's the law for a breach of the peace." Gasps all round. "Get out!" Cerdic pointed to the gate. "Get out and stay out. Now!" Cheeks flaming, Eata stalked away. Hild remembered his last brawl. Was it the same? Had young Rohan insulted Cerdic?

The mob shuffled nervously as Cerdic turned.

"As for you…" He lingered over his words to young Rohan. "I'll leave you to your father."

Old Rohan was baffled, his face a mixture of anger and fear. Hauling his swaying son to his feet, he grasped him by the tunic and slapped him hard, once, twice.

"Fetch my goad," he yelled in his face. In the horrified silence, the boy dragged himself away, returning with the long, supple rod Rohan used for the oxen.

"Traitor!" Rohan raised his arm and brought it down across the boy's body with a sickening swish. The boy flinched as the prick bit into his skin, but faced his father without a sound.

"Traitor to your lord." A second stripe. The boy moaned quietly. Blood welled from a gash across his neck.

"Traitor to me." Another slash split his tunic across his chest.

"Enough, Rohan." Cerdic stepped forward. "Have you anything to say, boy?"

"Sorry!" came a surly mutter.

"Manners!" barked his father.

"I'm sorry, my lord." He watched stonily as his friends sidled away. Hild shuddered. No explanation, no buck-passing, only bitterness.

"I take leave, my lord," Eata bowed formally as Cerdic swept to the door. He halted but said nothing. "M-might I take the pony?"

"Ride south," Cerdic barked in a gruff voice: he must have noted the pathetic bundle and single spear. "Away from our people. I want no more trouble." He swept inside, calling over his shoulder, "I expect you back for the spring muster." Soon the yard was empty but for Hild and Eata.

"Why, Eata? Why?" She looked at him closely. His lips were tight. So young, so stubborn. She shivered. The stars glittered. He'd be cold. And lonely. She remembered the scop's song: ...*careworn and cut off from kin, endure the winter roofless, aching with cold, stiff with frost... no comfort for the cheerless heart...*

"Wait here." Groping to the store, she felt along the shelves till she found what she wanted. "For scratches and wounds. Use sparingly." She pushed a pot into his hand and hugged him fiercely. Before he could pull away she whispered, "Keep safe. I want you back." All winter she remembered his arms tight round her neck.

* * *

It was still bitter cold when a traveller's bell rang in the forest. Hild watched and waited, eventually making out a packmule bearing an ungainly load which two robed men steadied between them.

"Welcome, brothers," she called, recognizing monks. "Come and rest."

"We've someone for you." A grizzled man helped a fresh-faced acolyte lift the bundle down.

"Who is it?" She felt a lurch in her guts. Eata?

Carefully, they set their burden by the fire and pulled away the wadding.

"A woman!" she cried in relief, then felt ashamed as she looked at the piteous creature. "Brigit, fleeces!" She turned back to the monks. "Who is she?"

"We were hoping you could tell us." The greybeard eased himself up.

"I don't know her." She frowned, scanning the hollow face and dirty white hair. Many people might know her – from a royal progress, the king's hall, serving Eostre – but not here, in Gododdin land. Brigit wrapped the woman in fleeces and trickled a few drops of ale through her parched lips.

"Small start," Hild sighed, pouring for the men. "Where did you find her?"

"On the moor. Half dead, unable to speak..." He broke off as Brigit placed broth and bread before him. "Except to say, 'Tell Lady Hild.' Over and over, 'Tell Lady Hild.'"

"Tell me what?"

"She's too weak to say." And he tucked into his meal. "Thought it was a boy. Asked the herdsman to shelter him. When we returned…"

"He was a she!" The youth chuckled.

Hild looked at the woman. Eyes closed, cheeks faintly coloured by wine and warmth, she was breathing heavily. "I don't know her. She looks – sounds… Is she…?"

"I'll try a little broth, lady." Brigit crouched down. Dipping a morsel of bread in the bowl, she laid it on the woman's lips. There was a feeble suck.

"He did his best, the herdsman, but food's short and…" the monk tailed off.

"We'll feed her up and keep her safe till she delivers her message," Hild decided. "You were on the moor, you say? Did you see anything of a young sprig on his own up there?"

"One of your lads? Missing? I'm sorry. We'll look out for him. But now… " He pushed to his feet. "Blessings on your kindness, lady."

"Won't you sleep? You must be weary."

"We're on pilgrimage." He shook his head. "Come, lad!" He shouldered his scrip and limped to the door.

"But the mule, brother?" The youth was slower to rise.

"Ah, yes! Lady, would you…?"

"Keep the mule in good trim? Of course."

"God keep you!" He strode off, crusts and dried fish in his satchel, his boy trotting in his wake.

Hild shuddered as she pulled the door. "Could be snow. They'll have a hard trek." *And so will Eata.* As she watched Brigit rub the woman's joints with warm grease, she wondered, for the umpteenth time, what had driven the boy to that desperate fight.

"What's this, then?" Cerdic blew in with a blast of icy rain. "Lost traveller?" It was common enough. He and the men took little notice.

While the cold lasted, the woman hardly moved. They met her bodily needs and sat nearby in the warm, mending and chatting.

Little Caitlin took to curling up on her fleece and treating her like a rag doll, setting her arms straight and stroking her hands.

"Don't disturb her, Caitlin," said Brigit. "She's very sick."

"It's all right," the little girl said firmly. "She likes it." Sure enough, the woman was watching the child through half-closed eyes.

One morning, Hild was startled to find the door open. The woman sat in thin sunlight on the bench outside, wrapped in fleeces.

"Ssh!" Caitlin whispered.

"Tell Lady Hild!" croaked the woman, tears flowing.

"I'm Lady Hild," Hild said, sitting beside her and taking her hand.

"Lady, you're making her cry," Caitlin reproached her.

"You can cry with happiness, you know," Hild smiled. "I think she's happy here."

She often found herself alone with the invalid when the spring rain stopped and the men rode out and the children searched for birds' nests.

"Lady Heri," the woman rasped one day. Her mouth worked, silently.

"It'll come. In time," Hild said gently. "Don't struggle."

"Lady Heri," persisted the woman.

"Hild, I'm Hild," she smiled. "Heri was my sister."

"Sister. Yes." The woman nodded. "Alive." That was all.

Shaking, Hild took up the spinning which Caitlin had, as usual, left beside her. Pull, twist, draw out, wind up, pull, twist, draw out, wind up… she let the rhythm soothe her. Foolish, to feel pain after so long. Foolish to listen to the ramblings of a half-mad stranger.

"Married. Heri."

"Yes." Hild nodded, not letting her fingers stop.

"Alive. Heri. Alive." Exhausted, the woman fell asleep.

Heri, fair-haired Heri. Golden bride, fit to be queen: flighty charmer, unfit to be queen. Heri, the other half of herself, sharing bed, jokes, disrespectful giggles. Plying her fingers faster, Hild felt again the loneliness of loss.

The woman was no burden. As the weeks passed, she dressed

herself, prepared food, fetched water, fed the geese and collected eggs. She sat mending and kept an eye on the children, even went out with them to search for primroses. Caitlin seemed especially drawn to her and often stroked her gnarled hand.

"Why's it so wrinkled?" she asked.

"Hard work," the woman smiled, dropping her spindle.

"Ma hasn't those scars," retorted the child, picking it up.

"Ma's never had to grub for food." That was all, but it set Hild thinking. No woman could keep herself alive like an outlaw: she couldn't hunt or trap or cook what she found. Fruits, berries, leaves were not enough to stay alive, especially in the winter. Was that what had happened? Suffering, not age, had whitened her hair. Where did she come from? Could it be true, what she said? Was Heri alive?

The life of their busy household suited the woman. Brigit was often absent, visiting young Rohan who had gone to live and train with the smith in the vill on the Firth. When she was away, the woman took charge naturally and the men responded to her, fetching wood, lifting water, rolling large jars. They brought and quartered deer or polecats for her to joint. She worked away, humming. All the more of a shock when Caitlin lurched to Hild in distress.

"Lady, you must come!" She pulled Hild to the pigpen. The sow was due to farrow and the woman leaned on the fence which fended off the dogs. Her cheeks were wet with tears. Gently, Caitlin took her hand. Hild drew close on her other side.

"What is it?" she said gently. "What's upset you?" No reply. "You've nothing to fear. This is your home as long as you wish. Nobody here will hurt you."

"Remember?" The woman turned fiercely, like a sleeper startled. "The pig girl?"

"The pig girl? Begu?" Hild started. "How do you…?" Gripping the woman's shoulders, she looked closely into her face. "Begu! Is it you?"

"The Begu you rescued," she nodded through her tears. "You and your mother. In the happy times."

"Our Begu!" Wonder and warmth filled Hild's voice, and she folded the woman in her arms. "How blind I've been! Begu, our friend from the past, and I didn't see."

* * *

About ten days later, Cerdic galloped up the track with the banished Eata.

"Met on the moors," Cerdic explained curtly as he dismounted.

"I was bringing my lord news," Eata cut in eagerly. He looked thin and dirty, but his arms and legs were muscled.

"Cutha," Cerdic barked, resenting the interruption. "He's back from Edwin's army. Not wounded but, well, sick in some way."

"Dazed," Eata burst out. "His men fear he'll harm himself."

"Hild, have you anything that might help?" Cerdic asked.

"Does he speak?" she asked.

He shrugged and looked to Eata.

"Just sits," said the boy. "Won't eat."

"I've something…" she hesitated.

"Could you…?" Cerdic was frowning.

"Dangerous. Very strong." She was thinking aloud. "It could kill…"

"Could you come, then? No, of course… "

"Wulfi…" She was torn. She owed Cutha much, but abandon her baby? She'd never left him more than an hour, and in Brigit's care.

"Lady, if you'd trust me," Begu said shyly, "I could care for Wulfi. Goat's milk, like we did for Princess Anfled. You won't be long. And I could always send for Brigit if need be." She fell silent, blushing. The men stared. Cerdic waited.

Wife or mother? Cerdic or Wulfi? Only Hild could decide. Who better than Begu, who'd cared for her mother, and nursed her from sickness? And with Brigit on call…

In the end Cerdic said, "I must go. Cutha may have news that affects us all."

169

7

THE GODODDIN

"**I** should have died with my lord," Cutha moaned. Ragged, stinking, sweaty, he was blind to everyone, immersed in grief.

"You have a duty to your men." Hild was sharp, knowing how hard it had been for them to bring him home through a war zone.

"They expected his wits to return," murmured Cerdic.

"He's not stunned now," she replied crisply, "just sunk in himself. What is there to rouse him – no household, no foodstock, no wife?" She looked round at the bare homestead.

"I don't understand." Cerdic shook his head. "Did his slaves all go with him? Or did they take the chance to run away?"

She shrugged. Unlikely. Cutha was a kind and responsible lord: so said the monks. "D'you want me to doctor him here?" Bleak prospect.

"We got off to a bad start." Cerdic was thinking aloud. "He commandeered my land for Edwin. But he's cared for it well…" he gnawed his lip, "and we were his house-guests."

"What are you saying, my lord?"

Cerdic took a deep breath. "We owe him hospitality."

In the end, Hild took him home with some of Cutha's long-suffering spearmen, who rode tight to keep him upright on his horse. Cerdic had heard rumours: Penda had amassed booty and returned to Mercia, but Edwin's lifelong enemy, Cadwallon, had stayed behind, ravaging Northumbria. With the best horses, a couple of Cutha's spearmen and Eata, Cerdic galloped off down the old road south. He needed to find out the truth.

Reduced to Eata's pony, Hild had a tough ride. Return journeys were usually shorter. Not this time. The track was slippery and the spearmen nervy. A dank mist dripped from the trees, shrouding landmarks. They stopped once, to ease their legs and swallow some ale. As dark fell, every creaking trunk, even their own echo, made the men take aim. Hild remembered the monks saying, *God made the wilderness; his spirit is there*. Oh, for their assurance! It was with relief that she pushed up the home track: shelter, a warm fire, and food.

"All's well," Begu whispered, leading Hild behind the screen. "Rohan's in the vill with Brigit. Wulfi's asleep."

"Will you see to Cutha and the men?" Hild dropped onto the bed and rubbed her aching thighs. Leaning back, she fell asleep instantly.

She woke abruptly. Wulfi! He'd not been fed. Rolling onto her side, she saw him burbling quietly and Begu snoring on a pallet, the feeding cup clutched to her chest. Later, she roused again to find Cutha wrapped in skins near the hearthstone and Begu sitting at the door with Wulfi in her lap watching Cutha's spearmen chewing flatbread round their camp fire.

"How did you come here, Begu?" she asked casually, sitting beside her. "I left you with Queen Ethelburga."

"Ah!" Begu swallowed. "The king sent her to the coast. Bass had a plan for her safety."

Hild shivered. She remembered the plan. "Ani and the boys?"

"All with her. Uscrea was cross, but his father said he was the future and Yffi would look after him. I think he knew, Edwin."

"Knew?"

"That his time had come."

Edwin had always looked death in the face, thought Hild: *A prince must die for his people.*

"A rider came in the night and the family sailed away."

"Couldn't you have gone with them?"

"She sent me to you, the queen."

Hild was surprised.

"'Tell Lady Hild,' she said, 'her sister is alive, with a new husband and a son.' She had planned to see you herself when we came north to Yeavering."

So it was true, what she said: Heri was alive, and a mother. What a lot they'd have to talk about! The startling possibility took away her breath. Then she said, "How did you find me?"

"Boat to Bamburgh. Then I walked."

Hild gasped. Riding from Bamburgh took three or four days. A girl on foot?

"Followed the old road. But everything was burned. No people. No food. Until the soldiers caught me…" Begu broke off abruptly.

* * *

With several days of drugged sleep and good broth, Cutha revived, but did not speak or smile. No thegn, Hild knew, would blench at wounds, corpses or worse. It was something more. She had to draw it out.

"Tell me about the battle," she challenged. "They were my friends, my kin, Edwin and his sons. I need to know. Osfrid… What happened to him?"

"When the king…" he started hesitantly. "The king was hacked down by Penda. Osfrid stood over him swinging Edwin's great sword. We tried to break through to him but…" He was shaking. His face was white and pouring sweat.

Hild gripped his hand. "Go on."

"Penda's men hewed, pushed, speared till we all went down. I saw Osfrid circled by five or six. Brave, magnificent, he charged like a boar, but useless, useless…"

"He was killed?"

He was looking straight ahead, eyes glazed. She didn't think he heard.

"They jumped him," he rasped suddenly. "Spears, axes, knives.

A mash of pulp…" Dry sobs racked his frame.

"What next?" She must force him on.

"We tried to get Penda, cut him off. Edi was with us. He went down…"

"Killed?"

"Captured." He swallowed convulsively. Hild handed him a cup and he drank without noticing. "Taken alive. He did everything: kicked out, wrestled, spat, rolled to break the rope. Penda came at him. Edi lurched towards his sword. Anything to die. But they were too many. Pinioned like a fowl. Helpless. I can't remember… I can't…" He faltered to a stop.

She waited.

"Why not me?" A cry sharp with pain. "I should have died. Dishonour…"

"What then? After Edi was taken." She was ruthless now. He must tell it to the end. "What then?"

"I can't…" he whimpered. "I ran away."

"Your men say not," she countered briskly.

"The battle was over. No one left to fight for. Must have fled."

"No one believes that." Hild shook him lightly. "All who know you, know you couldn't flee. Fighting at the centre, standing by your king, trying to save your prince. You must have been poleaxed. Doing your duty as long as your body held out."

"How can I know?" he moaned, tossing his head.

"It happens."

"I don't know. I'm afraid I failed him. Failed my lord!" Horror and bitterness in the anguished cry. He couldn't trust himself.

Hild sat a long time, thinking. In the end, she spelled out her thoughts.

"Women are afraid," she said quietly. "Each year when the men march off. Not knowing. It's a kind of fear. Worse than the worst news. That's the fear you have to fight now: not knowing."

A little later, she said, "Ethelburga was a Christian, like you."

"What's that to do with it?" He looked up.

"I remember her saying… She was torn, bleeding, very low. A

boy child died at birth. But it was not the death. It was the wound she'd dealt Edwin."

Cutha sighed.

"Edwin wanted another boy. She felt she'd failed him. She said, 'I can't see why God's keeping me alive.'"

Cutha nodded. He'd been close to Ethelburga.

"After a while," Hild continued, "she solved the mystery. 'God must have a purpose,' she said. 'Something he still wants me to do.'"

Silence. He looked drained. Had he understood? Would it help?

She poured him a cup of French wine from her diminishing reserve, hoping there'd be some for Cerdic when he came home… if he came home from riding among the enemy, bold as Thor. The not knowing. She could understand Cutha's fear.

* * *

Cutha started to tend his horse, then the pony as well. He rode the near fields, venturing along the edge of the woods. He was tethering his mount after his first moorland foray when Rohan swung through the gate.

"Lord Cerdic!" he shouted, dismounting urgently.

"Rohan!" Hild came to the door. "What's wrong?"

"I must see him. It's urgent."

"He's not here. What is it?"

"The Picts! They've bypassed us and gone south."

"Picts?" Hild came out to him. "How do you know?"

"Fisher Daigh saw ships. Packed with spearmen, he said. He was fishing behind the rock and tried to count. But you know him. Can only do up to three. So he tallied on his fingers."

"How many?"

"Ran out of fingers. Near a score, he reckons. It's what my lord's been fearing, Picts coming south. We must let him know."

"When was this?" Hild needed a clear picture.

"Dawn. He rowed back, came for me, and I've ridden straight up from the vill."

"You're sure they're Picts?"

"Direction's right." For the first time, Rohan paused. "Who else?"

Who indeed? Hild was thinking hard.

"Cerdic's somewhere in Bernicia," she said. "You can't chase after him till we're sure. Not even then. If the Picts aren't heading here, we've time. I'll ride to the headland."

"I'll come with you." Cutha startled them. "I'd recognize them better than you, but you know the way."

"Right. Rohan, will you tell Begu?"

With a sharp east wind in their faces, Hild and Cutha galloped hard. On the headland at the mouth of the Firth, Cutha scanned north for signs of an army, Hild squinted into the sun. She picked out the sharp hill of Lindisfarne in a luminous haze, and sails bellying nearby. Eight, she thought – perhaps more beyond.

Cutha found a fire roughly kicked out, some bones picked clean, and an empty bladder. A lookout, perhaps?

"Why so far south if they're Picts?" Hild mused.

"Raiding," Cutha said. "Easy pickings, with Northumbria in chaos. Lindisfarne, Bamburgh, Yeavering, Maelmin, and on the way back…" There was no need for him to go on.

"Right," Hild rapped. "To the farm under the cliff. That way!" They ran to the horses. "They'll start the beacons, rouse the Gododdin."

Side by side they galloped along the Firth, racing the fires which sprouted ahead of them, shouting to goatherds and woodsmen to pass the word inland.

"Didn't the Twister's son take refuge with the Picts?" Cutha had a healthy glow when they reached Doon Hill. "Could it be him? Circumventing the Gododdin to take back his homeland?"

"Makes sense." Hild slithered down. "That would mean we're in less danger. Ah, Rohan, here we are."

"Someone's come." He nodded at the door. "I'll stable your mounts."

"Was it the Picts?" Eata, gaunt and leggy as ever, bowled out and folded Hild in a crushing hug.

"You!" She disentangled herself. "Is Cerdic...?"

"He's fine! Sent me to fetch Cutha." Remembering his manners, he added, "Pleased to see you recovered, my lord."

"Nothing like an alarm to restore a man!" Cutha clapped him on the shoulder. "What does Cerdic want? D'you know?"

"Y-yes." Eata blushed, and hesitated.

"Out with it, Eata." Hild was exasperated.

"Lord Cutha, you're a father. Your lady went to her parents after you left, and took the household with her. They're all safe, and she has a baby boy."

"A boy!" Cutha shouted. "A son. Cuthbert, my son. God be praised!"

"We'll eat now," Hild said firmly. Cutha may well be exhilarated, but he was tired. "Eata will go with you in the morning."

"Is it the Picts?" Rohan persisted.

"Likely," said Cutha. "There were signs of a lookout on the cliff. We thought it could be the Twister's eldest son invading Bernicia."

"They'll welcome him with open arms," Eata chipped in. "The further south we rode, the more of Cadwallon's rampaging we saw. And fugitives, women and children mainly, fleeing from looting and..."

"Begu!" Hild saw her sway. Eata leapt up and caught her. Hild bent over her, fanning her face. "She was a fugitive herself," she murmured. "Bad memories."

In the morning, Begu busied herself as usual. Hild stood by Cutha and Eata as they mounted.

"Tell Cerdic we've roused the Gododdin," she said. "I'll ride to Din Edin."

"You can't go alone!" Cutha exclaimed.

"I won't be alone," she smiled. "Begu and Wulfi will be with me."

She waved them off as they dropped to the stream and wove up through the trees, Eata's red curls catching the light.

"Go with God!" she whispered. Not an adjuration to Thor, but the monks' prayer. It held more affection, somehow.

* * *

Far from berating her for firing the beacons, Gwylget welcomed Hild's quick thinking. Cerdic's reconnaissance in the south worried him, but he felt secure on the rock, he said. It was a natural fortress.

He walked the walls with his counsellors, checking the steep gulley at the entrance and the perilous drop to the lake on the opposite side. He renewed the stakes concealed in the brushwood of the trenches, added to the fringe of boulders stacked under the earth walls, examined the armoury, and made the storehouse secure.

Water was a weakness, Hild knew. What they collected in open tanks evaporated in hot weather. For now, the lads were charged with shinning down the crag with buckets to refill the tanks from the lake.

It was the hungry time of year, new growth barely showing. Uneasy that she'd arrived empty-handed, Hild was relieved to see Rohan drive in a couple of pigs and some geese, with other springtime offerings for the chief.

"Thought we could spare them. Did well in the woods this winter," he grunted.

"Any news?" she pressed.

"All's well, lady. Young Rohan's knocking spearheads out like he's shelling peas. Brigit sent this." A jar of crushed agrimony, All Heal.

"Cerdic?"

"Nothing."

From the embankment she watched him trot away. He'd be home tomorrow, she thought wistfully. *Home* meant a lot to her now.

She and Begu had taken an unbelievable time over the same journey. Begu kept slipping down from her pony to walk.

"Would you rather have stayed?" Hild asked pointedly.

"I'm sorry, lady." Begu flushed and her face crumpled. "I'll try again."

Only then did Hild understand. Begu knew what it meant to suffer *Cadwallon's rampaging*. Eata's description had made her faint. Once their blood was up, men's lust had no truck with women's pain. *Thor's blindness* was her mother's acid term. Begu was lucky to be alive, but she lived with the legacy. Hild was remorseful.

"Oh, Begu, I'm sorry!"

"It'll pass." Pressing her lips together, Begu persevered.

They settled comfortably at Din Edin. Hild felt the Gododdin were her people and her lord their protector.

Wulfi was too sheltered, she realized, as she sat with the women. Other babies crawled about together, lunging, snatching and chattering. He made straight for his mother, wherever he was put.

"Wily Gododdin! Knows where he's safe," old Gerda laughed. "Don't fret. He'll walk before you go home."

As always in the spring, she thought about the past. Easter here delighted her: the wooden cross at the heart of the township, its decoration of early flowers, and the thrilling night-time vigil. But could it take the place of Eostre's festival? It was not about the fields and cattle. This year Edwin was on her mind, especially on the black day of Christ's death. *A prince must die for his people.* She pictured Edwin's mangled body, hacked about and dismembered, and Jesus' body, tortured, twisted and speared. Edwin had said all princes die at their weakest. They both faced bloody ends with the patience of Eostre's slaughtered bull, dying for the people, he and Christ. A far cry from Thor with his hammer and thunderbolt.

One bright day came shrill cries from the walls: "Horses! Spearmen!"

"Come down off there!" The watch was peeved that young eyes had outstripped his.

"Cerdic! It's Cerdic!" Ignoring him, the boys dragged Hild up to see a troop of Anglian fighters galloping from the south. "Look! He's at the front. With the leader."

The boys vanished: to hang over the bank, no doubt, or rub down the splendid horses. The spearmen emerged from the gulley in a group, heavy swords hanging from jewelled belts; clearly men of rank. Cerdic crossed to Hild.

"Lady!" His face was furrowed, but his step was light. "You're well? The boy?"

"Wulfstan prospers, my lord, and your homestead. Eata?"

"Just behind, with the cattle we... er, liberated."

"Where from?" She was shocked. Old habits resurfacing?

"Cadwallon's ruffians," he rasped, briefly showing a gash inside the neck of his tunic. "You roused the defence, I hear. It was timely."

"Is that Cutha?"

"Yes. No vestige of his old trouble." He gave her a cursory hug. "Must see the chief."

She greeted Cutha in the hall where he was placed in the seat of honour at Gwylget's right, with other Anglians. Gerda served the guest cup in the age-old way. Cerdic took his seat at her left with Hild at his side. After they had eaten, he rose.

"My lord," he said. There was a rustle as everyone settled to listen; in this tight-knit community, everyone was involved in everything. "The Picts are no longer a risk. Their force is disbanded." A buzz of satisfaction. "But," he said forcefully, "we should guard against their old habits as they return home." There was knowing laughter; the Picts were notorious raiders.

"They were not out to get us this time, but to help Prince Eanfrid of Bernicia beat back Penda and regain his kingdom. Penda's forces routed them and have returned to Mercia with their booty." Cursory nods. The Mercian king may mean nothing to the Gododdin, but Hild shuddered at the thought of Penda among people she'd known.

"A new hazard." Cerdic raised his voice. "Cadwallon of Gwynedd, Penda's ally, has not gone home. He's marching north, near our borders, enjoying easy pickings. We're next in line." He had them gripped now. "Bernicia won't stop him. They're kingless and weakened by defeat."

One man cleared his throat but Cerdic did not yield the floor.

"Many of you know Lord Cutha." He bowed in his direction. "He and these Northumbrian lords plan action. They're riding to fetch Oswald Whiteblade. He's of age, a Bernician prince, and a strong fighter. They want him as their king."

Cerdic sat down. Gwylget let the comments flow:

"What about us?"

"Cerdic, do something!"

"Why don't we join 'em?"

Eventually, the old chief held up a hand. "You're right, my friends," he said. "This is our business. Northumbria is our protector. We should demonstrate our allegiance. Lord Cutha assures me Cerdic would be welcome to join his party. Let him go to speak for us to the Anglian prince."

"Cerdic! Cerdic!" The shouts of acclamation faded behind Hild as she walked to her lodging. He would go, she knew. His greatest fear was to let Gwylget down again.

"When?" was her only word as he joined her.

"In the morning," he groaned, squatting on a stool and lifting Wulfi onto his lap. "He's heavier." The child wriggled and thumped his chest.

"Put him down and he'll crawl to you," Hild said. But Wulfi made for Hild, hauling himself up by her skirts. "Up! Up!" He lifted his arms.

"Why you and not me?" Cerdic protested.

"You're a stranger. He's hardly seen you." Hild walked over to lay Wulfi in his cradle. "Besides, you ignored him. He was showing you he can walk!"

Cerdic flopped onto the bed. "I hope the brat doesn't scream all night."

"You're far more likely to disturb him!"

* * *

After Cerdic had left, a monk came to Din Edin to celebrate the feast of Pentecost. He was a small man, brown and wrinkled as a walnut, with warm eyes that Hild thought seemed to look deep inside her. His calm, resonant voice captivated her as he told a story that she found new and startling.

After Jesus died, he said, flames settled on his followers, not burning them but firing them up to speak out and tell his life story.

"God's Spirit," he explained, "giving them courage and strength for the task."

Like Thor in the sacred grove, Hild thought, rousing Edwin's army for battle. But the monks' Jesus was different. He didn't rouse men to fight and kill. He died for them. Strange way for a god to behave, but that was the point of their Easter festival.

"God letting his Spirit loose in the world," the monk was saying. "Like a bird, alighting where it is wanted. In hearts that are pure. In your heart, if you choose, to guide your mind and actions." And he ended with prayers, in the familiar way.

"Make clean our hearts within us," he cried.

"Take not your Holy Spirit from us," answered the crowd. The words which Brother James had written on her scrap of parchment. The words which Christ used. James said he needed the prayer too; it was easy to lose the Spirit if you didn't tend it.

Here at Din Edin, Hild had little to do except join the women and children. They were used to her quiet presence. She let her mind ponder on what the brown monk had said. She'd never heard of gods giving their spirit to humans.

When Ethelburga had given her a Gospel book, Hild could see no use for it. But now, as the monk sat on a tree trunk by the fire in the compound, chatting to the people that gathered round, she waited to ask him about the story. Could he mark it, so that she could read it again?

"You read?" he said with interest, taking the book. "You wish to study the story?"

"It's a new idea," she nodded diffidently. "The gods I know – if they gave away their spirit, they wouldn't be gods any more. Couldn't do the things gods do: dole out rewards and punishments. I mean –" She wondered if she sounded silly. His eyes pierced her confusion and she couldn't hide her scepticism. "A god giving away his spirit? His power?"

"You're right," he said. At once she relaxed. "Jesus gave up his power to become human. He lived a human life. Died as one of us, for us. Hard to grasp." He focused on Hild as he spoke, oblivious

181

to the screech of the men's whetstone or the children's giggles. His warmth gave her confidence.

"But you say – you monks, I mean – that he didn't stay dead but rose to new life. So his Spirit, his godly Spirit, was not killed. And he gave it to his friends in his place. Is that right?"

"Yes, it is." He nodded enthusiastically. "You have a good mind, lady, a rare gift. Use it. You see, if you get to know him, I believe you'll find Jesus better than the old gods. Read his story in your Gospel book. But…" He started to hand it back. "You won't find the story of the flames in here. It's from another book about what happened to his followers afterwards." Suddenly, he tightened his grip.

"But let me show you something Jesus said." He flipped through the pages. "Here, see." Moving his finger along the line, he translated the Latin into British: *Keep on asking, it will be given you; search long and hard, you will find it; keep knocking and the door will open.*

"If you persist…" Hild interpreted hesitantly, "God will give you his Spirit…?"

"He will! He does!" He gripped her hands. "He loves you. Wants you to have it. If you choose."

"What a remarkable man," she said to Gerda.

"Brother Aidan?" She nodded. "He never stays long enough. He has to be back on the Isle of Monks within the time his abbot allows."

* * *

"Sit up, Wulfi!" Cerdic barked, his voice carrying on the blustery wind. Four years had passed. They were at the end of the Firth, trotting south to a small seaport where Eata was arranging their passage.

"I'm tired," the boy whined, dawdling.

"Good posture's less tiring," Cerdic persisted. "Back straight!"

"Not far now, Wulfi," Hild encouraged him.

"He's no feel for it," Cerdic muttered.

"It's a long ride for a five-year-old. I think he's doing well." Hild knew Cerdic's irritability was really about what lay ahead: presenting the Gododdin tribute to the Northumbrian king on Gwylget's behalf. "Whoops! What's got into him?"

Wulfstan was galloping madly, whirling his wooden sword above his head and hallooing his father's warcry.

"That's more like it!" Cerdic grunted.

"Will he cope? He's bound to get bored." How well she remembered the tedium of court ceremonial, and her mother's nagging.

"It's time he learned to handle the flummery," Cerdic growled. "King Oswald's a decent chap. Got a young boy of his own. Well done, son!" Cerdic interrupted himself as Wulfi fell back to ride alongside, windswept hair spread across his glowing face.

"A lot hangs on that poor queen, wed for the sake of the anti-Penda alliance."

"Strange man, Oswald, for a king," Cerdic said. "Getting his father-in-law baptized! Comes of being brought up by monks. Did I tell you about Heavenfield?"

"Where you fought with him against Cadwallon?"

"Mm. Oswald had a vision, a flaming cross. Made the leathercaps erect a wooden one. Held it himself while they dug it in. When we were all lined up, he made us pray."

"Well, it worked," Hild chuckled. "You won."

"You won! You won!" chanted Wulfi.

"Thank God," Cerdic said fervently. "It's still there, the cross, venerated by the locals." Hild nodded. She'd heard the tales. Everyone knew someone who'd met a man who'd actually seen the cross mend broken limbs, cure lepers, or calm a frenzy. Northumbrians didn't resent Oswald's peculiarities. They'd put up with anything for peace and justice.

"I'll be interested to see this paragon," she said. "If I get the chance, crammed among the women. Take care of Wulfi, won't you?"

"Do you doubt it, woman?" Cerdic patted his son's shoulder. "That was quite a display, Wulfstan. Stay with us now, till we find Eata. Look! Down there."

There was a sheer drop to a tiny cove ringed by jagged black crags. The waves surged in on the high tide, tossing a fat-bellied cargo ship which stood at anchor. A couple of warehouses hugged the water's edge. Behind them, sheltered in a ravine, stood a decrepit thatched lodging. Carefully they picked their way down the steep track, Cerdic first, gripping Wulfi's leading rein, with Hild advancing cautiously behind.

It was a hard night on narrow boards under skimpy fleeces. Cerdic and Wulfi sprawled out, oblivious. Hild hung at the edge, wakeful with fleas, a howling wind, and anxiety. She couldn't forget that King Oswald's father, the Twister, had been Edwin's deadliest foe, and she was Edwin's kin. But surely, after ten summers, no one would recognize her as Eostre's maid; she was a matron, over twenty-three. And everything at Bamburgh would be changed.

But it wasn't. From the women's lodging Hild watched thegns, boys among them, stack their weapons at the hall doors and push through. Women fluttered past her, but she waited to watch the parade of subject lords bringing their tribute. Cerdic came well down the line; the Gododdin were a poor nation. Yet he had presence, walking tall in his finest cloak and silver arm rings. At his side, Wulfi burst into a frantic wave until kicked from behind by Eata, who carried Gwylget's tribute: a bone box containing a crystal goblet.

Cerdic's day was busy with royal ceremonies, and Eata never left his side. Hild took Wulfi exploring. Running down from the fortress, they skidded over the dunes, kicked their way through the sand, paddled barefoot, capered around in the sun making grotesque shadows, carved monsters in the wet sand, and bowled wizened apples to each other before they ate them. Hild became a girl again. There was no one to see, and their shouts were drowned by the booming rollers.

"Can we walk to the island, Ma?" Wulfi pointed at Lindisfarne, looking so close at low tide she felt she could touch it.

"No!" she laughed. "We'd get stuck in quicksands." So they drifted in a coracle round the marsh of a million birds, the child trailing his hands to catch tiny squirming creatures.

"I really need a string," he said.

"Oh, Wulfi," she sighed. "We'll fish for our supper, I promise, once we get home."

"Must we go in?" He nodded at the fortress, dragging his feet through the spiky grass. "It's so boring! I don't want to grow up."

Hild shuddered, praying Hreth had not heard. He ran off to pull primroses.

"Here's one for you." Selecting the fullest bloom, he reached up and gave it to her. Impulsively she flung her arms round him and held him tight. Wulfi wriggled under and out, cruising on widespread arms like a gull. She followed thoughtfully, sheltering the fragile flower in her hand.

In the hall, she could only identify the king by his royal circlet and chair. He wore a simple gown and his greying hair offset a bronzed, outdoor face. The food served was plentiful but no richer than at home; cuts of sheep with bread and radishes. Only the fruit glowed in the firelight. Wine circulated freely, but the atmosphere was subdued. Deep in conversation with the king sat a monk, judging by the familiar bare forehead, long hair, and homespun robe. Was it one she knew? she wondered.

Draughts round her ankles drew her eyes to the door where the thegn on duty was holding back a desperate crowd. Ragged and dirty, they were nearly all women and children.

"They hound him wherever we go," sighed Hild's neighbour, seeing her glance.

"Hound the king?"

"Four years, it's lasted." The woman shook her head. "Cadwallon's victims. Homes burned, men slaughtered, beasts stolen, where else can they turn? Look!" Snatching at the bowls of leftovers the servers passed out, the beggars started to squabble over them. "He's doing what he can, but it'll take years."

The scop tuned up for his ritual song: *Whiteblade, Oswald Whiteblade, sword of justice, sword of peace.* Oswald simply poured wine for his wife, flashing her a smile. Beside her sat a young lord waving a jewelled hand while cramming food into his mouth.

"Who's that?" Hild whispered. "Beside the queen."

"The king's brother. Always on the go, hunting, boxing, fighting. A dark horse, Prince Oswy."

"Typical younger son." Hild remembered Edi's ambition and rancour.

"Brother, no!" the prince suddenly cried. The room quietened and all eyes turned to watch. The king was handing his own silver dish to a thegn.

"Break it up. Distribute the pieces," King Oswald said quietly. "Silver will serve them better than a crust."

"No!" Oswy stretched over to seize his arm. "Buy loyalty where it counts. Give those vagrants treasure and you'll never be rid of them." There were nods of agreement.

"Loyalty's a poor thing if it has to be bought," Oswald said firmly. "This is little enough among so many." He rose, and the room rose with him. "Bishop Aidan will give thanks."

Aidan! The wrinkled monk with the warm, resonant voice and brown eyes. The monk who'd given her time, answered her questions, listened uncritically to her scepticism. The monk who saw inside her and understood.

"Father," he said, "we thank you for our food, and ask you to fill us with fervour for your service. Amen."

The king repeated his words exactly. Of course! Aidan spoke British; Oswald was translating for his Anglians.

"Let us tell you a story," he said, and the hall settled.

"A young thegn asked a lord what service he would require," said Aidan in a conversational style, the king translating, and adding, "Just like you, when you're in attendance."

"Fight for me?… Tribute?… Kneel and clasp hands?" Oswald muttered the men's suggestions into Aidan's ear.

"Here's the lord's answer," Aidan interrupted. "*Sell everything you have for gold…*" He smiled at the nods of approval. "*And give the gold to the poor.*"

Hild heard guffaws, protests and indignation that the bishop should encourage Oswald's eccentricity. Some were as puzzled by the answer as the question. "What do you think the young thegn did?" Aidan asked.

"Obey, of course!" came a quick reply, but others faltered.

"He hadn't sworn yet… Too much to lose…"

"What would you have done?" prodded Aidan. "If he obeyed the command, his lord said he would live for ever."

Oswald's thegns were young and living at peace; death was unreal and Aidan's tale senseless. They waited.

"Well, what did he do?" growled an old thegn near the door.

"He turned away," Aidan said. There were nods and mutters. Most men, though ashamed to admit it in the king's presence, would have done the same.

"The lord was sad," continued Aidan. "*It's harder for a rich man to earn eternal life*, he said, *than for a warhorse to bolt down a badger hole.*"

They burst into raucous laughter. It was a good joke, and they'd remember it. But Hild knew Aidan was disappointed he hadn't got through to them. How could he? How could a British monk understand Anglian thegns' values: gold to show your worth, fighting as the way to earn it? Monks were poor like the Christ they followed, giving away what they had. What had Aidan in common with Oswald's Companions?

He stood, gripping the king's arm, until quiet fell.

"The lord in the story was Christ," he said, "the Christ to whom your king swore allegiance." He was making it clear, Hild thought, that their duty was to their king, who in turn served Jesus. "This hand belongs to Christ's man. You've seen it do Christ's bidding. May it do so forever!"

When the queen and her women rose, Hild looked over at Cerdic, deep in talk. Eata was helping Wulfi roll his cloak into a pillow.

"Coming?" said her neighour.

"We've brought our son for the first time," Hild explained.

"It's not like the old days," the woman said. "Oswald's officers are strict. He wants restraint amid all this suffering. Some thegns grumble, but the bishop says it's the Christian way. Will you sleep here? This is a guest pallet."

Removing her embroidered overdress and veil, Hild curled into her cloak and lay down, lulled by soft talk and giggles. Suddenly, she was trapped among fighters, struggling towards Wulfi. As she reached out, he faded away, again and again and again. Stifled and panicky, she woke to see light under the door.

Pulling her cloak tight, she stepped over sleeping women and slipped outside. It was full moon. Leaning on the wall in the shadow of the thatch, she breathed deeply and mastered her trembling. This, she told herself firmly, was a place of cherished memories: where she'd revelled in summer and yearned for Erpwald; where James taught her to read and set her mind free.

Startled, she found she was not alone. On the far side of the compound, pale in the moonlight, stood Aidan with his arms upraised, praying to his man-god, this Christ who died and gave his living Spirit to his followers. What would he pray for? she wondered.

At least the king was on his side. Oswald's refusal to buy loyalty, his generosity and moderation, was impressive. He did not lack military skills, as his victories proved. But he saw war as a stepping stone to peace.

* * *

After the distress in Bernicia, Hild relished the harmony of her Gododdin life. Her lord was equable, her homestead welcoming, her household friendly, and Wulfi was her delight. In the next two years he grew past her elbow, standing out with his fair skin and light hair, a throwback to her father, but always with Cerdic's nose. The village boys took him fishing and taught him to swim, Eata showed him how to use a spear and took him hunting, Brigit's boys helped him shoot a sling and skin a hare, and Gwylget gave him a whelp from the royal litter.

From her hawthorn tree on the cliff edge, Hild looked down on boats beating across the Firth to the blue hills. The monks encompassed Pictland in their pilgrimages. She came across Pictish merchants in the vill at the water's edge. All was peace.

She remembered Aidan, driven by passion for this god who lived humbly as a mortal. She must look again at Ethelburga's Gospel book.

8

DIN EDIN

Disaster broke like a cloudburst at the end of a windless summer day. Cerdic, with other Gododdin men, rode up the rock of Din Edin windswept and hungry from a day's hunting, bringing a stag, a boar, and anxiety.

"Look!" He pointed out a red stain in the western sky.

"What a sunset!" Hild exclaimed.

"No! Wrong colour," he said sharply.

"Why?"

"Could be crops, a farmstead," he said. "The ground's dry." They watched as a billowing cloud blackened the evening sky. "Hell's teeth, a raid!"

"Who, d'you reckon?" he asked as other men gathered round.

"Westward. Could be Rheged, the old enemy," they offered. "Or pirates."

"From there, we'll be next!" he said.

"We'll be safe on the rock, won't we?" Hild asked faintly.

No one answered.

"Gaeth, take fresh horses and a couple of men," Cerdic ordered. "Suss it out." The man sped away. "You, check the stake traps, and you the missiles – boulders, spears, and so on. You, take a group to survey the walls. And you, check the armaments. Move calmly, avoid panic." He spoke with quiet urgency, in warleader mode; no time for niceties. "Hild, get Wulfi and the women indoors. I'm going to the chief."

The settlement was small and intimate. Men scurried to and fro, faces alight. Eata and other youths, infected by their mood, bellowed rowdily as they herded children inside the wall. The news spread. Hild's stomach sank. She remembered Edwin's captives, the survivors' ghastly wounds, Oswald's beggars. Not again! Not here!

"What is it, lady?" Begu was tidying up around their lodging.

"See that glow?" Hild put a finger to her lips and pointed. "Could be raiders. Cerdic's not sure. Keep Wulfi indoors."

"Ma!" As if he'd heard, Wulfstan ran up with his puppy. "There's going to be a battle. Can I go? I'm getting good with my spear."

"They're probably drilling the warband," Hild answered casually. "Good practice. Keeps the neighbours on their toes. I'm going to find Father. It's your bedtime."

"Can't I come?"

"Will you give the hound his supper?" She kissed him and pushed him inside.

Cerdic was deep in conference with Gwylget as men dashed in to report. The chief listened attentively.

"Further east?" he suggested. "Send warning?"

"I'd rather not light beacons," Cerdic answered. "It would alert the enemy. With your permission, we'll send a runner, start a chain."

"Food?"

"Store's full. Reserves in hand," Cerdic replied. "Four or five days' worth. More if we eke it out. Hild and some of the women could…"

"Missiles?"

"Likewise. Rocks and stones piled, arrows bundled, spears…"

"Clearly you have it all in hand," Gwylget sighed, finding it hard to be an onlooker.

"My lord!" Impulsively Cerdic knelt at his feet. "I swear to give myself to your service." His voice was low and hoarse with the memory of past failure. He placed his hands together and bowed his head, just as he must have done when first chosen warleader. The old chief laid a quivering hand on his shoulder, then pulled off his regnal ring and pushed it into Cerdic's hand.

"Take it," he said. "Sign of my trust. Go with God. And my blessing."

The emotion was tangible: an old man surrendering his power, Cerdic burdened by his trust, Gerda watching her lord yield to age. Hild felt the old woman's eyes on her: *I told you so. Cerdic's come through.*

"God be with you, lady!" Cerdic gripped Hild's hand and looked keenly into her eyes. "My lady is at your disposal," he said to the chief. Then he was gone.

"There's something you could do for me, Lady Hild." Gwylget had steel in his voice. "Find a couple of youths and send them in."

Outside, night had fallen. No women were visible, only men and beasts. Male sweat smelled acrid amid the dung, smoke, and food. Hild stood listening: grunts of effort, barked instructions, horses blowing, logs spitting, and anvils ringing. Spotting youths round a cookpot, she picked her way over.

"Two of you!" She sounded more confident than she felt. "The chief wants two helpers."

"What for, lady?" They looked her up and down in surprise.

"He'll tell you himself," she snapped, impatient as they unfurled slowly and sauntered between goats, dogs, and slaves dragging spearshafts. She wanted to prod them.

"Ah!" Gwylget nodded his satisfaction. On the table lay various pieces of ancient armour. "Know how this fits on, you two? Get it round me."

Gerda looked strained and tearful. Hild slipped out.

* * *

They knew they were in trouble when the scouts did not return. While they waited, men prepared for the worst and women hung on to normality. Frost threatened the evening as Eata turned up.

"Cerdic's taking the night watch. He's sent for his helmet," he said, lifting the long leather cap from a nail on the wall. "He said, could I ask you to get the women and children into the hall? He doesn't want anyone near the edge. Could be picked off or…"

"Fire." She knew the hazards. "I'll see to that, tell him. Does it look bad?"

"Strictly for your ears – he'd kill me if he knew – it may be Rheged."

Incomprehension choked her. "That old feud's been dormant for… well over a generation!"

"I've never heard of it," he nodded. "Seems there may be Anglians too. A shepherd saw…"

"Anglians!" Hild shrieked.

"Hush!" He clapped a hand over her mouth. "Sorry, lady, but it's top secret." His eyes were cold. "Prince Oswy's wife. She's from Rheged."

"You mean Oswald's brother is invading Oswald's sworn vassals? We've done nothing…"

"I must go!" He smothered her in a hard, affectionate hug. "Don't let on."

"Keep safe!" she whispered.

"I'll look after Cerdic." He was already at the door. "You'll be in the hall?"

She found Gwylget stamping stiffly round the table in his armour.

"You know it's my duty." He sounded furious. "A chief fights for his people. Too old to lead," he snarled bitterly, "but I can fight." Then he looked down on his lady, hanging on his arm. "You've been my strength," he murmured, patting her hand. "Be strong for me now."

Hild ran to summon Gerda's women. Finding servers huddled in the cookhouse, she set them to clear the hall. Only then did she summon the women, sending a message to the nearest lodging and asking them to pass it on. They obeyed without question, settling the children in cocoons of skins and cloaks, stifling the odd cry. Wulfi slept, arm flung across his hound's neck. Soon heavy breathing was the only sound.

Outside, a haloed moon hung in a chilly sky. A good night for seeing, but cold. Lookouts huddled at their posts. Quiet challenges dogged Hild's steps. She found Eata first, guarding his lord's back. Cerdic was hugging his knees on top of the western rampart.

"All in order," she murmured.

He nodded. "If I were them," he whispered, "I'd slip through the night and attack at dawn. It's what we're expecting. Go back and get some sleep. You'll need your strength tomorrow."

"You're sure it's an attack, then?"

"Well, the scouts haven't returned."

"Old Gwylget's armed and about."

"I know. He's heading the defence at the gateway. He's shrewd, won't panic and…" he paused, "there are worse ends than a fighting death."

Hild shuddered.

She strained her ears for the scouts. Bleats and shuffling from tethered beasts, murmurs from the sentries, the crackle as sleepers stirred the rushes, Wulfi burbling gently on his back in a streak of moonlight, Begu snoring lustily nearby. Nothing else.

Just before cockcrow when sleep was heaviest, it started: roaring, the clash of iron, the rhythmic thud of a trained warband. From the gate, she thought. Where the chief was stationed. Where the toughest were on guard. She forced herself to remember the towering piles of missiles, the steep rocky track, the deadly overhang, everything to trap an enemy.

"Battle at the gate," she murmured to Gerda. "I'll get a fire going, and gruel for all." Her calmness was infectious. The women distributed food while she partitioned the hall and allocated tasks: here, mothers to care for infants; here, girls to amuse young children; down the side, the whole length, childless women to aid the wounded.

"To the weaving shed," she ordered a cluster of young women. "Keep down, between the buildings. In silence. No risks, please. Scraps of cloth, wads of wool, goat's hair, moss – anything to staunch and bind wounds. Begu, fetch my smallest chest. Keep away from the edge of the cliff. Quick as you can. There'll be casualties soon."

The chief came first.

"No wailing," she barked, directing the bearers to his bed behind the screen. "The enemy mustn't know." Or our own men, she thought.

Gwylget was white, drenched with sweat, and unconscious. He flopped as they removed his head gear. Trying to strip off his leather jacket, they found a spearhead pinning it to his chest. The iron was barbed. Hild stood by with poultice and wadding as two of his bodyguard held him steady and a third wrenched the spike out. She watched the blood flow clean and packed the wound with unspun wool; the oil would help the healing. But the hole gaped wide, and he was frail. She held out her hand to Begu, waiting for a clump of moss. As the men raised him she packed his wound and bound his torso tight.

"Gerda?" he groaned, calling for his wife.

"Just here," Hild said, wringing out a cloth and starting to bathe his brow. The old lady took the cloth. She'd feel better, Hild knew, to be doing something. If fever set in, his chances were slight.

"For the pain," she whispered, handing over a small beaker of poppy juice. "Sleep's the best cure."

More men limped or were carried to the side of the hall. Hanging a cloak to screen what they were doing, she and Begu cut out splinters, dressed gashes, splinted broken limbs and tended the dying. Those fit enough carried out the dead; ceremonial could wait. The stream lasted all day, some returning to battle, others lying in the rushes or propped against the wall. There were times when it sounded like a banquet, with cries and calls mixed with children's laughter.

By nightfall, exhaustion had set in. Hild wrapped herself in her cloak and leaned against a pillar near her diminishing pile of dressings. From time to time she toured with a tallow to soothe those in agony, quieten the restless and settle the wandering dazed. Before first light it all started again.

The next day they ran out of cloth and tore up their garments. Begu brought all Hild had left and she donned a heavy ceremonial dress to free up the comfortable soft fabrics she'd been wearing. Irritability sprang from tiredness, and arguments shrilled.

"Stick to broth," Hild told the cooks. "Gruel if it runs out. We can't cook meat indoors."

They ran out with bowls to the fighters but had to give up as spears rained down, crazed beasts panicked, and the ground was slick with dung and blood. A couple of men she'd bandaged helped Hild gather and pile the enemy spears for their own men to send back.

The fighting sounded nearer. Stench, clashes, children screaming, beasts stampeding, men shrieking, piles of bodies, flames, smoke. Day turned dark but dark brought no respite. Time lost its meaning. No chance to eat, rest, or find out the state of battle.

At an hour when sleep called, the spears fell thinner. Men sank in exhaustion. Hild crept outside. Dodging between the horrors – men glaring with the whites of their eyes, cattle twisting in final agony, mangled corpses among dying men, hoarse pleas for water, for a dagger blow – she sought the western wall. Buildings had gone, there were gaps in the walls, the scene seemed unfamiliar, but Hild followed her sense of where the dark was thickest. If she was right, that would be where Cerdic was.

"Halt!" came the challenge.

"Eata! Thank God."

"Wait here!" he ordered. Crawling up the bank he stretched back to haul her up.

"We've made a hole in them," Cerdic grunted as she crouched beside him. "Eata, be my eyes for a moment."

Hild peered at him in the moonlight. His limbs seemed sound, but there were dark patches on his spear arm and forehead. Reaching up, she felt her hand sticky with blood. A new wound at the neck, or the old scar reopened?

"You all right?" she whispered, handing him a bladder of ale.

"Fine. But it's taking too many men and too much time." He slurped. "What of the women and children?"

"All right."

"I'd like you to get them out."

Hild gasped.

"I'll mount a sortie." He had it planned. "A charge from the gate. Give you chance to climb down the opposite crag. Down to the water."

"That deadly slope!"

"No more deadly than staying here," he hissed. His honesty was shocking.

"You mean, down the boys' slither-track?"

"It's got handholds," he nodded. "You'd have to keep them quiet. In small groups. At intervals."

"Aren't we surrounded?"

"Not on the crag side. It's just..." His men were spaced thinly round the walls, with only boys and old men to hand up spears and boulders. There was so much he was not saying, she realized. Die here, by fire or starvation. Or perhaps, just perhaps, survive by dropping down the crag. All those women and children in the hall... Wulfi and Begu... the sick and wounded. She shivered.

"Only... There's a group of horsemen riding round and round the rock. You'd have to keep your eyes skinned," he said flatly.

Hild felt sick. It was too much. She was no strategist. She couldn't lead a retreat. A retreat... that was what it was. She couldn't... he asked too much. Yet he couldn't spare men...

"If there's no other way." Each word heavy and exhausting. "But..."

He waited.

"What about the rest?" she asked. "The wounded... those who can't...?"

"We'll guard them." His voice was firm. "Men fight with a will when their families are safe."

Horror filled her. If one of those horsemen... If someone fell...

"God knows," he sighed. "We can only trust."

Had she really agreed to this?

"There's no one else," he said. "If anyone can do it…" The words were torn from him. "You're stronger than you know."

* * *

Calm and upright beside Gwylget's body, his lady endured the long vigil without complaint. No power on earth could stop the rot in a festering wound. There was no surprise, no lament, when the old king died.

"He wanted to die in harness," she said prosaically. "Will you help me?" Together they bared his bent body and washed him in water that was brackish but left him clean. Hild packed his gaping chest with fresh moss against the stench, and rubbed fragrances on his face and feet. They wrapped him in a cloak, tucking herbs in the folds, set his head on a rolled cloak, combed his hair and adorned him with his circlet and jewels. At his side they placed his blood-stained sword.

"A chief's state and a fighter's bier." Gerda nodded her satisfaction. "And he won't have to face the downfall of Din Edin." Closeted with her dying lord, she had still grasped their peril as surely as Hild. "Don't tell the people till you must. We want no wailing."

Covering the fetid corpse with one of her finest veils, she took her place at his side, thoughtful and still. "Go, my dear, and do your duty."

"These are your helpers." Eata led a group of youths to Hild. "He says they're the best. They know the rock." She wanted to hug him, as usual, but couldn't in front of his peers.

From a small overlap in the defensive bank, the lads showed her the place where they customarily scrambled down to the lake.

"Broke my leg," muttered one. He was quickly squashed, but the peril was obvious.

"We need a plan," Hild said. "Come where we can talk." In someone's lodging, far enough from the edge to escape stray spearshots, they squatted in the rushes, looking out at the starry night, debating the best way to lower women and children down the crag. These boisterous, impulsive lads had changed. Solemnly they discussed the best route, how to gain silence and how to avoid discovery. By the early hours they had their plan, but it was too light to start. They must wait another day and leave at nightfall.

Waiting was hard. Hild twitched at running feet and falling rocks. Action calmed her: tending the sick, dealing out drinks and dressings, jollying servers to share round the food. She made sure to speak to each woman in turn, establishing the group she would lead and the need for utter silence.

"Wear dark clothing, keep both hands free, take nothing but the children, move only when summoned, and silence – absolute silence!" The volume rose as they talked things through. As Hild turned to quell it, a high-pitched squeal silenced them all. Running in from the daylight, a child buried his face in Hild's skirts.

"Ma!" he sobbed, as she lifted him up. "Dead!"

"Show me!" She held him firmly and stood under cover while he pointed out where his mother had gone to fetch him a dark tunic. Handing him to one of the older women, she ventured out with two reluctant servers. The woman's crumpled corpse, head staved in, blocked the narrow alley.

"Carry her round the back, and keep the route clear to the crag top," she ordered, turning to face the aftermath. The child and his brothers sobbed, other infants joined in. "Bad omen," mothers muttered, looking askance. She'd known the risk but with escape so near it came as a bitter blow. Jaded and sweating in her cumbersome robes, Hild doubted herself. And Gerda, who might have braced the women, refused to leave her lord.

"Together in life, together in death," she declared. Nothing – duty to the women, obedience to the warleader, what Gwylget would have wished – would move her.

At nightfall, Hild led the first group to the top of the track where two youths waited.

"All in order below," one murmured to her as he turned to the women. "Use hands and arms for balance. Feel ahead with your feet. Go slowly. No talking. Ready?" With immense care he and his mate handed the first woman through.

Tucking her skirts up as if it were washday, she took her first slippery steps down the narrow track, her children gripping her from behind. Almost at once a lad supported her from below, and passed her down to a youth beyond. Hild saw the little family vanish from sight in the bracken, and turned to find another edging sideways and down. Each family passed as a unit, handed down from youth to youth. After an eternity, word came back up: they'd reached safety. Hild fetched the next groups from the hall.

She held her breath, wracked by nerves, blinded by night, hearing no fall or cry, no sound of discovery. Generations of lads had scaled this hazardous cliff, preferring the short cut. They knew bad spots, good cover, and the women were in the safest hands. At the bottom, she knew, they'd be launched on a path to the shore, with fishermen to scull them to safety by dawn.

It was agonizingly slow. Each group crept nervously forward, infants strapped to backs and chests. Some women jibbed at the brink, one fainted, children panicked, girls clung flirtatiously; all needed chivvying. Hild marvelled at the lads' resolution, their tirelessness and their control.

"Halt!" A sharp whisper came upwards. They froze. Hild strained uselessly. Then a faint jingling carried on the still air. Horse-harness, she prayed, not, please not, a man's war harness. Nearer it came, more distinct, with hoof-beats and heavy breathing. Horsemen traversing the rough ground of the lower slopes. A splash, a curse, a half-checked laugh, and a pause.

"On!" rang out a quiet command. In Anglian. They were close below, circling Din Edin. Slowly the sounds faded. And died. Ant-like the women resumed the descent.

Clashing of arms and challenges reached Hild from behind, on the other side of the compound. She sighed with relief. Cerdic had seen the prowlers. This was his diversion. She gritted her teeth and prayed it would work, shock them, drive them back.

Time for the last group, led by Begu.

"Ma!" Wulfi whispered in excitement. Hild put finger to mouth to quieten him. She could see him, he could see her, she realized. Dawn was breaking. No time to dally.

"Thanks," she mouthed to the lad who held her above the drop, "and good luck!" She let her feet find the track below.

"Fast as you can," he whispered. "I'm going back to help."

Last in line, she felt the chill of exposure like a wind in her back. One step at a time, downwards, crabwise, one hand gripping the ground, the other pulled by Wulfi. He stumbled, scree rattled, his hot hand slipped from her grasp. But he found his feet and clung to the ferns, hanging, finely balanced, waiting for her. Far below she glimpsed Begu's head bobbing through the furze. Everyone else was out of sight. She hoped they'd got away. Crouching, she slithered from foothold to foothold until she reached Wulfi and grasped him tight.

Where was the next youth? They ought to have found him by now. A corpse curled on the bracken like a mattress of down, the spear that had killed him dangling from his side. Had they suspected, those horsemen riding round the rock? Had they left spies?

"Down!" she rasped at Wulfi. "Keep still and hang on!" Gingerly she edged forward, eyes stretched, ears alert, clutching the knife in her girdle. Under the bracken she moved unseen, but she could not see. Stink of sweat, gulping breaths, a man climbing steeply, the bracken parting. A figure loomed up.

"No!" came a cry. Wulfi hurtled down from above, small sword flailing, slithering uncontrollably. "You leave my mother alone!"

"Oho," the man guffawed. "An enemy charge!" As he hurled his spear uphill, Hild rushed under his raised arm with her knife. His eyes bulged, he grunted, his back curved, and he tumbled, over and over, bouncing down the slope. Wulfi landed in a crushed ball at her feet. Blood gushed from his head, and one of his legs was bent backwards beneath him.

"Oh, Wulfi!" Hild sobbed, dropping her knife as she tried to lift him. He screamed in agony, passing out. "Oh, brave little idiot! Poor, poor babe!" She held him in her arms, kissing him frantically, unaware of a figure scrambling up to her.

"I'll take him, lady. Did he fall?" A youth lifted the child. "Come quickly now. At once. With me. Put your hand on my shoulder."

His tone was stern. She obeyed automatically and followed shakily down the track. "We should have been there for you but we've had deaths. Glad I got him, even if he took my spear. Steady, now. You'll feel better at the bottom."

Hild tried to concentrate, watch her step. The lad prattled; to encourage, or to hide his shock. Could be his first death. Could have lost mates. Did he kill the man, or was it her knife? Gone. Not in her belt. How would she cope? No ointments, no poppy juice. How to tend Wulfi?

"We're down!" Clearly relieved, the lad seized her hand and ran her to the shore. They were quite alone.

"Already on the water," he sighed. "Here, get in this coracle. I'll pass the boy." Hild stepped into the fragile craft, wobbling dangerously. "Sit down and steady it," he ordered. "Reach the paddle. Right, here's the child." Clumsily she tried to lay the inert Wulfi in the curved bottom. "Hey, don't rock like that." He waded into the sea beside her, pushing the little craft free of the sand.

"Jump in, quick!" she cried as he gave it a final heave.

"I'm going back," he shouted. "May be others to save. They're firing Din Edin. Go, go quickly!"

His words floated away, and she saw him running. The rising sun picked out the tufty sides of the rock and, away at the top, black ruins, the township in flames. What of Gerda? The wounded? Cerdic? She let herself sink in despair. The coracle twisted and skittered in the swirling currents.

Feebly at first, then with anger, she pulled at the paddles and swung to face the glare of the morning. Keep to the coast. Go with the tide. Mind the rocks. Keep going. Towards the sun. Into the wind. Pull, pull. Pull against pain. Pull for safety. Safety and help. Help for her baby.

"Wulfi," she sobbed. Bouncing and twisting, the light craft swooped like a frenzied dancer on the frothing waves. Tears streaked her face. Her hands slipped. She hadn't the strength.

But she had the will. Beat them down. Keep pulling. Pull, pull!

"Oh, God!" she cried. "Wulfi… Oh, God!"

9

BERNICIA

Flicker in the blackness, boots crunching on reeds, a jolt. Hild lay as uncaring as a slug.

"Still unconscious." A girl's voice, then the covers lifted. "Look!"

"Don't know her." A man, abrupt, offhand. "What's this?"

"Pouch from her girdle," said the girl. "Soggy. Hard to untie." And then an exclamation. "A book! Worked leather."

"A book!" he whooped. "Chance of a fat ransom."

"Oswy, for pity's sake!" she snapped. "Forgotten your monks' training? Leave it here for when she wakes." A light touch at her pillow.

"She'll read it?" The harsh voice sniggered and the boots retreated. "We had to nail them, sis. Their leader was in Edwin's pocket. The monks would've understood…"

"Not taking it out on a woman, they wouldn't!"

An Anglian man. She knew the voice. Resting her cheek on Ethelburga's Gospel book, Hild drifted back to nothingness.

In the quiet of night she woke alone. Her head swam when she tried to sit up. Sounds and sights floated through her mind: *Hope of a ransom… In Edwin's pocket… silver's for buying loyalty.* Like sun from a cloud, it spilled back: Din Edin, enemy horsemen circling, the moment of waiting, holding Wulfi back, and a voice under the crag. The Bernician prince! Oswy!

So, she was in enemy hands. And Wulfi? Where was Wulfi? She must find Wulfi. Determination gripped her: regain her strength, eat, exercise, listen.

She could have been a cookpot for all the heed they paid her, the women charged with her care. As they washed and fed her, they chattered and giggled, different girls each day: the lady Abbe this, and lady Abbe that; the endless fish in this godforsaken spot; the mystery woman they were lumbered with; Lord Oswy's wandering hands… When they left her alone, she paced and stretched, peeped between the timbers, listened for clues.

One morning she felt strong enough to reach the bench at the door. Sounds from her sickbed came to life. Drovers whipped cattle up to the great Anglian hall, carts creaked, and feet squelched in the mud. Children gambolled and giggled. Horsemen cursed as they pushed through, hounds yelping at their heels. Hild saw clusters of wooden lodgings, each with scavenging hens and a bleating goat, and sagging leather tents near a gorse-lined gulley which dropped to the sea. Busy and business-like, she thought approvingly, like Edwin's vills. Yet not quite, for she was struck by the friendly grins and greetings tossed easily in her direction. Was this how they treated a captive?

"So you're mending, sister?" A monk crossed from the track to sit beside her. Taking her hand, he flexed the fingers and weighed her wrist. "Still too thin, but improving."

"Who…?" His rich voice sounded familiar. "Who…?" She couldn't form the words.

"I'm Aidan the pilgrim. And you are Cerdic's lady."

"Where…?" She swallowed, shocked by his recognition.

"Lady Abbe took you in," he explained. "A crabber found you on the rocks. Thought you'd drowned and brought you here."

It didn't make sense.

"D'you remember a boat?" he asked.

She closed her eyes.

"No more now." He patted her hand. "God restore you, lady. We'll talk again."

A boat? Scenes ebbed and flowed. A coracle. Wulfi lying in the bottom. Wulfi… She must find Wulfi.

Before the next daybreak, she heard the unmistakable clatter of men striking camp. Clinging to the doorpost, she watched horsemen stream past, chucking up mud and churning the track. Ox carts lurched behind, leaning crazily under spearshafts and barrels. Oswy's warband marching away. Morning broke in a limitless sky. She felt lighter, brushed by hope.

"May I join you? Oh, look at that gull!" The girl opened her mouth in a carefree laugh, glowing with vitality and confidence. About Hild's own age, fair-haired, glittering with neck chains, she must be the lady Abbe. Hild watched the squawking chick chase its parent, dragging its wings and ducking. "Pathetic fraud!" the girl cried. "Should be catching his own food by now." She sat down on the bench. "Forgive my neglect. My brother takes a deal of cosseting. Now he's gone, we can be comfortable."

"My gratitude, Lady…" Hild began, but Abbe swept her thanks aside, chattering easily in British, asking nothing.

"Let's walk!" She jumped up and held out her hand. From that day onwards, they strolled together, further each day, until they left the buildings behind and reached the top of the cliffs. Dizzy from watching birds wheel over swirling waves, Hild staggered.

"No more gannets now." Prattling on without a hitch, Abbe steered her to a rock. "I used to spend hours watching gannets. My brothers taught me to climb for eggs. Steeped in bad ways, I was, long before they packed me off to the nuns. I'm still better at birds than psalms." She chuckled.

Hild smiled absently, distracted by the distant outline of Lindisfarne jutting from the sea and, in the other direction, a row of conical rocks leading to Din Edin. She knew where she was, at the end of the Firth, where she and Cutha had fired the beacons. Now she could search for Wulfi.

"Oh, my friend!" Abbe was watching her. "Don't look so anxious. You're my guest." She reached for Hild's hand. "I want to see you well and happy."

How could this impetuous girl be her enemy? But Hild knew she must beware. It would be all too easy to let slip that she was Deiran.

Through the dark days of winter, Hild held fast to her purpose. Cradled between frost-bound hills, booming breakers, and a busy life which made no calls on her, she grew stronger. On a day of scudding clouds, she tramped with Abbe along the cliffs to a sheer crag above sharp, black rocks surrounding a tiny bay. The tide surged up its sides and a ship tossed at the staithe, gangplanks down. She knew it: the harbour where she'd ridden with Cerdic and Wulfi to take ship for King Oswald's court.

"Off to Bamburgh," sighed Abbe, echoing her thought. "Wish we could go."

"Who…?" Hild froze. A line of men, roped together, shuffled at spear point along the quay.

"Prisoners of war," Abbe said casually, "for Bamburgh slave market." Hild looked with horror. "Oh, I don't want to go with them. Just… the sea road's open and I like Bamburgh."

Hild's guts clenched: captive Gododdin, Oswy's victims, too poor to bargain for their freedom, being hauled away to punishing labour. She'd seen the brutality and squalor of slavery, smelt the fear. Among the dark heads, bowed and lurching, was a scattering of white; even, she gasped, a redhead. Eata? She'd know by his jaunty step. But he was hobbled, roped in line, and too far below. Women straggled behind, with children. People she knew? She could have been with them – should have been with them! Her tears streamed.

"We've come too far." Abbe took her arm.

"No!" Hild pulled away and stood rigid, hands clenched at her sides, till the last screaming child was herded aboard and corralled on the heaving deck. "Lady Abbe," she said through gritted teeth. "Those are my people, my lord's people. Your enemy. I should be with them. But I fled. Fled with my child." Her voice cracked. "Seven years old. Lost…"

"His father?" Abbe asked quietly.

"Must be dead." Shock stopped Hild's tears. She'd not given Cerdic a thought, her grim-faced man, awaiting the end with his warband. Turning, she stalked away, stiff with remorse, anger and helpless failure. Abbe kept pace with her and, something she'd never done before, followed Hild into her lodging.

"I can't imagine your pain," she said gently, wrapping a fleece round Hild as she sobbed in anguish on the bed. "To lose a child…" In the flickering fireglow, Hild saw her fill a cup and blow on its surface.

"Drink this." Abbe helped Hild sit, and turned the sodden bolster. Mulled wine, some herb infused. The honey was soothing.

"I'm sorry." Hild leaned back with a sigh.

"Don't be. It's healing, to share sorrow."

Abbe spoke as if she knew. Dully, Hild remembered Cutha voiding his misery.

"Fathers do that, Aidan says. I never knew mine. He put God in his place."

God? The God of her mother and the busy monks who tramped the northern wilderness? And then she remembered: *Aidan the pilgrim*, he called himself. Aidan the preacher who listened to her doubts, looked into her heart, and encouraged her. Aidan, who'd been to see her here.

"I never knew my father, either," she croaked, responding instinctively in the Anglian Abbe had used. "I wish I could believe in your God."

"It's…" Abbe hesitated. "I think it's a matter of trust." She paused. "And trust is something you choose to do. An act, not a feeling."

"I wasn't brought up to trust," Hild said. "Edwin didn't even trust his kin."

"Ah," Abbe murmured sympathetically. "Edwin of Deira?"

Too weak to resist, Hild nodded. "My father's uncle," she whispered.

Abbe answered briskly, "My mother's brother."

Hild stared at her.

"Yes, we're kin," Abbe said. "Aidan told me who you were."

206

"I thought… but I'm… your prisoner?"

"My…? Oh, no!" Abbe cried, half laughing. "Come here!" She wrapped Hild in her arms, whispering fiercely, "Our fathers were enemies but we are not. We are cousins. Even if we were, Aidan says we should love our enemies!"

Side by side on the pallet, they sobbed and laughed together in the firelight; a closeness Hild never thought she'd know again after losing her sister. For the first time she spilled out the story of her life and loss. In return Abbe recounted losing father and mother in infancy, and being torn away by her brothers to Iona, where she grew up with the nuns until Oswald brought her back home.

"My mother used to say all men dealt death," reflected Hild. "It's for women to bind up the torn threads, to be Peace-Weavers."

"Peace-Weaver. A lovely name," Abbe smiled. "That's what we'll be, you and I." She got up. "And our first task is to look for your son. Together."

Princess Abbe was loved by her people. Once she had explained to them that Hild was like the sister she'd never had, and had lost her son, they all joined in the search for a seven-year-old boy with golden hair and dark eyes. Fishermen scoured the shore, priests enquired around the homesteads, the steward tasked plough teams, charcoal burners, woodsmen and cowherds to spread the word. He even sent out huntsmen with hounds. Abbe instructed her guards to enquire at Bamburgh slave market and alert any of Oswy's troops they could find. She paid a merchant to run his ship along the coast promising a rich reward.

Hild was endlessly grateful. Yet the painful scene at the harbour preyed on her mind. What about all the other children herded away by men with whips? Who was comforting their mothers? How were the old men now? And was it mischievous Eata she'd seen? Surely, news would have filtered through if Wulfi were still alive. Stabs of pain caught her unawares, and a grinding, hollow yearning. But she could only wait.

Taking her usual place at Abbe's side in the Great Hall, Hild saw a familiar figure ushered to the seat of honour.

"Please sit there, Aidan," Abbe said. "I want to talk to you. I thought you brothers did your own work, yet I hear you've been buying slaves."

"Ah!" he twinkled. "Not slaves. Brothers."

"You mean like when you say we're all God's children? That sort of brother?"

Aidan chuckled as he shook his head. "Future brothers. Boys I hope to educate so that, God willing, they'll become monks. Better monks than me."

"Haven't you monks enough?" Abbe sighed dramatically.

"Lady Abbe, your brother's kingdom is vast!" He laughed at her teasing. "I'm father and bishop to every person in it. My brothers labour with me to the limit of their strength, and still we leave hearts cold. Especially among you Anglians. These boys will carry God's word to every one of Oswald's people." Vision and practicality. Hild was fascinated.

Later, he walked her to her lodging, chatting easily about his pilgrimage. "We're walking the Firth till we meet our brothers from Iona. King Oswald wants us among the Gododdin to do what we can to ease their suffering. For instance," he stopped and turned to her, his eyes sad in the moonlight, "search for your Wulfstan."

Hild gasped.

"A deep, unhealing wound for a mother," he said gently, leading her to her door. "Lady Hild, you are always in my prayers, you and your son. God knows where he is, and holds him in his loving care."

Tears rolled down her cheeks. Aidan curved his open palm over her head.

"Father, soothe this aching heart. Cradle her in your arms. Enfold her in your love." A caress, light as wind, stirred her hair.

Later that night, she saw him outlined on the clifftop, arms raised in prayer. For a long time he stood unmoving. Praying, she knew, for her. Bitterness and grief flowed from her, leaving a calm spirit waiting.

* * *

It was her duty. Ready to forge a new life, Hild strode firmly through the spring rain, hauling a laden donkey behind her. *Cerdic's alive*, Aidan had said, *and he needs you*. She remembered the pain in his eyes when he brought no news of Wulfi. And his comfort as she battled towards a kind of acceptance.

Abbe's affection had helped. She dragged Hild out each day to cheer the labourers buckling under Christmas preparations: a king's lodging slowly rising, a corral for meat on the hoof, stabling for horses, stores for wine and spices from the boats, poultry feathers drifting like snow.

Prince Oswy did not join his brother for the Holy Day, but King Oswald welcomed Hild. She was kin, Abbe explained, related through their mother. Hild was shocked by his lined face and heavy tread, and by Queen Cyneburg's anxious hovering. Abbe worked hard to give him ease. When the Bernician court reassembled for Midwinter, trailed by the usual mob of beggars, there was unspoken regret. Hild soon realized why.

"March on Deira this spring!" Oswy urged. "Recapture our old lands. Time's ripe, now you're established. More subjects, more tribute."

"And more enemies?" Oswald retorted wearily. "Brother, we've regained our own Bernicia, prosperity's increasing, our borders are secure, Deira bolsters us against Penda. Do you want the hornet to sting?"

"Penda's getting on," Oswy sulked. "Seems a good moment." Hild watched his exotic Rheged bride sink her fingers into his arm, and Oswald pointedly bandy riddles with his son. But it wouldn't end there, she knew. Just like Edi, Oswy hungered for power. And his men were restive.

"Look!" One jerked his head to draw attention to Oswald distributing alms.

"Best join the line," sneered his mate. "It's the only way to get gold and prove we're king's men."

"Whiteblade!" they sniggered. Whiteblade: Oswald's brilliant, deadly sword now seen as a charlatan's weapon, polished bright and bloodless. Oswald probably knew what was going on but, thank the gods, he stood firm.

Hild's donkey pulled on his rope, bringing her back to the present. She had left the Firth below and climbed to the bend in the Doon Hill track. Looking back, she waved farewell to the two horsemen who had escorted her from Princess Abbe's vill, and surveyed the familiar scene: her homefields with the stream below, the forest beyond, the cluster of family graves, and the old homestead.

But it had changed. A tall, angular building faced her, with new planks just starting to weather. The palisade had vanished, and the animals and storehouse. The ploughland was choked with weeds, the coppice sprouting. Oswy's men had visited.

Inside she could barely see. The stench hit her. Flies buzzed among damp floor reeds. There were no herbs, merely hay sagging over a beam. The fireless hearth bore no yeast box or cookpot, only a litter of scraps and half-burned logs. Her old chest leaned gaping, broken and pillaged.

Forewarned by Aidan she looked straight at Cerdic, lying on the ground in a streak of sunlight. A mighty blow had sliced down the left side of his body, leaving deep scars studded with scabs and bulbous pink sores. One ear had been lopped off and the eye socket puckered over a sagging mouth. His left arm was truncated and the fingers of his sword hand were splayed. A useless carcass, glaring, repellent. Hild swallowed.

"My lord!" In a stride she knelt beside him and lifted his hand to her lips. His face contorted at the traditional homage and jerked away.

She waited, keeping hold of his hand, fully aware he would rather be dead. Cruel irony: of all people, she was least welcome, symbol of his humiliation, embodiment of his Anglian conquerors. *Be patient*, Aidan had said, *he needs your strength*.

"I've come home." She squeezed his shoulder and rose briskly. Stirring the embers, she heaped the scant logs into a pile which would catch, filled a chipped pot with wine from her pack and set it to warm. She unloaded the donkey, piled the crossbeams with food she'd brought, and tossed her bundle into a corner. From the water bucket, the only sign of a living home, she poured water into a bowl. On the window ledge was a broken axe-head, the sole blade except for the knife in her girdle. All other iron – pans and cauldron, pick and ploughshare – had disappeared: booty for Oswy's spearmen, those experts in dealing lingering death, divesting a home of life.

Cerdic followed her movements, glancing repeatedly to the door. Her heart sank. The news would crush him. He must be stronger before he knew.

Rolling her cloak, she bolstered him and fed him flatbread dipped in mulled wine. His fingers were stiff and swollen, swallowing was hard, he seemed unable to speak. But when she wiped his fingers, he pressed her hand, lying back with a sigh, and instantly fell asleep. Wearily she curled on the floor at his side.

"Dratted goose, gone again!"

Hild started up. Two lumpy figures rolled sacks from their shoulders, and stopped in the doorway, staring.

"Begu?" Hild scrambled to her feet.

"Lady Hild!" Limping towards her, a muffled figure wrapped Hild in a damp embrace. "Oh, lady, you've come home!"

"Caitlin!" Hild held her tight, voice wobbling. "Little Caitlin!"

"How long have you waited? I'll soon have a meal for you, lady." Begu slapped things onto the window shelf. "We've been foraging. Fish, beans – only a handful, they're scarce – bartered for goose eggs."

"Begu!" Hild gripped her raw, cold hands. "Let me help."

"Caitlin helps now. Go find that goose, Caitlin, before you cast your cloak." She waved the axe and Caitlin slipped outside. "Brigit's with her son. Rohan is – well…" As she chopped, Begu slipped into the old familiarity, oblivious to the squalor. That, more than anything, brought home to Hild their abject want.

"Rohan's old and frightened," Begu rattled on. "Farmhands lost in the fighting. A gash with the pick. Couldn't cope. Don't expect anything of him." She dropped the chopped roots into the chipped pot on the fire. "Young Rohan's going to put together a plough.

He'll come up with a borrowed ox when he can. Well, that's what he keeps saying, but…" She sighed noisily.

"Any news of Eata?" Hild asked.

"Must be the worst."

"I saw a chain gang. Prisoners, one redhead. I'm not sure…" Hild's voice choked.

"Lord Cutha brought Cerdic home. He'd been left for dead. They went there after… you know, in case…" She spoke as if he weren't there. "Cutha rebuilt our homeplace. It was gutted. He brings meat when they've hunted. Where's Wulfi?"

"I don't know." Hild put a finger to her lips. Begu stared with wide eyes. "They're searching…"

An unearthly howl enveloped them, hollow keening like a wolf. Cerdic, jaw fixed in a ghastly rictus, stared.

"Hush, my lord!" Begu hurried over and mopped his eye and nose. "We knew in our hearts, didn't we?" She cradled him like an infant, rocking and crooning.

"He was with me down the cliff." Hild faced them stiffly. "He was with me in the boat. After that…"

"Hope's been keeping him alive," Begu said bleakly.

* * *

"Poor lame Caitlin" was their strength. She bartered the luxuries Hild had brought, directed the building of a goose pen and a donkey shed, bullied her brother into ploughing, dug a vegetable plot, begged a piglet, and stirred Begu to tend the pen.

Only one thing brought balm to Cerdic. Again and again he asked for the story.

"We went last. Crawled down the cliff. Not a sound." Hild built the drama, hid her pain. "An enemy spearman lurked in the scrub. What do you think he did, Wulfi? Just like you." She shook her head. "He charged. Wulfi charged! Lunged forward. Tried to protect me. Wulfi! You should have seen him; you'd have been so proud."

Cerdic's mouth twisted.

212

With better food he grew strong enough to lean against the wallboards, then to sit near the fire, and eventually, with help, to reach the bench outside. There he watched the sprouting crop, the antics of the goslings, and Hild weeding. He took a few shaky steps, leaning on all three of them, to the earth mounds where the gate had stood.

But nothing healed his mind. The men, on rare days of field work, averted their eyes. The carpenter and the potter's boy spoke to the women and hurried away. Hild sighed. Men! Fierce for a fight, cowardly before the abnormal. Like the shipyard leather worker his mates dubbed "weird". She wondered what folk called Cerdic now. Only the visiting priests spoke directly to him, sitting either side, sipping sour ale.

"We pray for you, brother…"

"You may raise your eyebrow," said with a chuckle, "but we pray you grow in grace."

"Know God beside you, a friend, close as us."

Cerdic gave no sign, but Hild was heartened.

"Any news of Aidan?" she asked.

"Busy training his boys."

"Getting thinner. Walks miles, spends whole nights in prayer. Where he gets the strength…"

"The king gave him a horse…"

"But he gave it away…"

"To a lame man!"

They all laughed. The tides may swirl, as the riddle said, but Aidan was a rock.

Cutha came when he could. One day he arrived with stag meat and his son, Cuthbert, rosy-cheeked and fair. Hild's first thought was for Cerdic, watching another man's child. Then she noticed the boy, dismounting clumsily while Cutha stood by, thin grey hair blowing in the wind.

"It's the legs." He turned his back to face Hild. "He won't be helped."

"For you." The boy limped to Hild and handed her two brown fleeces, still matted with twigs, and a bag of wool-clippings.

213

"Cuthbert, just what we need." Hild bent to take them and, as he lifted his face to hers, gave him a kiss. "Warmth for winter," she said shakily over his shoulder.

"I'm a shepherd," he said proudly. "May I see your animals?"

"He has a way with beasts." Cutha followed Hild indoors to fetch some ale. "Roves the hills with the flock. I'm sending him to board over near Melrose. Save him struggling home each night."

"You'll miss him."

"But he's ready to go," Cutha shrugged. "He can't follow me, and he gets under his stepmother's feet. His friends are a rowdy crew!" Sadness and pride battled in his eyes. "Besides, he's made friends with the monks. They tell me he has an aptitude. He can recite chunks of Gospel. You ask him."

"I think he's busy," Hild said in wonder. Cuthbert was swinging his legs, sitting beside Cerdic on the bench, prattling away. And Cerdic – Cerdic was smiling!

Man's talk did Cerdic good: the crops, Cutha's new wife, child on the way, the fighting season, Penda on the move again, Oswald forced to muster.

"Oh, no!" Hild's thoughts flew to Abbe: both her brothers at risk, probably Oswald's boy too. Not her own Wulfstan, though: one small mercy.

"Land campaign," Cutha said. "Mercians near Gwynedd, so the king's moving west."

"Useless!" Cerdic thumped his knee.

"Me too, old friend," Cutha sighed. "Oswald's never used me like Edwin. I'm left at home."

Stories trickled through: a cargo ship saw Bamburgh in flames, merchants reported the palace at Yeavering razed.

"Yeavering, only two days' march!" Cerdic sent Caitlin to bid Rohan sharpen his sword. Hild said nothing.

No news before winter. Nothing till spring, when the monks got through. King Oswald had been killed in the battle.

"Massive blow to the neck," they said. "Penda nailed up his head and hands…"

"Oswald's tree, they call it…"

"Because of the miracles. A paralysed girl, a man's arm…"

"Even a horse!"

"A good end," Cerdic sighed. The priests agreed: thinking of the miracles, Hild supposed. Aidan taught there was no barrier between life and after-life. Oswald would have believed that too. She simply grieved for a good man.

Their life was humdrum. Hild worked to keep thoughts of Wulfi at bay. She tended the stock, weeded the fields, ground herbs, brewed ale, and served Cerdic. Not often was she free to climb to the hawthorn on the ridge. Eostre's ribbons flapped grey and wan, a faded reminder of the early years.

Her battered Gospel book was always with her. Ethelburga could never have foreseen the power of her gift to shield Hild from pain. In its pages she met a companion, walking with her through the fields, sampling the grain, watching the fruit ripen, admiring the flowers. He sailed over the water and climbed in the hills, weathered storms and begged water in the heat. He loved people, told stories, made jokes, and helped the sick in body or mind. He called God his father, like Aidan, and treated all men as brothers. And he promised his friends they'd stay in his father's care in life and death. She hoped he was real, this God, and that, as Aidan declared, Wulfi was in his hands.

* * *

She was under her tree when she saw a rider galloping from the east. As he branched up their track, she hitched up her skirts and ran down to Cerdic at the door. He asked for his sword. She bit her lip – it was a warrior's instinct – and took her stand beside him.

"Lady Hild?" The man jumped down, looping his reins over a tree. Long hair and jewelled swordbelt: a royal thegn. "I come from Princess Abbe."

"Begu, bring some ale," Hild called and turned back to him. "How is she?"

"In good health, lady. Her greetings and a message: will you come to her? My fellow is following with a horse if you choose to ride back with us."

"What's wrong?" rasped Cerdic laboriously.

"Nothing, my lord." The man bowed. "The lady promises a surprise."

"My thanks to your lady," Hild said, "but my life lies here now." It took their combined strength to raise Cerdic. How could she leave? Except… "Oh! Is it my son?"

"I'm sorry." He shook his head. When Begu appeared, he gratefully downed the ale and went to water his horse.

"You must go," Cerdic insisted hoarsely. "Bring news." She shook her head and put a finger to her lips. The thegn was at the nearby water barrel.

"Speak up, lass!" Begu propelled Caitlin towards them. "She's got an idea, lady." Shyly Caitlin suggested the smith should come and stay. He could leave young Rohan in charge of the forge.

"I like the smith," snapped Cerdic. "Good. Go pack your bag."

It was a fast and exhilarating ride. Hild arrived glowing, windswept, and stiff. In the two years she'd been away, the place had changed. Spearmen manned the gate in a defensive earth wall, the leather tents were back, spilling outside it, thegns galloped on errands, herdsmen butchered behind the cookhouse: King Oswy must be there.

"Hild! You've come!" Abbe ran to embrace her, tangling the reins and giggling like a girl. Taking Hild's bundle she led the way. "You're bedding with me. We're pressed for space. Oswy's here."

"I saw the transformation," Hild chuckled.

"His doing, mostly. Fit for a royal, he says. Silly oaf!" A shadow clouded her face. "I miss Oswald – you heard? Oswy's rescued his remains, thank goodness!"

They ducked under the lintel. Abbe's lodging had not changed. Flopping down on a stool, Hild recaptured her bundle.

"Mud to a swamp!" she quipped, unwrapping a guest gift of goose eggs and Gododdin wine. They laughed at the ill-suited proverb.

"You didn't need…" Abbe hugged her tight. "Are things very hard? The monks said… No. We'll keep that for later. You must dress for the feast. Oswy's brought his new queen. A political alliance, as you'd expect. But she's lovely. Only a slip of a girl."

Hild half listened as she unrolled her simple tunic, wool dyed with moss, her own lumpy handwork, including the braid round the neck and sleeves. For the first time in ages, she looked in a mirror: shadows under her eyes, springy dark hair, preposterous for a woman nearing thirty. Impatiently she spread a linen square over her head and anchored it with braid and hairpin.

"Mongrel to pedigree, beside you," she sighed wryly, looking at Abbe's casual elegance, "but it'll do."

They ran to the royal lodging. Hild stood in the doorway to catch her breath, and clung there in shock: one woman was combing the queen's long fair hair, another waited with a gold circlet, a third fitted her slippers, a fourth shook out a fur-lined cloak and the woman in charge hung a cross round her neck and handed her emeralds for her ears. Hild had stepped back in time.

Seeing Abbe, the queen turned, and cried, "Hild, my Hild! At last!" She leapt to her feet, scattering attendants, upsetting her stool. Flinging her arms round Hild, she held her close. "It's me," she whispered. "Don't you know me? Little Ani."

"Ani?" Hild stood helpless with shock. "I thought… Ani?"

"The screamy baby," Anfled chuckled in her ear. "Hild, how wonderful you came!" She swung round with a flourish. "Ladies, Princess Hild of Deira, my earliest friend. She was at my birth and baptism. Closer to me than my mother."

"You're not supposed to weep," Abbe chortled at Hild's shoulder.

"You never said…" Hild snuffled.

"Thank you, ladies. I'll manage now." Anfled sent the women chattering out, and drew Hild to the fire. "Oh, how I hoped…! Abbe knows – don't you, Abbe?"

"Ani… I'd no idea!" Hild was overcome. "You've changed." Her inane comment sent the three of them into fits of laughter.

"I mean… a fine princess of… seventeen, is it? You're so like Ethelburga: even the emeralds."

"They're hers. Mother died two years ago."

"Oh, I'm sorry." They fell silent for a moment. "And the boys?"

"We all escaped to Canterbury. But Mother thought they were still too close to danger. She sent them overseas, to a German cousin. They died of plague." She shook her head sadly.

"But you…" Hild hugged her afresh. "You came through it all."

"I've news for you. I met your nephew, Aldwulf, when I came through East Anglia."

"Aldwulf? Oh, Heri's boy."

"Yes, king of East Anglia now."

"And Heri? She's with him?"

"No."

"Ah," Hild nodded. Only to be expected; Heri was the elder.

"No, no." Anfled read her face. "That's what I wanted to tell you. She's retired to a religious house."

"Religious? Heri?" Heri, who cartwheeled down slopes and cavorted in the watermeadows!

"At Chelles, near Paris. Customary for East Anglian dowagers, apparently. Aldwulf says she's happily settled."

Feeling as plain as a dunnock among finches, Hild sat at table beside the queen. When Anfled took round the guest cup, Oswy bowed coldly across the vacant seat and she bowed back. But her eyes were all for Ani, serving the Mercian envoys, and the Rheged men who had come with Oswy's first queen, and the thegns from her own land of Kent.

"She does it well," she murmured proudly, "like her mother. It's a delicate task."

"Oswy's so relieved to have Kent on side," Abbe whispered back, "and a stronger link with Deira."

When Ani returned to her seat, it was to Hild she turned. "D'you remember the wooden horse we played with?" Reminiscing, questioning, listening.

218

"You're tough," Abbe exclaimed as they retired with the queen. "I never knew all that about your past."

The three women chatted far into the night and rose bleary-eyed for prayers with Anfled's dark-robed chaplain. It reminded Hild of Paulinus, and his monks' musical chanting, powerful as an amulet; more beautiful, but more impersonal, than the prayers of the bustling monks who cherished Cerdic. It was the same Christ, she reminded herself: only men and customs differed.

* * *

The east wind blew her home, with rain clouds veiling the hills. She climbed the Doon Hill track feeling refreshed, as if she'd been away a long time. Cerdic's pallor was ghastly as he watched her escorts unload foodstuffs, a fur-lined cloak for him, and a bundle of trinkets for barter. His face lit up only when the smith said he'd come again with the new coulter they'd planned.

The months resumed their pattern and time dragged. Under her tree, Hild hugged her knees in delight at the affection of Queen Ani and Abbe. She hoped Oswy appreciated his wife and sister. The very name made her shudder: Oswy, wrecker of her lord, her son, and her livelihood. *Love your enemies*, said the man in her Gospel book. How could she? *Act as if you do and it comes in time*: that was old Gerda, wife of the Gododdin chief, when Hild first wed Cerdic. Well, she grunted, she'd remember Oswy with his family and leave the rest to Aidan's God.

Cerdic grew gaunter. She only noticed at seasonal rituals – blessing the bounds, spring sowing, harvest – when she looked back to past years. She tried not to notice the steps in his decline: the day he couldn't reach the bench, couldn't sit, or roll over, or chew.

"Clean and comfortable – that's what matters," she jollied the women, hiding her distress. But he fidgeted, even inside Abbe's soft furs, and started to refuse food.

"Why?" he groaned.

"For me." She touched him tenderly, putting the cup to his lips, aching with his pain. "Courage isn't only for battle," she whispered.

"You are a gallant lord, and I honour you."

Mutton broth, herbal infusions, precious French wine. Weakness, pain, despair. Sleep, when it was a good day; the sullen prospect of bare beams when it wasn't. She sat by him, held his hand, and willed her strength into him.

Several winters passed, when ice bound the ground and food was scarce. Aidan's monks slithered up the track. No, Deira had not yielded to Oswy. Yes, Penda still threatened. Better news than that: Queen Anfled had a baby boy. *With healthy lungs*, they said, and Hild's face cracked in a rare smile. She recalled her struggles with Ani's infant screams. Aidan led the thanksgiving and name-giving, the monks said. Egfrid, the baby was called: Prince Egfrid.

And they brought Aidan's loving greetings. Loving greetings! On a sharp winter night like this, long ago, she'd watched Aidan praying on the clifftop, against all reason, for her. What a gift he had of spreading comfort!

The monks surrounded Cerdic in the usual way. One of them held a flask of holy oil. He anointed Cerdic and the men prayed quietly together, one of them taking Hild's hand to include her.

"Come, sister," he said afterwards, and led her outside.

"I feel useless," she sighed. "He's suffered so long, and so much." Six years' indignity, she thought – as long as his exile, and none of the warrior's glory.

"You've given him everything you could," the monk said gently. "Food, potions, strength of your body, love of your heart. Now he's weary. It's time to let him go. His soul is waiting to fly to its maker."

Numb with tiredness, she brooded on the bench. Snow thudded from the trees, ice cracked in the stream. Begu brought her cloak and put it round her shoulders. Hild was wrapped in regrets; her love had been too weak. Her throat tightened and her head drooped. A fiery sun was dropping fast when Begu took her hand.

"Lord Cerdic's gone," she murmured. "Very peaceful, lady. The monks held his hands and he gave one big sigh. They're washing his poor body."

Hild could not weep. She gripped Begu's hands and watched the light fade.

"He's ready, lady," said the monk's quiet voice.

Cerdic lay on his back in a crisp tunic. His dignity had returned, the haughty nose and stern jaw. She saw again his fierce defiance, his loyalty to his chief and people, his bravery. And she remembered the way he kept his word.

The smith and young Rohan hacked out a grave near his brothers, where the gate had been. After she'd placed Cerdic's sword and spear beside him, they bore him out and laid him there. Simply, the monks prayed over his body, the men put the earth back and heaped on stones they'd gathered to keep him safe from roving beasts.

In the past, she thought, they'd have shipped him across the water to Valhalla and a warrior's welcome. The Christian heaven was harder to see: fragrant meadows and sweet music, said some; or a valley between ice and fire where the soul was judged; or a banquet spread by angels. Then she remembered Aidan describing Wulfi *in God's loving care*. Hild clung to the words. Her family, in God's arms.

"Take your time, sister," said the monks as they left. "Wait on God."

She waited. The goats came into milk, frosts melted and buds swelled, boats launched, eiderducks flirted, cattle surged to pasture. In the township below, smoke billowed from bonfires of soiled floor rushes, hammers thudded with spring repairs, young women giggled as they beat their linen. Still she waited, bereft, and aimless.

Stories drifted into her mind: Jesus healing the little sick girl; raising his friend from the tomb; painting death as the entrance to God's homestead where there were lodgings enough for all who loved him. And she remembered about the Holy Spirit, *let loose in the world, alighting where it is wanted*. God's spirit of peace.

And then she knew what she would do.

PART 3

10

BETWEEN TWO WORLDS

She sagged onto a coil of thick rope, deafened by the quayside din. Sails cracked, animals brayed, sacks thudded, an adze shrieked along a plank, ships knocked against stanchions, and labourers cursed. She breathed in pitch, dung, spices, sweat, and sea.

Serene on its rock against scudding clouds, the fortress hid behind its wooden walls. Carts jostled down and up to the gates. Drivers lashed whips and oxen tossed horns at dodging pedestrians. Across the harbour she saw Lindisfarne: Aidan's home now, they said, near enough to the king, but a place of peace when the tide ran high. Stretching towards it like a longing arm was the spit of sand where she'd dreamed her girlhood dreams and frolicked with Wulfi. Bamburgh.

A month ago they'd left Doon Hill, bucking round the coast in a fat-bellied coaster which bartered at every inlet. She'd secured onward passage on a merchant vessel among the skins and hunting hounds to be exchanged for cinnamon and holy books. The crew sat on the staithe patching the sail.

"Lady, look who's here!" Begu thrust sturdily towards her, working her elbows, rosy with effort. Following with her basket was an upright figure, lean and bronzed, white hair whipped by the wind.

"Cutha!" Hild tripped over her bag and landed in his arms.

"You look better!" Laughing, he set her on her feet.

"More white hairs," she chuckled.

"But vitality in your eyes. Where are you off to?"

"Paris. My sister – you remember Hereswid? She's followed the East Anglian custom. Gone to a house of prayer. We're joining her."

"The fashionable choice," he nodded. "My Cuthbert had the same impulse. He's with the brothers at Melrose now. Prayer, study, peace. I envy you."

"But you're with the king?"

He nodded, looking up at the fortress. "We've just arrived. Won't you come and see Queen Anfled?"

She hesitated. To see Ani one last time! "We leaving on the evening tide. I daren't let the ship go. There's no word of another for East Anglia."

"Where's my man?" Cutha scoured the crowd. "Ardal, here! Ardal will safeguard Begu and your goods, and load them when the shipmaster's ready. We'll be there and back before tide-turn. Come!"

As they forged a path between the ox carts, Hild fed him scraps of news: one of Oswy's thegns had built a new hall on the Firth at the river mouth; Caitlin ran the homestead; the smith kept the land in good shape. Pausing for breath, she gasped at contorted stumps of blackened wood where the mighty gates had stood.

"Penda," grunted Cutha. "It's a miracle it's no worse. He fired the defences. Aidan saw the flames from Lindisfarne. Would you believe, he prayed and the wind turned."

Here was the concourse where she first saw Cerdic, the women's lodging where she'd slept; everything the same, even the chaos of arrival. Weaving between the queen's gaping chests, she shivered at the memory of Edi's villainy and Bass's plans for escape.

"Hild!" Queen Anfled opened her arms. "Why not come to me now? Shed your burdens, live an honoured life in my household. I'd love you to help rear this imp."

Hild chuckled, lifting Egfrid onto her knee. The pull was strong – love, nostalgia, weariness? At thirty-three, she was nearly as old as her mother when she died. But life pulsed strong in her. She must be free, stretch her mind, unravel the knots in her thinking, nurture her dried-up spirit. The prince in her Gospel, who died for his people like an Anglian king but lived, like Aidan, as one of the poor – she must seek him out.

"Regrets?" Cutha asked as they walked back. The wind had swung offshore.

"Of course. Parting for the last time…"

"She's doing well, Queen Anfled. Good for Oswy, and the people love her."

"It's you I meant. Do you realize you've been at every crossroads in my life – always there, always my friend?" They reached the quay. Hild placed her hand in his.

"We shall meet again," he said. "Here – or hereafter." The faith for which she struggled burned strong in him.

Begu was crouched on a bundle of ship's canvas under the curve of the prow. Hild raised her eyebrows at a nearby satchel and pannier.

"Still on the quay," Begu pointed. "A priest and a king's messenger. Safe company, I thought."

At a sudden hail from the master, dockhands loosed the ropes. Laughing, the two men leaped aboard, nearly missing their footing, and stumbled forward in a tangle of raised oars. The ship pulled gently away, nosing through anchored vessels. Hild stood at the bow, looking into the future.

* * *

Beyond the harbour mouth, the master rigged the sail and they sliced like a sword down the Bernician coast. A day later, south of the saltpans, they sailed by moonlight past the high crags of Deira. Bernicians were not welcome there – only Aidan because of his friendship with Oswine, the king. The crags gave way to little bays, one with upturned fisherboats reminding Hild of the poor herring woman years ago. While Begu snored, she drifted, buoyant, poised like a star between one world and the next.

Rounding Humber sandspit, they saw deep-sea vessels standing in the tidal stream like cattle, fly-bitten by skiffs. Hild and Begu wandered among the market stalls where men touted swords, sheepskins or slaves, and warehousemen tossed winejars hand to hand. The women sniffed peppercorns and fingered ginger roots.

Rain squalls drove them down the coast of Lindsey. Wet through, they crouched under the prow as the ship tossed crazily, the sail cracked, and the steering oar juddered. Skittering horses broke their legs and were flung overboard, dogs howled eerily, and the crew took to the oars again, warming the women with their toiling bodies.

"Like riding a colt," called Hild from the bulkhead. Begu spewed, the priest prayed, and the king's messenger lay prone. The master pulled under the lee of a promontory and they found themselves becalmed in a sea of mud.

"East Anglia." The priest pointed south to a grey smudge on the horizon.

"Fat spider," grunted the messenger, "waiting for wealth to drop into its web."

"At peace for a generation," explained the priest, "well placed for trade…"

"… when the tide comes in," snapped the king's man.

Landing at a riverside wharf, Hild and Begu plodded through a dripping township to the royal hall. King Aldwulf was the nephew Hild had never seen.

"My lord." She bowed formally to a young man with Heri's blue eyes and gold hair. "We thank you for granting us hospitality for the sake of my sister, Hereswid." She couldn't stop herself adding, "You look so like her!"

"I cannot say the same of you, lady," Aldwulf guffawed and his Companions sniggered. Hild flushed, conscious of her dark colouring and simple dress. "Welcome to our court," he continued in a lordly way, leaning back to belch. A male society, Hild realized, with his mother gone.

"May I? As mark of our kinship?" Poring over a box of dazzling finery, he selected a rope of amber beads to pin across her chest. "You will stay the winter," he stated. "No one will sail till spring."

The steward housed them comfortably, and they enjoyed the interlude, walking by the river, gathering berries, reading from Hild's Gospel book and chatting by the hearth. What would it be like, to live in a house of prayer? What would they do?

In the short, dark days of Yule, no one expected a battered vessel to berth. A thegn ran out of the hall, calling his men to seize the ship. When he reported back, the king announced, "It seems, my lady, to be some kind of priest for you."

Hild excused herself and, taking Begu, crossed the compound with the steward and a guard. At her lodging, surrounded by spearmen, stood a hooded figure in the pale garb of a northern monk.

"You bring news for me?" She stretched out a welcoming hand.

"Lady Hild?" He put his icy hand in hers and bowed. "My name is Utta and I come from Lindisfarne."

"Come into the warm, brother." She nodded dismissal to the guards. Begu prodded the embers and the sudden flare revealed a man with a shaven forehead, thin face and long, cold nose.

"It couldn't wait, sister." Utta wrapped his hands round the cup Begu offered. "Aidan sent me because I know the way. I sailed here to bring Queen Anfled to her marriage with King Oswy. Now he hopes I'll fetch you. Aidan asks you, implores you, to turn back."

The logs crackled, the door rattled.

"But Aidan knows," Hild gasped, "I'm following my sister to a house of prayer. I want to see her and know God."

"Know God, and serve him? That is your wish?"

She nodded. Utta hugged his cup and wrinkled his brow.

"What if God chooses differently?" he said, with a loud sniff. Begu passed him a wad of spinning wool and he blew his cold nose. "God speaks through his workers, men like Aidan, and Aidan needs you. Could this be God, calling you where he wants you?"

"Why should Aidan need me?" Hild seized on the sentence she understood. "He knows I was reared to the old gods, and struggle with this new belief. What could I ever do for Aidan, let alone his God?"

"Do you remember Christ saying: *Whatever you do for one of my children, you do it for me*?" Utta waited for her to nod. "*Whatever*." He thumped his knee in emphasis. "Whatever gifts people have, Christ uses them. Aidan's gift is his passion. He lives to spread the knowledge of Christ. He needs help."

In Utta, Hild glimpsed Aidan's burning eyes, and felt his fervour, gentle, yet fierce.

"He needs help of all kinds," the monk continued. "People to tell Christ's story. People to live out God's love. People able to see and seize the moment. Sister, I do not know you. I cannot say what Aidan has in mind. I only know he is a leader I am proud to follow, and he says he needs you."

She couldn't turn back now...

But Aidan. Aidan drew her, as he always had.

She'd nothing to give Aidan; she'd leaned on him...

But if he was calling for her...

Live quietly till the end, or labour for Aidan?

Her thoughts swung like a leadsman's weight.

"What's it to be, Begu?" she asked, as they lay in the dark. "On? Or back?"

"My place is with you, lady. Whatever you decide."

* * *

They ran fast before the westerlies while Utta talked about Aidan's vision and the obstacles he faced: language, the old gods, and the Anglian warrior culture based on riches.

"And he only has us. His boys, he calls us, a mix of Anglian and British."

"You're one of the slaves he bought?"

He nodded. "Our first task was to learn each other's language. God needs all tongues, he said."

Hild remembered how King Oswald's translations hampered Aidan's teaching. "What else did you learn?" she asked. Would Aidan expect the same of her?

"He hoped we'd become monks," Utta replied eagerly, "but only if we chose. So we learned the Latin of the Scriptures – psalms, Gospels and so on – reading and memorizing, writing, rhetoric…"

"Persuasion, you mean," she said wryly.

"… history, worship." Strange schooling for young lads more suited to the forest camps. They would have been – what? – fifteen? – ten years ago.

"But boys should be boys, Aidan said, so we played football. I was never much good." Utta grimaced. "Eata always got the ball off me."

"Eata? A fiery redhead?"

"Yes. Toned down now, of course. He's…"

"He's still alive? Eata? Begu, did you hear? Eata, our Eata. He's alive!" And she wouldn't have known if she hadn't turned back. Did it mean hope for Wulfi?

"He's a monk now, like me. Destined for Melrose, an area he knows. Was that where you knew him?" Hild nodded, grinning broadly at the absurdity of Eata as a holy man.

They'd reached the Humber without realizing. A skiff rowed out and someone hailed the boat and scrambled aboard.

"Easy to pick you out," he gasped. "Aidan's broken-down old tub!"

"Cedd!" Utta laughed. "At least it floats. Where're you heading?"

"God knows," Cedd shrugged, "or Aidan. We're to look out for him at the saltpans."

"Monster aboard!" hallooed a crewman. "Get ready to bail out!"

Cedd roared with laughter. An easy-going giant with the domed forehead and long hair of a monk, he worked his way through the oarsmen, slapping them on the back. Grabbing an oar, he threw off his robe and sat on the bench, pulling with the best, as far as the desolate estuary. Then he and Utta stood scanning the shore as they nosed into the tip of Bernicia.

"Anchor!" Cedd let out a deafening bellow. "Aidan! Over here!" Jumping overboard with a splash as mighty as the anchor stone, he strode shoreward breast-deep, shouting and waving. Aidan started to wade into the shallows. Cedd lifted him bodily and carried him back until the crew stretched out their arms and hauled him aboard.

"You've come!" Aidan cried as he spotted Hild. "God be praised!" Wringing out his skirts, he edged to the prow and crouched beside her in the yawing boat.

She smiled at his enthusiasm. "I'm not sure why."

"To be a beacon," he stated promptly. "To beam God's light and love to men."

"How could I ever…?"

"Be yourself," he replied. Rather airily, she thought.

"How?"

"The life you lead. That sort of thing." His voice was gruff with excitement. "Caring for people. Searching for God. Studying, thinking, simplifying…."

"But I don't have faith… knowledge…"

"And the way you talk with people. As equals, in an ordinary way." He paused, relaxing into his deep, warm tone. "You can't see with my eyes, sister. The faith and knowledge you worry about – I can see them growing in you. You're just what I need. And you came!" he said again, in wonder. "Thanks be to God."

"But… What do you want me to do?"

"Ah! Some preparation first. What will be new is learning to pray and keep the hours, just as you would in France. A short period of training, then… *infect* the community!" Hild as plague. They laughed. "We'll help you, I and my travelling priests. Men like Utta and Cedd. If at year's end you still wish to go to your sister, I promise I will get you there."

* * *

A small homestead, Aidan had said, at the mouth of the River Wear. They arrived at dusk. Next morning, she wandered down to the river. It was still too dark to see the sea, but she could smell it beyond the woods which sheltered her new home. Aidan's boat bumped against the jetty, willows rustled along the river, and startled ducks quacked indignantly.

God, you are my strength; at dawn will I rise to you. The priests had recited this litany on the boat. Today, for the first time, standing over the burbling water and watching the light spread, she made it her own.

A door banged behind her, a lantern wove through the gloom. She turned and strode purposefully indoors: the first day of her new life.

After morning prayers and a crust with a cup of ale, Utta sat with Hild to explain the daily pattern of worship, and how the prayers and readings matched. Blows of the axe, Cedd bawling measurements, farmhands groaning as they heaved beams into place for a chapel, drowned out his words. Utta led Hild upstream to a spot where the willows soughed gently. Lowering himself to the ground, he placed two well-worn books carefully on his skirts.

"I'm leaving you these," he said, opening the heavier tome with effort. "This is a book of psalms, holy songs. Jesus sang them himself, like all Jews. Each time we worship, we chant some – here, I've made you a list. Some we chant each day. Every dawn, for instance, at the daily service of Lauds, we sing these four great songs of praise." He turned to the end of the book. Hild bent to look at the even columns of curved writing. "Some psalms are angry," he went on, "some fearful, some joyous; the whole of human emotion is here. Try reading this short one."

"*Praise the Lord, serve the Lord with gladness, know that the Lord is God…*" Hild read hesitantly, but found with delight that as she ran her finger along the line, she could read and understand the Latin words.

"Excellent! You've a clear, deep voice," Utta beamed. "Now, the Gospel, the story of Jesus' life. You have one of those, I believe?" She nodded. "So, here's something different, shorter." He laid on her lap a flat folio. "The story of Ezra. He lived at a time when the Jews were divided, like Bernicia and Deira, and he was trying to re-establish the law of God. A bit like Aidan. Let me show you."

As he turned the pages and summarized the columns of writing, Hild leaned forward, picking nervously at the grass; Utta couldn't possibly appreciate how little she knew. But when he moved on to prayers, she relaxed. This was just like reading Brother James's prayer book when she was a girl.

Cedd's mighty shout called them to noon worship. They passed boatmen quaffing ale and a couple of fieldmen, tools discarded, chewing their tack in the shade. Indoors, Aidan read the midday office before they shared a simple meal.

"Utta's a clever chap," Cedd said fondly to Hild, "but let me show you what we've been doing." He led her into a plain wooden building, like a store.

"Fragrant!" she murmured, breathing in the scents of new wood and beaten earth. It had a cool, clean feel. Her chapel.

Cedd pointed to the single window, a roundel high over the door.

"The evening sun will strike through there onto the altar," he said, tracing an arc over his head to the worked stone set in an alcove at the front. "See the seven carved crosses? A great way to focus the mind."

"Empty crosses," she murmured, "because Christ rose…"

"Yes, and is still alive. You don't have to come in here to speak with him. He's all around." Cedd's arms wheeled. "But a special place can help." She nodded, remembering her tree. "Somewhere to join everyone's prayers together… once the thatch is on!"

Wandering to the altar, Hild recognized the book of Psalms. "Beautiful," she breathed, turning the pages. The leaves were velvety, the columns straight, the writing even, and each capital was the colour of blood. Lifting one side of the heavy volume, she closed it, letting her fingers run over the tooled leather cover. Cedd smiled at her pleasure.

"Our brothers love to beautify God's word," he said.

In the following days, Cedd introduced her to the crops, the fieldworkers and the riverfolk. God was in the whole of life, he said. Typically, he knew everyone's name. Utta sat with her, drafting a study plan. And every evening, Aidan prayed with her, and talked about faith and prayer. As her knowledge and understanding grew, so did her confidence.

But one morning, Utta gave her a shock.

"Not everyone will know the Lord's Prayer," he said. "You'll need some copies of that, and the Apostles' Creed. Let's make a start." Setting down a quill and a pot of oak-ink, he asked for a fair copy of the alphabet. Hild fingered the feather.

"I haven't done much writing," she sighed. "Well, none, really. There's been no need. But if Aidan thinks it necessary, I'll do my best." Biting her lip, she leaned forward and copied her first letters.

Credo in unum Deum… Surprisingly soon she was, slowly and laboriously, writing the familiar Latin words. *I believe in one God…* And she really did, she realized with amazement. It had taken an age to shake off Thor and the fear of woods and thunderclaps, but at last she was winning through. Her new God did not mete out erratic punishments. He loved her as his daughter.

"The Creed, summary of Christian belief," Utta explained. "That and Jesus' model prayer. The two basics." And with a new clarity she understood why each convert must take them to heart before being baptized. She remembered her mother and Cutha, and a lump came into her throat. How thrilled Lady Breguswid would have been!

Aidan planned to consecrate the new chapel before he left. Hild went there early and stood tracing the beams under the thatch, and wrinkling her nose at the stink of tallow. Cedd was right: a crimson glow from the west shone like God's blessing on the carved altar crosses but the winter sun struck low, through the open door.

A small sound made her turn: Begu watching from the back corner. Hild was stricken. Engrossed in learning, she had overlooked the enormity of this step for her loyal companion. Remorsefully she went over and took Begu's hand. They would stand together in the ceremony.

There was a heartiness in the priests' responses that night; relief in a job complete, perhaps, or the urge to protect the women with a wall of prayer. They processed round the building inside and out, reciting and sprinkling the holy water of purification. In the earth floor they inscribed alphabets to ensure a godly foundation, chanting *Unless the Lord build the house, they labour in vain who build it.* Aidan reminded them how God called the prophet Isaiah, filling the Temple with smoke to reveal his presence, and prayed that the Spirit of the Lord would fill the chapel and inspire the women.

Hild and Begu knelt before him and, with Utta and Cedd raising their arms in prayer, Aidan laid his hand in blessing on their heads. Silently, Hild begged Christ to give her the faith she'd need.

* * *

Homestead rhythms were the same the world over, governed by livestock and crops. In this woodland clearing which the sun reached briefly, the fieldmen worked harder than in Edwin's rich cornfields or Gododdin lands. A foot plough teased narrow strips of loam to raise patchy barley crops, the few cattle were driven to graze on the seashore, and Begu sweated over a small plot for onions, cabbages, fleabane and tansy.

Hild kept to the pattern of worship Utta had drafted. Before dawn, at Lauds, she read aloud the four songs starting, *Praise ye the Lord.* After her morning studies she read the psalm about God's faithfulness to his people and prayers set for that hour. The evening psalm was a plea for God's protection in the trials and temptations of life.

Unused to praying women, the workers kept their distance until their children thawed: a small girl showed off an outsize duck egg; a lad brought a couple of trout and stayed to heft water; his mates teased the billy goat and lurked in the rushes while Hild practised.

"You've found some worshippers," Cedd chaffed, arriving en route for Deira.

"*Suffer the little children…*" Too late she spotted his twinkle and laughed.

"You were reading in British?"

"It's what we speak. Besides, Aidan talked about *starting with the milk of simpler teaching.*"

"I can see why he was bent on capturing you!" Cedd guffawed, letting the children pull his skirts and crawl over him, oddly gentle for such a great bear. "Sister, may I celebrate Easter with you?"

Do this in remembrance of me. Cedd broke and shared a loaf of Begu's. Only a priest could serve the Lord's Supper; he was both monk and ordained priest. Though it was the night before the crucifixion, Hild's heart sang; Cedd's burly presence attracted youths, children, and adults. He invited everyone to the midnight vigil. At the dawn cry, *He is risen*, everyone tumbled into the Easter feast. The houseplace was crammed. Old men dozed by the fire, youngsters sported by the river, men gossiped and women cleared up.

"Thank you, brother, and God speed you!" said Hild, walking with Cedd to the jetty next day. He loped beside her, touching the tender shoots, cheering the weeders.

"It's going well." His eyes were warm as his hand engulfed hers. "I'll come again."

But her next guests were horsemen awaiting a ship, who spent their days hunting for the table. One of Oswy's thegns, Hild discovered, taking his son to Bamburgh for the first time. She bit back memories; the boy was about Wulfi's age. He joined in worship morning and night, reciting the psalms by heart.

"The Latin's musical," he confided over his ale. "I want to learn more. Perhaps become a monk."

"You wait," his father frowned over the boy's head, "till you're with the other young sprigs in training. There's nothing like it. Forest runs, catching your supper, cooking over an open fire…"

"But when I'm old…"

"If, Wilfrid, not when. How often have I told you? For a thegn there's no greater destiny than dying in the king's service."

"But which king, my lord?"

Hild was amused. The boy's courtesy was impeccable, but there was no hiding his stubbornness. She was sorry when he left. Years later, she'd remember this first meeting; the signs were there from the start.

During the Dog Days, travellers flocked in. Then, a woodsman needed his gashed arm dressed. It healed so well, others followed: a crushed foot, a thorn in the eye, a toddler sobbing over a duck with a broken wing, and a wandering dotard who needed minding while his daughter baited her man's fish-lines. Then Begu sliced her hand and a pregnant woman developed fever. Hild had come in winter; the hawthorn was blooming, and already she needed a sick room.

When the Lindisfarne boat pulled in, she sighed with relief. Cedd would help. But the children did not rush forward and the men knuckled their brows.

"I'm Cedd's brother," announced the newcomer.

"There are two of you?" The same look, the priest's robe, Aidan's boat.

"Four, actually – all Lindisfarne monks." His chuckle showed he was used to being mistaken. "I'm Chad." Now she looked, he had a smaller frame. The fieldworkers dwarfed him as they hovered for a story.

"Just a minute, friends," he called. "Let me take this weight inside first." Slapping his satchel, he turned to Hild. "Sister, will you take me to the chapel?"

He looked round appraisingly, nodded, and uttered a silent prayer. Extracting a large book from his leather bag, he placed it carefully on the altar.

"The world's creation. Genesis, the book's called. Aidan thought you should have it next." Hild felt excited. "You're daily in his prayers," Chad went on quietly. "He'll come as soon as Oswy spares him. I'm taking a message to Oswine, the Deiran king, so he sent the book with me."

"King Oswine?" Her closest living kinsman. "Will you tell me about him?"

She watched Chad in fascination. He had Cedd's enthusiasm and burning blue eyes, but a gentle voice and neat gestures.

"A generous man, Oswine. Gave us land in the moors for a house of prayer. A Christian, devoted to Aidan, a man like King Oswald." She remembered Aidan holding up Oswald's hand and praying it would live for ever, the hand that was cut off and nailed up by Penda, now in a casket attracting pilgrims to Bamburgh.

So Oswine, too, was a man after Aidan's heart. In his ascetic way, Hild thought, Aidan probably rationed his visits to Deira not because of Oswy's jealousy, though that would be a factor, but because he enjoyed them!

With her bandaged hand, Begu was clumsy and Hild took on her tasks. She began to understand why Aidan prayed at night: it was the only time. And he'd urged her to make sure each day to talk on her own with God. Twenty-four hours weren't long enough. Was this really what God wanted? Aidan would know.

Of course: he'd pray. Pacing the riverbank after dark, with none but the ducks to hear, she poured out her doubts. Feeling emptied, calmed, she waited.

No thunderclap. No still small voice. No answer.

"Press on, then," she sighed.

Harvest was due. The men struggled to gather enough for the busy household. Hild called on the lads who'd shadowed her. They responded with alacrity, clearing ploughlands, threshing grain, bagging some, soaking the rest for ale. They collected nuts and berries, filled the barn, added a shed on the end, culled the beasts, and pinned the skins under stones to dry. She gave thanks in the chapel and, remembering how they celebrated at Doon Hill, held a feast for them all. Presiding over this boisterous, jocular affair, she felt a surge of warmth and pride in her simple household with Christ at its heart.

When Aidan's boat returned, Hild sped to the river. First ashore was an agile youth in undyed robes. He stood holding out his hand while an oarsman gently lifted over the side an old man in monk's habit, with a domed crown and wispy white hair. The boy steadied him, placed a stick in his hand, and took him by the arm to lead him up the bank to Hild.

"Sister!" he called with a beaming smile. "This is Brother John from Lindisfarne. I am his eyes."

"Brother John, welcome!" Hild found her hand firmly gripped. "And you, brother. You are…?" But the boy had turned to shoulder two heavy bundles.

"He's Aetla," Aidan said as he shouldered a third.

Her heart leapt. "Oh, welcome to you all!" she cried, leading them up the slope.

"I thought John might benefit from the milder air of your riverside," Aidan said, close at her side, "and the lad volunteered to stay with him. John's his teacher. Though he has no sight, he brings a deep fund of knowledge – and some books. You may find him helpful."

"You don't know how I've longed to see you," Hild exclaimed. "So much to ask, if you've time?"

"Gladly," Aidan said, squeezing her arm. "Show me what you've been up to."

As Begu took charge of John and Aetla, Hild showed Aidan around. The fieldmen waved, fisherfolk unbent from their traps with a friendly greeting, and children began to tail them.

"People in monk's robes tell stories," she hinted.

"I shall not fail," he chuckled.

"Dark comes early. I'll invite them to our fireside."

At the chapel, Aidan suggested a prayer and, raising his arms in the familiar gesture, said quietly, "Father in heaven, bless our earthly life and work, so that we may bring glory to your name and love to your people."

As they stood side by side, she confessed her pressure, her fear that she could not live up to his dream. In the dim chapel, she was aware of his glimmering eyes fixed on her.

"You are not alone," he said at last. "Christ trod the same path. You cannot lose the way while you keep him in your heart."

That night Aidan talked as he had at Din Edin, easily, in his own tongue, to the families round her hearth. He told the story of Martha, busy with cooking for her guests, while her sister, Mary, chose instead to listen to Jesus. The balance between necessary work and feeding your spirit: how did you make room for both? Had he chosen that story for her, Hild wondered. Even Jesus understood the problem; she need not feel ashamed.

"I see good things stirring here, sister," Aidan said in the morning as they stood on the jetty, admiring the rich golds of the autumn trees. "The people warm to you, and you serve their needs. Keep close to God. Let him work through you."

* * *

During the winter, Hild extended the sleeping quarters, and adjusted the hours of prayer to fit the Lindisfarne customs of John and Aetla: Lauds at dawn followed by a simple breakfast and Bible study; Prime at the second hour, acknowledging God's great works, with prayers spoken by John and repeated by them all; after the day's work, which grew later as the days lengthened, prayers before the meal; and at the end of the day the plea for deliverance: ...*we have not forgotten you, O Lord, nor have our footsteps veered from your way. Redeem us, for thy mercies' sake.*

One frosty dusk, a small party approached from inland, a woman led on horseback by her son; wealthy, judging by dress and bodyguard.

"The lady Frigyd for the lady Hild," he announced formally.

"I am Hild." She was surprised to be known by name.

"Brother Cedd sent us," the woman croaked. "You know him?"

"A good friend." Leading her indoors, Hild looked askance at the mountain of bundles.

"My son, here. A good boy. What I should have done..." Frigyd sank down by the hearth, knotting her fingers. "My lord... a hunting accident..."

"He was with the king?" A Companion, Hild guessed.

"Now Oswy's gifted our lands away," Frigyd's voice sharpened.

Hild drew in her breath. Oswy! Yet he was only reallocating a dead man's land, as kings did. But in winter? Hild felt the old bitterness stir.

"You're welcome here as long as you need," she said reassuringly.

"Hunting, fighting," Frigyd started to sob. "I couldn't bear to lose him too. I wonder… would you? Book learning? A different kind of life?"

Hild's eyes opened wide. Frigyd wanted her son to study! A boy of age and status to join the forest camps? Cedd had sent him. The boy Wilfrid sprang to mind, and Aetla, and Cutha's son in the northern hills. Four young men seeking the new life. Was this Aidan's mission bearing fruit?

The lady Frigyd did not settle easily. Hild invited her for a walk, ostensibly to check on the cattle. Beyond the trees it was blustery, with a driving gale and breakers thundering onto the sand. Knotting their veils round their necks, they walked the windswept beach. Frigyd talked and talked: court life, fashion feuds, the endless travel, awkward stewards, unpredictable princesses. Finding Hild a sympathetic listener, she relaxed. When Hild and Begu stood at the loom weaving cloth for next year's garments, she dug out a rich robe to turn into an altar drape, stitching creatures in twining fronds.

The boys, Oftfor and Aetla, wrestled, fished and teased their blind teacher, appearing always tousled and hungry. Brother John proved an endless delight, talking. He discussed Christ's teaching and its meaning for their own world. She felt able to make suggestions and found him ready to listen and respond.

The ewe came into milk, the thorn buds swelled: the season of Imbolc. Undismayed by the teeming rain, the household filled the chapel with candles and gave thanks; a wet Imbolc meant a good summer.

The surrounding trees were bursting into leaf when Cedd boomed from the boat, bringing Aidan back. He joined in their simple life, and chatted easily with each of them.

"Is this what you had in mind?" Hild asked when she could wait no longer. "A community like this?"

"Do you sense God here?" he asked.

Hild sighed; travelling priests never answered, but asked a question in reply. And this one was hard.

"Sometimes…" She trailed off. For all her striving to hear God, nothing. Perhaps she tried too hard. Yet, since the arrival of John and Aetla, Frigyd and Oftfor, the load had been lighter; they shared it. Was that God's answer to her prayer?

Aidan sat forward, his dark eyes intent. "Sometimes," he said, "when I sail down the coast, the bays seem lifeless. But the birds return. Like God. Sometimes you sense him, sometimes not." He seemed so comfortable with uncertainty. "Ask John to tell you about Doubting Thomas. And he was an apostle!"

He'd not answered her question, but he'd answered her need. He was good with people: clever Utta now established at the Tyne crossroads, Cedd's boisterous humanity in tense Deira, industrious Chad at Lindisfarne. But what about her?

"Do you wish to go to your sister?" he said suddenly. "You promised me a year, remember?"

She was caught off-guard. Everything was so new and she'd been so busy that Heri had slipped her mind. And Aidan was suggesting she should go to France.

"I'm no use here?" she whispered.

"You mean you're willing to stay?" Aidan laughed in delight. "You have rare gifts, sister, and I think you're ready to pledge yourself."

* * *

She must have fallen asleep. The night vigil had been long, the chapel floor hard, and she ached. Feeling ashamed, she lurched to her feet and went out to greet the dawn.

When had she dropped off? Prayers of adoration; she remembered those. Thanksgiving, she'd completed. Confession? That was it! The long list of her failings – impatient, self-centred, ignorant. How could Aidan have confidence in her?

She leaned on the doorpost, realizing with a jolt her mind was drifting again. Supplication, not even started. Firmly she raised her arms and asked a blessing on Aidan's plans, his priests, and the four boys seeking learning. Sighing over Oswy's court who paid mere lip-service to Christ, she asked God to sort things out. Then she prayed for Ani and her boy, growing to be a handful, and Abbe. Oh, and Oswy.

"Grant peace in the land, O Lord," she murmured.

It was Pentecost, the day God loosed his Spirit in the world, the day she was giving herself to God. Lowering her arms, she rehearsed the dedication Aidan would use, and the promises she would give: to keep close to God, to surrender her will to his, and to serve his children.

A blackbird trilled. Day was here.

People thronged the meadow, waiting for the priests' procession. Lost in wonder, Hild followed where they led and knelt at their bidding. Aidan, dark eyes burning, put a fresh robe over her tunic and led her to the altar to receive the bread of Christ.

11

THE ISLE OF HART

"The place is made for you," Aidan said. "A peninsula near the royal estate at Hart. On the Tees delta where Bernicia ends. King Oswy wants you to go. He's even promised help. That's a sign of God's will."

Hard to believe. Until she realized it was the place where Oswy's lands faced Oswine's. Who better to send than a cousin of both?

"God's will," he repeated firmly. "You're the right person for the Isle of Hart."

And so they sailed into the sun past dunes and hidden rocks, until they rounded a headland with a shoreside settlement in a sandy bay on the south. The lodgings were smaller than any she'd ever seen. Behind them, on the lower slopes, were fenced brown fields, ploughed and sown, and corrals for horses. Among the scrubby bushes on the heights, a few cattle foraged among goats and pigs. Early in the season for grazing, she thought, but on this sunny slope life sprang earlier than in her Wearmouth clearing.

The sails flopped, the anchor dropped, and seamen carried Aidan and Hild's party ashore. Brother John had elected to come, with Aetla. When Oftfor chose to join them, Frigyd decided to follow her son. Begu's response was the simplest: "Need you ask?" In a group, they walked along the shore to the tiny thatched huts, glimpsing solitary occupants through the open doors.

"Preparing for Vespers," Aidan said. "Let's wait in the hall. Over there."

Looking where he pointed, Hild's eyes flew to the black cliffs across the water. Deira was her homeland, but it meant nothing to her after sixteen years in the north. Home, now, was where she made it.

Sister Heiu's welcome was unforgettable. Her face was etched with pain, her frame bent and crippled, but her eyes were beady and vital, full of urgency.

"Lady Hild, you've come!" Her fingers clawed Hild down beside her. "There's so much to do, and you'll make it happen. The time's right, the king's supportive, but," she looked pointedly round the room, "we are few and old."

"Powerful in faith," Hild said warmly.

"Anodyne!" Heiu bridled dismissively. "More than prayer's needed here. Action's called for — action beyond my strength. Not for me to tell you what. But it is for me to leave the Isle of Hart in good hands. Now you're here, I can take my useless carcass to the far side of York. God and my kindred will see me through."

"A hard journey." Hild imagined the bent old body tossing over ruts in a covered ox cart.

"But I've a strong arm to lean on. Brother Cedd's promised to see me safe. He's somewhere about." She looked vaguely round the hall. "Well, he'll be here for Vespers." She'd spur him like a horse, Hild thought. Heiu had force of character. The first woman ever to give her life to Christ.

A few days later, Hild watched them embark to sail up the Tees as far as the old Roman road. None of Cedd's chat-stops and diversions. Heiu's will would goad him to the end. Now it was up to Hild to carry on her work.

This community, more women than men, was completely devoted to keeping the hours of prayer, including two night-time services new to Hild. And before each act of worship in the chapel, they spent an hour of prayerful preparation in their lodgings. It was a concentrated and rigorous regime. Her people adapted, each in a separate lodging, except for John and Aetla. Aidan conducted a Mass before he left; there were no priests among them.

"Soon there will be," he told Hild. "Aetla. Brother John says he has the learning. I'll send one of the brethren to initiate him into pilgrimage." It was what Aetla wanted, Hild knew, and he'd be welcome everywhere, like the travelling priests at Doon Hill.

Her first challenge was to know the land. Visiting the fisher hovels near where they'd landed, she took Aetla and left him there to make friends. Next, she climbed the ridge to the top of the headland, looked over the northern slope where scrubland tumbled down to the sea, and returned through the fields. Chatting with the farmworkers, she learned that they made their own decisions, unless the king's bailiff intervened. How would they cope, she wondered, if visitors started flooding in?

One day, she decided to explore further, perhaps even walk to the king's estate. Windless sky, leaden water, sharp black outlines: a storm was on the way. Freed from Thor, Hild found nature's fury exhilarating. At the top of the ridge, she turned full circle, seeing how her land merged into a purple sea which stretched to a black horizon. The settlement below seemed to hold its breath, close enough to touch. Men laboured in little fields, worshippers flocked to a tiny chapel, fishermen like ants hauled boats ashore.

She turned to the narrow neck which connected with the mainland and struck out along the track across the marsh, heading for what looked like the rides of the king's chase, with a hut nestling in a hilltop thicket. A sudden gust snatched at her veil, the horizon fragmented, black clouds bowled across the sea, and heavy raindrops spattered down. She sped uphill, seeking shelter in the building.

Running through the thicket, she tripped in the gloom. A low wall, crusted with rotting food and a raven's corpse, surrounded a black pool. Water oozed through the stones at the roots of an elder which hung crazily over the edge. From the branches, supple as whips, flapped rotting strips of blanched cloth. The air was fetid, the ground slimy, the atmosphere sinister: Woden's place.

Suddenly, the storm broke. Drenched and blinded, she made for the hut but her boots sank, brambles clawed her skirts and her ears thudded like pursuing footsteps. Wrenching up her skirts, she floundered forward, arm outstretched, weaving between the trunks. In the doorway she stumbled, landing heavily on her knees. Looking over her shoulder, she saw only rain cascading from the thatch. A violent shudder rippled through her body.

Willing her eyes to settle in the dark, she crept forward until her hands touched a homely plaster wall where she turned and saw outlined against the open door a central roof post. With dry sobs she rushed to it and clung, feeling the Evil One near, insinuating, beating her down.

"Holy Jesus," she cried, slithering to her knees, "cast him out!" How could she have let this happen? "O Lord, have mercy on my unbelief!"

She could not tell how long she stayed embracing the post and laying her cheek against the rough wood. When she stopped shivering and crawled to her feet, she saw through the doorway pale sunlight and raindrops hanging like stars from the branches.

Walking back she castigated her carelessness. Woden spread poison everywhere. This shrine tainted the marsh where travellers crossed to her minster. Brother Cedd, she recalled, had endured weeks of prayer and fasting to cleanse his moorland retreat. She must do the same. Brother John would know the ritual.

The stormclouds had lifted, the air was clear, and her spirits revived as she reached the top of the ridge.

"Here!" she exclaimed, as a new idea took root. She'd crossed the marsh and stood on her own land. "Dominate that copse. Visible from sea and land." Her excitement grew. "Like a beacon, Aidan's beacon. At the apex of the island, pointing to God. Here! I'll build a church."

* * *

"Timber's no problem." Oswy's steward had instructions to give any help she needed. "And a bit o' good stone. Needs grounding, a structure as tall as you want. Labour'll be no problem after harvest. Till the king comes, around blackthorn time."

Hild had grown up cajoling royal bailiffs. Burly, windburned Ulf was a lamb.

"Wi' your permission, lady, I'll start on t'causeway. Strong fencing, it needs. Wouldn't do to lose oxen down that ditch on the way over with heavy loads. Besides, it'd give a bit o' dignity."

They walked the ridge, planning the site.

"Not too far from the track," said Hild. "I'd like your folk to feel it's their church too."

"What about them as tends it? They'll need lodgings nearby. And the sick." He was carried away. "Where d'you plan for them?"

"One thing at a time," she laughed. "First, a house of prayer."

Brother John was keen to dispel the miasma of Woden's grove. He sat with Hild, intoning passages from the prophets: *We have all been made unclean... We have dropped like a leaf blown away by evil... Burst open the heavens and come down!* Then, he asked Aetla to take him to the place, and spent a day proclaiming them at the top of his voice.

Aetla and Oftfor assumed the daily task of circling the knoll, chanting to expel the old evil. They hacked down trees and let in the light, turned the stones and erected an ash cross where the elder had been. Mustering woodsmen, they worked on the shelter, cutting a window to face the sun and fixing a crosshead on the central roofpost.

"They've transformed it!" Hild described the changes to John as he sat with her on the low wall, face to the sun, ears alert to birdsong and the gentle flow of channelled water.

"The change is tangible," he said quietly. "The stench of evil has gone."

"It's a place of peace," Hild complimented the boys, "a refuge." Aetla flushed with pleasure; it was his first priestly task. Kneeling beside her, he dipped a pottery beaker in the water.

"Drink, lady. It's good. We tried it when we were hot. May we leave the cup here for travellers?"

Conscious of her great failure, Hild tried at the first hour of the day, alone in her lodging, to listen for God. Folding her hands, she repeated the age-old prayer: *Kyrie, eleison; Christ have mercy.* Very occasionally, a sense of peace stole over her. All too soon the bell rang for Lauds, and breakfast, and work.

Before long, the fisher children began to crowd round for nuts or a story, lowering from their heads the heavy baskets of seaweed and winkles they'd gathered for the cookpots. When she saw the men's catch, she asked them to keep the kitchen supplied. She often left Aetla behind, helping to bait the lines as he chatted.

One day, climbing the ridge, she heard singing. Some of her monks, hems stuffed in girdles, were sharing toil and banter with the builders. Warily, she stepped inside the structure, admiring the rounded apse, the recess for a holy cup, and the oak frame towering above her as high as the king's Great Hall.

"Mind yer backs!" A massive beam swung close on cables tied at both ends and looped over the roof-ridge. Muscles bulging, men strained at the ropes to keep it steady.

"One, two, three!" Staccato grunts, rhythmic heaves, and the beam lurched up a notch. Hild stepped smartly out of the way.

"One, two, three!" Again the ropes creaked and the beam rose shuddering, vibrating, swaying gently between the uprights. At each heave, a sigh rose from the workers' families, who had brought the men's food and stood watching.

"Hang on, lads!" a voice bawled above. "Right! She's running sweet. One, two, three!"

Trapped inside, Hild craned upwards. The beam jerked to the top-plate. Men as lithe as squirrels caught the ends, set them on the uprights, and hammered the joints in place. A ragged cheer went up. The ground crew rolled their shoulders, wiped their necks, and slapped each other's backs.

"Midday!" Ulf's shout exploded beside her as she massaged her neck. "That's t'roof started," he huffed with satisfaction. "At this lick, it should be topped by Advent, given the weather."

Hild walked downhill through picnicking families. Men swigged from bladders, sprawling on the grass or lolling on sawhorses. Women crept among the wood piles gleaning chippings for their fires. They all smiled as Hild passed.

"Eh, you, stop that!" Ulf barked as lads flicked twigs into the cattle pen, risking a stampede. Jovial with his labourers, he was sharp with troublemakers. As he kept pace with her down the slope, Hild realized he was trying to tell her something.

"We used to watch from longways off," he stammered. "When t'king left, so did priests. Not fer us, the likes o' priests. But you…" He skirted a gorse clump. "Your men work wi' us, you come to watch… we feel part of summat." He took a deep breath. "Sorry, not fer me…"

"I'm pleased." Hild glowed. "And it's shaping well."

"Aye, they're not a bad gang," he growled, blushing. "Mebbe King Oswy'll come fer t'dedication?"

* * *

Ulf's men worked hard and, with the predicted gap for harvest, continued through the winter. The little handful of Heiu's monks surprised Hild.

"Chance of a lifetime!" They pleaded to help. "We won't neglect our prayer duties. It's a privilege, to build God's house."

"Truly, it's God's work." Hild was glad for the new church to be so blessed in the building.

Gently, she persuaded Heiu's company to help their near neighbours as foodstocks diminished in the new year: barley for the fisher familes and fish for the field folk. And she wheedled a jar of honey from Ulf to dose the frail and sick.

At the first sign of spring, Aidan sailed in. As usual, he kept the hours and joined in daily life, meeting Brother John's students, and walking the lands with Hild.

"Good to see this intermingling," he said. "Men of God among God's children."

"So long as we keep the hours," she said, betraying her anxiety: should she allow men dedicated to prayer to undertake manual labour? The new buildings on the ridge were well away from their shoreside chapel, where worship continued undisturbed. But she was already planning a sunny library for John under the lee of the new church.

"Sister, the monks' eagerness for this work is God-given," Aidan answered. "They are showing his love in sharing the labour."

To have Aidan to herself was rare, and she needed to share the painful failure which still, after a whole year, nagged in her mind.

"Let me show you something," she said.

They crossed the causeway, boggy with the high tides of spring. Even now, she felt shame as she approached Woden's old shrine. She should have foreseen the danger.

"This was the place? Mm, the usual sort of hilltop site." Panting from the climb, Aidan surveyed the pool in the grove, with its cross and shelter. "But Christ has defeated the darkness. The cross reigns now. You did the right thing, sister."

"But how can I be fit to serve God?" she wailed.

"Sit here." He dropped onto the sun-swept wall. "Do you remember Peter who denied knowing Jesus when he was condemned to death?" She nodded. "What must he have felt?"

The water rippled quietly. She could not imagine Peter's shame.

"Who did Christ choose to 'feed his flock'?" Aidan continued.

"Peter," she whispered.

"Who did Christ call his Rock? Peter, the man who knew failure."

"But…" Hild was thinking hard. "Christ lived beside Peter, understood his human weakness…"

"And Christ understands you," Aidan said. "We all fail, Hild." He sighed as he rose stiffly to his feet. "I fail, and keep on failing, to get through to the king's Companions. So I din into my ears what Saint Paul said: *Forget what is past and reach forward*."

* * *

Grateful as she was for Ulf's honey, Hild determined to produce her own. Along with her small armoury of herbs, it was invaluable for medicinal purposes, for mead, and for fragrant beeswax. Begu dug a herb patch at the edge of the fields where the gorse bloomed profusely. There, she and Frigyd fashioned frames out of withies from the marsh, filled the weave with old straw and dung, and set up a row of hives to await the bees.

Come they did, in early summer. But honey did not flow in time for her church dedication. No mead, then, and no wax candles; but Frigyd embroidered a beautiful altar drape, which Cedd blessed as he passed on his way to Deira.

"This as well," he said, unwrapping a silver chalice. "Queen Anfled sent it as a gift." And he blessed the cup to God's service.

"Will you stay awhile, brother?" Hild asked eagerly.

"Not this time. There is so much Aidan and King Oswine want doing in Deira."

The new church overflowed at the dedication. There were seats at the front for Oswy, Anfled and Hild. The royal party almost filled the church and Hild's people had to squeeze against the far wall. She found her seat occupied by Prince Egfrid, whose short legs jutted out as he waved his miniature sword. Frigyd raised an indignant eyebrow. Hild gave her a soothing pat and stood near the altar. When Aidan and his monks processed in, the two groups parted in a channel which immediately closed again like the Red Sea. As silence fell, Hild was conscious of the fidgeting and heavy breathing of her builders, fieldworkers and fisherfolk outside, craning to see and hear.

Aidan and his monks chanted the psalms and performed the rituals which she remembered from her Wearmouth chapel, adding this time thanks to God for the skill of the craftsmen who had raised such a great edifice to his glory. When the service was over, Aidan handed his bishop's robes to one of his monks and moved among the local people like an old friend.

For Hild, the feast in the king's hall was an anticlimax. After the exaltation of the dedication, court gossip seemed trite. She'd hoped for a chat with Aidan or Anfled but, after a quick embrace, the queen was swamped by royal duties and Aidan withdrew early, as was his custom.

Next to her, a young woman brilliant with jewels fixed fascinated eyes on the sturdy boots protruding from Hild's skirts. Just like Heri, she thought wryly, pulling her feet in. The Hart looms could still not cater for her height.

"I won't stand for it," the girl whispered to her other neighbour.

"Ssh!" He gripped her arm. Brother and sister, judging by their likeness.

"It's all right for you, Alcfrid," retorted the girl. "You get to choose."

"Alcfled, shut up!" He pinched her arm, and she subsided.

A tiny incident, which Hild would remember later.

After a stuffy night in the women's lodging, she left as the huntsmen were loosing the dogs. Her mind was busy. Aetla was waiting to be ordained. Begu, overwhelmed by broken limbs and gashes among the builders, needed a sick room. John had more boys to teach, and two potential novices. She had accepted a cottar's daughter to prevent her enslavement for debt, and that meant education for a girl and finding a way to help the father. The brothers who were to tend the new church needed lodgings nearby. Where could she find another potter? There was so much to do; a satisfying, fruitful life.

* * *

On a glowing autumn day she would never forget, Hild was on the shore when a familiar figure disembarked in the shallows.

"Brace yourself, sister," Brother Cedd cried as he hauled himself heavily through the surf. "Throwback to the old days. King Oswine's dead." Dishevelled, drooping with despair, he staggered across the beach and dropped into a soft dune, wringing out his skirts. "Murdered," he barked. "Oswine's been murdered. Cut down in his Companion's homestead."

Horror perfused his face. Hild could see why. A just king, chosen by his people, assassinated. And at the hearthplace of his sworn man.

"Hunwald didn't do it. He was killed too."

"Who, then?" she asked gently, slipping down beside him.

"Hunwald's steward, his… most trusted man!" he snarled bitterly.

She knew he was close to weeping. There was no comfort she could give, except to let him vent his feelings.

"The two allegiances most sacred to any man!" he bawled, beating his clenched fists on his knees. "Lord and king!"

After a long pause, Hild asked, "Did you bury him?"

"Yes," Cedd sighed. "Every honour a man could wish. A Christian burial. And we laid his thegn beside him."

"Was he caught?"

"The killer? Dealt with. But…" He rocked in anguish. "I told you, the bad old days have returned." For a long time he could say no more. "Oswy!" he suddenly yelped. "Oswy bribed the killer."

Hild went cold. "To get Deira," she said slowly. He'd always envied his father, the Twister, for ruling the whole of Northumbria.

"Uh?" Cedd stirred. "Oh, Deira won't have Oswy. They've chosen Oswald's son. Prince Ethelwald's king of Deira now."

Hild groaned at the futility. Deep in sorrow, they sat a long time.

"I must get to Aidan." Cedd brushed his sandy robes and started up.

"Stay the night!" She put her hand on his arm.

"Yes, please." He nodded, acknowledging her friendship with a wan smile. "I need to find out if I'm to stay in Deira, or…. Oh, I just need to talk to Aidan."

Silently, they trudged over the dunes and up the ridge.

"I'll go in here a while," he said at the church door.

Hild could see an agitated gathering below. Someone peeled away to run to her. Begu.

"Lady," she called, "Chad's here. Bad news from Lindisfarne. Aidan's dead."

* * *

From across Northumbria they came, Aidan's boys: Utta from Gateshead with his brothers Adda and Betti; Eata and Cuthbert from Melrose; Hild with Cedd and Chad from Hart; their brothers Caelin and Cynebil, and all the monks of Lindisfarne. They packed the sanctuary on the Bamburgh cliffs, and spilled out into the rain. Here Aidan had died waiting against a pillar for the tide to ebb so that he could walk home across the sands.

In my father's house are many mansions... Chad read. *I go to prepare a place for you...* Christ's promise. Oswine and Aidan would be there together now, Hild thought. And Wulfi?

The men chanted, *The Lord is my shepherd*, and she added her treble, glad to be there, *I will dwell in the house of the Lord for ever.*

Aidan's boys had not met for years. After laying him in his coffin for burial on Lindisfarne, they stood around reviving old affections. Hild heard her name. A crooked nose, a mischievous grin, and grey hair corkscrewing in the rain.

"Eata!" She grinned. "My young tearaway! And look at you now. Oh…"

"Hild!" He muffled her with one of his tight hugs. "Dear Hild! Don't give me away. Look, here's someone else you know."

Blushing and ruffled, she saw a lean figure, unfamiliar until he stepped forward with the old limp.

"Cuthbert!" She gripped his hand. "The only person who made Cerdic smile."

"A lovely way to be remembered." His face lit up.

"He's got a way with people," said Eata. "That's why he's our guestmaster."

"Your father?" She'd last seen Cutha here, at Bamburgh.

"Buried at Melrose. He came to us at the end. And you?" Pausing, he said gently, "This is a big change."

"Thanks to Aidan."

"He changed us all!"

Eata had been like a son to her, and Cuthbert had brought fleeces in her time of need. Now they stood together, colleagues in Aidan's great enterprise.

"Heaven is weeping for Aidan!" she exclaimed later, walking back through the rain with Queen Anfled. "So many mourners!

Thegns, labourers, boatmen – everyone loved Aidan." Entering the queen's lodging, she took Ani's cloak and tossed it with her own over a beam.

"Even my chaplain." Ani leaned back, pushing her hands into the small of her back. Taking the chair, she propped her feet on the firestone and loosened her plait to dry. "Being from Canterbury, Romanus didn't always agree with Aidan, but he said he was the most Christ-like man he knew."

Automatically, Hild picked up the comb. "How much longer?" she asked.

"Must have been Christmas." Ani shifted to ease her bulk.

"Any day now, then." Hild combed on. "Where's Egfrid?"

"With the men," Anfled said. "Hawking, mostly. A boar, once. It's good for him; he's been too cosseted. But Hild, they're on campaign," she sighed. "Facing Penda, at six years old!"

"And you sit and worry." Hild knew the dragging uncertainty. They listened to the fire-crackle and raindrops puttering.

"Soothing, you combing. Like when I was little." Ani felt her hair and took the comb from Hild. "Almost dry. Come and sit down."

"Oswy?" Hild settled on a stool by the hearth.

"Trying for alliances in the south. Sigebert of Essex, because Penda's on his border too. Kent, of course, through me. Oh, that reminds me... Paulinus has died."

"A name from the past!" Hild was drying her plait. "Paulinus baptized me."

"And me, I gather," Ani chuckled. "I don't remember."

"I do," Hild said drily. "Your father was proud of your voice. Thought he'd fathered a warrior."

"Shame!" Ani giggled. After a while, facing away, she said, "You heard about Oswy and Oswine?"

"Yes." Hild touched her lightly.

"He gets these impulses, you know. Afterwards, he's sorry, but can't admit it. I... do you think...?" Ani turned towards her. "If he set up a house of prayer..."

"Where?"

"Where it happened. Gilling, near the Swale. To show remorse."

"A memorial to Oswine. Good idea." Hild nodded. Remorse seemed unlikely for Oswy, but she understood Ani's desire to salvage his reputation. "Brother Cedd will find the right abbot."

"Oswy must." Anfled clenched her hands. "He must make his peace with God."

"Lady – oh, forgive me!" A dark-robed priest darkened the door, looking so like Paulinus Hild shook herself.

"Romanus," Ani beckoned, "you know Abbess Hild?"

"Lady!" As tall as Paulinus, but sleepy eyes; not one to challenge the king. He bowed like a courtier and turned straight back to the queen. "You remember Wilfrid? The boy you sent to Lindisfarne to serve lame old Cudda?"

"Hard to forget, young Wilfrid," Ani chuckled.

"He's here with a companion and begs leave to see you."

"Bring him in!" Ani turned to Hild. "You'll like him."

"I think," Hild said guardedly, "I met him once."

Swift and fluid, a pale young man strode in and folded himself reverentially at the queen's feet.

"My lady," he breathed, bowing his head.

"Wilfrid!" Anfled looked delighted. Rising, he stood before her, hands in his sleeves, eyes burning. "What is it?"

"Lady, Lord Cudda no longer needs me…"

"Rest his soul," Romanus muttered.

"After he died," Wilfrid ignored the piety, "Aidan let me stay and study for the priesthood. I crossed today with the brothers but, lady, something's arisen and I wish to beg your support."

"Tell me more." Anfled glanced past him at a thickset man waiting near the door. "Who's your friend?"

"May I present Lord Biscop?" Wilfrid said. "You'll have seen him among the king's thegns. He's travelling to Rome."

"Lady," Biscop said gruffly, with a bow. "The king's granted me land at Wearmouth. I want to found a house of prayer, monks, books. Young Wilfrid'd be useful."

"Ah!" Ani looked significantly at Wilfrid. "So you want the king's consent to leave? He's away at present." She thought, then turned back to Biscop. "How could Wilfrid help you?"

"Metal to my clay," he blushed awkwardly. "Born scholar. Knows all the psalms and stuff. I'm a man of action, raw beginner. Wilfrid'll choose for me."

"And your father?" Ani asked Wilfrid.

"He's accepted my choice, lady. In the end." A self-deprecating smile. "He'll not stand in the way of my calling." Wilfrid waited, a suppliant in every line of his body. How clever, thought Hild, letting his modesty, his vocation, plead for him: the queen was enraptured.

"Go then, with my blessing." She smiled affectionately. "Say a prayer for me at the shrine of Saint Peter."

"Lady!" His voice was breathy, mellifluous. "I shall ever be your slave."

"Biscop," said the queen, "on your way, could you take the abbess home?"

* * *

How she missed him! Oftfor mopped up knowledge like spilt ale, and asked quirky questions: Aidan would have loved him. Aetla, nearing thirty, awaited ordination which Aidan had promised. John was keen to start making copies of books loaned to them, and he wanted to discuss whether Pope Gregory's *Pastoral Care*, which he thought a good, practical handbook, should become part of their minster's training for priesthood. Hild could decide, of course, but Aidan would have relished it.

The next harvest was poor. Fieldwork was so hard that haywards and stockmen were too exhausted to tend their home plots, and their families grew thin.

"Beestings for the cowman," Hild reminded Frigyd as she sorted food in the abbey stores. "Give the swineherd the biggest piglet."

"But…"

"It's their due. Invite the hungry to share our meals. We'll overwinter fewer beasts, and rein in our appetites."

She tried to barter with Ulf for a load of cattle fodder. Not cheese, he said, but he could use ready-dried fish and three vats of honey for the king's visit.

But Oswy did not come. He sent for gold and men. Penda had slipped behind him and fired Yeavering, a short march from his fortress at Bamburgh. Oswy must buy him off, said the messenger, or fight without hope.

"If all the men go before sowing," Ulf moaned, "it'll be another paltry yield. Well, mebbe Penda'll solve it. Kill us all first." He heaved a gusty sigh. "As for gold, 'tis a king's job to win it." He lowered his voice. "Tha knows my thinking, lady? He's bin beat, King Oswy. He's amassing tribute for Penda."

Brother Chad confirmed Ulf's pessimism. He took it upon himself to visit Hild, knowing the minster needed a priest to celebrate Mass. From Aidan's monastery on Lindisfarne, he brought the Bamburgh news.

"Prince Egfrid's gone to Penda as a hostage."

"Oh, no!" How could Oswy play war games with his child? She couldn't forget how Penda had treacherously slaughtered Prince Edi after Edwin's downfall.

"He won't be on his own," Chad reassured her. "Princess Alcfled's marrying Penda's son and Prince Alcfrid his daughter." She recalled the brother and sister who'd sat near her at King Oswy's feast.

"All Oswy's children in Mercia?" she groaned. "A nice snare he's put them in!"

"God is with them," Chad said calmly. Hild bowed her head. She wished she had his assurance. "My brother Cedd's there too, and other priests: Adda, Betti..."

"I thought Penda was of the old faith."

"Oh, he is. A man of many gods. He doesn't mind who other people worship. Penda's children are to be baptized in Northumbria before they wed. And Cedd will lead the mission to Mercia."

"Who'll baptize them?" Hild was confused.

"Ah, I forgot you wouldn't know. Bishop Finan, the new man from Iona. Distantly related to Oswy, apparently."

"Ah well, Aidan was uniquely lovable," Hild said sadly. "Human warmth, self-denial, British volubility, shaky Anglo-Saxon…"

Chad returned her smile. "If you haven't heard about Finan, there's something else." He pushed away his cup. "No – good news. The queen has a baby girl!"

Ulf's men trickled home from battle, shattered. Hild and Begu tackled wounds and breaks. Easing haunted minds was harder. Monks who had themselves seen war unpacked the men's nightmares and turned their thoughts to peace.

Foodstocks, invalids, Ulf's anxiety, Aetla's frustration, Oswy's unreliability: all weighed heavily on Hild. At dawn she prayed for strength, at night she handed her load to God, and on her rounds she stamped out Saint Patrick's litany: *Christ be with me, Christ within me, Christ behind me, Christ before me… Christ in quiet, Christ in danger…*

Winter struck hard. Ice made tracks impassable and filled the infirmary with broken bones. When meat and leaves ran short, endless salt fish turned their stomachs. Youngsters brought offerings for the pot: a dead magpie, a hare frozen in its form, a fulmar, even a fox. Tempers frayed. When an overeager helper prodded the logs and the cauldron boiled over, dousing the fire and wasting precious broth, Frigyd gave full vent to her sharp tongue. Fieldmen huddled in the forge; blunt axe-heads, chipped knives – anything – justified a gossip in the warm. Ulf swung his whip and blackened the smith's eye.

The thaw brought floods. Seed stores rotted. They ground pea husks for bread and stomachs revolted. The elderly failed. Two of Heiu's people, Berchtred and Hildegard, died first and were buried near the chapel on the shore, with stones edging their graves. Fieldfolk, the oldest and youngest, were laid at Ulf's request within sight of the church.

Then, the whole cycle was repeated: waterlogged ground, scant ploughing, late sowing, infertile cattle, and again the warband summoned. The king was in retreat, they said; Penda was marching north. The new bishop could hardly have chosen a worse time to come.

* * *

Hild watched from the ridge as Bishop Finan's company picked their way over the marsh. His plain priest's robe and naked forehead might look like Aidan's, but his back locks were fair and he rode like a thegn.

"My lord bishop, welcome!" Hild sank to her knees, nose level with his boots. Lordly boots, supple leather. Sharply, she checked herself; he may have a great spirit.

"Lady Hild." Dismounting, he sketched the sign of the cross. A man in his late thirties, about her age, he strode vigorously beside her to his lodging. They'd built it halfway between the brothers near the church and the sisters by the water, with a bedspace, a recess for a servant, and the hearthplace where he could interview people.

Aetla went first, eager to have his vocation tested. The place held no fears; he had thatched it and transported books for the prayer desk. Some hours later he emerged, glowing with wonder.

The night before his ordination, Hild could not sleep. She knew what faced a wandering priest: lonely trails, injured feet, wolves, outlaws, cold, hunger. And she knew how rarely he would return for rest and renewal. Shrugging on a cloak, she climbed to the church. Remembering her own vigil, she stood and shared his.

To her delight, Brother Cedd came to stand beside him for his vows, and accompany him on his first pilgrimage. They shared the bond of all who'd passed through Aidan's hands.

"A fine young man." The bishop watched Aetla deep in discussion with Cedd and Oftfor over their meal. "A credit to you."

"Not me," Hild said firmly. "His learning comes from Brother John, his spirit is his own, and his model, I believe, is Brother Cedd."

"A-ah!" Finan lifted an eyebrow. "That should take him far. Cedd's done well in Mercia where the faith is new. I'm sending him to Essex, where it was once rejected. He's a man to make an impact, I believe."

"Oh, he does, my lord. But the East Saxons?"

"King Sigebert wants a chaplain. I recently had the pleasure of baptizing him with King Oswy as sponsor." Complacent he sounded, but understandably; a whole new kingdom for Christ.

"Cedd will move mountains," she said quietly.

"God willing." Bishop Finan crossed himself and, as if following a train of thought, said, "Sister, I should like to meet your Brother John."

"I'll bring him to you."

"No." He shook his head. "I'll go to him. After Prime?"

They tracked John down in his half-built library. Tree trunks were stacked outside, the branches chopped into logs and piled to dry inside the double doors. Standing in the litter of chippings, Hild and Finan heard young voices arguing.

"A poor king? Not how the world works. No gold, no thegns. No thegns, no warbands, and the land is overrun."

"Why gold? Don't they fight for honour?"

"My father said King Oswald wasted his gold." A thegn's son, Hild thought wryly, recalling the Companions' grumbles about almsgiving.

"There is one good king," John said mildly, "near the end of the book." Rounding the corner Hild saw him perched on a log, groping along the volumes beside him. The boys noticed her, but John could not see. "Here." He held out a book. "Find the name Hezekiah and read the column." Taking the book, a boy turned the pages.

"Brother John," Hild interrupted, "here's Bishop Finan."

"My lord!" The old man pushed himself up.

"Brother!" In two strides the bishop checked him. "Don't kneel to me. I bow to your gifts. These boys are fortunate."

"You heard them?" John chuckled. "We're studying the books of Kings and wondering why it's so hard for kings to be good. Your wisdom outstrips mine, my lord. Would you…?"

"The issue of our times: *Can a king follow Christ?*" Finan chose a tree stump in the boys' circle, pulled in his skirts, sat and leaned his elbows on his knees. Hild smiled; he might still be a scholar on Iona. And this must be a live topic for him, living with Oswy.

"Try another angle," he began. "What *can* a king do in the spirit of Christ?"

They were off: "Give to God's work – like land for our minster… help the suffering… justice, like Solomon and the two mothers…"

"But all kings do justice," countered one boy.

"Not always justly," said another. "Sometimes for their own gain."

"Wealth!" groaned Oftfor. "It haunts us. To follow Christ, we…" He struggled to voice what was in his mind. "We must upend our ideas."

"Upend?" puzzled voices chorused.

"Jesus overturned what they thought in his day," Oftfor persisted. "Remember the shame-faced widow giving her tiny coin to the Temple? It was her gift he praised, not the big sums."

"Why?" Finan encouraged him.

"Because," Oftfor hesitated, "she gave all she could."

"Ye-es?" pressed Finan.

After thinking, Oftfor said tentatively, "Because… she loved God."

"You've put your finger on it." Finan sat back. "Someone once said: *I shall show you, O man, what is good, what the Lord requires: to act justly, love mercy, and walk humbly with God.* Three things. Memorable." He repeated them, the students mouthing with him.

"That was the prophet Micah, speaking to those kings you're studying." He rose reluctantly and gave them his blessing. At the door, he turned back. "One day you'll be priests, some of you, and I hope you'll be able to 'upend' men's thinking. Men care about things. God values the heart."

Their eyes followed as he left.

"A good place for learning," he murmured as they started up the slope. "I see why your minster is growing famous."

As Aidan would have done, he blessed each patient in the infirmary, and paused to pray in the church. Hild watched his men assemble the horses near the causeway.

"You should know," he said, as he bade her farewell, "King Oswy can't hold out another season. Battle, tribute, hostages: it's all been useless."

Hild's heart sank. What could she do about the king's troubles?

"He's sworn an oath. If God gives Oswy victory," the bishop

said slowly, "Oswy will give God ten new minsters and – this is where you come in, Abbess – his baby daughter."

* * *

The toddler staggered towards Hild, arms flailing. Gathering speed on the slope, she tumbled and rolled over and over. With a sharp cry, Anfled ran after her; Hild sped upwards. Breathlessly they met where the baby landed.

"'gain," she chortled, "'gain!"

"Clever Elfi." Hild swooped her up. Setting her on her feet, she grasped her tunic and helped her stagger downhill, while Anfled cast about for what had scattered from her basket: breechclout, feeding bottle, and a favourite shell.

Against all the odds, late in the season, when torrents were raging and the ground was waterlogged, Oswy and his small army drove Penda into the River Went. The Mercians were killed; Oswy was left standing, lord of Mercia, Lindsey and Bernicia.

Fires burned high, piles of booty gleamed, and tables were awash with mead when the court gathered at Hart to burn the Yule log and feast on fat cattle from the midlands. Captured lords looked on, hoping to be ransomed. Their horses were corralled near the haybarn, their followers roped under the trees. Prince Alcfrid brought his Mercian wife and Egfrid home. His sister, Alcfled, stayed with her lord Peada to govern south Mercia in Oswy's name. In three short weeks, desperation had turned to riches and mirth.

Faithful to his promise, Oswy was to dedicate his baby daughter at Easter. Men had no understanding, Hild thought tartly, as Queen Anfled started an early weaning and brought Elfled to the minster each day. Hild moved into the lodging built for the bishop, so that Elfi could play without disturbing the community. Knucklebones, bladders, her prized shell and a new gift from a hedger, a hound woven of withies and dragged on a length of gut, littered the abbess's floor. They fed her soft bread soaked in broth, and she napped after noon psalms in a cradle by Hild's bed.

"You're not eating." Hild recognized the queen's anguish.

"I don't regret his promise," Anfled retorted bravely. "It's just…
I miss her. She'll have a good life, I know; better than many royal
girls." She sighed. "Like Alcfled, reared to see Peada as the enemy,
then wed to him against her will. And so young."

"You were just as young," Hild said.

"But I was lucky. I had a mother to prepare me. Besides, Oswy's
considerate – to me, at least – and Romanus came with me."

"He helps, the chaplain?" Hild was surprised.

"Reminder of home," Anfled nodded. "Elfi will be saved all that.
Better God's virgin than a man's pawn. And I know you love her."

Hild sighed. Love: youthful lust, patience in wedlock, a friend's
affection, the bond between man and lord, the visceral love of a
parent, ecstatic joy, and searing pain. She knew about love.

Blossom frothed when Finan and his pale-robed priests
processed into the church. The royal couple took their seats
surrounded by kin and household, with the baby on her mother's
lap. From near the altar Hild saw young Egfrid, back from Mercia
with Prince Alcfrid and his wife.

"Lift up your hearts!" Finan raised his arms.

"We lift them to the Lord!" the reply echoed beyond the walls.

Finan blessed the font, took the child and marked her brow with
a cross of holy water.

"*Exorcidio te spiritus immunde!*" he said softly, driving evil away.
Then he touched her nose, ears and chest. "*I anoint you with holy
oil.*" Elfi, perched comfortably in his arms, looked critically at the
oil stain on her new white tunic, and tutted, bringing a smile to
everyone's face.

"Elfled, daughter of Oswy, do you renounce the Devil and all
his works?" The child looked up, startled at his ringing tones.

"I do!" Oswy declared firmly on her behalf. "With God's help."

"Do you promise to love and serve the Lord Jesus Christ?"

"I do, with God's help," he said again.

"Do you render yourself to him alone?"

"I do."

"All you her kinsfolk, do you willingly and wholeheartedly render this child to God?" They must all swear. No one must ever reclaim her.

"I do," came a ragged response, and a sigh rippled through the gathering, followed by the declaration of faith, *Credo in unum Deum*... Finan enfolded Elfled's hands in a fine linen altar cloth embroidered by Frigyd with crosses of gold. Holding her up for all to see, he declared, "Elfled, daughter of Christ, I receive you in the name of the Father, and the Son, and the Holy Spirit, so that you may share eternal life with them in glory." Beckoning Hild, he drew her hands into the same cloth. "To you, Abbess Hild of the household of faith, I entrust this child that you may nurture and train her to be Christ's faithful servant until her life's end."

Deeply moved, Hild took the child and turned to face the gathering. Oswy stood approving, Anfled's jaw was set, and Frigyd had tears on her cheeks. The king and queen offered bread and, in a final symbolic act, moved close to Hild to receive with her the bread of the Sacrament.

> *I sing to you, most glorious, blessed one,*
> *object of our hearts' desire, you who bear the crown,*
> *you the source of every good...*

The ancient hymn rang out as Finan led Hild from the church to bless Elfled's new home. Oswy and Anfled rode away without looking back.

From now on, Hild's houseplace and Begu's care would be the core of Elfled's life. The first evening, Hild took her back to church to offer her dedication cloth at the altar. The next morning she took her to the beach.

Carrying the basket of toys, she trudged over the soft dune with Elfled under her arm. Breathless from the child's weight and from wading ankle-deep in soft sand, she sank down. No one was in sight. She pulled off her veil, shook out her hair, and leaned back, idly sifting sand through her fingers. The little girl paddled and squatted, searching for shells. Critically selecting the best for her basket, she hurled away the rejects, gurgling with satisfaction when they splashed in the water.

"Elfi, come here!" Hild held her arms wide, chortling at the child's lurching progress, then hugged her tight and tickled her tummy till they rolled apart giggling. "How I wish Aidan had lived to see you," she murmured. "A king's daughter given to God!"

Elfled scrambled off to make sand pies and Hild reflected on the other ceremonial service to take place before the royal party left. "Cedd in a purple silk stole!" she chuckled, remembering him manhandling Aidan. "A cuddly giant of a bishop, he'll be; warm, approachable, energetic, learned. A true Aidan's boy. Bishop of Essex, indeed!"

Eventually, wedging hairpins between her teeth, knotting her hair and pinning her veil on top, she called, "Home time, chick!" Shouldering Elfled, she felt the first twinge of age. "Over forty! Older than my mother when she died. Well, as Ethelburga said, God must still have work for me. And I think that work is you!" She gave the child a hug and climbed up the dune.

Once the new Bishop Cedd set sail for Essex with King Sigebert, life settled into a new pattern. The field children took to passing Hild's lodging, offering Elfi birds' nests, teasels or tufts of goat's hair. She gave them shells or bladderwrack, chattering incomprehensibly. The swineherd brought a pig's bladder which provided hours of fun as the children threw, kicked, and rolled it around. Sometimes Begu took them all to the sands. Elfi grew strong and bronzed in the fresh air. She liked to be clean. Forever covered in sand or mud, she would strip off and drop her tunic into the washing trough, running around naked.

"Court customs!" Begu chuckled, and instituted "working dress like the sisters"; the minster did not have an endless store of tiny tunics.

Hild took her to noon prayers where she growled in a tuneless drone during the psalms. Afterwards she had a midday nap. Oblivious of her former life, she settled happily in her new one.

In late summer, Aetla returned, gaunt but elated. Preaching at all the ritual trees up the Tees valley, he'd capped them with crossheads, superimposing a caring Christ on outworn beliefs. He spent hours with Brother John, sharing his enthusiasm and discussing how to make his message simpler.

As the months passed, more young men and women arrived at the minster to study or to serve in practical ways. They brought their own gifts: reading, writing, or teaching; pottery, basketmaking or gardening; skills in kitchen, infirmary or guesthall. Some came for help, like a hare-lipped girl, teased beyond endurance, or a pair of wounded fighters. Heiu's old people lived out their lives in prayerful comfort. Peace and a sense of purpose prevailed.

Ulf's distraught arrival came as a shock. It was another spring and Hild was viewing a recalcitrant bull on the north slope when Begu panted over the hill waving a headcloth.

"Hild!" She clutched her middle, breathing in gulps. "Ulf's here. Says it's urgent."

He was pacing up and down outside Hild's lodging.

"Lady, there y'are!" he exploded, when she arrived breathless. "I'm at my wits' end. She were allus outrageous, but it's beyond anything."

"What is, Ulf?" Hild stood panting.

"The wife's looking after 'er, but we canna keep 'er. Not without 'er women. Will you tek 'er, Princess Alcfled?"

"I thought she was queen of South Mercia!"

"Ay, so did we. But up she rides, no guards, horse in a lather, demanding food. A' course, we took 'er in. But we canna keep 'er. 'Tis not proper," he wailed. "She says she's pursued, we must protect 'er, and send fer the king. *Send fer the king,* I ask you!" His hair was on end. Sweat soaked his tunic and his hand trembled.

"Come in the shade." Hild settled on the bench, signalling Begu for cups of ale. "Did she tell you why she wants the king?"

"No. An' she won't, the likes of us!"

"Well," Hild said practically, "she can stay in our guesthall. I'll ask Frigyd to look after her." Ulf was out of his depth, but would she do any better? "Send messengers to let King Oswy know."

The girl rode in with Ulf later that day, flushed and bareheaded.

"Welcome, lady." Hild bowed.

"Where's Father?" Panicky and frustrated, she didn't glance at the room Frigyd had prepared, or the women ready to attend her. "I thought he'd come. But if they capture me…" She flung herself on the bed.

"Can we help?" Waving the sisters away, Hild sat beside her.

"I'm scared," she moaned. "They'll never forgive me." Then anger took over. "They wouldn't let me hunt, ride, fly my falcon, anything. As for him! Don't do this, don't do that. Had to be in charge, be seen to be in charge. King, huh! A man who couldn't rule a hawk!"

"Peada, you mean?" Her given husband?

"I hate him!" she cried hysterically. "Couldn't stand him. Got rid of him. Rode away… to Father."

Hild put a cup to her lips. "Take a sip. Help you sleep." Had she really done what Hild thought she'd heard?

"Father!" Alcfled spluttered. "I did it for him." Hild felt her brow, tucked a fleece round her and held her hand. The girl grew drowsy, whimpering in her sleep.

"He had to go… I couldn't bear him…"

* * *

Ulf supplied a couple of guards and a kestrel so that Alcfled could hunt the king's lands. Frigyd offered her silk embroidery. The sisters provided veil and robe of their softest wool. Nothing matched her expectations.

Remembering Queen Anfled's pity for the girl, Hild forced herself to sympathy. Born in the Rheged court, wrenched away to a different culture when Oswy regained his homeland, petted and pampered, then summarily despatched to wed a Mercian enemy: small wonder she was petulant. But what had she done?

Hild went to the chapel to think. These days, it was the one place she could be alone. Not this time. A strange man knelt at the altar. He had the shaven crown, cropped hair, and dark robes of a Canterbury monk. A visitor in the guesthouse, she supposed.

"Abbess Hild!" Rising, he met her at the door.

"Welcome, brother!" Who was he, to know her name? She looked at his spare frame, the deep furrows between nose and mouth, and the tapering fingers. He waited expectantly.

"Are you travelling far?" she asked politely.

"Across the world," he cried exultantly, "with the teachings of the Holy Father."

"You've been in Rome?"

"And Lyons, and Canterbury. Five long years." He flung out his arms expansively. Something about the gesture stirred Hild's memory.

"Wilfrid, of course! The years have changed you, brother," she apologized.

"More than years have changed me, Abbess," he said sternly, his deep eyes burning in the old way. "God has tested me. Shipwreck, persecution, twice saved from death. Why?" He paused dramatically. "To fulfil God's purpose. Bring glory here."

Hild waited, brows raised.

"I've sat at the feet of holy men, heard beautiful music, sung liturgies, everywhere the same. Throughout Italy and France, evidence of God's greatness."

"Come and eat, brother, and tell us of your travels."

Neglecting his broth and scattering breadcrumbs, Wilfrid held the community spellbound with tales of his perilous journeys, the princes who welcomed him, the marriage and great province with which they tempted him.

"But my calling is a greater one," he declared. A sigh swept round the hall. They thrilled as he told of his stay in the house where Gregory lived until he became Pope and sent missioners to Britain. They lapped up his memories of reading in great libraries, studying with Archdeacon Boniface, standing where Peter the apostle had stood, and receiving the blessing of Pope Eugenius himself.

"Everywhere God's majesty," he cried, "striking men's hearts with awe!"

"But what of God's love, brother?" asked Hild. "Jesus led a simple life, draining himself to live out God's love to man."

"He showed us God's power to conquer sin and death. For that, Abbess, we owe the greatest praise and glory."

They were both right, Hild thought; looking at a medal from different sides. He was too young to remember shrinking in awe from the old gods. A loving Christ, to her mind, was closer to men's need.

Next morning, they walked together to the fish huts and jetty Ulf was building.

"Where do you go from here?" Hild asked.

"Lindisfarne, to report to the bishop, then the king. But I'll call in on Benedict Biscop at Wearmouth. His chapel is of pure white stone from France, and he has craftsmen to carve it and make glass windows. A small, but glorious, beginning!"

* * *

Some weeks later, noon prayers over, Hild had tucked Elfi up for her nap when she saw a rider dismount at the causeway and stride down the slope, leaving a posse of horsemen clustering on the ridge.

"Lady," he shouted, "a word!"

She recognized the impatient stride, tossing hair, glittering pommel and, as he drew nearer, the face red with fury and lips taut as a cable: King Oswy, unheralded and in a rage.

"My lord!" She bowed politely.

"I've come to see my daughter," he snapped, stopping in front of her. "Lead the way." About his height, Hild looked him straight in the eye.

"Napping, I hope," she said affably, turning to bend under her lintel and gesturing to Begu. "You'll take a cup of mead, my lord? Or wine?" Rounding the partition, she dropped her voice. "Here she is."

Elfled was asleep on her back, covers thrown aside, one chubby fist above her head, the other clutching her battered withy hound.

"Silver hair!" he exclaimed. His own was darker and shot through now with white.

"It's the sun," Hild murmured. "She loves the outdoors."

"A healthy child." A proud smile tweaked his lips. Hild hoped Elfi had drawn his sting. He downed the wine and crossed to the door. "Heavens! She makes her mark." Kicking the litter of playthings aside, he lowered himself onto the bench. "Now, what about my other daughter?" Pause. "The one you're hiding."

"We're giving the Lady Alcfled refuge." Standing above him, Hild spoke coldly. "She is deeply troubled."

"So she should be. Have you any idea what she's done?"

"Run away," she said flatly. "From Peada of Mercia."

"Christ's wounds!" Oswy exploded. "Worse than that. She's poisoned him!"

Hild swallowed and sank onto the bench; it was worse than she'd feared.

"Mercian troops are massing." Oswy's voice shook. "Alcfrid can't get through to me. They refuse to deal with him. They're electing their own king. *No more of Oswy's brats*, they say. No more of Oswy's brats!" His voice rose in a crescendo of disbelief until he was shouting and thumping his knee. She could almost feel sorry for Oswy; all his political machinations subverted by his own daughter!

"To kill a prince!" he howled. "They want his blood price, naturally. A fortune! She's a dangerous bitch, a mad hound ready for the cull."

Hild turned and looked levelly at his contorted face, so like his daughter's. "She's a girl, my lord," she said firmly. He looked at her, uncomprehending. His Companions, Hild realized, would have echoed his indignation, stoked his fury. "Something must have made her do it. What do you think it was?"

"You tell me!" he roared. There was silence. "She knew what was at stake," he groused quietly. "I told her. It was to hold my rule in Mercia."

"She's not behaving like a killer," Hild said slowly. "The horror is driving her wild. What she did, she did for you, she said. She said that only you would understand."

Oswy chewed the inside of his mouth. A man of action, he'd probably never considered feelings, even his own. He sprang to his feet and paced up and down, trampling Elfled's toys. Hild sat with head bowed: *Grant him insight, O Lord, and a merciful spirit.*

"She must be punished," he groaned, gazing across the settlement to the sea. "I'll have to show them she's been dealt with… Pay a hefty murder fine, let them have their Mercian ruler." He turned to her, calm but cold, his voice grating with self-control. "Fetch her to me."

Hild bowed acknowledgment. "It may take some time, my lord. She rode out earlier. I'll arrange food for you and your men."

Willingly Hild's people scattered in search of the princess. She was needed in the guesthall, they were to say. If Hild could prepare Alcfled, the worst might be averted. She sent a messenger to take her instructions to Ulf.

The afternoon wore on. Hild circled the buildings like the rest and then went into the chapel to pray that Oswy's violence would abate. As she emerged, she stopped, her heart in her boots.

Near the guesthall, Oswy and his daughter stood eye to eye, their hostility palpable, her fling for freedom battling against his pride. The evening sun cast their shadows across the grass. Arms at their sides, too far apart to touch, they swayed like snakes. Hild saw Elfi picking up her toys, Begu spreading cloths on a hurdle, fishermen pulling across the bay and herdsmen returning from the hill. It was a scene of peace, except for the king and his daughter.

He moved to touch her brow with a formal kiss. She sketched a cursory obeisance and stalked into the guesthall. Hild moved.

"Abbess!" Oswy waited, his face drawn and white. "I'm indebted for your care of her." Hild bowed acknowledgment. "I'll send women and guards as soon as I can. She's forbidden from my court and her brother's. I'm banishing her." He nodded towards the bay. "Over there, in the black hills of Deira. She must make her own life in exile." Wearily he walked uphill to the horses.

Banishment was a living death. *Broken the exile's heart, severed from country and kin.* How would Alcfled cope?

The girl shrugged off offers of help or comfort. Her dark eyes roamed emptily and she lashed at her horse. Ulf heard from her escort that she only barked with mirth when her kestrel tore into a living creature. At the end of winter a sullen company attended her over the water.

With them came a messenger for Hild. Oswy wished her to leave Hart. She was to go south and found one of his ten new minsters.

12

THE BAY OF LIGHT

On an ebbing tide the boat pulled across the bay to a headland shielding an estuary. Bay, estuary, cliff: the same as the Tees, Hild noticed, but in miniature.

The oarsmen had to pole across the mud to the River Esk, carving a turbulent brown course at the cliff foot. Fish jumped in the shallows, waders prodded for worms, and herring gulls wheeled overhead, keening mournfully in the bleak, grey sky. The men tied up at a skewed and broken jetty.

There was no sign of life, only a sheer gulley where a rope dangled. Heaving a sigh, Hild started to clamber up, hauling hand over hand, scrabbling for a firm footing. The rope jerked and Aetla laboured behind her. At the top she bent over, panting heavily.

"Oh, look, Aetla!" she pointed, exasperated. If they'd nosed further inland, the boat would have reached a wharf from which a regular track climbed to where she stood. There were hovels and coracles at the water's edge, fish traps poking out of the mud, and men hammering and whistling on a tethered ship.

"Well, here we are," she muttered. Ahead, the land sank in a shallow basin dotted with huts and bushes, stunted and leaning away from her. On the left, cliffs overlooked the sea. Where they met the estuary, a protruding arm curved protectively across the river mouth.

"Abbess!" Aetla stood looking down. "An old firepit. Heaps of rusting spearheads, never used."

"And that," Hild pointed along the cliff, "looks like some sort of farmstead." She started towards a squat building, its thatch black with age. As she and Aetla approached, a gaggle of geese lumbered up from a muddy pond, cackling aggressively. Immediately a wolfhound ran forward snarling, followed by a burly man wielding a heavy staff.

"What d'you want?" The man held the stick across Aetla's chest. "You're new."

Aetla, who'd met worse on his travels, murmured, "I am Brother Aetla. This…"

"Hrumph! What d'you want, then?" The man gripped the hound which crouched ready to spring. "Food, I s'pose." He sniffed. "Hi, son!" he hollered at a boy in the doorway. "Tell yer mother, bread and broth for a new priest and… Who's this?"

"Abbess Hild," Aetla replied. "We've sailed from Hart and tied up below."

"Below? You've come up the boys' rope?" Surprise made him less hostile. "Why here? No one comes here."

"Would you like them to?" Hild's question startled him.

"The new king," he sniffed. "Be good if he showed interest."

"Which king?" Aetla was curious. The man ran grubby fingers through his hair and his hound sniffed round their feet.

"Can't rightly say," he muttered, "not since good old Edwin." A heavy sigh. "Has he sent you, then? The latest?"

"In a manner of speaking." Aetla was discreet.

"Udric! Let them eat!" shrilled a woman, waving her ladle. Grudgingly the man jerked his head to let them pass. "Don't mind him." Shooing the geese away, the woman drew them inside. "It's an awesome task, tending the king's land, and he frets dreadfully."

Hild sank gratefully onto a log by the firestone, and the woman handed her a bowl of thick broth with crumbly cheese. The hound eyed each spoonful greedily.

"Son, outside with that beast!" snapped his mother and the boy clicked his fingers. "Follows him everywhere. Daft about creatures, him!"

Sidling back in, the boy stared like his hound. Old Udric pushed him along the log and demanded, with a sniff, to know their business.

"King Oswy has given me these lands for a minster," Hild said decisively. "A household of men and women dedicated to God."

The man sniffed, scratched his head and, after thinking hard, said, "You mean, you'll live here? I'll work for you?"

* * *

Rising early after a hard night by the fire, Hild walked past the pond and watched dawn rise over the sea. A brisk west wind puffed her skirts before her like sails, and whipped her veil over her head. Gripping it tightly, she looked over the fields and realized, in the low light, that each building was capped by a network of ropes, securing the thatch with heavy stones at their ends. Early summer, yet not a single green shoot on this windswept clifftop.

She turned round and her clothes snapped behind her. That smudge on the horizon was the Isle of Hart, where the minster faced the sun; here, the promontory jutted north. She set off along it, feeling the west wind blowing her sideways, and waves sucking at the base on either side.

It was a bleak, dejected place. Her hips ached from yesterday's climb and sleeping on the floor. Living on this hill would be trying; she was an old woman. Was Oswy punishing her as well as his daughter? Twice already she'd started afresh in a new home, and another beginning was wearisome. Sighing, she reminded herself that Christ's disciples left the familiar behind; Gregory, too, and Aidan.

Letting her eyes wander inland, she traced the River Esk as it wound between wooded banks into the far, blue moors. *To the hills I lift my eyes, from where my help comes.* The psalm soothed her.

"Lord, your will be done," she breathed. "Just make sure you give me the strength I'll need."

* * *

Queen Ethelburga had fled from here when King Edwin was killed, Udric explained as he showed them the lands. The army had never collected the spearheads he'd made, though they'd have been useful, heaven knew! This was an out of the way place; few ships called, news came late, and he couldn't keep up with the changes. Still, at least it made for a peaceful life. And that, he supposed, was what they wanted.

Chuckling ruefully, Hild followed him into a rectangular building with a sagging thatch.

"The royal lodging." He held his arms wide, sniffing uneasily. It stank of decay. The earthen floor was puddled and the beams freighted with cobwebs. Still, repair was possible, it was a good size and well situated, with its back to the sea and oversight of life on the slope below. It would do for her lodging.

Young Udric, trailed by his friends and hound, raced ahead as they turned left across the ploughland. The cottars tied to these home fields worked for Udric and lived off their own plots. Beyond the boundary ditch, lean cattle grazed the clifftops, and herdsmen were clearing the byre of winter dung.

Veering inland, they ducked under nut trees at a springhead, and followed the burn crosswise down the slope, glimpsing at its mouth the wharf where Udric had moored their ship. The boys jumped and splashed in the shallows, racing twigs downstream and noisily disputing the winner.

Trees grew thick on the opposite bank. Woodsmen's axes thudded, and Hild saw new planks piled to season. Women beat their washing at the stream edge and hung it to dry among the apple trees. Calf and beaver skins were stretched on tenterhooks, fish dangled from drying racks and, in a cluster of workshops, half-completed lengths of wool hung on untended looms. Craftsmen crouched over horn and pot, lads shinned up to patch roofs with fresh reeds. All the activity of a vill, Hild observed, but no joking or songs.

Udric steered them away from the fishing hovels up the main track to his farmstead. As they skirted the old queen's lodging,

Hild saw clouds of smoke gust horizontally across the skyline, and children cavorting round the firepit.

"New forkheads for tilling," muttered Udric, leading them beyond the sweating smiths to the neck of the tapering spur, and turning. "There!" he sniffed. "All in plain view, except…" he waved vaguely behind, "those ruins. A Roman lighthouse, they say. Probably why it's called the Bay of Light."

Bay of Light. Hild gasped. Lighthouse! *A beacon, beaming out the love of God.* Just what Aidan wanted. Was this a sign from God?

Udric started towards the farmstead. Suddenly he stopped, nose lifted like a scenting cur. Hild caught faint musical sounds: a traveller's horn, perhaps, or a bell. Suddenly, young Udric exploded into motion. Hurtling back down the track, he flung himself bodily at a figure striding from the river path onto the wharf. All the boys crowded round, and they tumbled back uphill in a group, the bell clanging wildly.

"Well, then!" Udric sniffed with satisfaction. Hild was dumbstruck.

"You've found me out!" Bishop Cedd gave his booming laugh. "I've been at my bolt-hole in the hills. Udric's the man with the boat that takes me back to Essex. But you, Hild," he gave her a brotherly hug, "I'm so glad you've come."

"You knew?"

"One of Oswy's ten minsters." He grinned. "And it's good Aetla's with you."

"I'm thinking of staying a while," Aetla said, with a sideways glance at Hild, "to pray and purify."

"No one better." Cedd clapped him on the shoulder and Aetla glowed. "Shall I ask my brothers as well? They helped me sanctify Lastingham."

* * *

Hild loved this spot at the tip of the promontory. It was midsummer, when the sun rose and set over the sea. The path to Valhalla, they used to say. She saw in it God's love pouring into his world.

Sitting on the ruinous heap of squared stones, she looked to the west where her abbey of Hart sang praise to God from cockcrow till day's end: on each visit, she'd found the brothers and sisters faithfully keeping the hours of prayer. Turning east, she saw beyond the fields the abbey herdsman move quietly among his cattle. After nearly four years, she knew his loping strides, his quiet eyes and silences. She'd watched his deftness with sick cattle, his shrewd eye for a vellum calf, his quick and painless culling. Once, in the early days, she'd sat out a shower in his crude shelter and tried to draw him out. He only smiled and ruffled the hound's scruff.

"You'll get nowt from Caedmon," sniffed Udric. "He's a close one. Turned up with the old queen. Good with stock."

"Caedmon, you say?" She remembered Ethelburga naming the half-hanged British lad and promising, *You'll always have a home with me.* Hild wondered if he recognized her from the past, but he said nothing, merely smiled like a man content with life.

A rattle of stones made her turn. Over the cliff edge popped a boy with a basket of rock on his back. She chuckled, recalling her first ungainly ascent by the workers' rope. The lad jumped down into the firepit where, these days, they fashioned beauty: medallions for book covers, neck crosses, bells for travelling priests. She marvelled as the hard-won metal oozed from the fire, or an ingot mutated into filigree under the master's tongs and the lads' polishing. Small wonder they used to think it goblins' magic.

"Mother Hild!" Elfled ran towards her.

"Careful! It's slippery!" Both sides of the spur were crumbling into the waves.

"I've learned it," Elfi crowed. "Will you hear me?"

"Go on, then," Hild smiled. At six years old, the child's mind was growing as fast as her body. Her daily task was to memorize lines from a psalm. She had by heart *O be joyful in the Lord*, and was beginning a song of comfort.

"Levavi oculos meos in montes," she intoned. *"I have raised my eyes to the hills…"* Reciting the first half without a hitch, she danced round begging for more.

"Come here, then." Hild mouthed each line, and the child watched and repeated. *The Lord is your safety... The sun shall not burn you by day... nor the moon by night... The Lord will preserve you from evil.*

"That's enough for now," Hild finished. "By the time we've travelled to York and back, you'll have mastered the whole thing. Now, Lauds, breakfast, and..."

"Off we go," they chimed. Swinging hands, they edged their way back.

* * *

Aetla, with staff and scrip, was going on pilgrimage into the hills. They parted when Hild's path descended to the River Derwent and Aetla carried on to the peat-gatherers' shacks and the outlaws' camp.

"Rash and violent, maybe, but no risk to me," he assured Hild. "They long for the human contact they lost as punishment for their crimes. *I will go in the strength of the Lord,*" he quoted. "*O God, you have taught me from my youth, and I will declare your wondrous works.*"

Elfi rode in front of Bosa on his horse; Hild lagged behind. For years she'd ridden nothing swifter than the abbey donkey. They planned to stay a night in Derwentdale with Bosa's kindred. He was a thegn who had recently entered her abbey, seeking to study for the priesthood. He'd do well, she thought, judging by his quick understanding and ease with people. Her diverse community, with sisters and brothers, married and celibate, travelling priests and home-based monastics, could not offer him the uniformity of the men's minsters, but Bishop Cedd pressed her to welcome trainees, citing her success with Aetla and Oftfor, and Brother John's scholarship.

Many men could recite the Scriptures, like Elfled, but Hild believed that priests needed deep learning if they were to help people understand Christ; vagueness was worse than ignorance. John excited his students' minds. He was collecting a library: histories, commentaries on Scripture, philosophy and practical guides, many of them copied in their own scriptorium. Hild's great joy was to read and discuss with him.

After splashing along the river meadows, Hild was glad of a warm lodging in Bosa's home. The child was asleep before being tucked up, but Hild lay awake. It was four years since Elfled had seen her parents. How would she cope at court?

When she was presented, she made her bow, backed to Hild's side, clung to her hand, and looked wide-eyed at the glittering throng. The court stared back, piqued by their fame and simplicity. Queen Anfled watched fondly.

"Elfi, there's your mother." Hild urged her forward. "That lady, the queen. Go to her, and be kind." With relief, she watched Elfled allow Anfled to draw her close, put an arm round her, and hold out a small piece of honeycomb.

"I like that." Prince Egfrid stretched across. "Give me some."

"That's rude." Elfi's piping treble cut through the babble and she closed her fist. "You should wait to be offered."

Hild gave a wry smile, Oswy let out a guffaw, and Egfrid flushed crimson, snatching back his hand.

"Elfi," the queen murmured. "This is your brother, Egfrid. Will you share a bit with him?"

"Sister, forgive me." The boy bowed formally. On the cusp of manhood, he was embarrassed at his childish impulse and needed to save face. "May I show you my falcon? Over there, by the door."

At a nod from Hild, Elfled went to the perch where the bird sat hooded. Gingerly she stroked his feathers.

"Oh, I like *him!*" she suddenly volunteered, bending to fondle Egfrid's wolfhound at the foot of the pole. "Prettier than our cattle hound."

A titter rippled round. Egfrid, persisting despite his friends' sniggers, conducted her round the King's hall. In piercing tones she asked about the spears on the walls, the dais, chairs with backs, the footstool for the king's spokesman, Egfrid's jewelled knife, and their relationship.

"I've two mothers," Hild heard her declare. "Mother Hild *and* Mother Queen."

"It's a good thing she's not here all the time," King Oswy chuckled.

"She'd have us bewitched!"

Hild captured her for bed in an annexe of Queen Anfled's lodging. Gingerly Elfled touched the hanging tapestries, a mirror on a stool, and fading flowers peeping through the straw, but she lay down sleepy. Hild left them together as Anfled pulled the fleeces round her.

"Bedtime prayer first." Elfi's announcement followed Hild, and she heard the child recite her litany perfectly.

She sat watching the moonlight on the river. It brought back memories. Here, in York, Heri danced through the meadows, Bass lost his leg, Erpwald rode out of her life. She'd been Egfrid's age, on the brink of maturity, Eostre's maid for the year. Little did she think, when Paulinus dunked her in this river, that his God would take over her life.

* * *

The next day Bishop Finan was to reconsecrate the old chapel where Edwin was baptized. Hild went there early. They'd hauled stones from the Roman ruins to build a skin round the wattle, and stretched the thatch to cover the wider walls. Not steep enough to slough off snow, she thought, but a protection for Christ's first footprint in Northumbria.

Before the door stood a raised cyst for Edwin's bones, newly reassembled after Penda's violent dispersal, surmounted by a simple wooden cross. Standing there, preachers could reach crowds far greater than the building would hold. Hild slipped into the dim sanctuary where, so long ago, she'd watched Paulinus baptize the infant Anfled and her own mother.

"*The heavens are yours and the earth is yours: the world and its fullness you created....*" A bent figure was reciting Prime, kneeling before the guttering altar candle. Hild shared his devotions, gradually registering his accent: not British, not Anglian, but familiar, as soothing as a lullaby. When she saw the small figure struggling to rise, she moved to his aid.

"Tch, useless old knees! Oops!" he chuckled, stepping awkwardly on his hem and grimacing as it tore. Not for the first time, Hild thought, taking in the faded black habit, clumsily patched. "*Grazie*, sister, *grazie!*" And he waved her away as he regained his balance.

The face, the voice, the humility. Memory stirred.

"Brother… James?" she whispered, looking down at him. "I thought you went back to Italy."

"I stay," he said simply. "Stay always. And you…?" He peered up at her. "Tch, useless old eyes!"

"Remember Bamburgh? Teaching a silly girl to read?"

"Hild! Often I wonder. You are little Hild?" They laughed at the epithet, gripping each other's hands.

"I thought you were far away," she said. "Why didn't you flee with Paulinus and the other priests?"

"Ah," he chortled. "Couldn't let that old viper, the Devil, poison my flock."

Still gripping his hands, Hild looked down affectionately at the small frame, bony now beneath the thin robe; at the beady eyes, and smiling mouth. All the lines slanted upward, etched by laughter. A man with a clear conscience.

"Abbess! Oh!" Bosa stopped in the doorway. "The queen's waiting."

"Oho!" James twinkled. "Not little Hild, but great Hild, yes?"

As Hild joined the royal party beside the cross, Elfi slipped a hand in hers. Bosa took his place in the line of priests behind Chad, Cedd's quieter brother, who bore aloft the Gospel book for the altar. James bowled merrily along at the tail, raising his voice as sweetly as in the old days, while the chanting procession circled the building inside and out.

Bishop Finan pronounced the dedication. Frail and withered, he leaned on the two royal chaplains, Romanus from Bernicia and Coclin, Cedd's third brother, from Deira. Finan was no older than her, Hild recalled, but burned out by his labours.

The prayers for Edwin's soul were entrusted to Brother James as he was the only priest who remembered him. King Oswy stood in full regalia, head bowed, with Prince Alcfrid and his wife a pace behind; symbolic homage crucial for Oswy's reconciliation with

Deira. Queen Anfled guided her two children to the plinth which covered her father's remains. Egfrid laid a wooden sword and Elfled a bunch of flowers.

"I picked them this morning," she announced, darting back to Hild.

"Lord, may your servant rest in peace, for he recognized salvation and brought it to his people," ended James.

The Amen rumbled far beyond the chapel enclosure. Only then did Hild see the crowd outside the fence. Prince Alcfrid moved easily among them, greeting many by name, as he ushered the king's party to the Great Hall. He'd ruled Deira well for his father, she thought, remembering his sister, Alcfled the outlaw, whom her priests visited fruitlessly. The procession moved slowly, she and the queen at Elfled's pace. Behind them the priests, as usual, chattered boisterously. A familiar figure tapped her arm.

"Eata, what are you doing here?" she exclaimed. His green eyes glowed affectionately. "And Cuthbert! I thought you were both at Melrose."

"We're Deirans now, like you," Eata chuckled. "Prince Alcfrid gave land at Ripon and Bishop Finan sent me to found a minster. Cuthbert and others came too."

Hild turned to Cuthbert. "Your father would have been pleased by today."

"Yes, he was Edwin's man." Cuthbert's thin face lit up. "No human is perfect, but Edwin made the right choice for his kingdom."

"And your new house, it prospers?" Hild asked. There was a discernible pause. Cuthbert looked uneasily to Eata.

"It's early days," he said quickly. "Our northern ways need adjusting to meet Lord Alcfrid's wishes." He paused, then added urgently in an undertone, "We need your prayers, Hild."

* * *

That night, once Elfled was asleep and the queen had discarded her court finery, she and Hild sat wrapped in fleeces over the dying fire.

"Hild, my mind's going round and round," Anfled confided.

"You're the one person I can tell. You may have ideas, and you'll keep it to yourself."

"What is it?" Hild prodded the fire. "Elfi?"

"No. Well, I'll miss her all over again. Such a gem. But no, it's Oswy."

Hild froze; when trouble loomed, it was always Oswy.

"And Alcfrid." Ani's voice sharpened with misery. "His own son! Oswy says Alcfrid's too popular, changing Deira to suit himself, a threat to the kingdom. I'm worried, Hild. It's the old impetuous Oswy, the one who killed his cousin, the one I have no hold over…"

"You're afraid he'll…?"

Anfled nodded. "Alcfrid has a point, you see. It's the church."

"The church!" She'd assumed faith had no problems for those reared to it.

"Oswy and I have different customs. His bishop keeps Easter at the wrong time for my chaplain. Until now, it hasn't mattered. But this year Oswy was feasting a week before I finished the Lent fast. No queen to serve his guest cup. He wasn't pleased."

Hild opened her mouth but Anfled cut her off. "And Alcfrid's begun to listen to priests like Romanus, who thinks all priests should be tonsured, and Wilfrid who has come back full of enthusiasm for Roman ways. He even said Bishop Finan's like a Druid, all beard and flowing hair!"

"Hair!" Sort out the clashing calendars; but hair?

"The tonsure represents Christ's crown of thorns, Romanus says," Anfled answered flatly.

"I see." So it was serious. Hild gazed helplessly into the dying embers.

"But there's worse," the queen continued hoarsely. "Oswy thinks this is all an excuse; that Alcfrid really wants to split the kingdom, have Deira and Lindsey for himself. I'm frightened, Hild. Oswy's ruthless, and it's his own son!"

Ani was right, thought Hild; Oswy could be relied on to pick a quarrel.

"Could you… I wonder…" So urgent was her impulse to help

that Hild started speaking before she'd worked out what to say. "What if you all sat together and talked it out?"

"We've tried. It's a running sore," Anfled moaned.

They talked late into the night. There was no solution.

* * *

Over the moors they galloped into the teeth of a gale. Hild's skirts ballooned wildly, so she pulled them up through her girdle; there was no one to see. The forest tossed and creaked alarmingly. Uprooted trunks and fallen branches blocked the track. Out on the homestead fields, Hild's veil whipped off. Her pony shied and danced erratically past field huts where roof stones clattered and doors swung, banging.

"Thank God you're safe!" Begu cried, hauling in their packs. "Bosa, pull the door and make it fast. I've a meal for you all."

The gale persisted, driving the spring tides up the estuary, submerging the wharf and flooding the fisher cottages. Day after day the winds howled, fierce enough to bowl grown men over. Night-time was worst. Lying under groaning beams they heard roof stones bang the walls, beasts whinny, and shutters crack. Eventually, the barn roof blew off, the mesh of ropes ripping like a spider's web. Chunks of thatch and wattle cartwheeled away and bowled over the cliff. Men struggled in blind confusion, torches veering, shouts lost in the wind. The thatch caught. Flames roared. Coughing and retching they raced to drive out poultry, trample sparks, and hurl precious storage jars and baskets as far away as they could.

"Pray for rain at tide turn," Udric yelled, tugging at a smouldering beam with his bare hands. Hild staggered around in the dark, gathering old and young into her lodging.

The morning after the fire brought grey drizzle and a flat sea. Hild viewed devastation as bad as a cattle raid: smouldering ruins, grain bags shredded, straw draped over bushes, lodgings gaping, stock scattered. Udric counted everyone into the church at the head of the track. Lauds was a hoarse affair but they sang praise to God; no lives were lost.

Setting the monastics to keep the hours, Hild shared out the work of recovery: ruins to dismantle, timber to fetch, reeds to gather, ropes to twist. Caedmon coaxed cattle from the woods where they'd stampeded. Young Udric and his mates cleared the beck of fallen trees, disentangling branches from the leather workers' skin-steeps, and heaving away trunks with the ox-team. Runaway swine foraged on the waterlogged fields till the swineherd and his children drove them inside a roofless hut. Brother John's students collected the vellum and drying racks which lay strewn across the crop rows, crusted in mud.

Begu treated injuries and looked after the infirm, while Udric's wife organized the women to retrieve any stores they could and prepare cauldrons of hot broth. Brother John occupied the young children in his library. Hild left Elfi chin in hand, absorbed by the tale of Saint Paul shipwrecked on Malta. When she looked in later, Christ was stilling the sea but Elfi was fast asleep.

"Worst disaster since the old queen fled," lamented Udric, sniffing furiously. "It'll be a hungry season. Takes time for the growing."

Hild nodded. "We must have no waste and no one going short," she said. "Your wife's got women salvaging stores. I'd like you to muster men for building a hall large enough for everyone to eat and sleep in until their homes are rebuilt. And I mean everyone, Udric, including the fisher families."

"But we don't mix, lady. Never have."

"They're God's children too, and they need help. And don't you dare pretend we shan't all need their fish!"

No one had leisure for Elfi. She missed her starring role at court. When young Udric brought her an orphaned hare, she announced coldly that she wanted a kestrel. Hild caught her mincing like the queen's women, and was annoyed when a tanner delivered a thong the child had ordered to string her shells like beads.

"When they're all up to their eyes!" she snapped.

"Don't fret; she'll grow out of it," Begu chuckled. "She dunned me for a headcloth, down at the washtubs."

"That'll come soon enough. Then she'll want rid of the pesky thing."

But they watched uneasily as she sulked on the mud island in the estuary.

"I'll lay stepping stones to the far side," Udric sniffed. "Stop 'er getting caught by the tide."

"You're too busy." Hild was irritated.

"Done in the shake of a lamb's tail, lady," he retorted, "if we pull together, like you say." And when he had to ride round the bay to check the damage, he offered to take Elfled. "Give her an outing. She likes to dig her heels in. I'll find 'er summat speedy."

Afterwards the child took to spiriting away any idle pony to race along the sands as far and fast as she could. Or she slunk along the cliff to the herdsman's shelter and crouched beside his hound. Caedmon's calm soothed her as well as his beasts.

* * *

Oftfor strode down to the wharf, where coracles lay smashed, fisher hovels had floated away and the boat was stranded in the mud. He stood tall amidst the ruins, every inch a thegn's son, fair hair streaming in the wind.

"Foolhardy to rebuild here!" he cried, pointing. "Why don't we clear those trees over the burn and build where the ground rises?"

"We'd be further from our traps," muttered the headman.

"With coracles outside your doors and a good view?" countered Oftfor. "Coracles have been known to walk!" There was a titter. All eyes swivelled to Elfi.

"A lot of heavy work." Pessimistic, the head fisherman.

"But we'd be safer," his wife chipped in. "I think it's a good idea."

Thank goodness for a woman's common sense, thought Hild. "Oftfor will see to it," she announced, turning away.

Elfled pulled on her hand. "Does everyone know about the coracle?" she asked. It went missing until a ferryman spotted it upriver, with Elfi perched on the nearby bank.

"Well, he lost a day's work, chick – a day's food for his family. It's his livelihood. He asked all round."

After a long silence, Elfled said, "He hasn't said anything."

Hild looked at her thoughtfully. "Because he was glad to get it back. But also, I think, because you're you. A princess. He may even be afraid you'd be angry."

"But that's unfair! He should be the angry one. Can I make it up to him?"

"Too late now, chick."

"But I can say sorry." And she ran off.

Turning up the track, Hild heard singing which she hadn't previously noticed. A column of dark-clad monks swung along the river path, reminding her of Paulinus advancing to battle at Woden's grove.

"Abbess, it looks as if God has sent us in your time of need." The leader broke away, pointedly surveying the desolate fields and gutted buildings.

"Wilfrid! Brothers! Welcome." Her mind whirred: how could she feed another seven men? She stretched out her arms. "We are short, as you can see, but what we have is yours to share."

They kilted their skirts and sang as they worked, hacking wood, clambering up ladders, and raising beams. In the refectory, Wilfrid was greeted enthusiastically by those who remembered his traveller's tales. This time, he was sterner.

"Frugality and self-discipline!" he cried, scattering crumbs in the old way. "The rules in Italian monasteries. I want to establish them here." His voice was mellifluous and his smile bewitching. The company was entranced. Sourly, Hild asked herself what was new about frugality and self-discipline; her people pooled what they had and followed a strict timetable of worship, study, work, and prayer. They didn't talk about it; simply lived that way.

"We've made a small start at Ripon, and Prince Alcfrid's pleased," he continued. So that was it! Wilfrid was working on Eata's monks to change to Roman ways. He was at the root of Cuthbert's unease, Queen Anfled's tears, and the antagonism between King Oswy and his son!

"But Christianity's been established in Italy for centuries!"

Hild exclaimed. "Here it's in its infancy." She couldn't believe imported ways were better for Northumbria than those developed by Aidan to suit the people. Especially if they split the royal house.

"Never too soon to demonstrate God's laws," Wilfrid declared. His brow was clear, his eyes shone, he knew he was right; he'd discovered it all at the Pope's feet.

"But when people love Christ, they follow his example." Hild was defiant. "They don't need rules."

Once the workers' hall and fisher cottages were complete, Wilfrid's party turned their attention to the old boat, marooned in the middle of the Esk. Hauling it to the wharf, they caulked the timbers, adzed and sanded fresh oars, and worked alongside the ropemakers and saildressers to prepare for a voyage.

"We're sailing to Stamford," Wilfrid explained as Hild accompanied him to the boat. "Prince Alcfrid's given me land to set up a monastery in the Italian style. We'll even be near enough to Canterbury to brush up our singing."

"What about Brother James at Catterick?" Hild asked. "Doesn't he sing in the Roman style? He came over with Paulinus."

"Mm." Wilfrid nodded. "Rather out of practice."

Nothing, Hild thought sadly as he jumped aboard, was good enough for Wilfrid; he left no space for other people.

"Such beautiful music!" exclaimed Bosa, holding a dripping rope as singing reached him across the water. Wilfrid stood by the helmsman, timing the rowers by the rhythm of their psalm.

"They're greatly gifted," Hild sighed. "But God hears the music of the heart."

* * *

Months later, Hild was hailed in the fields by a cottar's child; Udric wanted her. Always so nervous, the steward, so frightened of doing the wrong thing. She started the slow ascent to her lodging.

"Have to find a stick," she muttered, pausing to catch her breath and straighten her back. It was good to see the land recovering:

to the right of the track, fruit trees laden with blossom and fields bristling with shoots; ahead, Begu's bushy herb plot.

Someone waved from the abbey kitchen: "Udric... wants... you!" Waving back, she passed between the guesthall overlooking the river and the abbey dormitories, men at one end, women at the other.

"Nearly there!" she sighed, looking up to the church standing squat and solid against the winds, midway between her lodging and Udric's clifftop farmstead.

"At last!" His accusing cry carried on the wind, and she saw him run down, both hands waving, to wait at her door.

"Summat strange, lady. Can't fathom it." He was breathing heavily.

"Udric, don't spread alarm." Hild drew him inside. Sinking breathless onto her chair, she pointed to a stool. But Udric stood sniffing, fidgeting with his belt, at a loss for words. "What's the matter?"

"Cattle prodder," he managed. "You'll think it daft."

"What?" she asked patiently.

"Dumb as his beasts. I wouldn't believe..."

"Udric!"

He jumped, let go of his belt, and grasped the pillar as if holding steady in a storm. "Well," he sniffed. "The herdsman... Caedmon... he's seen..." A loud sniff and a long pause.

"Yes?"

"... seen an angel." He backed defensively against the pillar.

"Yes?" Hild said with studied calm.

Udric swallowed. "He said the angel... told him to sing!"

She waited.

"He showed me, sang to me – Caedmon!" His voice rose steadily. "I mean, he never speaks, let alone sings. When the harp's going round in hall, he skives off."

"But he sang to you?"

"Yes, I made him. Prove his story."

Hild thought for a while. "Send him to me after work."

His burden lifted, Udric lurched out, mopping his nose on his arm.

The cattle were in their stalls and Hild was at her reading desk when Caedmon knocked.

"Old friend." She led him gently to the bench and they sat with his hound at their feet, looking towards the setting sun. "I know your love of peace, and your tenderness for God's creatures. Tell me about your vision."

"An angel." He turned to look her straight in the eye. "Couldn't be anything else. Last night in the byre. A voice said, 'Sing.' 'I can't,' I said. 'You can,' it said. 'I don't know any songs,' I said. 'You know God's creatures,' it said. 'Praise his creation.' And I did."

Hild knew the man of old. He'd never hurt beast or cheated man. Honest as spring water. She had no doubt he spoke truth.

"A dream?" she asked.

"Perhaps," he answered without offence, "but the song is real."

"Can you sing it now?"

"I could when I woke." In a low, gruff voice with a rhythmic lilt he sang:

We must praise
The Maker's skill
And his design,
A master's work.
The roof of heaven
His first creation,
Then earth below
as home for man...

The short lines, the beat, the meandering tune, the common words. Like a scop's tale, or the impromptu lay of a thegn in his cups. A strange amalgam: praise to God in a drinking song. For all Udric's warning, Hild was astounded.

"Sounds better with a bit of thrumming on the old harp," Caedmon chuckled.

It was growing chill. Hild took him indoors and sent Begu for Bosa. He came running, with Oftfor and John close behind. Unfazed, Caedmon told the tale and sang the song. They sat amazed.

"From the heart, brother," John sighed appreciatively. "You sing what you know. A gift of God."

"Could you do it again?" Oftfor chipped in. "Another song, if we give you a story?"

"I don't know," Caedmon replied bluntly. "Give me one."

Hild nodded to her desk and Bosa read about Adam and Eve, twice. Caedmon wandered off with his hound. Next morning he sought Hild out with the Garden Song, as he called it, in the same style: tender green of bursting leaves, soft birds' feathers, sharp tang of buds, virgin freshness tainted by man, the sin which drew God's pity, bringing Christ to earth.

Hild took him to the chapel at noon. With no vestige of shyness, he told the brothers and sisters of his vision.

"How, Caedmon?" A single voice broke the stunned silence. "Why, after all these years?"

"I don't know," Caedmon said. "I've listened to you, and the men over their ale. I heard those visiting monks, their sweet singing… but me, never. God must have laid his hand on me." And, wielding his harp, he sang both songs.

"Good beat," cried a travelling priest. "Catchy things that folks'd remember. Will you teach me?"

That was the start. Caedmon was often seen leaning against the chapel wall, fondling his hound, waiting for someone to translate the Latin readings. His fluent creations put the community in ferment, learning, practising, singing as they tilled, wove and sewed books.

"Is it quite proper," Bosa asked Hild, "mixing humdrum and divine?" She thought of Cedd, long ago, assuring her God was in the whole of life; and Aidan saying God's Spirit was alive in men whose hearts were pure.

"Work and worship," she said briskly. "We offer both to God's glory."

* * *

Hild sat at the foot of the preaching cross outside the church, eyes shut against the sun, relaxed by the rhythmic schlurring of the waves. An offshore breeze brought her the chink of the forge, children's games, cooks clattering, the creak of the guesthall's well bucket, and someone, somewhere, singing Caedmon's Garden Song.

All was ready for the new bishop's coming. Seeing the battered Lindisfarne boat manoeuvre at the wharf, she heaved herself up to begin her slow walk to greet him.

"Lord Bishop." She knelt.

"Just bishop, if you must, my dear." He blessed her, helped her up and loped beside her up the track, a lean, bent man in sandals and dusty robes. He spoke fluent Anglian with an Irish lilt, as well as priestly Latin and his native tongue. "Colman will do. What better than my baptismal name?" And he slowed to her pace and took her arm.

He was not a weak man – she'd heard he trounced Oswy's Companions for greed – but he was humble. He stayed with Bosa and his fellow ordinands through their night vigil and, when he gave them the blessing, he didn't reach down but knelt before them, embracing them as brothers in Christ. Afterwards he led a singing crowd to the beck and baptized new converts: Udric and his family, fisher families and, to Aetla's delight, some of his ruffians from the moors.

"They've repented," he explained, "and want to make good their crimes."

"D'you like my shells?" Elfled greeted Bishop Colman in their lodging. Hild was embarrassed; the child had become inseparable from her necklace. But Colman crouched to look.

"Did you find them in the rockpools?" he asked. "See, this one clamps down to keep the water out, this shuts up like a door – oh, and here's one of those coiled snakes, heavy as stone." Dark and fair heads together, they worked their way along the thong. "God's so lavish!" he sighed as he stood up.

"Now I'll recite for you," Elfled announced, leading him to Hild's chair. "This is what Mary said," she explained solemnly, "when she heard baby Jesus was coming. *My soul is happy in the Lord…*"

"Child," he said at the end, "you have the greatest treasure in the world."

"Oh, no!" She looked slyly at Hild. "My brother has a kestrel."

Colman chuckled. "How old is his kestrel?"

"About three."

"Well, he'll die before you grow up. But the treasures in your mind will last the whole of your life."

In the next two years, Colman became a regular visitor. *My circular pilgrimage*, he called it, sailing down the coast, calling at Hild's abbey, journeying overland to Alcfrid's royal vill at York and returning up the Great Vale to cross into Bernicia and follow the Roman road north. Hild marvelled at his inexhaustible urgency and the way he poled himself along like a boat.

She loved him for joining in with whatever was afoot. He sang Caedmon's songs with tuneless gusto. One year he dedicated a little retreat she'd built at the far end of the bay. Another, he trained her in testing the vocations of those who offered themselves. And there was the time she consulted him about an outlandish idea.

"More and more people come to hear the preaching," she said. "They gather round the cross outside the church. Often the stories and prayers blow straight out to sea. Such a shame when they've come after a long day's labour. I'm thinking of building them a chapel."

"A chapel for the people? Wonderful idea! I'll come and dedicate it."

These were peaceful years. Hild gradually delegated her responsibilities. Bosa planned the eight daily services, Frigyd oversaw the guesthall, Oftfor led some of Brother John's seminars, Aetla led the growing team of travelling priests, a lay brother ran the kitchens, Udric had charge of the fieldworkers, and Begu looked after Hild and Elfled with loving care.

Hild saw everyone who asked: youths seeking book learning, wrangling cottars, men fleeing justice, the sick and aged, even visitors curious to see a woman who read books and taught men. She examined all who offered themselves, watched how they settled into the rigorous regime, supported those who were admitted, and studied each morning with the group of novices, among whom was Elfled.

She was learning to read. Choosing a Gospel story, Hild read the Latin words expressively, running her finger along the line. Elfi picked out phrases she understood and guessed others, until she could read the Latin with meaning herself. She sat in on Brother John's discussions, enjoying the cut and thrust of debate, and had her own ways of working things out.

"What's a parable?" she asked Begu at the wash tanks.

"Well," Begu answered, "the Prodigal Son, the Ten Talents…"

"Yes, but why call them *parables*?"

"Oh dear, Elfi," Begu sighed, "you'll have to ask Mother Hild. No, not now! She's busy, and we've to spread these shifts to dry. Here, take the neck while I twist."

"Why didn't he wash the disciples' hands?" Elfi persisted. "Why only feet?"

"It's not as if she's careless," Begu sighed, relating the incident to Hild. "Her spinning and weaving are fine…"

"Better than mine," Hild chuckled, making a mental note of the questions.

"She mends and kneads with the best. But her mind floats away where I can't follow. Words, always words. It set me thinking. Should you try her at writing?"

"Writing!" Hild gasped. But it made sense, and so Hild and one of the brothers taught Elfi the basics and she joined the scriptorium.

"Self-discipline is what she's learning," Hild told Begu, almost missing the old flyaway Elfi. "While the light lasts, no one utters a sound. You can hear quills crawling over vellum!"

"She's developing a good grasp of the meaning," reported Brother John.

Hild was delighted. "Brother, who would have dreamed…"

"… we'd nurture a female scribe?" he chortled. "God's full of surprises. So long as she still has chance to stretch her legs."

"Oh, she goes wild, running about with the calling bell at service time. And she walks the rounds with me. I want her to feel ready in time."

"Not for years yet, Abbess." John briefly touched her arm. "She's still a child."

Fun, Hild thought. That's what John meant. Had Elfi enough fun? She hunted with young Udric, lathered a horse racing along the sands, or giggled with the girls among the nut trees. But she seemed naturally serious.

"You should have seen her admitting the new man," Bishop Cedd chuckled as he sauntered with Hild to the refectory. He was staying in the abbey while Udric prepared the boat for his return to Essex. Elfled caught his sentence as she ran past.

"Brother Tatfrid couldn't speak for coughing, so I decided to put him in the infirmary and told him not to talk," she announced and ran on.

"You say he comes from Eata at Ripon, this Brother Tatfrid?" Hild asked Cedd.

"From Ripon, yes." Cedd hesitated. "But Eata's gone back to Melrose."

"Why?"

"Prince Alcfrid's brought in someone else. My brother, Coelin, told me – he's the prince's chaplain. Alcfrid's committed to tonsures, the Roman Easter, and so on. He got it from the bishop of Wessex, a Frenchman called Agilbert."

"And dismissed Eata?"

"No. Eata decided to leave the prince a free hand. Alcfrid's brought in a monk from Stamford."

Hild clutched Cedd's arm. "Come in here, where we can be private." She led him to a log in Begu's herb patch. Scents wafted up and insects hummed busily. Pulling his worn robes round his knees, Cedd basked in the evening sun and waited.

"Is it Wilfrid?" she asked. "The man Alcfrid's chosen?"

He nodded. "I knew him at Lindisfarne – a clever, driven youth. And he has a healing gift."

"Yes," Hild sighed. "A talented man. Cedd, do you see anything of the Kentish monks when you're in Essex?"

"Quite a bit," he answered. "In London, mostly, where both our kings berth their ships. Why?"

"Do you get on?"

"Of course!" Cedd laughed his full-throated laugh. "We share the same goals." Of course; he'd get on with anyone. *Love God and love your neighbour.*

"And Wilfrid? Do you see him at all?"

"Not really; my minster's in south Essex and he's the far side of East Anglia. We once met by chance. King Sigebert kept me with him when he viewed an East Anglian church for us to copy, and Wilfrid was there from Stamford. It was tall, and built of stone. He approved. Why do you ask?"

"No reason, really. An unease. A feeling he's trying to impose himself in Northumbria. Prince Alcfrid and the queen are fond of him, and he's… ingratiating, somehow."

"But he's in no position to act against the wishes of his bishop!"

"No. I suppose not." If Cedd had been his bishop, he wouldn't dare, she thought, looking at her old friend's certainty and strength. But she still wasn't sure. During daily prayers for names in the abbey's Book of Life, she added her supplication for the fraught royal household.

"I remember your fondness for Eata," Cedd said gently. "Wilfrid's not better; just different."

* * *

Hild decided she'd better go and see this Brother Tatfrid whom Elfi had admitted. If he came from Wilfrid's Ripon, she might have to handle a clash of customs.

He was crouched in the sunny angle between the infirmary and the church, listening with closed eyes to the brothers chanting on the other side of the wall. As Hild approached, he looked up and flipped off the cowl which protected his tonsured head.

"I hear Elfled visits you," Hild said with a smile. "I hope she isn't a nuisance."

Tatfrid beamed. "I feel like her tutor, Abbess. She asks good questions and I enjoy shaping answers to suit her."

"Parables?" He nodded. "Redemption?" It was Elfi's current preoccupation.

"A hard enough doctrine for anyone," he chuckled, "let alone someone who's never had to buy anything
!" They laughed.

"Hear that?" He suddenly raised a finger. "Lovely!"

"Fieldworkers," she smiled, "singing Caedmon's Creation Song." His obvious tolerance was reassuring, and his gift for listening.

"Mother Hild! Are you coming?" Elfled was hopping up and down outside their lodging. "I've something for you. Come on!"

"Patience!" Hild reached the bench and sat with folded hands. Elfi took a stand near the fleabane and recited:

> *"I saw a stranger yesterday,*
> *I put food in the eating place,"* counting on her fingers,
> *"drink in the drinking place,*
> *music in the listening place.*
> *And in the sacred name of the…* something or other…
> *God…"*

"Threefold," prompted Hild, imitating the counting. "Father, Son, Holy Spirit."

> "Yes, well… *in the sacred name of the threefold God*
> *…The stranger blessed me and my house,*
> *my cattle and my dear ones.*
> *And the lark sings, Often, often, often…"* sounding like a cuckoo.

"The stranger is Christ in disguise," they finished in unison.

"Frigyd taught it to me," Elfled explained.

"Well done, chick!" Hild gave her a hug, then surprised herself by wondering if Elfled was getting too old for that.

"She said it's her rule for the guesthall, because Jesus said, *Whenever you do something for someone, you're doing it for me.*"

"And that's why we keep a guesthall, so we can always welcome people in need."

Elfled nodded, satisfied. "Mother: redemption. Brother John's always on about it, and I haven't worked it out yet."

"Love at a price," Hild answered. "You know Bishop Cedd, and Brother Chad, and the other Lindisfarne men?"

"Mm." Elfi curled up on the bench, ready for a story.

"As boys, they were captured in war and taken to Bamburgh market to be sold as slaves. Aidan rescued them. Heaven knows how he paid because he was so poor, but he bought them, freed them, and gave them a home. Aidan 'redeemed' them."

Elfled nodded.

"God redeemed humanity in the same way."

"You mean... God rescued us and set us free? Paid for us?"

"Yes. With love. And with pain and blood when Christ died on the cross. The threefold God, remember? Father, Son and Holy Spirit. God, the redeemer."

* * *

What happened soon after took Hild by surprise. In the old days, she'd have blamed a spiteful deity. King Oswy himself hove into view.

At first, she thought it was his herald starting up the slope while the bodyguard offloaded horses at the wharf. Then, recognizing Oswy's impatient, bandy-legged stride, and remembering his temper, she abruptly left the infirmary, crossing the rough grass at a trot. Only when her breath ran out did she slow down, smoothe her skirts and pull her veil straight before turning into her lodging.

Oswy sat in her chair, cup in hand, feet on the hearthstone.

Elfled, her light woollen tunic stained with grass, stood before him, holding forth.

"I work in the scriptorium, making books. Brother John helps me understand what they mean. Do you know about redemption?"

"Ah, Abbess!" Oswy's eyes beamed relief. He looked older, with thinning hair and dark patches round his eyes; worry lines, too, making his nose jut out.

"Elfled's a good scholar, my lord," Hild said, omitting her livelier exploits. "Thank you, Elfi. Why not go and find Caedmon's puppies?"

"Or your brother," Oswy suggested, "down at the ship."

"Oh, yes!" A child again, she whisked away.

"Abbess, I've come for advice. But seeing Elfled… Will you bring her to see her mother?"

Hild recalled the effect of their last court visit. She took her time fetching a stool and placing it opposite the king. "My lord… you gave Elfled to God. His abbey is now her home."

"Umph!" He flushed.

"One day," Hild swallowed, "she'll lead prayers for your kingdom, the role you chose for her. But not if she gets… distracted."

"Ah!" He bent to ease his boot.

"Tasting luxury that can never be hers – it gives her the wrong idea, unsettles her."

Oswy's face darkened. His cold blue eyes scanned Hild under lowered brows.

"She's a credit to you." Hild looked him in the eye, refusing to be intimidated. "And you're always welcome here."

"I understand," Oswy barked, bristling with unspoken anger. He turned aside abruptly and Hild wondered what he would do.

He made a business of picking up his cup, and she refilled it from the jug on the hearth.

"Well, the other matter," he snapped. "The queen tells me you were baptized by Bishop Paulinus."

"Ye-es." What was this about? "But ever since Bishop Aidan, I follow the ways of the people. We all worship the same Christ. The differences are slight."

"It doesn't feel like it!" Oswy exploded. "My son Alcfrid… he's fallen under the spell of some monk and is making an issue of it. Wants to break away from the kingdom."

"Oh, no! Bishop Colman…?"

"Colman's in a fix. Under pressure all round. Even one of his own monks. Irishman called Ronan. Used to make Finan spit fire." At each phrase, Oswy beat his knee in the old way. "And now, Alcfrid's dismissed the monks Finan sent him."

"Eata!" Hild breathed.

"Brought in some youngster from the East Anglian border where they follow Paulinus," Oswy spat out. "Been to Rome. They're right, we're wrong, according to him." He sighed heavily. "So, what do I do? That's what I want to know."

Hild froze; Oswy pouring out his troubles to her! And she had no answer. Ever since the trip to York, she'd found nothing better than the same old thing, which Ani had said was useless.

"Could you… perhaps… talk it through with the queen and prince?"

"We've talked and talked, the three of us. With Finan, ages ago. With Colman recently. Nothing comes of it. Anfled thought, as you have a foot in both camps…" he tailed off despondently.

There was a long silence.

"What are the main issues?" Hild asked at last.

"Several little things – well, they seem little to me. Singing, robes, hairstyle – is it better to wear a crown of thorns, or shave your forelocks so God can beam into your brain?" He gave a short, harsh bark. "But the real nub of it is Easter."

"The timing…" she nodded.

"The queen's fasting when I'm feasting." He started pacing. "A king's table without a queen's welcome. We've coped till now, but with Alcfrid stirring things up…" Irritation brought him to a standstill. He stood like a wolfhound awaiting a whistle.

"If there was an easy solution, you'd have found it, my lord." Hild was thinking frantically. "All I can suggest is a formal meeting, on neutral ground; a structured debate, with bishops, in a prayerful and brotherly spirit."

"Neutral ground!" Oswy leapt on the words. "Here? Where the traditions meet?" He slapped his thigh, man of action once more. "I'll ask Colman, and tell Alcfrid to bring a bishop. Here? Before next Easter?"

* * *

So much hung on this meeting: Aidan's vision of love in Northumbria, the unity of the king's court, and the future of all the priests she knew. Hild felt as if she were shouldering the cares of the kingdom.

Pushing closed the door of the women's dormitory, she noticed violets sheltering at the foot of the wooden wall. The older she grew – and she must be fifty now – the more she delighted in the early flowers. Their deep blue cheered her.

The guesthall was full of royal Companions and she had lent her lodging to King Oswy, but the bishops and chaplains would be the main players. The abbey church, she'd decided, was the best place: in God's house, before his altar.

A wet wind drove in through the door, creating puddles at the entrance. Candles along the walls guttered, the lamp over the altar swung erratically, pages of the Gospel book fluttered on the reading desk, and a smell of damp earth rose from the floor. She stood for a moment in prayer before the side altar dedicated to Saint Gregory. Who better to aid the deliberations of his beloved Anglians?

With a jolt she left quickly; there were no seats for the royal party. By the time she returned, the scene was set. Like opposing armies, dark-robed followers of Rome huddled on the left, and northern priests on the right. Moving to the altar end, she tried to draw the sides closer to form a circle like a council of elders round a king's hearth. No one budged.

Bishop Colman, deep in thought, fingered his neck cross and looked stiff in formal robes: a rusty pallium, and a forked mitre sticking up like horns on either side of his head. Bishop Cedd towered beside him, in his bishop's pallium but bareheaded, chatting quietly to his brothers, Chad and Coelin. Slightly apart, Brother Ronan, who had harried his bishops, responded uneasily to her nod of greeting, then crossed the floor to talk with the queen's chaplain. Someone moved aside to make room for her in Colman's group. Surprisingly, it was Tatfrid, sporting his dark habit but engrossed in something Bosa and John were saying.

A sudden squall made the candles flare. Hild glimpsed Brother James crouched on the basebeam behind the Roman priests, leaning back wearily with closed eyes; he'd worked happily with Aidan's priests for years. In front of him, the French bishop Agilbert stood in the dignity of his richly embroidered pallium and tall mitre, warily scanning the room while his chaplain, Agatho, whispered in his ear. Agilbert was Prince Alcfrid's choice of bishop. How would he manage, Hild wondered, with his execrable Anglian? She could barely understand him in their common language of Latin! His Wessex king, she'd heard, had lost patience and brought in a British bishop. Offended, Agilbert was leaving for France when Prince Alcfrid summoned him to be his spokesman.

Hild's heart sank. If only some of the Bernicians had come: persuasive Utta, or Eata and Cuthbert. On the northern borders they often faced down devotees of paganism and won them over. In a meeting already split down the middle, such skills were sorely needed.

Two lay brothers entered to place Oswy's chair and a stool facing the altar. Hild nodded her satisfaction. A hush fell and all eyes turned to the door. A lone figure strode in, cast round appraisingly, and made for Agilbert. He knelt, was graciously raised, and stood conversing quietly, the only Anglian who could speak fluent French: Wilfrid.

The thud of a grounded spear signalled the king's approach. Oswy swept in, reflecting the lamplight from his jewelled sword. Prince Alcfrid followed with long, leisurely strides, pausing to smile at Wilfrid before he took the stool. Among the king's Companions, young Egfrid sloped in with his hunting hound.

"Bishops, brothers," Oswy started, glaring over his shoulder until silence fell. "I have no Christian learning but, as your king, I have a duty to resolve the differences which bedevil my church." His voice rang, his chin jutted. "We Northumbrians are one people, we hold one faith, we serve one God, we have one hope of heaven." His hallmark slap on the chair accompanied each statement. "So we should follow one rule of living. Which rule, is for you to decide. From today, everyone will adhere to it."

His cold eyes cowed the room.

"Easter," he announced. "Colman, bishop of Northumbria, you first. Describe your tradition, how it started, and why."

Colman inclined his head and edged forward so that he could face the king and see everyone in the room. Speaking in conversational tones, he was almost drowned out by gusts of wind driving rain through the doorway and roundel above.

"The Easter I observe, my lord, I inherited from my elders on Iona, the men who chose me as your bishop." Beads of sweat started on his brow. "All our forebears followed the same custom, and they were men beloved of God. To abandon their tradition would not be easy, for we know from history that they're the customs established by Saint John in all his churches, and blessed Saint John was Jesus' dearest companion."

He gave a little bow and wiped his sleeve across his face as he stepped back. Hild could smell his sweat; a staged debate was quite unlike joyously expounding God's love.

"Thank you, Bishop," Oswy said magisterially. "Will someone shut that door? Bishop Agilbert, will you please explain your observances, their origins and authority?"

Agilbert stepped forward and span on his heel in the gloomy lamplight.

"You allow, yes, my priest Wilfrid speak for me?" His head was bent in supplication. "We think same. Also these." He swirled his pallium to encompass his company. "We uphold world church. Wilfrid speak best. He speak Anglian."

Oswy nodded curtly.

"My lord!" Wilfrid hesitated as if taken by surprise. As he moved to the middle, a faint smile crossed Alcfrid's face. Hild saw and felt angry; they'd planned this!

"The Easter we observe," Wilfrid started quietly, "is kept in Rome where the blessed apostles Peter and Paul lived, taught, suffered, and were buried. It's the same throughout Italy and Gaul, where we travelled widely." He used the rhetorical plural of his Roman training. "We understand it's the same in Africa, Asia, Egypt, Greece, and wherever Christ's church has spread." As he warmed to his theme, his voice vibrated and he flung out his arms, ending up pointing at Colman's party. "These Britons and barbarians from two little islands at the world's end are the only people to flout Christendom."

There was a sharp intake of breath; a newmade priest to attack church elders! Hild looked to see if Oswy understood the enormity of this behaviour and caught Prince Egfrid guffawing, roused from toying with his hound.

"I'm surprised, Brother Wilfrid," Colman said mildly, "that you should disparage as great an apostle as John, renowned worldwide, and so close to Jesus."

Nods of relief at Colman's moderation. Wilfrid had gone too far; it did not do to savage Saint John. After a pause, Wilfrid lowered his head and his tonsure gleamed.

"Far be it from me," he said humbly, "to lambast an apostle for adopting the Jewish Passover. They all did in the early church; Peter, James, even Paul to start with. But it was Saint Peter preaching at Rome who ordained that Easter Day should always follow the Jewish Sabbath, for it was the day after the Sabbath that Jesus rose from death."

A sigh rippled through the church; relief that Wilfrid had retrieved his gaffe on the Roman side, disappointment that he'd reinforced his argument on Colman's. Exchanging an exasperated look with Chad, Hild stamped her feet silently to warm them, and pulled her cloak tight against the draught which made the altar lamp swirl.

"After Peter's declaration," Wilfrid went on with ostentatious restraint, "John's followers in Asia changed, and the Council of Nicaea confirmed the true Easter."

He'd had his say. Hild, and everyone else, looked to Oswy. But Wilfrid did not return to his place beside Bishop Agilbert. He slipped his leash.

"You and your people, Colman," he barked in the bishop's face. "You follow neither John nor Peter nor the ruling of the church."

Gasps all round. Brother James heaved himself forward to lay a restraining hand on Wilfrid's arm. Cedd stepped in front of Colman as if to ward off the attack. Hild screwed the end of her veil into a knot so tight it made her fingers numb. Would the king permit this frontal assault on his bishop? She glared at Wilfrid, close in front of her. Shorn round head wobbling on long white neck, he looked like a wrung chicken – or one waiting to be wrung. *God forgive me*, she gulped, horrified by her own disgust.

"Brother," Colman said in amazement, "are you really saying that our father Columba was wrong? Despite the amazing miracles God worked through him?"

"Columba? Who can say?" Wilfrid shrugged. "Our Lord himself said that at the Day of Judgment, many would claim to have worked in his name…"

…and he would disown them. Hild and every priest there could complete the quotation. Indignation swelled: Saint Columba of Iona rejected by Christ? Cedd's mighty fist curled tight. Chad and Coelin moved to restrain him. Hild stood at Colman's other side. She heard a groan as Tatfrid collapsed to his knees.

Across the church she saw James duck in shame and Romanus pale with horror. Bishop Agilbert looked puzzled, and Ronan sidled across to push between Hild and Colman and stand up for his rightful bishop. Wilfrid stood impervious, white with passion, poised to drive home his spearpoint.

"God forbid I should accuse your forebears," he cried. "We should always think the best of men we don't know – men who simply loved and served God, and were loved by him. How could we hold anything against men who knew no better?"

310

"Patronizing youngster!" hissed Brother John.

"Bad manners," muttered Bosa. "From a thegn's son!"

Fascination gripped Hild. Could he not see? Surely he wouldn't dig himself in deeper?

"But you," Wilfrid thundered, "you and your companions do know better. You've heard the decrees of the church. You refuse to follow them. Do you expect the whole world to bow to you, a misguided gaggle from the remotest corner of earth?" He spat out the words with contempt. "Even if your father Columba – our father, too, if he really did belong to Christ – even if he was holy, does he outstrip the blessed apostle Peter? Peter, to whom Christ said, *You are the rock on which I will build my church*? Peter, to whom Christ promised the keys of his kingdom of heaven?"

Oswy sat up. *Kingdom* did it, Hild thought. Kingship was his business.

"Colman!" he hissed. "Is this true? Did Christ really say that to Peter?"

Colman stood straight, facing the inevitable. "He did, my lord."

"Can you make as strong a claim for your Columba?"

"No, my lord," he said firmly.

"Well!" Oswy leaned back. "Do you all agree? This promise was made to Peter, and he was given the keys of heaven?"

"Yes, my lord," stuttered the clerics, echoed by a sudden clatter of hail.

"*And whatever you bind on earth shall be bound in heaven…*" Agilbert quoted in Latin. The priests nodded. There could be no dispute about Christ's words to Peter.

"That's all right, then," Oswy said. "As Peter's the gatekeeper, I'll go with him. I don't want him to turn away or shut the gate when I reach heaven."

He stood up, swung round, strode through the tight knot of his Companions and hammered for his herald to open the door. The court followed him out.

The priests were left with a view of the driving rain.

311

13

THE HACKNESS DREAM

Bruised by the Easter dispute, the meeting adopted Roman tonsures on the nod. Hild fled to pace the bean rows and compose herself. The decision she could accept, but not the way it was made. Did God really work through the manipulations of a self-serving whippersnapper like Wilfrid?

Thy will be done, she whispered over the beans. Of course a single Easter would unify minsters, travelling priests and bishops. Of course it would bring peace to Oswy's court.

Oddly, the smaller matter of the tonsure bothered her more. Her monks must abandon a lifelong, deeply personal habit. The long hair of their high calling was as much part of their identity as it was for princes and thegns. Well, Christ was one of the poor, not the mighty. And the tonsure, the crown of thorns, was like the arms of the cross, curving until they joined, embracing the world in love. Northumbrians understood symbols – think of Thor's hammer and Woden's ravens; men would respond to this.

This thought enabled Hild to preside calmly at the feast in the guesthall with bishops Colman, Cedd, and Agilbert nearby and King Oswy opposite in the seat of honour, flanked by princes Alcfrid and Egfrid.

"None of this touches the heart of the faith," Cedd murmured in her ear. "Christ's love is what matters." She smiled her thanks and turned to converse in Latin with Agilbert, who was sailing with

Cedd to Essex en route for France. When the king rose to his feet, she was glad to sit back.

"Lords, bishops," Oswy said, "my thanks for a task well done. Many of you journeyed far. You can return happy in the knowledge that Northumbria is again united." At his side, Prince Alcfrid applauded vigorously. Wilfrid, ostentatiously humble at the low bench by the door, smiled with satisfaction. Dear old Brother James and Brother John talked through it all, heads close, while Tatfrid and Bosa shared a joke. She drew a breath of relief; her men seemed unscarred.

"Above all," Oswy continued, "let us commend Abbess Hild, who had the idea of this synod of bishops, and her community for their charitable welcome. It's a wild place, this White Bay. They say the name comes from the sun's daylong presence in summer. To my mind, it's more likely from the foaming breakers that roll in, summer and winter, whenever the wind is lively." Nods and chuckles round the hall. "And so I now bestow upon this Abbey of Whitby in the Bay of Light a small homestead in the sheltered vale of Hackness, to be a house of prayer and calm retreat."

Startled and gratified, Hild bowed her thanks.

Too overwrought to sleep, she walked along the cliffs. The rain had blown over and the wind had dropped. The sea shone luminous under a clouded moon. She was soothed by the wash of the waves and the sound of cattle tearing grass. Feeling for a familiar rock, she sat and looked back. Lanterns darted like moths among the buildings; firelight flickered between the planks of the workers' hall; an explosion of mirth was doused by a slammed door.

"Mother Hild?" The voice in her ear made her jump. Elfi settled at her side. "I've been thinking. You never get cross with me."

"I don't know about that!" Hild chuckled.

"Not like Udric's father. He beats him, you know. Hard."

"Mm." Hild had noticed. Old Udric was a good, if anxious, steward; he didn't raise his hand to anyone else, as far as she knew. "It's a matter of training, chick. Young Udric will follow his father. He must learn to run the homestead, not just the beasts."

"He's good with beasts!" Elfi was indignant. Then she subsided. "You're training me like that, aren't you? To follow you."

"One day, Elfi." Hild was caught off guard. She'd started at Elfi's age, but she wanted the girl to enjoy her youth.

"Well, as I see it, Udric has to be tough and hard. So does Egfrid, following his father. But you…" From her bold start Elfled began to waver. "I've been watching you. Worrying, planning, straining to help… Mother, I'm not like you. I could never do that."

"Elfi!" Hild put an arm round her and hugged as Elfled burrowed into her like a toddler in a fright, torn between the child she was and the future she glimpsed. "I'll let you into a secret. I used to run off with horses and coracles, feel the wind in my hair, lie dreaming in the sun."

"You!" Elfled giggled, pulling away and peering up.

"Yes, me!" Hild retorted. How old and staid she must seem to the ten-year-old! "It's part of being young. You want to be free, be yourself. It's not wrong. It's natural."

There was a thoughtful silence.

"In time, you grow beyond it," Hild mused. "Find yourself ready to move on."

Elfled did not stir.

"Elfi." Hild sat up straight and said firmly, "I'm proud of you. Spirited, clever, generous. You'll be a fine woman, chick – a far greater abbess than I could ever be. When the time comes."

A door banged, making them jump.

"Caedmon!" Elfled whispered. "He comes to see the cattle every night."

"I didn't know that!"

"Oh, he's proud of his gift," Elfled assured her. "Wouldn't want to go back. But he'd rather sleep in the byre than in the men's dormitory."

* * *

After Lauds, Hild sat on the warm stone at the base of the cross listening to Wilfrid teach Bosa Roman psalm-singing. Last night's moon hung low, labourers bent over the rows, Young Udric moved among the pigs, women pruned nut trees by the beck, and tanners trod hides. Frigyd stood with her note tablets at the guesthall door overseeing her helpers as they carried trestles and pallets back where they'd come from. A shrill laugh by the stepping stones revealed Elfi cavorting in the shallows, shrieking at Egfrid's attempts to spear a salmon. A group of thegns waited at the wharf for Oswy and Alcfrid, who were closeted in Hild's lodging with Bishop Colman. Everyone else had left.

When the king and prince strode down to their ship, Colman stayed behind.

"It's not a matter of injured pride," he said, drawing Hild onto the bench by her door. "Having fought the fight, as Saint Paul would say, I leave the rest to God. It's simple practicality. I told the king he needs a neutral bishop for a fresh start."

A new bishop. Hild went cold. Colman had what was needed. When the arguments were over, he'd stood awaiting silence, his arms raised for prayer: *Lord, we praise you for showing us the way. Go with us from this place and help us by your Spirit to grow together in Christ.* Simple, tolerant, wise.

"I've suggested an Anglian." He'd read her face. "Man called Tuda. Studied in southern Ireland where they follow Canterbury. He'll understand." He patted her hand. "Eata will go to Lindisfarne as abbot, and Cuthbert will be prior of Melrose in his place." All good news. Fancy her two spirited boys stepping in Aidan's footprints!

"But you?" she asked. "What will you do?"

"Return to my roots. In Ireland I shall be free to wait on God. You know how precious that freedom is." She nodded.

He'd soon overtake James and Chad, she thought, as he bowled away at his usual trot. She pictured the three of them on the river path, grimy white and rusty black moving in harmony, symbol of the future.

* * *

Sharp shears, they'd need – larger than women's clippers, smaller than Caedmon's tools; and a tiny blade to shave the crown. There'd be enough hair to stuff a… No! Better to place it on the altar. A small offering in return for Christ's great sacrifice. She'd ask Brother John about a special litany.

Acting on the thought she sped to the library.

"Abbess, welcome!" As usual, he surprised her with the pinpoint accuracy of his hearing. "We're discussing with Tatfrid all the things we have in common."

"Good idea!" She saw Oftfor at his side, with Bosa and Tatfrid making a circle. "May I consult you about the tonsure? How to introduce it? Perhaps a special service at Easter? What do Roman priests do, Brother Tatfrid? Can you remember your tonsuring?"

"A long time ago," he sighed, "but I'll do my best." As Bosa made notes on a wax tablet, Tatfrid recalled the special prayers, John and Oftfor suggested psalms and readings and Hild encouraged them with questions.

"Shall we look in Gregory's writings?" she suggested. "He may say something."

"*Be patient, don't force it,*" Tatfrid quoted ironically. "*Use what men know – places, times. Win them with love.* Abbess, I deeply regret…" He broke off abruptly. *Gregory would have handled things differently*, Hild thought he meant to say.

Tatfrid, who had been tonsured at Ripon, advised the metalworkers on the size and shape of the shears, and trained two brothers to use them by letting them loose on his own neglected growth. And he comforted those who were distressed, especially a very old brother so upset he ended up in the infirmary.

One good thing, Hild thought: they'd need purging of lice less often, sparing her small crop of tormentil and fleabane. But exposure to sun and rain? Brother James used to have a cowl, rather like the sacks fieldworkers tied round their necks to pull up against the weather. So did Tatfrid. Lending him an abbey robe, she took his to the weaving sheds as a pattern, so that new garments would be ready for Easter.

* * *

Bosa conducted the Tonsuring Mass in Holy Week. Leaving him in charge, Hild took Aetla back to Hart, with Tatfrid, to repeat the ceremony.

Looking back as the homebound ship left the jetty, Hild's spirits lifted. Ever since autumn they'd been fixated on the king's council: now, they could return to their calling. She and Elfled exclaimed at the golden gorse tumbling down the ridge, spied clefts stuffed with primroses, watched gulls circle like bodyguards, and peered into the sun-flecked blue depths. Under the dark cliffs of Deira, Hild mouthed her usual prayer for the exiled Princess Alcfled, bitter as ever.

"Cold!" Elfled shuddered. The light was fading. Hild opened her voluminous cloak, wrapping it round them both so that they swayed together. Suddenly, the sails flopped.

"Oars!" bawled the master. "Storm coming. Need to race it!" Sailors shinned up to untie the sails and scuttled to their benches, cursing as they tangled the cumbersome oars. "Fast stroke. In, out, in…" He banged his hand on the planking. "Nice and sweet, now. Keep it going."

The boat cut along, raising a bow wave. Hild and Elfled leaned to watch the water creaming along the sides.

"Brrh! It's getting dark!" Elfled rolled herself tighter into their cocoon.

"We're all right, chick." Hild hugged her. "They know the way."

But soon she could not see the curling water for the gloom, and sensed unease mounting in the weary crew.

"Pray for us, brothers!" one grunted, and Aetla started a psalm of comfort.

"The gulls've gone!" Elfi shrilled. A single bird diminished to a white dot against the leaden sky. "Not a sound! Well, just oars."

"Calm before the storm," Hild said.

The cold bit keenly as the light died.

"Sit down, Abbess," Tatfrid called. "Safer, if there's lightning."

"Heave to!" cried the master. "Anchor!"

Men pushed past, dragged out a huge rock, and heaved it overboard with a mighty splash, guiding the snaking rope. They lashed the end to the ship, the anchor bit, the vessel bucked and lay still.

Hild found the master at her side. "We've rounded the nab, lady. Not far to go. But I don't like the look of this. We'll wait it out."

The boat rocked gently. No wind. No thunder. Blackness. Silence.

"Taking its time," he growled. "We're near home. You'd see, if only…"

"And not yet Vespers," she murmured. The middle of a summer day, black as a moonless night, still as ice. Tucked inside Hild's cloak, Elfi seemed to be asleep.

At long last, weird light faintly spreading, a kind of dawn.

"In the wrong place!" Aetla pointed. "That's where the sun should rise." Everyone looked to the leaden east as light and warmth flowed back behind them. Small flutters over the water. Cry of a shag. Explosion of gulls.

"Phew!" The master was sweating. "Thought the sky was falling."

"God giving us a surprise," Hild smiled.

"Lights at night I've seen." He shook his head. "But never night in full day."

"But the light's come back." Hild pointed. "Look! Our headland."

"And a wind!" The master edged back to the steering pole. "Hey up, boys! Set the sail! Back to normal." They scurried to pull on the stays, heave up the anchor, and coil the dripping rope.

As they left the shelter of the cliff, Hild looked inland expecting to see the sun. A black disc hung haloed with bright light. Too bright; painful. She shut her eyes and the image burned red behind her lids. Elfi stirred. Hild squeezed her hand but kept her head wrapped.

"Look!" Aetla pointed ahead. "The people like ants nosed by a dog!"

"We'll soon be there." Hild was relieved. The church crouched among the buildings like a mother hen brooding chicks. She willed the ship forward; her abbey needed her. She'd heard of black hours, but never lived through one. God was always beside them: she believed that now. But this was frightening, like the end of the world.

A memory stirred: *Famines, earthquakes, changes in the sky...* Gregory, was it? *God sends them as a warning. Look to your soul!*" That was it! The black hour, he said, was God's reminder to be ready for the Day of Judgment.

Udric, pallid and sniffing, was straining to hold his place at the front of the mob seething at the wharf. "Know what day it is, lady?" Leaning forward he gripped Hild's arm, almost hauling her from the ship. "Beltane. Are the gods angry? Is it bad luck?"

"Nonsense, Udric!" Hild rubbed her arm, shocked. In her seven years here, there'd been no whiff of the old gods: they were dead and done. She slipped her hand into the crook of his elbow. "Help me uphill. Show a calm front."

"Hild, Lady Hild!" Begu panted down to meet her. "Did you see?"

"The black hour?" Intentionally casual, Hild turned to check Elfled was there.

"Where were you?" Begu's voice was shrill. "The sun snuffed like a candle! I watched it all. Hild!" She forced Hild's attention by blocking the path. "I was at the washtubs and saw it in the water. It was like... like..." She waved her arms. "Like a cookpot!"

Elfled giggled.

"The round top, Elfi." Begu turned to her eagerly. "As if someone slid the cover on, and then slid it off again."

"God's surprise," Elfled explained. "That's what Mother called it."

"God's warning," Hild corrected her absently. "Can you hear...?"

"Caedmon's Song!" Elfled exclaimed.

"They're in the people's chapel." Udric pulled her forward.

At the cross they found Bosa, arms outstretched, ushering people inside.

"Abbess!" He flushed. "We asked ourselves what you would do. Give praise, you always say, so..."

"Quite right, brother!" Hild panted. "*Your heart shall rejoice, and your joy shall no man take from you.* Saint John, I think, quoted by Gregory. And he hadn't even heard of Caedmon's songs!"

"Gregory again," Tatfrid chuckled. "We should write a book about him!"

* * *

Summer turned dry and windy. Cracks opened in the soil and crops shrivelled. Begu brought Hild the news.

"There's murmuring," she said through pursed lips. "Woden's anger, Thor's revenge. Folk are fearful since the sun went black." Two good spears were broken in the river near the stepping stones. Trees were festooned with dead crows. A hammer was driven so hard into the oak on the hill they couldn't pull it out.

"Tree'll grow round it in time," sniffed Udric, shifting from foot to foot. "Trouble is, fruits won't swell. Folks're hungry, and it'll get worse."

The sickness followed. A cargo boat unloaded a seaman covered in boils and vomiting profusely. He died before reaching the infirmary. They buried him between the kitchen garden and the orchard.

Brother John's death was the first to strike home. Oftfor found him still warm, propped in bed with the granary cat curled on his feet.

"There's nothing of him!" he cried in anguish. "When I washed him for the shroud, he was oozing with boils. After sixteen years! Why couldn't he tell me?"

"His suffering's over," Hild said gently, comforting herself as much as Oftfor. John had helped her learn, inspire the young, innovate. And he had answered her doubts. When he was buried near the altar wall, she sang praise to God for his fruitful life, but in her lodging she let the tears fall. Only Begu saw her pain.

Hardly was John underground before others sickened: jaundice, vomiting, delirium. Yellow Pest, they dubbed it; when the body could take no more, pouring out pus and life together.

"God's wrath!" The whispers spread. "Is he angry at all these changes?"

"Plague is nothing new," Hild said sternly. "What is new is that Christ shares our suffering. Pain is what he chose. For our sake." But would the suffering never end? Council, eclipse, plague: all in one summer!

She prayed to God to strengthen her priests, working among the sick, trying to banish fear. The infirmarian pushed in extra pallets and commandeered the help of all with skill or will, sprinkling lavender on oil lamps and linens, to counter the stench of rotting flesh. Hild worked with the herbalist to find cures. Agrimony, the usual standby, could not touch this epidemic. She sent children hunting tormentil and bilberries to brew tisanes for diarrhoea, and ordered Begu to mash yarrow and goosegrass plasters for the pustules. Mint and golden oregon soothed the guts of those with nausea. To quieten delirium and dying groans, she brewed a strong poppy syrup with meadwort, praying the honey would last.

No cure worked. Children and old folk died at random, taking nurses and priests with them. The orchard cemetery swelled, and they built a special chapel there. A second row of graves for the religious crept along the altar wall.

News arrived at the wharf. Canterbury was stricken, with the bishop and king both dead. At Jarrow, only the abbot and a nine-year-old boy survived. Prince Alcfrid was sick and Derwentdale prostrate from York to the coast, with kin groups wiped out, plague victims left to starve, and corpses abandoned. Priests died burying the dead, and there was no bishop to ordain more. Aidan would not have abandoned them like this, or Colman. Where, oh where, was their new bishop?

Udric spotted the royal ship tossing through an easterly gale. As the tide was low, it stood off in the bay and lowered a boat. He ran to find Hild.

"No one must come up here," she said. "Tell Frigyd. I'll go down to the guesthall."

She found Oswy throwing off his wet cloak and kicking the logs to life. Taking a tray from Frigyd, she set bread, cheese and warmed mead on a stool beside him.

"We're homeward bound, Abbess. Egfrid's with me. May he see his sister?" He leaned back, watching his boots steam. "Met Aldwulf of East Anglia. He said to tell you his mother has died."

It was a brusque announcement, but Hild could not grieve. She was over fifty, and Heri was older. The sisters at Chelles would have tended her lovingly.

She took a stool facing the king. His narrow features ebbed and flowed as the fire guttered. Lacking several teeth, he chewed hard at his cheese. The wind howled in the rafters.

"What a gale!" He swallowed and hunched forward, toasting his hands. "Wulfhere – you know, the king the Mercians chose after Alcfled…"

"I remember." She cut in to avoid a rerun of his daughter's crime.

"Wulfhere was consecrating his new church to Saint Peter. A grand affair in the Fens. Lots of princes and bishops… Cedd from Essex, Damian, new bishop at Rochester. I was asked to be sponsor." He flushed: pride at his role in a holy ceremony, or at being acknowledged Mercia's overlord? "There was a great wooden cross. I had to say, *I, Oswy, friend of this monastery and abbot, support this foundation on the cross of Christ*, and put my mark. Just the thing, according to Wilfrid."

"Wilfrid?" She frowned. "Oh, of course, he's at Stamford."

"Heading for France, actually." Looking sheepish, he rattled on, "With no bishop at Canterbury, it seems we've no one this side of the channel to consecrate him."

"Consecrate?" Hild was aghast. "Wilfrid?"

"Tuda died before he got here. Plague." Oswy sounded embarrassed. "Alcfrid and I… before he died… you know he's died, Alcfrid?… we thought Wilfrid…" He peered at her pathetically. "… keep us in line. You do see?"

She did not see. Wilfrid! Priested at the youngest permissible age, self-opinionated, confrontational. As a bishop, Wilfrid would mean trouble. It was one thing for Aidan's men to accept change; quite another to be bullied into it. Stony-eyed, she listened to the creaking of the rafters.

"I'm weary, Hild," Oswy said in a small voice. "Not much longer for this world." He picked up his cup and put it down, untasted. "My only wish now – leave the kingdom united, and go on pilgrimage." He stopped, then breathed one word: "Rome."

So, his conscience was kicking in. High time! Wheedling, he was wheedling! Blaming Alcfrid, acting old and pathetic! Indignation burned in Hild. She eyed him across the flames, sickened, full of mistrust.

"Will Saint Peter let me in, cousin?" Like a child seeking reassurance.

She waited before saying coldly, "Who am I to say? I face God's judgment just like you."

"You've no deadly sins to your tally," he retorted. He had plenty: the firing of Din Edin, Cerdic's lingering death, Wulfi's loss, Oswine's murder, Alcfled... and he asked for comfort?

Edwin would have despised Oswy's moment of weakness, she thought. But Edwin had not lived to be as old. And times had changed. Love, conciliation, forgiveness: these were not Edwin's values. They were new teaching, Christ's teaching. Something Oswy needed...

Something Aidan had charged her with...

To spread God's love...

"One thing is sure," she said slowly. "We're all sinners, one way or another." She, especially, with this unrestrained bitterness, this cruelty to Oswy! *He that doesn't love, doesn't know God*: the stern warning flashed into her mind.

"God loves us all." She was thinking aloud. "He'll not leave us out in the cold if we're truly sorry." She must ask God to purge her and forgive. "Remember the thief on the cross?"

They watched the fire flare, sink, and flare again. At peace.

Just like two old friends. Absurd.

"She died, you know," Oswy whispered. "I never saw her again." Alcfled, the daughter who murdered her man. Hild didn't know but she grunted in understanding.

The door slammed open, caught by a gust, and Egfrid breezed in, a typical seventeen-year-old, rosy with exertion, fair hair snaking across his wet face.

"Shut that door!" Oswy yelped.

"Sorry. The men are following." He dropped his cloak and pushed back his hair. "Is that cheese?" He stretched out a hand. "I'm ravenous! Been racing along the bay. My sister nearly won." He glanced sidelong at Hild, mischief in his smile. "Not quite, though. Well brought up, y'know."

"Better than you," Oswy barked, "if you can't greet the abbess properly."

"Only teasing," Egfrid chuckled. "You fell for it!" He knelt respectfully for Hild's blessing. "I was telling her about that woman we met at Aldwulf's court. The one I plan to wed. Etheldreda. Remember?"

Oswy groaned.

"I know you disapprove of her. But you'd like what Elfled said." He waited, tantalizing Hild as much as his father. "*I should give it time*, she said. *Your feelings might change now you're home.*"

"Hmph!"

Thoughtfully, Hild left them to it.

Begu served her broth and told her someone, no one knew who, had coppiced the stand of trees at the opposite arm of the bay and jammed hammers into the boles.

"I'll act in the morning," Hild sighed.

"Young Udric said his father's not well," Begu added. "May be catching it."

"God forbid!"

She stood at her desk in prayer, handing her pain and shame to God. She could not earn his grace, but she could ask for it. And for Oswy.

Sleep would not come. A headache speared behind her eyes. Pain and rumbling loosened her gut. Heavily, she staggered out to the waste pit round the back. Vomiting and venting brought some relief. Feeling limp, she edged back crabwise. Her head whirled. Flopping back against the timbers, she slithered down the wall, gathering splinters and collapsing on the ground.

* * *

Someone was there. Shouldn't be; couldn't remember why. "Go away!"

"It's only me." A familiar voice.

"Elfi?"

"No. Elfi's safe. Far away." A hand stroked her hair.

"Begu." With a grunt, she turned over.

For many weeks she wavered between life and death, dimly aware that her lips were moistened, her body bathed, and her bed freshened; conscious only of pain in legs, head, and gut. Utter weariness. A fuddle of sensation and whisperings.

One day, Begu's furrowed face and trailing hair hung over her.

"Tickles," she rasped.

"At last!" With a choking laugh, Begu wrapped her in a tight hug, rocking to and fro, pushing back her hair with shaking fingers. A small dumpy figure, she heaved herself up and went round the screen. Twigs snapped, logs clattered, water splashed, a pan banged. She returned, hair plaited, tunic neat, a drying clout tucked in her girdle.

"How d'you feel?" She put down a bowl of water.

"Weak." Hild gasped as her face was briskly swabbed.

"Plague. You caught it." Begu chattered breathlessly. "But you've won through. Took a long time. But you're back." She mopped her eyes on Hild's drying rag. "At your age! You're a marvel. Oh, I must tell Elfi. Stay there. I'll be back." Flurried, chuntering, she vanished.

"Mother!" Elfled bounced on the bed, lifting Hild in a hug. "We thought you'd… Let me look at you." She sat back. "Oh!" Another hug. "Haven't seen you for ages. Begu wouldn't let me."

"Always under my feet," Begu grumbled. "Besides, Lady Hild sent you away."

"You, more like, you old dragon!" Elfled retorted. "Seriously, Mother, she never left you. Kept everyone away. Scratchy as a cat with kittens. Just opened a chink to take in what we brought." It all came out: how Begu spooned potions into her, stayed at her side, slept at her feet, and kept the lodging sealed.

And when Elfi whisked away, Begu told how the girl had defied them all, refused to flee to Hart, made up pallets, stripped victims, bathed fevered bodies, ground medicaments. She'd organized a bed for herself among the women and kept the hours. Between whiles, she swam and rode, talked with young Udric, rallied the workers, sorted the quayside fishbaskets, and set wolfhounds on the rats. As the plague ran its weary course, her zest and toughness earned respect, then admiration, then love. Elfi had come of age.

"Begu told me to pray," Elfled explained later. "I tried, but I was no good. Bosa did all that. You used to say, *Don't just offer prayers – help them along.* So I did."

"Bosa?"

"He held prayers every hour. You were dying. Everyone came – the travelling priests, and Abbott Eata from Lindisfarne. He gave you the last rites!"

"And I never saw him. What a waste!" Eata always conjured a smile. She pictured his red curls and cheeky grin, his ferocious loyalty to Cerdic. What a miracle God worked, preserving Eata for Aidan!

But she wept when they told her that old Udric had died, Aetla had not come home, and Bishop Cedd, her beloved giant, was felled like a sapling at Lastingham.

"Not to attend his burial!" she groused. "Not to give thanks for him, or welcome his brothers from Essex!"

"Just as well," Begu said tartly. "None of them survived. Only Chad and a boy."

It was many more weeks before Hild was strong enough to sit outside in her felt cloak. Dreamily, she traced the moors folding into the distance, edged by valleys so sharp they could have been carved; saw sea mist roll into the estuary; listened to hammer blows at the staithe; watched Elfi splash over the ford and ride west. She smiled at Frigyd airing fleeces outside the guesthall, waved as a boy raced past late for lessons, hummed to the cooks' singing as they dug up turnips, and idly watched a man lope downstream, hop over the stepping stones, and start uphill towards her.

"A welcome sight, sister!" Chad's voice. She wouldn't have known him! Ah, the tonsure.

"I was so sorry about Cedd…" She tried to rise.

"Don't get up." He sat beside her. Begu brought a cup of ale.

"You've come for a ship, brother? You're leaving?"

"Not for ever." With a smile Chad drained Begu's cup. "I shall return. When God's purifying wind and rain have done their work. I'm for Canterbury. King's orders."

"How is he, Oswy?"

"Ailing, anxious. Says he can't wait any longer. I'm to get myself consecrated bishop and come back post-haste."

"But…?"

"I know. No one less fitting," he chuckled. "Just the only one left."

"Brother, I didn't mean… There's no one better. But Wilfrid?"

"No word for nearly two years." Two years? That long?

"Thank God Oswy's seen sense," she said. "You have Aidan's heart."

"Pray for me, Hild. There's much distress: sickness, death, starvation. Men have no leisure to mourn. They must scavenge the scrubland for scraps to eat."

"Spring will be a long time coming," Hild sighed. "God grant you strength." She could see Chad, like Caedmon with the cattle, moving quietly to bring relief. "Would you like some of our men? With donkeys? To carry food and firewood?"

"You have some to spare?"

"We like to share," she said.

* * *

Hild now had leisure to keep the hours and recite the psalms, glad to find she still could. Her abbey ran like a ship before the wind: Bosa led services, Frigyd welcomed visitors, young Udric supervised the farm. The infirmary, kitchens, and scriptorium were all in good hands. People had grown used to consulting Elfled, and she dealt with much of the business.

She sailed to Hart, as Hild would have done, to find out how the plague had affected them, and returned with an old cloth.

"They said it should stay with me," she said doubtfully.

Hild fingered the fraying gold embroidery round the edge. "It binds us, you and me, in God's service," she said. "Bishop Finan used it at your dedication."

Elfi folded it thoughtfully and took it away.

The plague had left an ache in Hild's gut. Not as troublesome as the ache in her heart; so many folk had gone. If God still had work for her, she must stir herself.

First, to give praise in God's house. The Saturday night vigil was too much, but she set out to join her people at the third hour. It was like a wedding, Frigyd said. As Hild climbed the track, leaning on Begu, resting every few paces, everyone ran to greet her, clapping, chattering, pushing in to see, to touch.

"A chair!" Tatfrid shouted, struggling against the current. "Let me through to fetch her a chair." Holding it aloft, he preceded Hild and set it before the altar in the people's chapel.

Familiar faces in flickering candlelight, pale robes, heartfelt singing, well-loved psalms, Elfled and Begu beside her, holding her arms aloft during the prayers. Behind, sniffling and shoving, farmhands, fishwives, tanners, smiths, basketmakers, all celebrating. Caedmon raised his voice: Life and Joy, a new song about Christ's birth. Hild remembered the voiceless boy at Bamburgh years ago. His new, God-given voice would ring to the end of the world.

* * *

Trouble came with a rush of children to Hild's door.

"Ssh! Don't bother the abbess." Begu tried to sweep them away.

"But it's the king!" Oswy's unscheduled visits had become legend. A little boy wormed past Begu, jumped up and down and announced, "The king's here!"

A horseman galloped along the cliffs in a swirl of purple with an armed posse. Dismounting, he tossed his reins to a guard, lifted the gold cross he wore in his belt like a knife, and made the sign of blessing over them all. The children watched in awe. Not the king; Bishop Wilfrid.

"Abbess, may I beg a night's lodging for a small fee?"

"You are freely welcome in our guesthall, my lord," she said, seeing from the corner of her eye Begu send the lad to warn Frigyd. "You and your men. Have you come far?"

"Only from York. But my fee: news of Brother Aetla."

"Aetla?" Hild gasped. "We thought he was…"

"No, very much alive! My monks found him in the wilderness, all but dead of the Yellow Pest. He's still with us, learning Benedictine ways."

"Aetla, alive!" Her voice wobbled. "Wonderful!"

"I've been to France to be consecrated." He followed her indoors. "Twelve French bishops – Agilbert was one – lifted me on a golden chair and laid their hands upon me. Each one of them was consecrated in the direct line of bishops going back to Saint Peter. It was humbling."

A strange word, thought Hild, for a man resplendent in finery. Her people wore homespun and shared everything. She couldn't remember the last time anyone had gone against a decision they'd made together.

"You took a long time," she said mildly.

"I made pilgrimage to Saint Peter's tomb," he explained, seating himself in her chair. "A great church has risen over his bones – something I want to copy here."

Hild passed him a cup of ale.

"I've made a start. At Ripon I'm digging out a crypt for holy relics." He tossed back the ale. "At Hexham, I'll start with the crypt."

"Another church?"

"I'm the king's bishop!" he flared. "I have that power, even though I'm debarred from my diocese. Not for long, though!"

From a low stool, Hild looked him in the eye. She thought it unlikely Oswy would change his mind again, and Chad, she knew, was loved by the people.

"I told Chad he wasn't properly consecrated," Wilfrid went on. "Do you know, when he found the Bishop of Canterbury had died, he simply went along the coast to the next bishop, the man who ousted Agilbert? Unbelievable! Bishop Wine was, admittedly, consecrated in the Roman way, but he's not allowed to consecrate a bishop on his own!"

"What did Chad say?" As Wilfrid's voice rose, Hild kept hers low.

"He's quite prepared to submit." *Submit*: a warlord's term! "We're going to put it to the new Bishop of Canterbury, a Greek called Theodore."

"Theodore?"

"Name means *gift of God*. Comes from Tarsus, like Saint Paul. Been in the Syrian monastery in Rome. I'm going to Canterbury to ask him to sort out Northumbria!"

What Wilfrid wanted, Wilfrid would get. On this bitter thought, Hild caught her breath. *The Father inspires whom he chooses*, Saint John said. And to see how unpredictable God's choices were, you only had to look at Christ's disciples: Judas, a rabid nationalist, alongside Matthew, who worked for the Romans!

Love your neighbour, Christ said, *love your enemy*. It was foolish to compare everyone with Aidan. The young had new vision. It was time for her to hand over, and mend her soul. Let Theodore sort them out!

The farmstead Oswy had gifted was a day's journey away. Begu and Frigyd went to look it over, travelling on the abbey donkeys with Tatfrid walking alongside. He would pray and cleanse the place.

A snug homestead, they reported, in a sunny valley, with trees full of bird song and a clear stream running through open meadows. Crops were sprouting, the apple trees drooped with blossom, and the cattle had pelts so soft the scriptorium would covet them. It seemed a dream.

But there was no chapel. Bosa sent relays of novices to help Tatfrid. They gathered in the harvest, blessed the household and told them stories of Jesus. The lodgings they built for themselves would become the women's dormitory. Their greatest work was a simple chapel, built with a calling bell, so that a single tug would ring the hours of prayer. Before winter closed in, Bishop Chad sailed from Lindisfarne for the dedication.

Elfled asked if he could spare her some time before he left. After the day they spent together, she emerged full of quiet joy. With Hild's blessing, Chad held a quiet service for her, before her mother and the religious community, finishing with a Mass. She had chosen to rededicate herself to God of her own free will.

Hild was content. Everything was moving to its appointed end.

* * *

God, it seemed, had other plans. Prince Egfrid rode in, with guards and a spare horse.

"Abbess," he said, "I've come to fetch my sister. Our father is near to death and asking for her."

Hild was waiting when Elfled brought her father's body home. It was a boisterous March day with the gusty wind Oswy hated. Should she choose light covering for ease of movement or heavy wool for warmth? Pulling her felt cloak off the peg, she shrugged it on, gripped her stick, made her painful way down to the wharf and sat on a bollard.

Much of an age, they were, she and Oswy. An odd sympathy had linked them at the end. Like her, he was reared under the old gods and lived to see a world transformed: his realm was the widest ever, and he died in his own bed. Remembering his fear that Saint Peter would shut the gates in his face, Hild was glad she'd written his name in the Book of Life; the abbey would pray for his soul every day till the end of time.

The cliffs were fringed with silent crowds as the royal ship nosed in. Wet oars flashed in a pale sun. Elfled stood at the prow with her brother. Winter had dragged and Hild had missed her. She strained for a sight of Queen Anfled.

The moment the ship touched the staithe, Egfrid leapt ashore and knelt for her blessing: pleasing courtesy in a new king. He helped Hild up from the bollard. The first thing she did was open her arms to the widowed queen.

"Dear Ani," she whispered, "now you can be at peace."

"Oh, Hild!" Anfled clung to her fiercely, her bones brittle through her furs.

"He asked to be buried here," Elfled whispered, passing Hild her stick. "I couldn't refuse."

"You did right, chick," Hild whispered back. "It's his abbey, in a way."

She clutched her cloak and moved to Bishop Chad, waiting in his green woollen pallium, wooden cross held high, as the doleful procession formed.

The old king's bodyguard shouldered his coffin and, followed by King Egfrid and his mother, led the way up the track. Elfled supported Hild, but Egfrid's Companions overtook them and, before long, they found themselves surrounded by a double line of priests chanting in the new, antiphonal style. Hild spied Wilfrid's purple at her heels and, with a surge of delight, Aetla among the singers. Young Udric held back the locals, and the religious community waited at the cross to pray over the body in the church.

The old king's Companions sorted out the night watch while the company gathered in the guesthall. Hild led King Egfrid to the seat of honour and signalled Frigyd to send in the food.

"My lady," Hild heard Egfrid say to his mother, "I'd like you to take charge when I'm away. You've done it before and I'll feel secure."

"So soon?" Anfled frowned. "Shouldn't you first circulate among your people?"

"Picts on the move," he replied. "Testing a new king, as usual. But I'm not called *the sword's edge* for nothing! And I want to fetch my queen."

"The sooner you breed, the better," said Anfled, "but couldn't Wilfrid fetch her? He knows East Anglia and has a silver tongue. Who better?"

"A priest?" Egfrid sounded sceptical.

"A priest fetched me. Not even a bishop. A man called Utta, I recall." Hild smiled, remembering Brother Utta's impact on her life.

"Well, I'll head for York, start the muster," Egfrid temporized. "March once we're wed. Could you settle her in?"

"Not a good idea, two queens in one bower," replied Anfled firmly. "That's why dowagers return to their homeland."

"But you can't go to Kent. They're all dead!" Egfrid squawked.

"I know," the queen smiled across at Hild. "That's why I plan to ask your consent, my lord, to retire here, if Abbess Hild agrees."

Hild beamed. Anfled would supply the worldly wisdom Elfi lacked, and loving company in her lonely role.

Despite the herbs and incense lavished on his coffin, Oswy was ripe for burial. They laid him deep near the great wooden cross before the abbey church. The crowd stretched to the cliff edge, straining to hear Chad's quiet committal. "*Blessed are the dead who die in the Lord*," Wilfrid's brothers chanted.

Egfrid stood to attention as the grave was filled. Hild thought of Lilla, Edwin's murdered Companion, buried at the border of his lands so that his spirit would guard his people. Was it the same for Oswy? Chad would know.

She caught sight of him gesturing to Wilfrid. Purple pallium fluttering, Wilfrid stepped onto the plinth of the cross, raised his arms and let his voice ring out in prayer. His words were spontaneous, powerful, musical, even. Many eyes were moist when he finished.

"Beautiful," sighed Anfled.

"Amen," murmured Elfled with feeling.

Hild said nothing.

14

LIGHT OVER THE LAND

Queen Anfled lodged in the guesthall while she made arrangements to disband her household, and spent time with Hild learning about abbey life.

"What about night services?" she asked nervously.

"In time, when you're ready."

"Does everyone read?"

"No, but you'll soon find you remember the psalms and prayers we use every day. Praising God is our foremost duty. We study to deepen our understanding of Christ and his teaching. And we each work according to our gifts."

"But I have no gifts."

"Ani, you have what we need. Experience. Our task, yours and Elfi's and mine, is to deal with worldly matters and protect our people from distraction, so that they can live a life of devotion, goodness, and purity. And, of course, we set an example," she said, smiling wryly, "or try to!"

"Devotion, goodness, purity," Anfled pondered.

"We pray each day for the king and his people. And for the names in the abbey's Book of Life. I'll show you: past members, friends… Oswy's already there."

With all newcomers, problems were likely to arise. Hild should not have been surprised. They started when Elfled burst into Hild's lodging.

"I told her we share everything," the girl cried. "No one's rich. We're all as poor as each other." She was flushed and near to tears.

Taken aback, Hild grasped whom she meant. "Did you explain why, chick?"

"Like the early church, I said. Only… it's no good her thinking she can become one of us if she doesn't follow our ways."

"Your mother needs time, Elfi, like any other novice. Time to pray, to learn, to see if it's right for her… and she's not free till Egfrid agrees – and he's got other things on his mind."

"He wants her here, I'm sure of that. So she's got to learn!" She stormed out.

This was not the warmhearted Elfi that Hild knew and Chad considered ready to lead. Once she calmed down, Hild would need to talk it through with her. She leaned back and listened to the chanting carried on the wind from the church – the one she'd dedicated to Saint Peter because he understood human weakness…

* * *

"Hild?" said a quiet voice at the door.

"Ani, come in!" She glanced at the wind-burned cheeks and clear brow. "I'm glad you're here. It's doing you good. You look so much better than when you came."

Anfled pulled up a stool at her feet. "Elfi," she announced baldly. "She's not sure how to treat me. Seems edgy, on guard. Has she said anything?"

"Yes." Since her outburst, Hild had noticed Elfi act first and report later, as if proving she had the right. "Do you begin to see your future?"

"All I can see, Hild, is a life of prayer," Alfled replied. "Not as easy as it sounds, Bosa says. But to learn to pray, give thanks, ask for God's help, assist where I can – that is my wish."

Hild spotted Elfi at the door, vanishing in a blink.

"Will you, d'you think, miss the authority you've held?"

"How can you ask?" Anfled stood up so abruptly, her stool fell over. "You know me better than anyone!"

"Forgive me, but…" Hild looked straight into the hurt eyes, "it's easy to despise power when you have it. To live under another's rule can be hard, especially if your ideas conflict."

"Do you think I don't know?" Anfled's voice was very quiet. Her face was white, her fists clenched, and her chest heaved. She turned her back and looked out to the hills. Hild kicked herself; Ani had endured Oswy.

"I'm sorry," she whispered.

In a while, Anfled turned and sat again. "Your life, your Christian life, is new to me. How could I understand what it is? I come not as a queen, but as a learner."

"Elfi knows she's destined to take my place. At sixteen, she's stretching her wings," said Hild. "Perhaps she's afraid her duty to you requires her to surrender that future."

"But I'd never hurt her!" Anfled cried.

"I know. And you have experience she lacks. You'll help her in worldly affairs, give her love when Begu and I leave, guide her in ruling wisely…"

"But not if she rejects me."

"Shall we talk with her?"

"May I try on my own first?"

* * *

Hild was disappointed when Chad returned to Lastingham. He knocked on a day when Begu had pulled the door and hooked it tight against thick fog rolling in off the sea. Hild drowsed in the firelight, full of memories: Ma, Wulfi, Abbe, Cedd… How blessed she'd been! *Favoured*, Paulinus would have said.

When Begu let Chad in, she shifted awkwardly in her chair, weary from the pain in her gut.

"I should bow to a bishop," she apologized.

"Bishop no longer," he said cheerfully, slapping the green pallium rolled round his satchel strap. "It's a burden best carried this way." Dropping it to the floor, he took a stool.

"You're resigning? Oh… Theodore." The new Bishop of

Canterbury had confirmed Wilfrid in his bishopric. "I hope he realizes what he's losing."

"It's not important." Chad stuck out one worn sandal and wiggled his brown, chapped toes. "My feet will enjoy a respite."

"They deserve some winter boots! We'll find some in the store," Hild said briskly, admiring the agility of his worn frame. Then she sighed. "You'll be missed."

"Perhaps," Chad said doubtfully. "I'm no good at court. Persuasive rhetoric is not a skill I have, but I can and will pray for the man who does!"

Wilfrid.

* * *

Wilfrid was known far beyond Northumbria. While Chad was in office he'd lived at Ripon but worked in Mercia and the south, built his church at Hexham, and restored those at York and Lindisfarne. He saw no reason to confine himself. Hild had some sympathy; he couldn't abandon his new converts. But what he had done at Ripon left her aghast. King Egfrid told the tale, on a visit to his mother.

"I've never seen anything like it!" he exclaimed. "More splendid than my royal halls, for all the tribute I gather. There were princes and bishops, men from Canterbury, priests from north and south – wherever Wilfrid's been, and he's been all over."

"For the dedication of his chapel?" gasped Elfled.

"The queen and I were guests of honour," Egfrid nodded, "but there were gifts from other kings – he read an exhausting list. The altar was draped in gold and purple. *Royal colours for the King of kings*, he said. Each of the four Gospels was laid open, written in gold on purple vellum. They're kept in a box made specially, covered in sheet gold, studded with jewels – takes six men to carry! And the feasting lasted over three days."

Wealth and worldliness: what had they to do with God, who chose a thorn crown and a slave's death? Hild shook her head, remembering the lad so full of promise.

"Where did he get the gold?" asked Elfled.

"Kings' gifts," Egfrid said. "If I'd realized how rich he was, I wouldn't have given him the chapels in the north-west. Or let Etheldreda grant him land near Hexham."

"How is your wife?" asked Anfled. "Is it working?"

"Ye-es." Egfrid passed quickly on. "But tell me, lady, how do you find your new life?"

All was not right in the king's household; nearly three years, and still no heir.

"Never an idle moment," Anfled answered eagerly. "We pray for you and the kingdom…"

"Good!" Egfrid guffawed. "Christ wouldn't approve my doing down the Picts!"

"… and study Christ's life and teaching, and I work…"

"Work?" Egfrid's eyebrows shot up. "What do you do?"

"Well… I just help Mother Hild and Elfi. They run the abbey."

Set an example, Hild had said when Anfled arrived. Ani had something Hild thought she herself would never attain: true Christian humility.

* * *

Unexpectedly, the Bishop of Canterbury visited the Bay of Light. At the Pope's behest, he was examining the state of the English church. In the past, Hild would have vacated her lodging, but Anfled took him to the guesthall, asked Frigyd to provide for his needs, and called Elfled to welcome him on behalf of the abbey.

"Frigyd's in her element," Begu tittered, "chatting up a queen and a bishop! She visits them each morning to ask what they need for the day. Oh, she's tight-lipped, never indiscreet. But it makes her feel important to know their plans."

Hild chuckled, but wondered if she gave Frigyd – and Begu, come to that – sufficient recognition for their loving service.

It was not for some days that Frigyd asked if the bishop might call on Hild.

"What a place of harmony and holiness," he said, stooping

under her lintel. True, she thought; however Ani had resolved Elfi's early defensiveness, they were now a team.

He settled in a second chair, made specially by the carpenter so that she no longer had to surrender hers to guests. His head was almost bald, with a token fringe. Someone – Wilfrid, probably – had told her that eastern monks shaved their heads completely. He had the round shoulders of a scholar, piercing yellow eyes in a brown face, and a smile like Cuthbert's, mobile and transforming.

"Greetings, Abbess!" he said in accented Latin.

"My lord!" She tried to sink to her knees.

"Lady Hild, do not disturb yourself!" Taking her hand, he bowed over it. "I'm honoured to meet the abbess of whom I've heard so much."

She must have looked puzzled.

"Benedict," he explained. "Benedict Biscop of Wearmouth. We met in Rome and he brought me here. And now I've seen for myself how justified your reputation is: your diverse community, the scholarship, how your priests serve God's children beyond your boundaries, and the singing. Nowhere else have I heard such praise of God."

She must remember to tell Caedmon.

"How goes your pilgrimage?" she asked.

"It's a sorry tale." He gripped his rich, gold neck cross with a large crystal at its centre, the only adornment he wore with his simple robes. Perhaps it contained some religious reliquary, a sacred amulet; she'd heard of such things.

"Maybe you don't wish to tell," she smiled sympathetically.

"You're experienced and independent," he said, "perhaps the only person able to grasp my thinking and advise me."

"Advise, I doubt!" she chuckled, shuffling in her chair. "But I'd love to hear about the future."

"This land," he frowned, "has few leaders. No bishops in Kent and Wessex because they're dead, none to the west of Mercia because there never have been, none in the north-west where the chapels have been looted…"

For Wilfrid's Ripon, Hild remembered.

"Priests," Theodore exclaimed, "good men, struggle to walk from farm to farm. You have no centres, only scattered settlements. The only bishops I've met live with their kings, subservient to royal commands." He gazed into the fire. "We need more places like this," he murmured, "with God at the heart, stretching out to serve the people."

And he told her his ideas. "It's what Pope Gregory planned when he first sent the mission to the Anglians. Twelve bishops, led by Canterbury in the south and York in the north. But I'd like to see each nation with its own bishop. A man for the Deirans, one for Lindsey, one for the Mercians, and so on."

Wilfrid, she was not surprised to hear, was making difficulties: Theodore did not say so, but she could interpret.

"Will you be meeting King Egfrid?" she asked.

"Why?"

"Since before his father's day, bishops have served the king. His realm is vast, from this coast to the western isles and north to Pictland. Wilfrid is his bishop."

"The king's domain is not my business, but the bishop's is. He needs to know his people, be a father to them, an inspiration to his priests, and an adviser to his king. I'll be discussing it with King Egfrid and Bishop Wilfrid."

"You have my support," Hild said firmly. "I like your plan."

"I'm glad you said that!" Theodore pounced on her words. "Will you give me some of your priests to be bishops? They're open-minded, used to travel, friendly, firm in principle, and imbued with Christ's Spirit. Just the sort of men I need for the Severn Valley, Wessex, Bernicia…" Theodore's list was a long one.

Hild was amazed; her men as bishops all over the land! But Theodore was right. Like Aidan, they could draw men to God.

"In return," she grinned, "may I ask a favour?"

He chuckled. "I knew I shouldn't get away with it!"

"Did you notice Oftfor? He's a natural scholar and has outgrown our resources. Will you take him to Canterbury? He'd love to learn your Greek tongue, the language of the Gospels."

"And will you take one of my mine? A youth called John, whose parents live this side of Humberwater. He's promising and, with training like yours, could carry the Gospel to his people."

"Another Brother John," she said pensively. "We shall welcome him."

* * *

"Intolerable!" The cry of a fractious child. Wilfrid paced fretfully, purple pallium fluttering, tormented by frustration. "You're kin to both dynasties; I thought you'd understand. Northumbria must remain united."

"Wilfrid, Theodore has good reasons," Hild said gently, wishing he would stand still; he was giving her a headache.

"I think the king's got to him, blaming me for Etheldreda giving herself to God."

"The queen? You mean…?" Hild was dumbstruck. "But she has duties!" How could the kingdom be secure without an heir?

"She was wed before. She's much older than the king, almost too old for his purposes. It won't harm the East Anglian alliance because their King Aldwulf is your nephew. I'd like to see her settled in Princess Abbe's minster on the Firth before I leave."

"Leave? Again?" Hild sighed. So much to take in: Abbe with her own community at last; Wilfrid undoing the marriage he'd made; the kingdom without a queen!

"Theodore and the king are robbing me of my rights."

"Wilfrid, Theodore's plan is nothing to do with the king. What's wrong with it?"

"Out of date." He flicked a hand in disdain. "It's Gregory's, from generations ago! Based on Roman military rule." He cast up his eyes in exasperation. "*Forts in south and north, with colonies strategically located to control the natives.* Bishops, strategically located," he snapped, standing over her. "Twelve!"

"Like the apostles," she murmured. "Each of you a pool of inspiration, feeding rivulets to nurture the land."

"Twelve, with me at York, just for Deira!" Wilfrid exploded.

"Northumbria's mine! Egfrid's Northumbria. Bernicia, Deira, Lindsey, Mercia – he's lord of them all. I was consecrated Bishop of Northumbria. Theodore can't take it away!"

"Don't walk out again," she pleaded. "Your people need you. That's why Oswy had to put Chad in last time you went away."

"I am God's representative. No one can displace me!" he stormed.

"Christ is God's representative," Hild said firmly. "And he's alive in men who live like him."

"Pope Vitellian won't let Theodore get away with this!" He swirled round and swept out.

"God go with you!" she called, leaning back against the warm wood of her chair. Wilfrid's instinct was to fight – and glory in wealth and power. He was a thegn's son; it was his inheritance.

* * *

It is good to give thanks and sing praises unto your name, O Lord; to show your loving kindness in the morning, and your faithfulness every night…

At least she could still teach her novices to praise God, and practise love. Abbe, long ago, had said faith was not a feeling but a decision, an action. Christian love was like that; you had to work at it. She would never achieve perfect love, or perfect faith. But she trusted God to lend her what she needed for the tasks he set.

Sometimes she felt useless, watching Elfled and Anfled shoulder the responsibility for abbey life. But she could not seem to regain her strength, and the prospect of a moorland journey by ox cart, then being strapped to a board and lowered down the hill to Hackness, was daunting.

One of her deep pleasures was Ani's company. Sharing so much of the past, they could chat in easy intimacy.

"It's good he's here," Anfled said one day as they strolled up to Oswy's grave. "He so wanted, at the end, to make his peace with God. I've been wondering… could we bring my father, too?"

Hild smiled. "Edwin and Oswy, rivals and enemies, lying side by side near the women who tie them: you, Elfi, and me."

She leaned on her stick as they watched lads kick a bladder on the grass near the guesthall. A rhythmic creaking drew their eyes to a boat crossing the estuary. A young monk leaped onto the staithe and bounded uphill.

"Can it be…?"

"Mother Hild!" he called.

"Oftfor!" they chorused.

Hild perched herself on the plinth of the preaching cross, noting his maturity and eagerness.

"How is everything?" she asked.

He first bowed to Anfled. "My lady, I bring greetings from your Kentish kin."

"Thank you," Anfled smiled. "Tell us. How is Canterbury?"

"Marvellous!" he cried. "So many books! Theodore's monastery in Rome sends new ones. And I'm learning Greek. And I may be going to Rome!" He rolled his eyes in wonder. "But I come as bishop's messenger. Theodore asks if Bosa may go back with me to be consecrated Bishop of Deira!"

A lurch of happiness swept through Hild.

"But Bosa's not the first," Oftfor chuckled. "Chad's already installed as Bishop of Mercia. With a horse!" The women laughed: Chad on horseback! "Too much to be done, Theodore said; a horse would be quicker."

"A good thing," said Hild. "Chad's older than me and his feet are bad, but it won't come easily to him to ride. Like Aidan, he aligns himself with the poor."

Oftfor lifted his bulky satchel over his head and dumped it at his feet, extracting a bundle and holding it out. "From Bishop Theodore, for you."

Taking it, Hild unwrapped the cloth. "A roll of old vellum?"

"Unfurl it." Oftfor chuckled as if he were offering a child a treat.

"Oh, look, Anfled. Here… and here!" She pointed. "Gregory!"

"Yes. Jottings," said Oftfor. "Recollections from some Canterbury brothers and their contacts in Rome. The bishop said he thought Tatfrid might use them; he likes the idea of a Life of Gregory."

* * *

Wilfrid preyed on Hild's mind. These days, she couldn't blow worries away with a brisk walk. She envisaged him subtly canvassing the Pope's archdeacons, winning his argument but missing the point. *O God, grant him vision*, she prayed.

She roused to the sound of chanting: *I look to see the goodness of the Lord. Wait on the Lord, be strong…*

"Mother Hild!" Elfled lifted her up; she'd slumped in the chair. "We shouldn't have left you alone."

"I was thinking."

"Heavy thoughts!" Elfled teased. "You dropped off." She had her back turned, pouring a drink. Hild wondered whether to say anything. She shared most things, and Elfi might have to manage Wilfrid one day, but she didn't want to expose him unnecessarily.

"It's a shame," was Elfled's response. "He's an inspiring preacher, heals the sick, helps the poor, comforts the distressed, works all day, and prays all night. It's just… he can't see himself. He needs to show the obedience he preaches. Surrounded by too many flatterers, I suppose, like my brother."

How shrewd she'd become! Still, she was approaching twenty.

"I've prayed," said Hild, "but how can a Roman bishop know what's best for Northumbria, or understand Wilfrid's grandiose ambitions?"

"Why don't you tell him? He'd listen to you."

"A letter, you mean? Something I've never done."

"*Don't just pray: help it along* – that's what *you* say. Write to the Pope. Shall I help you draft it for the scribe master to copy? I'll fetch some parchment scraps." She whisked out of the door.

Hild sat, palms upturned, eyes closed in prayer.

Elfled returned with her mother. "Heavy burden," she trilled, "so the more oxen, the better!"

"Cheeky chit!" Hild gurgled. "All right, here's what's on my mind." She described again Aidan's vision of a Christian land, with priests showing Christ's way of love; and Theodore's plan to realize the vision. And she talked of Wilfrid, tainted by his courtly

345

upbringing, seduced by the splendour of Rome, fighting like a thegn to hold on to land and power. "If he wins," she fretted, "every priest, every baptism must await his pleasure. Spirits will dull. Work will stop. Remember the Yellow Pest?"

"I thought Theodore was to decide for the Pope," Anfled said.

"Wilfrid's appealing against his decision," Hild sighed.

The letter hung over them for days. They talked, drafted, scratched out, ripped up. How to express their fear without belittling Wilfrid?

"We're trying to protect an infant church," Hild said. "We mustn't make it worse."

"Should we send a gift?" asked Anfled. "Isn't it customary?"

"A gift?" Hild remembered the old Pope's gifts to Edwin and Ethelburga.

"This." Anfled fished from under her plain woollen robe a long gold chain with a jewelled cross. "My grandmother's. What better use for it now?"

She and Hild sat on the log in the herb patch while Elfled read out the final version:

To the Most High Vitellian, Bishop at Rome, from Hild, Abbess at Whitby, loving greetings in God.

Whereas it has pleased Theodore, Bishop of Canterbury, to appoint twelve bishops across the Anglian peoples, according to holy Gregory's plan, we beg and beseech you, in the name of our heavenly Father, to endorse Theodore's dispensations without amendment, for the benefit of God's work among these peoples.

Queen Anfled of Northumbria, servant of God in this abbey, and her daughter Elfled, who was dedicated from birth, send loving greetings and a gift to assure you of their good will.

May God's blessings be upon you.

Hild sighed with relief. Now it was in the hands of God.

* * *

The day was drawing in. Her breath hung in the air. Autumn was beautiful this year. The sunshine had tempted her up to the church. Begu and Frigyd had left for Hackness and she was to go before winter set in. She was ready. The abbey was in good hands.

She thanked God for it all: Elfi and Ani united, the next generation of men, her men, spreading God's love, and life continuing around her. Sitting at the foot of the cross, she watched sunlight dappling the sea, labourers leaving the fields, children splashing across old Udric's stepping stones, pigs and cattle browsing.

A wet nose startled her, pushing under her hand.

"Hello, Scruff!" she murmured, combing the old hound's mane. "Where is he, then?" Caedmon might sleep in the dormitory, but he always kept a hound at his side. A sharp whistle. Scruff lolloped down the track, ears bouncing. Watching him enviously, Hild started to haul herself up.

"Wait, Abbess! I'll lend you an arm." Bosa was coming along the cliff. "I thought I'd find you here." He settled beside her. "I shall see you in Hackness, but I wanted to visit this place once more."

"I hear good things of you, Bosa."

"Thanks to your teaching," he said. "Mother Hild, do you realize how far your light, your inspiration, spreads now? Your men all over the land, taking Caedmon's songs to the people, and your faith in God's love?"

A jewel in my lap, lighting the whole land: Ma's words, so long ago. Could they really apply to her now? She sat thinking.

"The sun's going." Bosa took her arm. "Let me help you."

Elfi was at the door, a bundle in her arms.

"Mother, look what Caedmon's brought." She unrolled two fluffy sheepskins into Hild's chair.

"Bosa," Hild said, lowering herself into the softness, "my work here is done. My lord bishop, will you give me your blessing?" She bowed her head.

She felt his hand touch her lightly, trembling. "Hild, child of God, may Christ's Spirit burn bright in you so that you know his love and joy, always."

AUTHOR'S NOTE

Hild never did reach Hackness. She died in Whitby on 17 November 680 at sixty-six years of age, two years after Bosa was consecrated bishop in York.

Aetla became bishop of the West Saxons at Dorchester-on-Thames. Tatfrid was nominated bishop of the Hwicce (Worcestershire and Gloucestershire), but died before he could be consecrated. Oftfor, after studying in Canterbury and Rome, did become bishop of the Hwicce. Two other Whitby men followed in the next generation: John of Beverley and another Wilfrid were both bishops of York.

The book about Gregory was completed, perhaps after Hild's death, and survives today as the earliest Life of Gregory the Great by an anonymous monk of Whitby. It is thought to be the first work by an English writer.

As I write, in 2014, it is exactly 1,400 years since Hild was born, and 1,350 years since the Synod of Whitby in 664. Her life story was first recounted about forty years after her death by the Jarrow monk Bede, in *A History of the English Church and People*, but he gives no information about her between the ages of thirteen and thirty-three. In her day, royal girls were invariably married off for dynastic or political purposes; modern scholars think it unlikely Hild escaped this fate. The case is best argued by Professor Christine Fell in *Hild, Abbess of Streonaeshalch*, a paper for a symposium entitled Hagiography and Medieval Literature, held at Odense University in November 1980.

For me, Bede's words that all who knew her used to call her Mother, are significant. This was long before the courtesy title was given to women heading nunneries. Bede attributes it to Hild's goodness and grace. Surely it also suggests personal experience from which she could offer effective practical help to people in every kind of human difficulty.

Hild must have been sent north: how else could she have become well known to Aidan? In my novel, her husband and child are not historical, nor is the Gododdin chief, though the unexplained sack of Edinburgh and the rebuilding of Doon Hill are. All other major characters are historical except for Cutha, Brother John, and the various stewards. Inevitably, everyone thinks and, for the most part, speaks through my imagination.

The Anglo-Saxon language rejoices in clusters of vowels and consonants which are difficult for modern readers to see and to say. I hope people who love the language will forgive me for simplifying names, either by using forms already familiar (as Ethelburga for Æthelburh), or by reducing them (as Elfled for Ælfflæd), and for mostly keeping modern place names.

Among the many scholars to whom I am indebted are: Kathleen Herbert, *Looking for the Gods of Lost England*, 1994; N. J. Higham, *An English Empire: Bede and the Early Anglo-Saxon Kings*, 1995; J. Marsden, *Northanhymbre Saga*, 1992, which interprets some of the Welsh sources; Christine Fell, *Women in Anglo-Saxon England*, 1984; Barbara Yorke, *Kings and Kingdoms of Early Anglo-Saxon England*, 1990, and *Nunneries and the Anglo-Saxon Royal Houses*, 2003; H. Mayr-Harting, *The Coming of Christianity to Anglo-Saxon England*, 1972; Michelle P. Brown, *How Christianity Came to Britain and Ireland*, 2006; Leslie Alcock, *Kings and Warriors, Craftsmen and Priests in Northern Britain AD 550–850*, 2003. The main Anglo-Saxon texts are available in Penguin Classics.

Recent archaeology in north-east England has proved exciting. Extremely useful to me were: Robin Daniels, *Anglo-Saxon Hartlepool and the Foundations of English Christianity*, 2007; Stephen J. Sherlock, *A Royal Anglo-Saxon Cemetery at Street House, Loftus*, 2012 (the dark hills of Deira); Anna Ritchie and David J. Breeze, *Invaders of Scotland*, 1994 for an introduction to Doon Hill. The English Heritage archaeological investigations at Whitby since 1996, led by Buzz

Busby, Sarah Jennings and Tony Wilmott, still await publication, but interim conclusions are exhibited in the site Visitors' Centre, and I am grateful for several illuminating conversations with the archaeologists.

I should also like to thank most warmly: Tony Collins and the talented team at Lion Hudson; Sandra Oakins for the map; the University of York for allowing me to use their library; Veronica Sembhi, my first, persistently demanding reader; Anthea Dove, mentor and gentle critic; and my husband, who has lived patiently for years with a third person in our marriage.

Jill Dalladay
Whitby